DAY

ZER

Books by Kelly deVos
available from Harlequin TEEN and Inkyard Press

Fat Girl on a Plane
Day Zero

KELLY DEVOS

DAY
ZERO

ink
yard
press

ISBN-13: 978-1-335-00848-0

Day Zero

InkyardPress.com

Printed in U.S.A.

For Evelyn.
My spark and hope for a bright future.

TONIGHT

I will save the world.

It's taken months to build the perfect guild, get every-one to level ninety-nine, mine ore, forge the best armor and train for the mission. Now I've got a foolproof plan to kill the dragon, charge the Cataline Hills and save the Elysian Fields. I'm ready for the raid. Tonight.

Well. Almost.

I get out my phone as I enter the empty history classroom. Dropping my backpack on the floor near my usual desk, I notice that there's one item on my list that doesn't have a checkmark.

Snacks.

It's not a raid without cheese puffs and Extra Jolt straw-berry soda. I'll have to stop at the store on the way home from school.

But after that, I will save the world of Republicae. When I

do, my virtual world will be happy, peaceful and predictable, which is cool because my real world is such a mess.

A complete. Total. Mess.

For example.

MacKenna enters the classroom and slides into the seat next to me. "Hi, Jinx."

My shoulders tense at the sound of my horrible nickname.

No one loves to call me a jinx more than my stepsister.

She's come from her journalism class and, as usual, carries all the electronic tablets she uses to write her stories. She dumps the stack on her desk and fiddles with a strand of her long, black hair. I reach up to touch the bun on the top of my head and confirm what I already knew.

I, too, am a mess.

Waving one of the e-tablets in front of my face, MacKenna says, "Look at this. The science teacher caught some jackasses called Jules and Becks making out in the chem classroom. That's what they want me to write about."

I roll my eyes at the bright image on the screen. All I see is a photo of two people having a lot more fun than I am. On the wall in front of us, the cracked, oversize classroom clock ticks away. I'm waiting. For the bell to ring. This is my last class of the day.

I'm ready for this Monday to be over.

MacKenna keeps talking. She taps the e-tablet screen with her thumb. "Mr. Johnson killed my article about that snotty soccer mom from The Opposition who got pissed at the school secretary and threw a drink in her face at the winter banquet." She pokes the picture again. "For this. He said we have to limit our reports to student life."

I pull my laptop out of my bag and position it on the small desk. A few clicks later and my digital history book stares back at me on the screen, the red, white and blue flag waving in an animated loop. "He probably wants people to focus on lab work and not locking lips. Anyway, do we really need to be so political all the time?"

At the front of the room, the teacher's faded red leather chair sits empty.

And the bell doesn't ring.

MacKenna rearranges the e-tablets. "You been to the front office recently? The secretary is still wearing an eyepatch. An ice cube bruised the lady's eyeball and she can't see right. All because she wore a T-shirt from The Spark. How are we supposed to forget that The Opposition and The Spark are almost at war? Twenty years from now, people will still be talking about the election. *Nobody* will remember that Becks put his tongue down Jules's throat. Life is political, Jinx."

Her life might be political. Mine is complicated. I pretend to read my book.

The classroom fills up and people say hi to MacKenna as they pass. After our parents got married, we moved to a new house and I changed schools. We've been here at Rancho Mesa High for six months, and she knows everyone in school. Meanwhile, no one remembers my name.

It's just as well. I've always been more comfortable with computers than people.

"This is how it is," MacKenna continues, now with an audience of several members of the debate club leaning out of their desks. "I'm going for the Most Likely to Be a Media Mogul backstory, not Pathetic Underachiever Who Overcame Adversity to Succeed Later in Life. Writing public service announcements about driving less than five miles an hour in the parking lot or what to do if your e-paper stops working in the middle of a test is not going to make that happen. You know—"

Oh, here we go. *In Boulder...*

MacKenna continues to scowl at the pictures. "—in Boulder—"

"I think class is about to start."

"—we had a real newspaper. Monthly. In print. To learn how they did things in the old days. You know, real journalism. We wrote *real* articles. I did a big exposé on cash that was missing from the school slush fund. Then the principal hired her nephew to repave the parking lot, and I broke the story. Now thanks to..."

MacKenna trails off midsentence as my mom breezes into the room, her long mahogany-brown hair flowing behind her. She pushes up the sleeves of her red cashmere sweater and places a stack of books neatly on the corner of her desk. As usual, she looks like a movie star playing a teacher.

My face heats up. Mom is great, but it seems like there ought to be some kind of rule against being in a class where your mother is the teacher and your stepsister is in the next desk. But since the last round of school budget cuts, there's only one history teacher and only one junior history class. So here we are.

MacKenna's glare bounces from Mom back to me. I know MacKenna hated to leave Colorado, but I don't know why she's so desperate to blame me for the situation we're *both* in. Our parents met at some celebrity golf tournament for the bank where her dad, Jay, works. I mean, it's not like I set them up or something. Mom married Jay over the summer, and they're happy and that's good. But it's not like I love sharing a bathroom with a stepsister who spends more time doing her eyeliner than it takes me to download the latest *Republicae* patches.

Mom falls into the squeaky red chair, opens her laptop and makes a few taps. The words CAUSES OF THE NEW DEPRESSION appear in green block letters on the e-chalkboard. It's been a long time since the LED panels have been replaced, so once in a while the letters blink and disappear.

MacKenna's shoulders slump. "Anyway. I'm stuck here," she whispers.

I don't think anyone besides me is listening, and most of the class breaks out in laughter when the board briefly reads, C US S THE N PRESS ON.

Mom clears her throat. "All right. For the first half of class, we will begin our discussion on the historical and financial causes of the New Depression. Then we'll start our book reports. Please flip your e-texts to page 187..."

After making a couple more clicks on her laptop, Mom rises from the red chair. An image of a small crowd standing in the rain in front of the White House appears on the e-chalkboard.

"As you know," she begins, "this morning, Ammon Carver was inaugurated as the country's next president, following a surprise victory for The Opposition in a very contentious election. The defeat of The Spark and David Rosenthal—"

"Everyone's for Rosenthal!" someone calls from the back.

The class erupts into a frenzy. MacKenna unzips her hoodie to reveal a T-shirt with the words Everyone's for Rosenthal in blue script on the front.

Sure. *Everyone's for Rosenthal.* Is class over yet?

Mom gives us one of her annoyed teacher looks that silences everyone. She continues louder than before. "The election results are widely believed to be the result of complex feelings about the New Depression. Our discussion will help us understand today's confusing events."

My whole life has been a confusing event.

I scroll to page 187 and stare at a picture of a nearly abandoned suburban neighborhood below a headline that reads "The Dangers of a Two-Party Political System."

At the front of the room, Mom paces on the cheap blue carpet. "Maybe you have heard The Spark say that this is an age of moral crisis. The New Depression arose from the need to pay for and atone for injustices of the past. Or maybe you've heard The Opposition say that this is an era of economic crisis created by bad decisions made by The Spark over the past ten years."

"Or *maybe* those are the kinds of things people say when they don't know what they're talking about," MacKenna mutters. "The kinds of things they hope aren't actually true."

I tune out the rest. The fact that Ammon Carver and The Opposition spent the past couple of years successfully blaming David Rosenthal and The Spark for everything going wrong with the economy is a frequent topic of conversation around our house. If I need to know which senator signed off on the bill that quadrupled the price of bread or who increased taxes on gas, Mom will be very happy to repeat her lecture.

Mom keeps talking and talking and talking.

"The Spark became the party of identity politics, and their willingness to spend tax dollars on programs to secure civil rights is an important part of their platform. This means that…"

I keep watching the clock. *Tick. Tock.*

"With a powerful pool of backers, including the Carver family and First Federal Bank, The Opposition has tried to position itself as the party of rugged individualism, but its main objective has been to block attempts to levy taxes on the rich. Without a way to raise funds for..."

I log in to the *Republicae* forum and post another reminder about the raid to make sure my guild knows the attack plan.

Finally, Mom concludes with, "Okay. For tomorrow, read pages 190–205 and be ready for a quiz on Wednesday." She clears her throat. "And now, on to book reports. Any volunteers?"

I'm not really surprised when my stepsister's hand shoots into the air. MacKenna Novac is always ready. She was born ready.

Mom nods, and MacKenna heads to the front of the room.

I smirk. Mom will take the volunteers first and then call us in alphabetical order. Which means it'll be at least Friday before we get to me. Which is why I'll be playing video games tonight and not writing a book report. My smirk shifts into a smile.

The fun is short-lived though. My breath catches as MacKenna pulls a familiar orange book from her backpack and carries it in front of her with her arms outstretched dramatically. The same way that the priest carries the Bible at church.

"This is *Dr. Doomsday's Guide to Ultimate Survival*," MacKenna says in a booming voice.

A couple people laugh.

It takes everything I've got to stop myself from groaning.

I'm expecting Mom to do something about this. Put a stop to it. But she's got a smile that borders on amused. She grabs her laptop and moves to a table in the back of the room.

MacKenna connects her own laptop to the e-chalkboard as she talks. "By Dr. Maxwell Marshall."

A larger-than-life picture of my father's bearded face fills the screen. MacKenna has managed to convert old news archive footage into a video loop, so every few seconds Dad squints or nods.

Yeah. Dad.

Here's a little pop quiz about him. Guess which option best describes my dad:

(A) He was a halfway-normal computer science professor until he became convinced that society was teetering on the edge of Armageddon.

(B) He quit his job and wrote a book. Dr. Doomsday's Guide to Ultimate Survival. It's illustrated and every bit as ridiculous as it sounds.

(C) Ammon Carver was Dad's old buddy from his army days. They stayed in touch.

(D) All of the above.

The correct answer is (D).

Sigh.

MacKenna leans on the desk. She has a few small, bright-colored note cards in her hand. "Dr. Marshall is a noted computer science professor famous for his hacker exploits, study of cryptography and the creation of complex data models at Arizona State University. Up until last year, he worked as a consultant for The Opposition and for Ammon Carver personally. Marshall's work became the basis for The Opposition's election victory."

My father's work.

The best-known piece of Dad's work, D00MsD4Y, was a worm he designed to teach his students about file server vulnerability. A few years ago, someone unleashed it into the real world. The worm doubled in size every eight seconds and took down seventy-five thousand servers in less than ten minutes. Comerican, the only survivor of the airline wars, had to cancel all its flights for three days. Police precincts in seven states resorted to using notepads to keep track of emergency calls. The only reason Dad didn't end up in jail was that the cops needed his help to stop the thing.

I open a new window on my laptop and pull up Dad's archive.

His code fills the screen.

```
push    6C6C642Eh    ; [EBP-8]
push    32336C65h    ; [EBP-0Ch]
push    6E72656Bh    ; [EBP-10h]      Push string kernel32.dll
push    ecx          ; [EBP-14h]
push    746E756Fh    ; [EBP-18h]      Push string GetTickCount
push    436B6369h    ; [EBP-1Ch]
push    54746547h    ; [EBP-20h]
mov     cx, 6C6Ch
push    ecx          ; [EBP-24h]
push    642E3233h    ; [EBP-28h]      Push string ws2_32.dll
push    5F327377h    ; [EBP-2Ch
mov     cx, 7465h
push    ecx          ; [EBP-30h]
push    6B636F73h    ; [EBP-34h]      Push string socket
mov     cx, 6F74h
push    ecx          ; [EBP-38h]
push    646E6573h    ; [EBP-3Ch]      Push string sendto
```

Like all his stuff, it's clean. Precise. A tiny little packet of code. Just 376 bytes. There's something about it though. Dad says that, to catch bad guys, we have to think like they do.

To understand why they do what they do. Malware. Bots. Worms. Ransomware. He writes these to show how they work and how to stop them. The code was supposed to be helpful.

Instead, it was...ominous.

MacKenna changes the image on the screen to a picture of a traffic jam. "Dr. Marshall's theories on everything from social media use to traffic patterns helped The Opposition suppress votes. For example, in Georgia, they were able to spread a rumor online that Carver had defeated Rosenthal by noon that day. Experts estimate that Dr. Marshall's rumor was responsible for a significant decrease in voter turnout among Rosenthal supporters who—"

Dad left The Opposition last year for reasons that aren't clear to me. I snort. "It wasn't my dad's rumor, MacKenna. He only wrote the program that—"

The first few rows of the class turn to face me.

I snap my mouth shut and make a show of examining my laptop screen.

Mom makes her way up my aisle and clears her throat again. "Miss Marshall, if you'd like to pass feedback to the presenter, please do so using the online form." She pauses near my desk, stares at the D00MsD4Y code on my screen and stuffs her hands in the pockets of her brown corduroy pants.

I minimize the code window.

"Let's stay on task here," she says.

"Um...okay, Mom—uh—I mean, Mrs. Novak," I stammer.

MacKenna almost jumps at the sound of her own last name. She continues her presentation but with less enthusiasm than before. "Two years ago, Dr. Marshall became convinced that not even the antidemocratic antics of The Opposition would be enough to save the world. He adopted the nickname Dr.

Doomsday and wrote this book." She holds up the safety-orange paperback manual again. "It's a weird combination of survival advice and bizarre ramblings. The reader is told to always carry waterproof watches. Oh, and also that the world is going to end at any minute."

I turn in my seat to check on Mom. She's returned to the table at the back of the room and is sitting there serenely, making notes in her grade book. Like it doesn't bother her at all that she's basically listening to a lecture about what destroyed our family.

It bothers me.

Mom spent a long time trying to pass off Dad's obsession with prepper doomsday drills as a midlife crisis, until last year when she finally decided she'd had enough and tossed him out. I get it. It's not fun to spend all your weekends in an underground bunker trying to figure out if you can live without plumbing, or at seminars on how to suture your own wounds.

The fact that Mom is for The Spark and Dad is sort of for The Opposition didn't help.

At the front of the classroom, MacKenna reads some passages from Dad's book and puts a couple of his illustrations on the e-chalkboard. She concludes her report with, "*Dr. Doomsday's Guide to Ultimate Survival*, a top-selling and often-quoted book, perfectly represents the way that The Opposition has used paranoia and propaganda to seize power."

MacKenna ends her presentation by putting Dad's giant face back up on the e-chalkboard. She snaps the book shut and returns to her seat.

Someone in the front row mutters, "It isn't paranoia if people are really out to get you."

A blonde girl speaks up. I should probably know these people by now, but truthfully, I prefer my online friends. "Do you think it's true?" the girl asks. "What they said on the news? That President Carver wants to disband the Senate? That he's considering martial law?"

A nervous energy surges through the classroom, and everywhere I look I see worried faces.

"We won't know anything for a while, and we need to remain calm until we do." Mom glides up the aisle and turns off the image of Dad's nodding head. "Excellent analysis as always, Miss Novak, although a bit off topic as your book choice doesn't address any of the causes of the New Depression. I'm afraid I'll have to deduct some points for relevance."

MacKenna frowns. "The relevance is that The Opposition doesn't actually care about fixing the economy. They've done as much as anybody to cause the New Depression, because it helps them. It keeps people desperate enough to do anything."

Mom smiles. "You'll need to do a better job making that connection in your written report or you're looking at a B here."

The bell rings. I close my laptop and shove it in my backpack. Mom stands by the door, saying goodbyes and giving out homework reminders.

Before MacKenna gets up, I lean toward her. "That was mean."

She drops her backpack on top of her desk. "It was the truth."

I swallow the lump in my throat. "I'm sorry you hate me, but that was a pretty crappy way to get revenge. And to scare the hell out of everybody."

She cocks her head to the side. "I don't hate you, and I don't want revenge."

My face heats in an equal mixture of embarrassment and anger.

MacKenna stands and comes closer. "Listen, there's something that you need to know—"

I don't get to find out what I need to know.

Mom waves us toward the door. "Girls, you need to get a move on it. Charles is waiting."

Charles is my little brother. He goes to an elementary school around the corner, and we pick him up each day after school.

The classroom is clear, and Mom's formal demeanor falls away. She approaches our desks. "MacKenna, Ted—Mr. Johnson showed me your article about the incident in the school office. Your piece was well written, well researched and deserves to be on the school website. I'll speak with him and see what I can do."

A kind of disgusted frown crosses MacKenna's face. "I can talk to him myself, Stephanie."

Mom tucks a strand of shiny hair behind her ear. "I'll at least put in a good word for you."

We both finish putting our stuff away, and Mom walks us to the door.

In the hall, there's an argument in progress between the school's two football coaches. Strictly speaking, the teachers aren't supposed to talk politics at school. But they find ways to air their differences. One of the coaches wears a red shirt and the other a blue one. They make jabbing motions at each other and the names "Carver" and "Rosenthal" drift up the corridor.

Mom stares at the scene. "Do you ever wonder what is wrong with this world?"

Farther up the hall, a student in a black baseball cap crashes a library cart into the double doors.

This breaks Mom out of her reverie. "You should get on the road. People are on edge today. I want you to go straight home."

I try to give her a reassuring smile. "Everything will be okay, Mom."

MacKenna swings her backpack over her shoulder. "Think so, do you?"

I cross my arms. "My dad made us do survival drills for floods, hurricanes, droughts, famines, nuclear war, foreign invasion and the collapse of the government. And do you know what happened?"

"What?" MacKenna asks, sounding genuinely interested.

"Absolutely nothing. Every day, I wake up, and everything is the same as the day before. Life goes on." I step out of the doorway without waiting for a response.

MacKenna is a few steps behind me in the hall.

"Until it doesn't," she says.

The coaches stop talking as we get closer.

"Go straight home," Mom calls after us.

DR. DOOMSDAY'S GUIDE TO ULTIMATE SURVIVAL

RULE ONE:

ALWAYS BE PREPARED.

Outside, it's sunny with an empty blue sky that stretches on forever.

I swing my backpack over my shoulder as we cross the mostly empty campus. The town can't afford to plant winter grass, so everything on the ground is yellowing and dry. The kid who crashed the library cart zooms by on an electric scooter, a blur of dark hair and green camouflage clothes, missing us by only a foot or so.

MacKenna jumps back. "Hey, watch it, Navarro!"

"You know him?" I continue to stare, watching the scooter move across the uneven, rocky parking lot toward the football fields. This info shouldn't have come as a surprise. She knows everyone.

"Um, yeah," she says as she walks and digs in her bag for the car keys. "He's in my Physics class. Oh, and his mom runs the district nutritional services. He's the guy who tossed me out when I tried to break into her office."

MacKenna sets a fast pace. She might have hated me at first sight, and she can't stand living in the outskirts of Phoenix, but she positively loves my little brother and doesn't want to leave him stuck at school.

"Wait. You broke into someone's office?" I ask, struggling to keep up.

"I *tried*," she says as we arrive at the shiny white Prius 18 that Jay bought for us after the wedding. "I'm telling you there's something up with those tofu nuggets they serve on Thursdays."

We hesitate in front of the car. She's about to say—

"That story's got legs."

We're supposed to share the car, but MacKenna usually insists on driving. This would probably have been okay, because I don't like to drive anyway—drills where we practiced rolling out of a moving car is what passed for driver's education with my dad—but MacKenna's way of rebelling against her move from Boulder has been to stubbornly refuse to use autodrive or to memorize any of the street names or directions. If I don't pay careful attention to where we're going, we end up lost.

MacKenna slides behind the wheel and gets the car going. The library cart guy is gone as she steers us onto the street.

I want to ask more questions about both the mysterious boy and when MacKenna manages to find time to break into the school, but I have to focus. "Turn right on Howser," I tell her when it looks like she'll miss our turn.

The drive to Cory Booker Elementary takes about five minutes from Rancho Mesa High. The neighborhood around the school has held up pretty well. The houses are old, and their brick designs look better than some of the newer stuff you see farther out in the suburbs. Charles is sitting on the curb with his copy of *The Encyclopedia of Tropical Plants* in front of his face. He's probably the only eight-year-old in the Grateful Gardeners Book Club.

"Whatcha doing?" I call out the window as he gathers his stuff then tumbles into the backseat. As usual, Charles is wearing a gray blazer and neatly pressed khaki pants, and, no, that's not the school's uniform. It's his dress-for-the-job-you-want outfit, and I guess the job he wants is that of a ninety-year-old landscaper.

"Researching the practicality of growing Dendrobium cuthbertsonii here in a greenhouse environment," Charles says. When I don't respond, he adds, "Orchids," in a know-it-all tone.

MacKenna laughs.

Her expression turns serious as she exits the school parking lot. "Which way?"

"Left," I tell her. "I need to stop at Halliwell's."

"Why?"

Part of me doesn't want to tell her, but she's going to find out anyway. "Snacks," I say.

MacKenna frowns. "Stephanie told us to go straight home."

I tug at the ribbing of my T-shirt, which suddenly feels too tight around my throat. Since when does MacKenna pay attention to what Mom says?

"It's on the way. I'll be in there for two seconds."

Charles leans forward. "Maybe they'll have this week's seed packets for my Click N'Grow."

For a couple minutes, it's quiet except for the occasional sound of Charles turning one of the thick pages of his book.

"You know what Phoenix needs?" MacKenna says as we

continue through Rancho Mesa. "More suburbs. I mean, why only cover half the planet with your urban sprawl when you could gobble up the whole thing?"

Sigh.

Glancing in the rearview mirror, I meet my brother's eyes.

"Jinx," he says, "in my class, Tommy said democracy is dead and Dad killed it. Do you think he did?"

"Well—" MacKenna starts to answer.

"No," I say. "That's just some dumb kid repeating what he heard at home. Dad didn't do anything wrong." Well. Not technically, anyway.

"Right," MacKenna says, under her breath.

I turn around and smile. Try to be reassuring. It's clear from Charles's worried squint that he heard MacKenna.

"But Dad is for The Opposition?" Charles asks.

"I guess," I say. My smile fades. "As much as he's *for* anything." Dad's always been more theoretical. It's hard to explain that our father has become this odd bundle of obsessions with computer science theories and survivalism. I barely understand it myself.

Charles closes his book and looks out the window. I face forward again, haul my bag onto my lap and get out my half-drunk bottle of water from lunch.

MacKenna adjusts her designer sunglasses. I'm surprised she doesn't make more snappish remarks about Dad. I'm even more surprised at the nervous frown that remains on her face.

"You're really worried about the inauguration? That something is going to happen?"

She hesitates. "I don't know. Not... Not exactly. I mean, I'm not sure what's going to happen. I guess that's the problem. There's something about the world right now that feels off. Unpredictable." She pauses again. "I'm... I'm going to the Rosenthal rally at the university tonight. You should come too."

I'm in the middle of a sip and almost spit out my water. "You think Mom doesn't want us to stop at the market but she's going to let you go on campus tonight?"

"Toby will be there," MacKenna says, indignantly.

Toby is MacKenna's brother and a freshman at ASU. He lives in the dorms.

"I doubt it. Mom's worried that there's going to be some kind of riot. She'll probably make us all be home for dinner."

We stop at a traffic light, and MacKenna turns to face me with a smile. "You're the one who keeps saying that nothing is going to happen. That life will go on. Why don't you prove it and convince your mom to let us go?"

I'm thrown back against my seat as we speed away from the green light. "There is no way on earth you're getting out of the house tonight, and I have my…"

"Video games?" she finishes.

In the backseat, Charles snickers.

I exhale in relief when MacKenna pulls the car into the Halliwell's Market parking lot. Because of the Sugar Sales Permit waiting list, old stores like these are the only places that carry Extra Jolt soda. I have to buy it myself, because Mom won't keep any in the house.

She thinks too much caffeine rots your brain or something.

Halliwell's is a squat brown building that sits across the street from the mall and is next door to the town's only skyscraper.

The First Federal Building was supposed to be the first piece of a suburban business district designed to rival the hip boroughs of New York. The mayor announced the construction of a movie theater, an apartment complex and an indoor aquarium. But the New Depression hit, and the other buildings never materialized.

The First Federal Building alone soars toward the clouds, an ugly glass rectangle visible from every neighborhood, surrounded by the old town shops that have been there forever. Most of the stores are empty.

We park in front of the market.

Our car nestles in the long shadow of the giant bank building.

Charles gets out and stands on the sidewalk in front of the car.

MacKenna opens her door. She hesitates again. "Listen, I know you might not want to hear this or believe it. But my book report wasn't about hurting you or getting revenge. I'm trying to get you to see what's really happening here. That Carver's election is the start of something bad. We could use you at the rally. You're one of the few people who understands Dr. Doomsday's work. You could explain what he did. How he helped Carver cheat to win."

"I've been planning this raid for months," I say. My stomach churns, sending uncomfortable flutters through my insides. I don't know what it would mean to talk about my father's work. What I really want to do is pretend it doesn't exist. Pretend the world is normal and whole.

I reassure myself with the reminder that there's no way MacKenna is going to the rally either.

Out of the corner of my eye, I see Charles give us a small wave. Before MacKenna can say anything else, I get out and grab my backpack.

Inside Halliwell's, I pick up a blue basket from the stack near the door. The small market is busy and full of other people shopping after school or work. The smell of pine cleaner hits me as we pass the checkout stations. They are super serious about germs and always cleaning between customers.

I leave MacKenna and Charles at the Click N'Grow rack near the door to check out the seed packets that my brother collects. Dad got Charles hooked on this computerized gardening that uses an e-tablet and a series of tiny indoor lights to create the ideal indoor planter box. Each week, they release a new set of exclusive seeds. Their genetic modifications are controversial.

All the soda is in large coolers that line one of the walls of the market. They keep the strange stuff in the corner. Expensive root beers. Ramune imported from Japan. And! Extra! Jolt! I put a few bottles of strawberry in my basket. I snag some grape too. For a second, I consider buying a couple of bottles of doughnut flavor. But that sounds like too much, even for me. The chips are in the next aisle. I load up on cheese puffs and spicy nacho crisps.

MacKenna and Charles are still at the rack near the door, and I try to squeeze by them without attracting any notice. I usually don't buy unhealthy snacks when I'm with my brother. I smuggle them in my backpack and have a special hiding space in my desk.

My brother has type 1 diabetes, and he's supposed to check his blood sugar after meals. He can have starchy or sugary snacks only when his glucose level is good or on special occasions.

MacKenna grimaces at a packet of seeds in her hands. "I still don't like this one. It's pretty. But still. It's…carnivorous."

I have to hand it to her. She really does have *a look*. She's pale and white, like me, but she manages to seem like she's doing it on purpose and not because she's some kind of vampire-movie reject. Her glossy black hair always rests in perfect waves, and if the journalism thing doesn't work out, she could definitely have a career in fashion design.

Charles smiles at her. "It's a new kind of pitcher plant. Like the Cobra Lily." He points to the picture on the front of the seed packet. "Look at the blue flowers. That's new."

"It *eats* other plants," MacKenna says.

"You eat plants."

"But I don't eat people," MacKenna says. "There's got to be some kind of natural law that says you shouldn't eat your own kind."

Charles giggles.

So far so good. Until.

My brother trots up behind me and dumps a few packs of seeds in my basket. His gaze lands on my selection of soda and chips. "Can I get some snacks too?"

Crap.

I freeze. "What's your number?"

Charles pretends he can't hear me. That's not a good sign.

"Charles, what's your number?"

He still doesn't look at me. "I forgot my monitor today."

"Well, I have mine." I kneel down and dig around for the spare glucometer I keep in the front pocket of my backpack. By the time I get it out, MacKenna has already pulled Charles out of his blazer and rolled up the sleeve of his blue dress shirt. I wave the device over the small white sensor disk attached to my brother's upper arm.

After a few seconds, the glucometer beeps and a number displays on the screen.

221

Crap. Crap. Crap.

"Charles! What did you eat today?"

My brother's face turns red. "They were having breakfast-for-lunch day at school. Everyone else was having pancakes. Why can't I have pancakes?"

I sigh. Something about his puckered up little face keeps me from reminding him that if he eats too much sugar he could die. "You know what Mom said. If you eat something you're not supposed to, you have to get a pass and go to the nurse for your meds."

My brother's shoulders slump. "I couldn't go to the nurse. Hummingbirds were visiting the Chuparosa and…"

Charles is on the verge of tears and frowns even more deeply at the sight of my basket full of junk food.

"Look," I say. "There are plenty of healthy snacks we can eat. I'll put this stuff back."

"That's right," MacKenna says, giving Charles's hand a squeeze. "We can get some popcorn. Yogurt. Um, I saw some really delicious-looking fresh pears back there."

"And they have the cheese cubes you like," I add.

We go around the store replacing the cheese puffs and soda with healthy stuff. I hesitate when I have to put back the Extra Jolt, but I really don't want to make my brother feel bad because I can drink sugary stuff and he can't.

We pay for the healthy snacks and the seed packets.

I grab the bags and move toward the market's sliding doors.

I end up ahead of them, waiting outside by the car and facing the store. The shopping center behind Halliwell's is mostly empty. The shoe store went out of business last year. Strauss Stationers, where everyone used to buy their fancy wedding invitations, closed two years before that. The fish 'n' chips drive-through is doing okay and has a little crowd in front of the take-out window. Way off in the distance, Saba's is still open, because in Arizona, cowboy boots and hats aren't considered optional.

I watch MacKenna and Charles step out of the double doors and into the parking lot. Two little dimples appear on Mac-Kenna's cheeks when she smiles. Charles has a looseness to his walk. His arms dangle.

There's a low rumble, like thunder from a storm that couldn't possibly exist on this perfectly sunny day.

Something's wrong.

In the reflection of the market's high, shiny windows, I see something happening in the bank building next door. Some kind of fire burning in the lower levels. A pain builds in my chest and I force air into my lungs. My vision blurs at the edges. It's panic, and there isn't much time before it overtakes me.

The muscles in my legs tense and I take off at a sprint, grabbing MacKenna and Charles as I pass. I haul them along with me twenty feet or so into the store. We clear the door and run past a man and a woman frozen at the sight of what's going on across the street.

I desperately want to look back.

But I don't.

A scream.

A low, loud boom.

My ears ring.

The lights in the store go off.

I've got MacKenna by the strap of her maxidress and Charles by the neck. We feel our way in the dim light. The three of us crouch and huddle together behind a cash counter. A few feet in front of us, the cashier who checked us out two minutes ago is sitting on the floor hugging her knees.

We're going to die.

Charles's mouth is wide-open. His lips move. He pulls at the sleeve of my T-shirt.

I can't hear anything.

It takes everything I've got to force myself to move.

Slowly.

Slowly.

Leaning forward. Pressing my face into the plywood of the store counter, I peek around the corner using one eye to see out the glass door. My eyelashes brush against the rough wood, and I grip the edge to steady myself. I take in the smell of wood glue with each breath.

Hail falls in the parking lot. I realize it's glass.

My stomach twists into a hard knot.

It's raining glass.

That's the last thing I see before a wave of dust rolls over the building.

Leaving us in darkness.

DR. DOOMSDAY SAYS:

THOSE WHO PANIC DON'T SURVIVE.

A handful of lights flicker on.

The first proof that my ears still work is MacKenna's voice. "Oh God. What the hell. Jesus." She's crouched next to me, breathing heavy, her toes curled over the edges of her wedge sandals.

On the counter in front of where we're hunkered down, the cash register's computer screen reboots with a large timer counting down from twenty minutes. This, and the scattered fluorescent lights, must be the store's backup power system. Next to the register, a stack of plastic dancing turkey figurines shake in unison from side to side. This is going to be the last thing I see. My last moments on earth will be spent thinking *Gobble till you wobble.*

I put an arm around Charles and hug him tight as I fight off waves of panic. Flashes of cold chill my blood. Hot acid rises in my throat. My stomach lurches like it's been kicked. I'm not sure whether to let myself throw up or to do everything I can not to throw up.

"Susan. What's happening?" Charles asks. Loud. Right in my still-ringing ear. He must really be scared, because he never *ever* calls me by my real name.

"It's going to be okay," I say.

MacKenna doesn't look at me and starts to rock on her heels.

We all jolt as another round of thunder booms outside.

From somewhere in the store, a woman screams, "We're gonna die!"

That does it.

Deep breath.

I can almost hear my dad's voice. *It's not the smartest or the strongest who survive. It's the people who stay calm, who stay rational.*

Always remember this one, simple thing.

Don't stand around waiting to die.

I tap Charles on the arm. "I think there was some kind of an explosion at the bank next door. You have to treat this like one of Dad's bomb drills. We've done it a thousand times. We need to do it again now. Just like we practiced."

Charles and I stand, but MacKenna stays huddled on the white tile floor. I reach out my hand to help her up. "We have to go." When she doesn't move, I add, "Now."

"What the everlasting hell are you talking about?" she asks, still not moving. "Go? Go where? We need to wait here until someone in a Kevlar suit shows up to wave us out. *Going* is the worst damn idea I've heard in all my life."

I check the view from the store's glass doors. A red-orange glow flickers through a dark fog. My blood runs cold again. "Something's going on with that building. And when big buildings fall down, they tend to fall on the things around them." For a second, I freeze. "Wait. You don't think…that Jay is in there? Do you?"

MacKenna's dad is the head of security at the bank. On most days, he works in the skyscraper that's currently on fire.

She shakes her head. "No. He took the day off. To fix the pool motor."

"Okay. Good." *Deep breath.* "We have to get going, then."

MacKenna still doesn't get up. She pokes her head around the counter to get a view of First Federal. "Someone was probably in there though."

I put my hand over my mouth to keep from throwing up the burrito I had for lunch.

"*Get going.* It's the first step in the drill," Charles says. His eyes are wide and he's got his hands balled into tiny fists. Dad taught him to recite the Latin names of different kinds of roses to avoid a panic. But he hasn't resorted to that yet.

"The drills?" MacKenna repeats and stares at me. "You actually want to follow the instructions in that ridiculous book?"

But Charles puts out one of his hands and MacKenna takes it. I don't have time to consider what it means for our relationship that she would rather take advice from an eight-year-old.

At least we're up and moving.

"Okay. Okay." *Breathe. Breathe. Breathe.* "Step two. Supplies. Like we practiced." I grab a couple of the reusable bags from a stand near the cash register and toss one at Charles. "You do first aid and I'll take sundries."

"It's gonna be okay, right?" he asks.

"Yeah. Yes. Of course," I say as I run my sweaty hands down the front of my jeans. "As long as we stick to the plan."

He takes the bag and jogs down aisle two.

"Hey, Charles. I love you," I call after him.

He stops and panic fills his face. "No, Jinx. No. That's not part of the drill."

My mushiness has managed to terrify my brother more than the explosion. I have to keep him calm. "Show Mac-Kenna what to do, okay?"

MacKenna bites her lip and takes off after him. She hasn't said anything since Charles helped her off the floor. I see the tail of the chevron-printed skirt of her dress whip around the corner as I'm stuffing sunglasses from a kiosk into my bag.

It helps that we're at Halliwell's, where we've done most of our drills. I already know that face masks are on aisle four. On my way, I snag a lighter, a few light scarves, three base-ball caps, several bottles of water, a flashlight that already has batteries in it and a small toolkit.

I meet MacKenna and Charles at the back of the store.

"Okay, let's go over it. First-aid kit."

"Check," Charles says.

"Rubbing alcohol?"

"Check. Jinx. I swear. I got everything. I promise."

"All right. Let's move."

Keep calm. The calm survive.

Walking fast, we pass a few people who are sitting on the floor, crying and tapping their cell phones over and over. The woman in the front is wailing uncontrollably and from some-where else in the store a man yells, "Shut up, lady!"

The store manager runs out of a break room and blocks our path to the back door. He braces himself in the hallway between the restrooms and the exit doors.

"We have to get out of here," I tell him.

I see this guy every time we stop at the store, and it's like he's gotten older and frailer in the last three minutes. "We can't… No… We can't go out there. The power. The phones. They don't work."

"'Don't stand around waiting to die,'" Charles whispers.

Listening to my brother quote Dr. Doomsday terrifies me even more.

"If the manager thinks we should stay, maybe, maybe, maybe we should stay," MacKenna stammers.

Keep calm. The calm survive.

I need the manager to move out of the way. This building is a billion years old and there's no telling how long it will withstand the chaos outside. My pulse keeps pace with the tick of the large clock on the wall. Our chance of survival is slipping away.

"You'd expect that. Cell towers only have a certain amount of bandwidth." I try to step around him. "Everyone within a ten-mile radius is probably trying to use their phone. You get signal collision and tower overload. We need to get out of here."

A couple paces in front of me, a woman kneels in front of a crying toddler. A boy in a blue shirt with a train on the front. A tiny version of my brother.

I pull the manager's sleeve. "We need to get *everyone* out of here."

We share a look. My brown eyes into his blue. It lasts less than a second. But I can tell.

He's afraid too.

Afraid that this is the start of something.

The manager takes light steps, like he thinks the ground will give way beneath his feet, and moves in the direction of the mother and her son. He helps the woman up and says, "We should be ready in case we need to leave."

I dole out the face masks, hats, scarves and sunglasses to

the three of us. Charles and I put ours on. MacKenna wears the hat but doesn't put the face mask on and does not wrap the scarf around her mouth and neck.

MacKenna is barely functional. "I don't... I can't..." she keeps repeating.

Okay. Okay. We can do this.

A siren blares in the distance. There's another crash.

An expression of horror crosses MacKenna's face. "You still want to go out there? We *can't* go out there."

"You need to put on your mask," I tell her. "For the dust."

It's getting even darker inside the building as the dust and smoke grow thicker outside. Help won't be here anytime soon. "Okay. We'll go out the back. We probably won't be able to see. But it's a straight shot across the parking lot to Saba's. We should be able to go through and into the alley behind the shopping center." To Charles, I add, "Like we practiced."

MacKenna snaps the strap of the face mask. She's regained a bit of color in her face. "Oh, you *have* lost it. If we're going outside, let's at least get to the car."

The wails of the sirens grow louder. I'm getting that hot, panicky feeling in my throat again. "I'm taking my brother out the back. If you want to stay here, fine. If you want to get in the car and try to drive it around a flaming building, also fine."

Charles parrots our father. "'Never get in a vehicle unless you have a clear exit path.'"

We take a few steps while MacKenna stays frozen, staring at the keys.

Tires screech.

Glass shatters and tinkles.

Another scream, this one cut off.

Metal scrapes the tile floor, and the sound is far worse than fingernails scratching a chalkboard. Our white Prius is on its side and being shoved through the storefront by a large pickup truck. It rolls and skids across the store, pushing over several cosmetic counters. Dozens of tubes of lipsticks fly into the air.

Breathe.

Because the calm survive.

A shelf in aisle one teeters back and forth. It falls over, knocking down the shelves next to it. They fall like dominoes.

With a series of clicks, the last of the lipsticks roll to a stop.

There's a hiss, probably from damaged two-liter soda bottles.

And then silence.

Even through my mask, I can smell the isopropyl alcohol and iodine that's spilling onto the floor from a nearby rack. I instinctively reach out to adjust my brother's mask.

MacKenna's eyes are so wide that her eyeballs might fall out of their sockets. She must be thinking the same thing I am.

The woman at the front of the store is dead.

MacKenna's voice shakes. "Okay. Okay. I…uh…guess the car's not a good idea after all."

Smoke and dust pour into the market through the gaping hole created by our car.

I grab my brother's hand and pull him toward the employees-only exit door.

The situation is finally becoming clear to everyone else in the store too. People scramble off the ground, and we find ourselves in a mass movement toward the rear door. I'm relieved to see the manager crowding up behind me.

MacKenna struggles to put her mask on as we move. The man next to her snatches the scarf from her other hand. There's no time to object as we're jostled outside.

It's a war zone.

I can see less than a couple feet in front of my face.

Sirens, screaming, thuds, crashing, cracking glass.

Burned plastic. Rotten garlic. Even through the mask and scarf, the stench makes me gag.

The taste of ash fills my mouth.

I grab on to my brother's jacket, but I need to keep my other hand in front of me to feel my way. MacKenna's decided to stick with us, and I feel her hand next to mine on Charles's collar.

We walk as fast as we can. With my arm extended, I manage to keep from smacking into light posts. There's nothing we can do about the parking blocks. I hear MacKenna grunt a few times. I'm wearing Cons but she's got sandals.

The dust has cleared a little by the time we get close to Saba's. We've gotten separated from the other customers at the market and ended up alone at the boot warehouse where my dad gets most of his shoes. Luckily, no one has thought to lock the door.

The three of us hurry inside.

We're one step closer to safety.

Some of the tension in my shoulders falls away.

The instant I shut the door behind us, there's a series of loud pops and a tone like an off-key oboe.

A silhouette, a ragged chunk, of what could only be the First Federal Building lands on Halliwell's, releasing another storm of smoke and dust.

A numbness spreads over me, but I shake it off.

Because I know one thing.

We *are* getting out of here.

DR. DOOMSDAY'S GUIDE TO ULTIMATE SURVIVAL

RULE TWO:

DON'T WAIT FOR HELP. THERE'S NO GUARANTEE ANYONE'S COMING.

Saba's is devoid of human life.

There's only one emergency light positioned above the expensive boots. The rows of Fryes and Luccheses and Tony Lamas cast long gloomy shadows. Pendleton shirts hang from half-empty racks, but we're alone. The store's employees must've had the same idea as us.

Get away from here as fast as possible.

MacKenna breaks into a fit of coughs. It totally sucks that her scarf got stolen. Only the fact that I've been wearing my mask and kept my scarf wrapped around my face has kept me from choking on a mouthful of dust.

It's got to be about five thirty.

Hot panic returns as I realize.

The sun sets early in January.

It'll be dark soon.

Completely dark.

We have to hurry.

I feel my jean pockets and realize that I don't have my cell. "Do you have your phone?" I ask MacKenna.

She coughs again. "It's in my purse. I dropped it…back there at Halliwell's."

We share a tense glance, and I try to push the thought of the car and the woman who died out of my mind. I have to focus. The store has an antique wooden phone attached to the wall behind the cashier counter.

When I pick up the receiver, the line is dead.

We'll have to go for help.

It's barely any quieter in the store than it was outside. I follow a narrow hallway past a small office and a tiny break room. When I reach the back of the store, I find a door flapping open that leads to an alley, letting sounds of pandemonium inside. Poking my head out, I look around. The dust has settled a bit, and it's possible to see ten feet or so ahead. Even though I can't see all the way to the street, I'm reassured. The Saba's employees must have been able to use the alley to get away.

I wipe my sweaty hands on my jeans, but that only makes things worse as the dust from my pants sticks to my palms. My fingertips become gooey and grimy.

I kneel in front of Charles. "Okay. We're going to take the alley to the main street. There's a minimart on the corner of Eighth Avenue and Powell. We'll go that way. Hopefully, they'll have a working phone."

"We can call Mom?" Charles asks.

"Sure," I say in a terrible, fake-cheerful voice.

"I'm calling 911," MacKenna says.

Moving into the dusty alley, MacKenna and I hang on to Charles as if our lives depend on it. We bump into each other a few times. Charles keeps whacking me with his Halliwell's bag. The smack of the heavy bottle of alcohol against my thigh doesn't feel the way it should, doesn't hurt the way it should.

"How much farther?" Charles asks. He actually kind of yells it out, and that's when it occurs to me that the blaring sirens are getting louder and louder the farther that we walk toward the main street.

A bit of sensation returns into my fingertips.

We're walking toward help.

My step lightens and my breathing slows to a normal pace.

"It's about a mile," I yell back. "We're halfway there."

The alley runs behind one of the older suburban neighborhoods where overgrown oleander bushes cover chain-link fences, shielding the houses from view.

MacKenna pulls on my sleeve. "We could try going to one of the houses."

I shake my head. Dr. Doomsday would *never* approve of that plan. "We have to stick to the drill." It has gotten us this far.

By the time the alley dumps us onto Eighth Avenue, the dust has cleared into a haze that reminds me of the light fog that sometimes rolled over Point Loma when my parents would take us there on our annual San Diego vacation. A long line of black-and-white police cars and ambulances blocks off the street to prevent traffic from moving toward what's left of the bank. Red and blue lights flash in every direction.

As we approach the cars, I loosen my scarf and take off my mask, then drop the mask into one of the Halliwell's bags. MacKenna and Charles do the same. Two police officers run in our direction.

"You from the bank?" one of them yells. A thick layer of dust covers his blue uniform.

I shake my head. "From the market."

We all instinctively turn in that direction. In the distance, there's a new skyscraper—a pillar of thick smoke that rises to meet the darkening sky. A swarm of fire trucks is positioned halfway between us and what's left of the bank.

He nods and ushers the three of us behind the blockade, toward a group of ambulances where paramedics are waiting. We're the first to arrive. We sit together on a stretcher as med techs swirl around us.

As they check us out, small groups of people I recognize from Halliwell's filter in. I see the market manager. For a second, I wonder if I should offer to pay for the stuff I took. In addition to everything else that's happened, I've become a shoplifter.

Next to me, Charles is murmuring, "Rosa persica, Rosa phoenicia, Rosa pimpinellifolia…"

I reach for his hand and squeeze.

They take the manager away in an ambulance before I can say anything.

The paramedics want to send MacKenna to the hospital as well. Charles and I are both wearing our Cons, but she's been in sandals. Cuts cover her feet, and the heels of her cork wedges are soaked in blood.

A paramedic bandages up her feet. As he hands her a pair of hospital slippers, he says, "We'd like to take you to Rancho Mercy Medical to run some—"

"I'm fine," MacKenna says.

"…Rosa pinetorum, Rosa pisocarpa…"

"An X-ray would help us determine if there's any glass we haven't—"

"I. Am. Fine."

She doesn't seem fine. She clenches Charles's hand as if she'll be sucked into a black hole if she lets go. Soot falls from her dark hair each time she moves her head. White ash frosts her eyelashes, and dirt is smeared all over the part of her face that wasn't covered by the mask.

The paramedics ignore MacKenna's words and talk among themselves. I can make out only part of the conversation over all the noise. "We should probably…all of them…monitor… smoke inhalation…the parents."

I lean around Charles and yell, "Your dad would want you to go to the hospital."

A bit of red flushes MacKenna's cheeks and she glares at me.

The conversation between the medics goes on. "…the boy especially…"

My brother doesn't look so good. I get one of the paramedics' attention. "Charles has type 1 diabetes. His blood sugar was high when I checked it earlier."

There's more murmuring between the adults. "He doesn't have a SNAP?" one of the medics asks.

Diabetes could be cured with a mini pancreas implant, but since The Spark nationalized the medical industry ten years ago, there were long lines for expensive procedures.

I cough. "He's waitlisted."

The second medic leans closer to Charles and mutters, "The Spark," under his breath.

My brother stops reciting rose species and bursts into tears. "I want my mom."

I do too. "Do you have a phone? Can we call our parents?"

Mom does always carry my brother's meds.

MacKenna takes Charles's other hand. "We're okay. We're gonna be okay."

It's the police who call our house, and then we're loaded into a patrol car and driven a few miles to the parking lot of the Appliance Warehouse. It's crammed with cars parked every which way and news trucks and more ambulances. We're driven through the crowd to the side near the store entrance where authorities have set up a series of white tents that look like the ones used for special events. Like when the warehouse sells refrigerators for half price on the day after Thanksgiving.

We're ushered into one of the tents. On one side, a short, balding man is showing his phone to a cop. He's describing his wife. "She just went out for a bottle of cough syrup," he says.

I pray to God that he isn't talking about the woman who got run over by our car.

A little while later, Mom and Jay break into the tent. As always, they look like a pair of vacationing celebrities. Or like they just came home from brunch and golf. Mom's wearing a tweed jacket over her cashmere sweater and has pulled her thick brown hair into a glossy ponytail. Jay's wearing a designer striped rugby shirt and a pair of perfectly pressed khakis. Like Toby, he's tall and pale with almost black wavy hair.

"Thank God. Thank God," Mom says as she rushes forward. "When we got the news, I thought… I told you to go straight home…but…but nevermind that…"

Jay follows right behind her and pulls all of us into a tight hug. It's equal parts reassuring and awkward. I want the world to think I've got it all together, but relief is surging through me.

We'll be okay. Mom will take care of everything.

Even though I'm using all my willpower to hold them in, a couple of tears squirt from my eyes. I dab them away before anyone can see. Except MacKenna. I know she sees me but she isn't crying, and she pushes herself off the stretcher without saying anything.

Charles clings to Mom, and there's more hugging, and Jay asking over and over again if everyone is okay. I glance behind him. It's stupid, but I'm hoping to see Dad. My rational brain knows that Dad is probably in the middle of the desert somewhere trying to build a shelter out of a poncho and a pile of river rocks, but part of me was hoping he'd show up.

Of course, he doesn't.

Instead, on the open side of the tent, reporters are craning their necks to get a look at us, and everyone seems to be filming us with their phones. I guess surviving a disaster has suddenly made us interesting. The sun has gone down and it's dark. Camera flashes go off. A crew sets up large floodlights in front of the tents. A bunch of the cars in the parking lot have their headlights on. Those people are lucky the great Maxwell Marshall isn't their father. Dr. Doomsday doesn't let you drain your car battery during an emergency.

One of the paramedics brings us some snacks and a few bottles of water.

I take out a small bag of pretzels and give them to my brother. "You have to eat."

Charles doesn't touch the pretzels. "I'm not hungry."

"You have to eat," I say with a frown. "Stressful situations can cause changes in—"

He rustles the bag open, making as much noise as he can with the wrapper, and makes a show of putting a single pretzel on his tongue.

Mom takes the empty seat on the stretcher next to Charles and fishes an insulin pen from her purse. She checks his blood sugar, gives him a dose of his meds and then finds a tissue and busies herself trying to dab dust off his face. It's a total waste of time, because Charles looks like he's *made* of dirt.

"Jinx is right," she says. "You need to eat."

Charles takes another pretzel from the bag.

A few feet in front of me, MacKenna has inserted herself into a four-way debate. There's a doctor and Jay trying to get us to go to the hospital. A cop who wants to ask us questions. And MacKenna, who keeps saying things like, "We're fine," and, "We want to go home."

As usual, she hasn't asked us what *we* want.

Also, as usual, she's right. Because right now, all I want is to curl up under my quilt with my laptop, binge-watch *Popeye the Foodie* and never come out. Next to me, Charles yawns.

Mom gets up and joins Jay. "I think she's right, Jay. Their injuries seem minor. We can keep an eye on them and call for help if we need it. The kids should get some rest."

You'd think MacKenna would be glad to have the backup, but her lips press into a thin line.

Jay nods. "All right. But everyone is going to have a full checkup tomorrow."

They give us an extra first-aid kit and take us around the back of the store, letting us dodge the news crews and crowds that have been getting larger and larger in the appliance store parking lot. The police have put up tall lights on stands here and there, creating pockets of darkness and light. Jay carries Charles, and MacKenna and Mom walk fast.

I end up behind and I stumble, dropping one of the Halli-well's bags.

Because I'm so tired and generally so damn clumsy, I kick the bag with my next step, sending it skipping along the con-crete before it smacks against the Appliance Warehouse wall.

A guy steps out from the long, deep shadows created by the store's tall stucco wall. Most of his face is shrouded by a baseball cap, but he looks like he's about my age. The hat has an odd logo on it—a golden medallion—and dark, crisply cut hair pokes out from underneath it. He's wearing some kind of black or blue uniform, but I can't place it. He leans out of the shadows long enough for me to get a glimpse of gingerbread-colored eyes.

It's the guy from school. The one MacKenna called Navarro.

"You dropped this," he says. He picks up the bag and holds it out to me.

"How are… Why are… What are you doing here?" I stammer.

He hesitates with our hands inches apart on the bag handle. I'm frozen. Waiting. For him to come closer or maybe for him to say something else. My fingertips heat up.

MacKenna breaks into another round of coughs.

"Jinx," Mom calls. "We need to get home."

As I realize that my family and the two cops kept walking and are now standing about ten feet away, staring at me, my arm falls. Navarro has released the bag into my grip.

And he's gone.

I realize my mouth is hanging open.

Jay loads us all into his black Suburban. We're given a police escort out of the immediate area past the roadblocks and barricades. Once we come to Powell, the officer waves us off and we continue alone.

The Suburban's clock says it's 9:04 p.m.

After a few blocks, things start to seem pretty normal. The power is on. We pass house after beige house until we get to our subdivision, Copper Point. Our family is pretty lucky. Jay makes good money at the bank, and we live in a nice, new subdivision where the houses all have copper roofs and the community has a gate. Our house is easy to spot. It's been two months since the election, and we're the only people in our neighborhood who haven't taken down our blue Everyone's for Rosenthal signs. They're all lit up at night by the expensive lawn lights Jay installed. MacKenna even still has glittery letters that spell THE SPARK in her bedroom window.

As soon as I walk through the door, the smell of Mom's famous chicken chili hits me and makes my mouth water. Bowls and bags of chips are stacked on the counter. It feels like it's been a million years since Mom was in the kitchen this morning, chopping peppers and onions.

Jay makes sure we're okay and then disappears into his study. I doubt that the city is letting anyone go near the disaster area, but he probably has a lot of calls to make.

"I'll help Charles into the bath. Why don't you girls get cleaned up and we'll grab a quick bite," Mom says.

"I'm not hungry," MacKenna says.

"Me either," Charles says.

Honestly, I'm more tired than hungry, but I know Charles needs to eat.

I glance around the kitchen. "Where's Toby?"

MacKenna gives me a look.

Mom ushers us down the hall. "Once we heard about the explosion, I told him to stay put at the dorms. Go clean up and we'll have a bit of dinner. We'll keep it brief. I know you are all tired."

Bookcases line the hallway, and my gaze settles on a row of bright orange copies of *Dr. Doomsday's Guide to Ultimate Survival*. I don't know why Mom hangs on to copies of Dad's book or why she keeps them right here for us all to see every day.

MacKenna makes a beeline for the bathroom that we share, and I hear the water turn on a second later. It kind of sucks, because the fact that I'm absolutely covered with disgusting grime is getting more gross by the second. I smell like I've been chain-smoking for thirty years. I take off my filthy clothes, stuff them in a tote and temporarily put on my Code Camp T-shirt.

I slide behind my desk and open a couple of drawers. I've got some old devices, but without the data card from my phone, they're useless. Not having a phone is going to be a real problem.

And.

I just saw someone die. And here I am in my same blue room.

Through the open closet door, a pile of discarded teddy bears stare at me. Despite their cheerful expressions, they're strangely sinister. I get up and close the door.

Our bathroom is in between our two bedrooms with a door that connects to each room. After I hear MacKenna close her door, I head in there. There's only a tiny bit of hot water left, but even a short cold shower is a little bit of heaven. I didn't know it was possible to be this dirty. I scrub ash from behind my ears, from that spot on my head where I part my hair, from where it got stuck in my bra.

Back in my room, I throw on a pair of yoga pants and a gray T-shirt and open the hall door.

The whole house is as quiet as a museum after closing time. No scraping of spoons in chili bowls. No chitchat.

It's absolutely silent. The tiny hairs in the back of my neck stand up.

I walk down the hall and into the empty kitchen. Someone has abandoned an open bag of shredded cheese and a pile of corn chips on a paper plate. The bar stools at the kitchen's marble island are pulled out at odd angles. Jay's laptop is open.

I turn my head. From my position, I can see everyone silently clustered around the large television in the family room with the volume strangely low.

I'm about to move in that direction when an alert sounds from Jay's laptop.

The console window is open. A script has been recently executed.

```
16:55:01 janders CRON[69210]:
(root) CMD ( cd / && run-parts /opt/dayzero/)
```

In spite of the fact that I'm dead on my feet, my heartbeat picks up. This is weird. Super. Super. Weird. Jay isn't especially techie. He certainly wouldn't be running code in the console window. And the code isn't anything I recognize. I have no idea what it's designed to do.

Day Zero.

What the hell is that?

MacKenna gasps at something happening on the TV screen.

I approach and stand next to Mom.

The screen is filled with images of flaming buildings all over the country, shots of crying people searching for their lost loved ones and the occasional image of an anchor trying to explain how or why this could have happened.

Headlines scroll by.

I struggle to make sense of everything.

In wake of attacks, President Carver declares state of National Emergency.

On screen, troops roll out of Luke Air Force Base.

They cut to a press conference. To a close-up of David Rosenthal.

The Spark's defeated leader leans closer to the camera. Rosenthal's weary face covers the screen. "Our worst fears have been realized."

Mom reaches out and squeezes my hand.

"The collapse of civilization has begun."

Rosenthal's face disappears and the screen goes black.

My superpower is pretending everything is okay when it's not.

But even I have to admit that Tuesday is off to a weird start.

I sleep in late and by the time I roll out of bed and hit the kitchen, everyone else is already up. MacKenna is on the sofa with her hair pulled back in a ponytail. She has her nose in a book. That part is pretty normal, but she's also flipping between several different news stations and pounding out notes on her e-tablet.

Both Mom and Jay are home. Jay because someone blew up the building that he works in and Mom because the town closed the schools for the day. She probably would have had to stay home anyway, to take us all to the doctor and for the way that parents want to hang around and observe you after something traumatic happens.

According to the news, a bunch of roads are still closed

due to the explosion, and an air quality advisory is in effect because of the dust.

On TV, a long line of tanks and desert camo Humvees proceed down Main Street toward the remains of the First Federal Building. We find out that the explosion at our bank was one in a series of what is believed to be deliberate attacks. President Carver will address the country later today.

Jay looks like he always does in a pair of slacks and a polo shirt in some cheery color. Today, it's the orange of a popsicle. He's outwardly calm. But he's doing like a thousand things at once. He's chopping fruit for some kind of salad and answering his phone and checking emails on his laptop, which is still on the island in the kitchen. Every couple minutes he asks one of us if we feel okay.

Mom is out on the patio. Through the sliding glass doors, I can see her pacing as she talks.

Charles sits at the breakfast counter in his plaid pajamas, his reddish-brown hair sticking almost straight up. He watches Jay cut cantaloupe, his legs swinging in sync with the chop of Jay's knife. My brother jerks his chin in Mom's direction. "Dad called a few minutes ago."

That's reassuring, I guess. At least Dad's checking on us. Maybe he'll even want to talk to us.

I hear the front door open and slam. MacKenna walks into the kitchen. "What the hell happened in the yard?"

Mom comes inside. "Language, please, dear."

Nope. My dad didn't ask to talk to me.

Perfect.

MacKenna focuses on her own father. "Dad. Where. Are. My. Signs?"

Jay points to the device in his hands and mouths *I'm on the phone.*

My pulse picks up. At first, I'm a little worried that the tanks we saw on TV might have started rolling down our street. But MacKenna is angry, not scared.

"What are you talking about?" I ask.

She jerks her thumb toward the door to the garage. "Go see for yourself."

Charles tosses me a bottle of water as I pass. I'm twisting the cap off when I see what MacKenna means. In the garage, all the signs from the yard are stacked in a huge pile on Jay's worktable.

It's a chilly morning, but my blood is practically icy.

Jay is getting rid of the signs that we support The Spark. Literally.

It strikes me that MacKenna managed to collect *many* posters.

The Spark for a New Generation.

Some are professionally printed and some she must have made herself.

The Spark for Prosperity for All.

Bold type in various shades of deep blue.

Inside the house, I take a seat next to Charles where someone put out a plate for me. I stab a steaming pile of biscuits and gravy with my fork.

MacKenna stares at her father.

Jay is finally off the phone and doesn't look at us when he says, "I couldn't sleep. I thought it might be a good idea to tidy things up a little bit. The election has been over for a while now. You know, *Everyone's for Rosenthal.* But still. Better safe than sorry."

Jay Novak was out before dark removing MacKenna's political signs from the yard.

Even worse, he didn't throw the signs away. While we're eating, he returns to the garage. After breakfast, I follow

MacKenna back out there, and all that's left of the signs are a few posts sticking out from behind one of the heavy storage cabinets.

He's hidden the signs.

When MacKenna gives him an accusatory stare, he mumbles something about not wanting to take up too much space in the trash can.

Mom comes into the garage carrying a laundry basket full of the dirty towels from our showers last night. She's holding up better than Jay.

But she's not the head of security at a building that just had a massive breach of security.

She's in a pair of yoga pants and a tunic top and manages to move to the corner of the garage where we keep the washing machine without seeming stiff. She gives me and MacKenna a reassuring smile while she measures the laundry detergent.

"You girls need to get dressed," she says. "You have an appointment with Dr. Piacintine at ten."

I roll my eyes. I don't know how old you have to be to not go to the pediatrician anymore, but apparently, even at seventeen, I haven't hit that magic number yet. I've been seeing Dr. Piacintine since I got the chicken pox in the first grade. He still gives me a lollipop.

"You should take those letters out of your window," Jay tells MacKenna.

It takes me a second to realize that he means the blue, backlit letters that spell THE SPARK.

"Why?" she asks.

"Oh, because. You know. It seems like the right time," he says, staring at his phone.

She steps closer to him. "Why?"

He's pressing the screen and doesn't answer.

"It's still a free country, right?" she says.

"Yes," Jay answers. "But these attacks are serious. They don't know… I don't know… This is a good time to err on the side of caution."

"We know about the attacks," MacKenna says. "We were almost killed in the attacks."

Once again, she's speaking for all of us, but I wasn't up at the crack of dawn reading the news. I don't know anything about the other attacks.

Mom's smile falls into a worried frown. "You girls should get ready."

Jay frowns too, and for a second his expression is appropriate for the crappy situation we're in. He pats MacKenna on the back. "Good idea. And don't worry about the letters. I'll take care of them. There's no reason you should have more to worry about, after what you've been through."

MacKenna's on the verge of arguing, but Mom puts an arm around both of our shoulders and herds us back into the kitchen. "We need to leave in ten minutes."

I make sure that Charles is getting dressed and then I run to my own closet and jam on a clean pair of jeans, a T-shirt and a hoodie. I watch TV while I wait for MacKenna. Clicking through the channels, I see that, rather than explaining what happened, most of the news stations have moved on to figuring out who to blame for the attacks. Attractive people blame The Opposition. Or The Spark.

When we're all ready, we return to the garage.

Mom and Jay are still there, standing close together, speaking to each other in hushed tones.

"I think we should at least consider speaking with a lawyer. You don't know—" Mom is saying.

"I haven't done anything wrong and any investigation will show that," Jay says.

"Yes. But, Jay, in cases like these—"

Jay leans against the Suburban and sighs in frustration. "Stephanie. Don't you believe me when I say that I will handle this situation in the way that's best for our family?"

"I'm worried about what's best for *you*," Mom answers.

Jay sees us first. "I have a conference call in a few minutes. Keep me posted about what the doctor says."

Mom nods and walks to the driver's seat. I help Charles in the back. MacKenna gets in on the other side, sitting next to my brother, leaving me to sit in the front with Mom.

"What was that about?" I ask.

Even though she's clutching the steering wheel so hard that her fingers turn white, she says, "I think it's important that Jay is protected, especially since we don't know how the bank will decide to handle things." Her gaze drifts to the rearview mirror, to my brother's small face. "We can discuss the rest later."

In the backseat, MacKenna squirms around. "Why would my dad need a lawyer?"

"He probably doesn't," Mom says. Mom puts the car into autodrive and turns her attention to her phone. Her words have a finality. We won't be discussing this further.

I consider asking Mom if we'll be able to get new phones but then think better of it. She has a lot on her mind, and I can probably solve that problem on my own.

Rancho Mesa Pediatrics is about a five-minute drive from our house, but the appointment itself takes forever. Mom does a bunch of paperwork while Dr. Piacintine changes the bandages on MacKenna's feet. When she can't answer questions about what she might have stepped on to his satisfaction, he orders a tetanus shot. Meanwhile, I have a physical and the nurse asks a bunch of questions that seem designed to figure out whether I'm mentally stable.

As Charles is having his diabetes sensor disk recalibrated and MacKenna is getting her shot, I wait outside in the courtyard. The doctor has a large swing set and slide a few feet from the front door of the office. Several kids travel together down the slide with smiles on their faces.

They're happy.

It's still cool and cloudy outside.

A familiar figure looms in the shadows.

Dad.

"How did you know we'd be here?" I ask.

He ignores my question and comes closer. "Jinx," he says, with the kind of impersonal nod that would be perfect for a coworker or a store clerk. "I'm relieved that you're all right."

Dad's in full-on Drill Mode. He's in his utility jacket and khakis, his beard unkempt.

I remember a time in the past, before The Opposition, Ammon Carver and the drills, when Dad used to hug me.

That was a long time ago.

I suck in a deep breath and fight off the combination of dread and sadness about to overtake me. "Dad. Did you see the news? About the explosions? About Ammon Carver?"

"Yes," he says flatly. He stares at me. "I have to go off-the-grid for a while."

"What? Why?" Hot panic threatens to overtake me. "They're saying you're responsible for—"

"I know what I did," he interrupts. "It'll be better for you and your brother if I go away for a while."

"Better?" I ask, grateful for the anger I'm now feeling. "Didn't Mom tell you what happened? We almost died!"

"Safer," he corrects. He gives me a small, sad smile. "I'm very proud of you. But, of course, with your training, I'd expect nothing less."

He glances to his left and, in the far corner of the courtyard, a tall, gaunt man smoking a cigarette watches two children play on the swings.

"Dad—" I begin.

Again, he cuts me off. "Jinx, I need you to take care of your brother. I need your word."

What does he imagine is going to happen to Mom?

"Dad—"

"Your word, Jinx. You'll keep Charles safe?"

"Yes, Dad. But where are you going? Are you in some kind of trouble?"

Dad stroked his beard in his maddeningly calm fashion. "Not yet. I'll contact you when it's safe."

It doesn't seem to bother Dad that those two statements don't go together at all. Desperate to be seen or heard, I wave my hands around. "But you helped him. You helped Ammon Carver. He's supposed to be your friend. And now he's president. Doesn't that mean anything?"

Dad considers this. "Yes. Just not what you think."

My father hasn't spent enough time listening to me to even know what I think.

A woman carrying a crying baby ushers several sick children out of the doctor's office.

"Stick to the drills and you'll be fine."

With that, Dad turns to go, and I'm left there wondering if I should chase him down. If it would make any difference if I did.

He's halfway across the parking lot and climbing into an

old pickup truck when Mom, MacKenna and Charles come out of Dr. Piacintine's office.

"I really hate that old dinosaur of a doctor," MacKenna says.

"He told you to take a lollipop," Charles answers.

Mom squints at Dad's disappearing form. "Was that your father?"

"Dad was here?" Charles cranes his neck in each direction.

"He left us." I'm unable to keep the bitterness out of my voice.

"I'm sure he'll be back," Mom says.

She's speaking more to Charles than to me.

My anger flares up at her. "Why are you always covering for him?"

"I'm not covering for him." Mom stares into the vacant space as if she expects Dad to return. "He's just afraid."

This one time, I force myself to say what's really on my mind. Hoping for some kind of an answer to fill that hollow space in my chest. "That something terrible is going to happen?"

"That if you spend too much time fighting dragons, you become one yourself."

I don't know what that even means, and Mom doesn't say anything else.

She's lost in her own thoughts as we drive home.

When we get home, MacKenna's window is cleaned out.

THE SPARK letters are gone.

Our house looks exactly like every other one on our street.

DR. DOOMSDAY SAYS:

**DON'T RELY ON STATE-SPONSORED AUTHORITIES.
THEIR MISSION MIGHT NOT BE TO HELP YOU.**

Back at home, Mom tries to make us take a nap.

I do go to my room, but I sit at my desk and power on my desktop computer.

The feeling of my fingers on the cool keys comes as a relief. Something familiar.

The instant my screen is working, a bunch of messages from Terminus pop up.

Terminus is probably the closest thing I have to a friend. We used to see each other in real life every week in computer club back when his name was Harold and my dad wasn't busy preparing for the end of the world and things were normal. Terminus graduated last year, but he's still one of the best *Republicae* players of all time. Some Silicon Valley millionaire even offered him fifty grand for his account. He's that good. He didn't bother taking it, because he's got some other data mining operation going on and he still does raids with me.

Oh. Yeah. The raid.

Terminus: It's 6:30. You there?

Terminus: Helllllooooooooo...

Terminus: Where the hell are you? The whole guild is asking.

Terminus: You missed your own raid.

And. Well. I missed the raid because I was in some...some kind of catastrophe? I type a message to Terminus.

Me: Hey? You there?

While I wait for him to answer, I open a browser window and do a search for the explosion at First Federal Building. The images that fill the screen aren't of the Rancho Mesa branch. The worst attack was in New York. The explosion took out three massive buildings.

Whoever was responsible for the attacks targeted five cities.

Boulder, Ann Arbor, Seattle, New York and Rancho Mesa.

I open another window and check out First Federal. I already knew that the banks were owned by Ammon Carver and that his family had been building banks forever. But they must own hundreds of buildings. Why would someone blow up those five?

As I click around I realize. These are all cities known for data storage.

The buildings were all file storage locations.

Someone was out to destroy banking records.

But this raises more questions than it answers. A bank like First Federal would have scanned all its physical records and would have backups of their backups. Any data loss would be temporary. They'd be able to make a full recovery. Probably in less than a week.

I can't make any sense of this, and I'm relieved when a new message from Terminus starts to come through.

Terminus: Where have you been?

I take a deep breath and type a response.

Me: Have you seen any of this First Federal stuff? We were trapped in Halliwell's across from the branch downtown.

Terminus: No way.

Terminus: You're screwing with me.

Me: Nope.

Terminus: You okay?

Me: I think so. Mom made us go to the doctor this morning.

Terminus: Yeah. You talk to Marshall?

I hesitate. It's hard to unpack all the weirdness with my dad. Plus, Terminus has his own issues. He used to be my dad's top student from our computer club. But that was before. Before Dad went so far off the rails.

Now, Terminus feels abandoned.

I can relate.

Me: I saw him.

Me: He said he's going off-the-grid for a while.

Three animated dots linger for a long time.

Terminus: Probably for the best. There are a lot of people who want to blame him for what's happening.

I don't know what to say, and there's a quiet knock on my door.

Me: Gotta go.

Terminus: Text me later.

Terminus: And don't worry about the raid. I logged in to your account and played as you. The guild is occupying the Cataline Hills.

Me: Thanks.

Mom comes in and sits on my bed. It's the first time we've been able to talk since everything happened.

I move away from my desk and sit next to her.

She kisses me on the forehead. "You've had a rough twenty-four hours."

As she wraps her arm around my shoulders, I realize how much tension I have in my arms and neck. I desperately want things to get back to normal.

"Jinx, I know things seem bad right now, but I hope you know that no matter what happens, I would do anything to keep you safe," she says. "Your father would too."

I stiffen. "I think Dad went away."

Mom smiles reassuringly. "I'm sure he's off on one of his drills."

"This sounded different," I say.

"Don't worry, dear. Come have some lunch. Also, this would be a great time to catch up on your homework. Even

The Opposition can't change the fact that your book report will be due once school starts up again."

Spoken like a true teacher.

She leaves, and I spend a couple of minutes searching for my laptop before realizing that it was destroyed in the explosion. Along with my phone. I'll have to replace that too.

I come into the kitchen where Mom must be making sandwiches, because there's a stack of lunch meat and cheeses on a plate on the counter. Jay's laptop is there again. Only this time it's open to a website.

For a law firm.

Once again, the kitchen feels eerily deserted. I look around and see everyone else clustered at the large living room window that faces the front yard. Jay's arms are crossed. Mom peeks through the closed blinds. Red and blue lights shine and flash through the wedge.

The cops are here.

I'm about to go over there to see what's going on when a loud beep sounds from Jay's laptop. The console window opens and a message appears on the screen.

The wolf is shaved so nice and trim.
Red Riding Hood is chasing him.

And then.

TORK IS COMING.

Mom opens the front door.

Rows of police officers block the front door and the outside entryway.

Jay's laptop has been hacked.

What is happening?

And who or *what* is a Tork?

I fight the urge to use Jay's laptop to figure this out.

Mom has let a few cops into the foyer.

I try to reassure myself. This must be routine. But when the floodlights in the backyard activate to reveal a dozen officers in black SWAT uniforms surrounding our pool, I know something's gone really wrong.

Mom's voice shakes. "Jinx, can you take your brother?"

I slam Jay's laptop shut and tuck it under my arm, trying to conceal as much of it as possible. I don't know what's wrong with it. And then suddenly I remember the code I saw yesterday when we got home from that mess at the bank.

Day Zero.

Maybe the computer has gotten some kind of a virus. But it shouldn't be left lying around until I figure it out. Receiving cryptic messages in the console window is *not normal*.

Waiting for Charles at the hall entrance, I hope no one notices the laptop. My brother walks over to me at a pace that's maddeningly slow.

Step. By. Step.

Light footsteps echo off the tile floor and fill all the quiet, empty space.

While I struggle to take a full, deep breath.

When he's an arm's length away, I grab him and tow him down the hall. Mom didn't say where to take Charles, and my room is first, so I take us there. I shut the door and give my brother a gentle shove toward my bed. "What did you hear?"

Charles lands with an *oof* on my blue bedspread. "They were asking about Jay."

This morning, Mom and Jay were clearly worried about something like this.

But still.

Jay is one of the most honest people I know.

Suddenly, the laptop is a hot potato. I open the closet and stuff it under the pile of teddy bears, repositioning them as best I can.

"What are you doing?" Charles asks.

"Think, Charles. What did the cops say?"

My brother yawns. "They just asked Mom if Jay was home."

I fidget with the tail of my T-shirt. "Okay. Wait here."

Without stopping for him to object, I return to the hall. MacKenna is leaning against the wall, watching Mom and Jay. They're a few feet away in the foyer, speaking in hushed tones.

"You don't need to consent to an interview," Mom says. "We could call Phil Hartwell. Or maybe the bank's in-house counsel. Or wait for them to come back with a warrant."

Jay's lips pucker. "I'm head of security for the Rancho Mesa branch of First Federal. It's my responsibility to assist the police."

Mom frowns. "All I'm saying is that it would be better to understand the angle of the investigation before you answer any questions on the record. If we call Phil—"

"Stephanie, I haven't done anything wrong. That's what any investigation will show."

MacKenna steps forward. "Jesus, Dad. Do you always have to act like you were born on the Fourth of July? Are we really gonna pretend like truth and justice always prevail?"

Jay smooths his orange shirt and turns to his daughter and kisses her on the forehead. "I understand your concerns, and you're not wrong. But MacKenna, I'm *acting* like a man whose first responsibility is the safety of his family."

Leaning back toward Mom, Jay says, "I'm going with them."

The shuffling and mumbled conversation of the police in the foyer fills the tense silence following those words.

Mom moves to block his path. "I don't think that's wise."

He kisses her forehead. "Everything will be fine, I promise."

He leaves the three of us there.

Mom remains in the foyer, blocking the police from getting any farther inside. They clearly want to search the house, but she quotes Thomas Paine and tells them to come back with a warrant.

After Jay goes, the cops in the backyard leave too, but a few black-and-white cars remain in front of the house. Watching us.

We go through the motions.

I'm dying to get back to my computer. If I could connect Jay's laptop to my machine, I could run some diagnostics. Plus, Terminus has a contact that used to have the log-in info for all the local police systems. I could do a search for Tork, or try to get my hands on the police files. But Mom makes us stay in the living room. She probably wants to watch us for symptoms of shock.

Mostly so Charles will eat, Mom makes us lunch then gives us all busywork to keep us near her. As the afternoon fades into the evening, we have dinner. I force down mouthfuls of cheese pizza. The slice is cold and clammy. The cheese tastes like plastic. I check my brother's blood sugar and give him a small injection using the insulin pen.

I suspect he's found where I'm hiding my candy bars.

Afterward, Mom gets a call and takes it on the patio. A few minutes later, Charles pulls out one of his big gardening books and curls up in the oversize suede armchair. MacKenna and I sit together on the sofa.

In spite of everything, I find myself thinking of Navarro.

"You know that guy from the parking lot? He was at the appliance store. Do you think he's…" I trail off, considering how to finish my thought. *Do you think he's following us? Do you think he's dangerous?*

As usual, she guesses what I really want to know. "Um. Do I think he's hot?"

MacKenna flashes me a grin, which quickly fades. "Yeah… but what was he doing there?" She picks up an e-tablet from the end table and scribbles something down. "When we get back to school, I'll follow up. If there's a story, I'll find it."

Does Navarro have a story?

We're silent again.

We watch the news.

And we wait.

A little after 6:00 p.m., a graphic appears on the screen. *Stay tuned for a message from President Ammon Carver.*

A couple minutes later, an image of Carver in his usual tailored dark suit and red tie fills the screen. He's posed in front of a row of large golden eagle statues that have their wings folded in front of their bodies.

"Does it seem like my dad has been gone a *long* time?" MacKenna asks, unable to keep the nervous edge from her voice. She's doing her best to read a book called *The Savage Storm: Inside the World of Ammon Carver.*

"Does it seem like my mom has been on the phone a *long* time?" I say. Mom has been outside, pacing, arguing with someone on the other end of the line.

Neither of us answers the other. If we did, we'd have to acknowledge how we feel.

I change the subject. "Have you heard from Toby?"

MacKenna shrugs. "I don't have a phone, and Dad told Toby to stay at school until things settle down."

Whenever that will be.

Carver begins to speak.

"My fellow Americans, it is with a heavy heart that I address you this evening."

I shiver at his gravelly voice.

"Last night, shortly before 7:00 p.m. Eastern Standard Time, five First Federal facilities became the latest target of domestic terrorism. I know you will join me in offering thoughts and prayers to the victims of this violence. I wish I could stand before you and say that these attacks on my family's financial institutions—banks that have been the motor of our national prosperity for nearly a century—were directed toward me alone. However, early credible intelligence indicates that these dark deeds were the work of The Spark under the direction of the organization's leadership at the highest level and, therefore, a direct assault on our republic. November's election was a hard-fought battle, and my hope was that we'd be entering a period of hard-won peace. But this will not be possible when our rival political party and its candidate will not accept the results of a lawful election. I am saddened to report that authorities are seeking the whereabouts of David Rosenthal, who appears to have fled the country—"

MacKenna drops her book. "Wait. What? That can't be right."

Rosenthal. Her hero.

On screen, Carver continues.

"We will do whatever is necessary to bring those responsible to justice and secure—"

I pull my blanket around my shoulders. "That sounds really sinister."

MacKenna casts me a dark look. "Carver's whole presidency is sinister. You know, some people think he murdered his own mother."

"I'm not into those conspiracy theories," I say.

"Nobody knows where she is. That's not a theory."

"Yesterday, I declared a national state of emergency. Where necessary, I have called up state troops and authorized the use of—"

"Ten years ago, she was dropped off in front of a cruise ship and never seen again."

Mom comes in from the patio and gives a haggard glance to Ammon Carver on the screen. "Soon the world is going to be a very different place." An odd expression crosses her face. Like she regrets saying that. She sits between me and Mac-Kenna on the couch, picks up the remote control and mutes the television. "That was Phil. You know, that lawyer Jay plays golf with. He's got a few contacts at the courthouse, and he made some calls. He thinks they're treating Jay like a suspect."

MacKenna eyes Mom warily. "A suspect? Suspected of what?"

Charles freezes and looks up from his book.

She folds her arms across her chest. "We should get off our butts and do something to help him." MacKenna sounds tough, but her face is pressed into a worried frown.

"There must be something we can do," I say.

Mom sighs, and her shoulders slump. "I'm going to try. Phil put me in touch with a criminal attorney. She's going to meet me at the precinct and stop whatever questioning is going on. I need you girls to hold down the fort here." She rises, and I hear her in the kitchen getting her purse out of the hall closet.

Mom's statement takes the edge off MacKenna's fear. At the sound of the car starting in the garage, she flops back. I realize that maybe she feels alone. Toby is still at school, and Jay has been gone for hours.

"Mac, it'll be okay."

She gets up. Charles has fallen asleep in his chair. She covers my brother with a blanket and when she sits down again, she says, "Don't start calling me Mac and talking to me like we're gonna start our own girl gang. Things don't always work out okay just because we want them to."

Stepsister fail. I'm not someone she trusts. I also kind of think that Rosenthal's loss in the election is one more thing she blames me for. We keep watching TV.

We keep waiting.

MacKenna turns up the TV volume. Above a headline that reads *Where Is David Rosenthal?* a blonde woman is giving a report. A profile of Rosenthal.

"Born in a Borough Park one-bedroom apartment, Rosenthal is the son of Polish immigrants who struggled to manage their hardware store and make ends meet."

It's getting late. Mom's gone, Charles is asleep and Mac-Kenna clearly doesn't want to talk. This is the perfect time to make a break for my computer. To find out about Jay.

Or about Day Zero.

"…married his high school sweetheart and attended a city college…"

As I get up, MacKenna calls out, "What are you doing?"

"…spent long hours as a community organizer, working to address the low income…"

"I have to check something."

"Right now?" she asks.

I don't bother answering as I enter my room. I jiggle my mouse, open a private network window, cloak my IP address and route my connection through a bunch of different random locations, before finally contacting Terminus.

I'm praying that he's awake and that he gets my notification. Luckily, it takes only a minute or so before a message comes through.

Terminus: Hey

Me: I don't have much time. There's a bunch of cops here. Do you still have that file from the script kiddie you met at Infocon? The one with all the usernames and passwords for local police departments?

Terminus: The cops are there? Why?

Me: Do you have the file or not?

Terminus: Maybe

Me: They think my stepdad had something to do with the attacks on the banks.

Terminus: Did he?

Me: Are you seriously asking me that?

Terminus: Okay. But are you saying what I think you're saying? That Rancho Mesa's finest are hanging around your house and you want to choose this exact moment to hack the PD mainframe?

Me: I have to figure out why they think Jay has anything to do with this.

Terminus: I'll do it. Hang on.

I want to object, but the truth is that it's safer for Terminus to log in. He's already got the file, and he has better hardware than I do. Mom made me give all the really good stuff to Dad when they split.

Meanwhile, I search the web for *Tork*. Nothing particularly relevant comes up. There's a company that sells medical scrubs. A band based in Pittsburgh. It's also a brand of lug wrenches.

Quiet footsteps are coming down the hall. A new message from Terminus appears in the server chat window.

Terminus: It's bad.

MacKenna pushes my door open without knocking. "What are you doing?"

I'm starting to get nauseated again, like when I get off the Zipper at the state fair. "I told you. I have to check something."

Me: Tell me.

Terminus: Their theory is that someone used sonic interference to trigger something explosive that had already been placed in the buildings.

Me: Like what?

Terminus: Maybe Tannerite.

I bite my lip. Before he left his job at the university, my dad had been working along these lines. Investigating whether hardware could be vulnerable to sonic attack.

MacKenna approaches my desk. "Check something? Like what?"

Me: Marshall was never able to get that to work.

Terminus: Well maybe somebody did.

Me: They can't possibly know one way or the other. Any evidence must be buried under tons of rubble. It will take months to sort it out.

Terminus: They brought in Marcus Tork.

Tork.

I quickly open another search window and type in the name. The only result that gets returned is a profile for an insurance salesman in Milwaukee.

"Hello?" MacKenna waves her hand in front of my face. We both jump as the home phone rings.

Me: You know him?

Terminus: No and that's really saying something. The PD mainframe says he's some kind of counterterrorism specialist.

Me: Great.

The phone rings again.

"Could you answer that?" I ask MacKenna.

I don't know what's worse. The fact that this Tork guy is after us. That we can't find any information about him. Or that someone is sending messages about him to Jay's laptop.

It's all scary as hell.

Terminus: One of the facilities was under an off-site security audit. Tork was able to get the server logs from that location. Jesen Novak's credentials were used to access the security system right before the attack.

Ring.

"Why can't *you* answer it?" MacKenna shoots back.

"Please?" I plead with her.

Terminus: They recovered a code fragment from the bundle that

Ring.

Terminus stops typing for a second. Like he's at a loss for what to say.

My stepsister leans around my desk to get a look at my screen.

"MacKenna! Can you *please* answer the phone?"

Terminus: Someone uploaded. It addresses the building's built-in speakers.

Ring.

MacKenna sighs and moves away from my desk. A few seconds later the ringing stops.

Terminus: They recovered an IP address.

I almost hold my breath, waiting for his answer. I can check the logs from our router. Jay was home all day yesterday dealing with the pool repairman. I'll be able to see what IP address his computer used to access the internet.

This could prove him innocent.

Terminus: 192.68.63.231

I connect to the router and check the listing of IP addresses that it assigned today. There's a bunch of entries from the morning when we were all using our phones, followed by a gap and then a pickup around four o'clock.

16:22P	192.68.1.1	SSDP
16:39P	192.68.1.105	SSDP
16:52P	192.68.63.231	TCP

Oh. God.

The cops think the attacks came from our house.

MacKenna is in the hall.

Terminus: You gonna check the router log?

Me: I have to go.

Terminus: Okay.

Terminus: Jinx? Be careful.

Me: See what you can find out about Tork.

I do a secure erase of our chat and close all the windows as MacKenna enters my room.

She holds out the cordless phone from the kitchen. "Stephanie wants to talk to you."

Before I can even say hello, Mom's tense voice fills the speaker.

"You need to get out of the house."

DR. DOOMSDAY SAYS:

FAILURE TO UNDERSTAND YOUR ADVERSARIES IS DANGEROUS. FAILURE TO IDENTIFY THEM CAN BE FATAL.

"What are you talking about?" The phone shakes in my hand.

"I don't know… I just…" Mom's voice is stuffy and hoarse. Like she's been crying.

Hearing her lose it freaks me out. She used to do all the drills with Dad. She'd be out in the desert for weeks on end. And she *never* lost it.

"Mom. Mom. What's going on?"

She tries to conceal a sob with a cough. "I'm not even sure I understand it myself. They think Jay had something to do with… And they're not arresting him. But they won't let him go either. Not legal. Not legal." She blows her nose and is able to continue on in a more normal tone. "All I know for sure is that they're on their way to search the house. I need you to get Charles and go to your father's house. Wait there until I contact you."

I suck in a deep breath. It's been a while since we spent

any time at Dad's house. "He's probably not home, and what do I do about—"

A door or maybe a metal drawer slams in the background. "I can't talk now, Jinx. They're coming. Go to your father's house and wait there until I call you."

The line is dead before I get to ask any questions. *What should I do with Jay's laptop? What should I do about the router?*

Frantic.

That's what I am.

Like that one time I had eight shots of espresso while cramming for a test.

It's almost midnight.

MacKenna stares at me.

"Mom says the police are coming in to search the house." I stand up but have to brace myself on my desk. "You should pack up whatever you need for the next few days."

"Search the house? What are they looking for? Where's my dad?" Her voice sounds the way I feel inside. She picks at the bright unicorn pattern on her flannel pajamas.

But we have to get moving.

"I told you everything she told me. She said she'd call us later. We have to go."

When she continues to stare at me, I add, "Now."

"Where are we going?"

"My dad's."

MacKenna cocks her head to one side. "Does it matter at all that I don't want to leave home in the middle of the night to hang out at Maniac Manor?"

Sigh. "Does it matter at all that any second now, the cops *outside* are going to be coming *inside*? Does it matter at all that we don't have cell phones, so if we don't go somewhere with a phone number Mom knows, she won't be able to call us?"

My stepsister gives me an irritated look as she shuffles out.

Jay's laptop has to be what the police are looking for, and it will be better for all of us if they don't find it.

When she's gone, I head to my closet. I guess the upside of having a father who's constantly suspicious of everything and everybody is that you end up with the right gear for situations like these. After digging around a bit, I find a yellow duffel bag with a concealed compartment in the bottom.

I get Jay's laptop from under the pile of judgmental teddy bears and slide it into the compartment. I need something to conceal the weight of the computer, so I step into the hall to the bookshelves and take a couple of MacKenna's books.

I'm not sure why I do it, but I grab one of Dad's books. I add *Dr. Doomsday's Guide to Ultimate Survival* to MacKenna's copies of *Annika Carver, Teen Titan: How Ammon's Daughter Charmed The Opposition* and *The Modern Guide to The Spark*.

Charles and I have clothes at Dad's, so I don't need to pack much. I stuff my feet into my Cons and throw on a hoodie. There's a broken laptop with a dead battery in the bin next to my desk where I keep spare parts. It's an older model than Jay's but close in color and size. I take it with me as I leave my room.

Next, the kitchen. The only thing left to do is to pack Charles's meds. I go to the cabinet where Mom keeps the blood glucose meter and test strips.

I swing the cabinet door open. "MacKenna. Are you almost ready?"

After dropping the meds into my bag, I fish the spare car keys out of the junk drawer and put the old laptop on the counter in the spot where Jay usually checks his email as he eats his Shredded Wheat.

In the living room, all the noise has awakened Charles.

He opens his mouth in a huge yawn. "Jinx. Whasgoinon?"

I kiss his forehead. "We have to go to Dad's."

"Dad is home?" he asks in a small, hopeful voice.

"No." I hate the disappointment in his face. "Mom just says to go to his house and wait there while the police look around here."

And I want to get far, far away with Jay's laptop.

MacKenna meets me at the door to the garage pulling a large suitcase on wheels. She's changed into a pair of designer leggings with cutouts at the knees and an off-the-shoulder, sparkly sweatshirt. We head outside. I turn on the light. Jay's shiny black Suburban is parked in the same place we left it.

I press the button on the wall to lift the garage door. The instant it lifts off the concrete, we see a pair of shiny men's dress shoes.

We watch in horror as the door rolls up.

Slowly. Panel by panel.

Revealing a pair of thin legs in dark pants. A man. Hands in his pockets. Behind him a row of officers in uniform and behind that, a line of cop cars with the red and blue lights flashing.

Even before he steps into the light, giving us a perfect view of his blond hair, his sharp, chiseled features, his nose like an arrow, I already know.

This is Tork.

It's the same man who was outside the doctor's office earlier. I had assumed he was following Dad, but what if he was actually watching us?

Tork smiles except, coming from him, it's more like a threat. "Miss Marshall. Miss Novak. Good evening. Or rather, good morning, I suppose I should say."

"Uh…uh…" I stammer.

"Hello," MacKenna says in a way that means *screw off*.

"Going somewhere?" he asks pleasantly.

"And you are?" MacKenna asks.

"Marcus Tork," he says with an even wider smile. Stepping closer, he removes his hands from his pockets and hands MacKenna a small white card. "I'm on point for the investigation into the attack at the Rancho Mesa First Federal Bank."

I have no idea what *on point* even means and the bag in my hand has a weight to it, a weight of guilt. We have to go.

Doing my best impression of a calm person, I say, "My mom says you're searching the house."

As usual, MacKenna has her e-tablet and is making notes. "Care to comment on the investigation?"

Tork ignores her.

I keep talking when I know I should shut up. "Mom told us to wait at my dad's while you search." I need to stay calm. *The calm survive.*

"Ah yes. Where is the great Dr. Maxwell Marshall these days?"

Charles's face puckers into a grimace.

Stepping around Tork, I load my brother into the backseat of the Suburban.

I slam the car door and when I turn around, Tork takes the yellow duffel bag from my hands, holding it with ease in arms that are unexpectedly muscular. He rifles around in the bag and pulls out MacKenna's Annika Carver book.

MacKenna shoots me a dark look. If we weren't in a total emergency, I'm sure I'd be up for another lecture about touching her stuff without permission.

"Catching up on your reading?"

It takes every ounce of my self-control to keep from shaking as I nod. Everything I have to breathe. "My laptop got destroyed at the market."

"Right. It's been one helluva day." His gaze travels toward

MacKenna's huge suitcase. He jerks his chin in her direction. "Do I need to bother searching that?"

MacKenna lets go of the suitcase's handle and gestures at her bag like a model on a game show presenting a prize. "Feel free. You could use a little insight on how to incorporate some color into your wardrobe." With a shrug, MacKenna makes her way to the passenger side of the Suburban, tosses her bag in the back.

Before she gets in, she says, "My dad's innocent. In case you're interested."

"Then I'm sure the investigation will exonerate him." Tork's response is lost in the slamming of MacKenna's car door, and it's for the best anyway. Tork sounds sure of something, but it's *not* Jay Novak's innocence.

Tork takes a step closer to me, and I reach for my bag. The second he releases it, I snatch and hold it close. He puts his hand on the driver's side door to stop me from opening it.

His smile fades. "Dr. Marshall is said to be a man of great capability, and I'm sure he did his best to prepare you for what lies ahead. But however resourceful you might think you are, Miss Marshall, there's something you need to know."

Tork grabs my wrist. My skin burns at his touch.

What lies ahead?

Tears pool in the corners of my eyes. I have no choice but to dab at them with the sleeve of my hoodie as Tork looks on.

His eyes narrow. "I'd rather destroy this world than let the wrong people control it."

He lets go of me. Why shouldn't he? I've shown him I'm weak. He walks toward the police cars parked at the end of our drive.

Tork is out of the garage when he stops and swivels his head in each direction, taking stock of the scene on our street. A few neighbors are outside in their pajamas. Over his shoulder he says, "I'm rather like your father in that respect, I think."

More tears. "You…you don't know anything about my father."

I'm sure my pathetic stammering must be too quiet for him to hear over the police radios and commotion in the street.

But he does.

With his back still to me, Tork says, "Neither do you."

And there it is.

A pronouncement that sucks the energy, the shock, the feelings, the life from me.

"Clear," Tork shouts to the other officers.

Sniffling, I get behind the wheel of the car. It's a huge relief to toss the yellow bag into the backseat next to my brother. A cop moves the car blocking the driveway and allows me to back out. There doesn't seem to be any point in closing the garage door, so it's still open as we drive away.

The cops let us go out the back way, dodging the news vans parked at the end of the street. Maybe I'm finally losing it, because I think I see Navarro again, standing in front of the alley that separates our subdivision from the next one.

I slow down and blink a few times.

The alleyway is empty.

MacKenna flicks Tork's card onto the dash. "Did Stephanie say anything about my dad?"

"No." I whisper the lie.

Charles falls asleep as we drive on in silence.

Dad's house—our old house—is in the middle of nowhere, about thirty minutes east of Rancho Mesa on the far side of Castle Rock. This was part a matter of preference, as Dad was never what you'd call the neighborly type, and part pragmatism. Nice, neat suburban communities don't let you build doomsday bunkers underneath your house. Or skin rattlesnakes and turn them into disgusting jerky in your backyard.

The rows of identical homes give way to older neighborhoods full of a mishmash of different kinds of houses spaced farther apart. The New Depression hit this area hard, and every third house is boarded up and abandoned. Eventually, we pass the gas station with the minimart. It's the end of civilization. The last outpost before we get to Dad's.

I make the turn onto the series of dirt roads that lead to Dad's house. It's barely two in the morning, and it's also January, so the sun won't rise for hours. I nearly miss the turn in the dark.

We arrive at the two-story, concrete block number that would be the perfect location for an old-timey, cheesy sitcom. By Rancho Mesa standards, the house is ancient. It was built in the old days when construction was still booming by an architect who wanted a place to retire. I doubt it's ever been remodeled, and God only knows what kind of remarks MacKenna will make once we get inside and she sees the avocado-green fridge and the psychedelic yellow, geometric wallpaper in all the bathrooms. This place is certainly a far cry from the McMansion she left behind in Colorado.

It's dark. Quiet. Abandoned.

I take the little emergency flashlight from the glove compartment and climb out of the Suburban.

After opening the back door, I wake up my brother. "Come on."

His eyes flutter open as he jumps onto the gravelly dirt. I reach into the next seat and grab the yellow duffel bag.

The creosote rustles in the breeze.

Far off in the distance, a coyote howls.

"This. Is. Awesome," MacKenna says. She drags her suitcase across the dirt and takes Charles's hand when she comes around to our side of the car.

Using the flashlight, I guide us to the side door, the one off the empty carport. Dad's usual truck is gone. Everywhere I point the flashlight is covered with a thick layer of dust. I realize how uncomfortable I am. I used to live here, and now the silence, the space, the echoes, the emptiness, fill me with dread.

I fumble with the keys until I get the right one into Dad's oversize dead bolt lock.

Pushing the door open, I shine the flashlight all around. I can't keep myself from gasping.

We haven't been here recently.

But someone has.

DR. DOOMSDAY'S GUIDE TO ULTIMATE SURVIVAL

RULE THREE:

STAY TOGETHER. STAY SAFE.

The carport door opens to the kitchen where all the drawers and cabinets have been ripped open. Whatever was left in the fridge when Dad took off is on the linoleum floor. I take one step inside and nearly trip over an empty milk jug.

"Maid's day off?" MacKenna asks. But the zinger lacks its usual punch. For one thing, the delivery is so halfhearted and for another, she's backing away from the door as she speaks. She puts her arms around Charles protectively. "We need to get out of here."

"And go where?"

The fact that there's no answer to this question is what forces me to go farther inside. I drop the yellow duffel bag next to MacKenna's suitcase and walk into the kitchen. Something crunches underneath my shoe. I lower the flashlight to find a floppy disk under my heel.

"Do you think Dad did this?" Charles asks.

"No." I don't think even Dr. Doomsday would be nuts enough to destroy his own house.

I try flipping the kitchen light switch, but whoever trashed the place smashed the lightbulbs in the fixture that hangs over the table. The room stays dark.

"Jinx. We shouldn't be here," MacKenna says with more force.

There's a mess everywhere I shine the light. A lot of Dad's old tech has been dumped all over, and there are piles of batteries, fan assembles, wires and different kinds of disks. Paper is everywhere too. Mostly it looks like stuff from my father's teaching days—old term papers and quizzes. Dad hasn't taught a class in two years. I don't even know why he kept the stuff. A set of blueprints, maybe for the bunker, have been tossed under the kitchen table.

A sense of unease builds inside me.

Whoever was in here was searching for something.

Did they find it? Are they coming back?

MacKenna is right. It isn't safe to stay in the house.

I pull my hoodie around me and fight off a shiver.

"Okay. We'll go to the bunker," I say as I do one last sweep with the flashlight.

"Are you for real? The *bunker*? That sounds even creepier. And how do we know that whoever was in *here* isn't waiting in *there*."

Charles can't help but yawn. "No one can get in the bunker."

Exhaustion sinks in, and I desperately want to crawl in a bed and never come out. "It'll be light in a few hours. We can get some rest and then decide what to do."

"Maybe my dad will be home by then," MacKenna says.

The yellow bag taunts me from the doorway. "Maybe." I

leave the kitchen and shut Dad's front door. There doesn't seem to be much point in locking it.

The bunker is about a quarter mile from the main house with an entrance concealed inside a large silver shed. I point the flashlight in that direction.

MacKenna stops. "If no one's here, whose cars are these?"

"Dad keeps a bunch of old cars around." There's a Chevette he inherited from his grandfather, a couple of clunky station wagons and an old truck with a camper. "If anyone comes by, he wants it to be unclear how many people live here."

I don't mention it, but the cars are also loaded with supplies. They're backup plans.

MacKenna snorts. "Well, it is. Unclear."

I start walking toward the shed.

Dad changes the lock to the shed all the time and keeps the key in a heavy, fireproof safe concealed by a pile of garden hoses. It takes me a couple of tries to get the combination right, but I'm able to get the key.

This whole thing is starting to seem like a drill.

Charles must be thinking this as well, because he says, "You have to put the key back," as I'm about to go into the shed. "And hurry. I have to go! Bad."

I return the key back to the safe and then open the shed door. "I have to start the generator."

"Perfect," MacKenna says, crisply pronouncing the *p*.

The shed is stuffy and dusty and smells like sweaty shoes. It's also cramped. The generator is definitely bigger. The portable, pull-cord model is gone. It's been replaced by a huge beige Generac unit the size of an air conditioner. There's an LED screen on the front that reads Active. I shine the flashlight on a metal pipe connected to the unit. It's labeled "Natural Gas" in Dad's cramped script. This gas model must be ready to go anytime. The old generator could power the bunker for forty-eight hours. I get the sense that this does more and lasts longer.

The actual entrance to the bunker is a stainless-steel hatch in the corner of the shed, which Dad has concealed behind racks full of boxes of Christmas decorations and old books. We squeeze behind the racks and I give Charles the flashlight to hold while I kneel down. The hatch has an electronic keypad lock.

The combination is the date he met Mom.

I keep thinking he'll change it. And he doesn't.

The heavy hatch opens with a creak and, until the automatic fluorescent lights turn on, we stare at a bleak, dark hole in the ground.

I go first down the thick, reinforced steel ladder and have MacKenna hand down the bags. I feel a little bit better that the yellow bag is down here. It should be safe in the bunker. I'm in the landing alone while Charles tries to cajole Mac-Kenna into going down.

"This is the drill," he tells her. "I promise."

"Is there…uh…anybody down there?" MacKenna asks.

"No," I say.

But she's skeptical of my response. "How do you know if you don't check?"

The landing, a tiny space between the hatch and the interior door of the bunker, is so small that I'd practically be on top of anyone else who happened to be down here. And there's no way in hell that anybody could get past Dad's security.

"There's no one down here, MacKenna," I say, wishing that, for once, she could trust me. "The bunker door is secured by a fingerprint scanner, a retinal scanner and a password protected lock. There are a series of motion detectors in the bunker that do a sweep every thirty seconds. There are two indicator lights on the outside of the door. One that indicates if any motion is detected and another indicates if the system has been tampered with in any way. My dad installed the thing himself."

That last part might not inspire much confidence in MacKenna, but it reassures me. My dad is many things, and one of those things is an unrivaled master of designing and coding security systems. I turn toward the bunker door.

Both sensor lights are green.

Normal.

A few seconds later, MacKenna's Doc Martens clank against the ladder.

Charles follows right behind her, but he isn't strong enough to close the hatch.

There's this awkward thing where we're all shuffling around in the tiny space, our shoes squeaking on the concrete floor, while I make my way to the ladder. I climb up again.

Below me, Charles does a little dance. "Jinx. I have to go bad!"

Using my body weight, I pull the hatch down and lock it. We're in.

"I'm going as fast as I can, Charles."

"Go faster."

MacKenna smiles and ruffles his hair.

I wriggle my way to the front of our little trio again and enter my password using the keyboard on the wall. Then my fingerprint on the pad. Then the eye scan.

"Okay, I see your point," MacKenna says. "No one *could* get in here."

The heavy, hydraulic door to the bunker does not open.

Instead, the small, square terminal mounted to the wall beeps and a question appears on the screen.

Who gave you your nickname?

Dad was getting more paranoid by the day. He'd added another layer of authentication to his already over-the-top security system. When had he done this? When was the last time he'd been here? I type in my response.

Nick Beamer

"Who's Nick Beamer?" MacKenna asks.

The door to the bunker opens. Charles hits the light switch as he rushes by me.

I shrug and let MacKenna pass me. "Some little punk from the second grade."

Charles is halfway to the bathroom and yells, "She killed the class turtle."

My face heats up. I shut and lock the bunker door. "I did not. Squirt was a billion years old. And anyway, you were wearing diapers when all this happened. How would you know?"

"Mom told me," he calls back. The bathroom door slams.

For some reason, I keep talking. "I had a bad year. A beach ball bounced off my head and ruined Becky Halverson's birthday cake. On the field trip to the petting zoo, a goat ate a map out of my pocket and then barfed in the bin with all our sack lunches. Nick Beamer started calling me a jinx. Dad said that the way to deal with it was to own it. To call myself Jinx to show it didn't bother me. And the nickname stuck."

The wheels of MacKenna's suitcase squeak each time she takes another step. "So, are you bad luck, then? Like a broken mirror?"

I scowl at the back of her head. "Maybe. I mean I didn't get sent to Europe for my sixteenth birthday like some people I know. Is that luck? Or fate?"

MacKenna ignores this comment. She's busy looking around.

Dad's got the place organized like a miniature army base. Bunk beds line the walls. One half of the room is basically a mess hall with pallets of food stacked to the ceiling, a refrigerator and stove in the corner and a long, stainless-steel food service counter that divides the room. The opposite corner is the communication center with computers and radios set up on a motley collection of desks we got from garage sales.

"Ah. The famous basement. Where you guys are storing more food than Noah had on the ark and practicing Krav Maga," MacKenna says.

That's it. I whirl around and confront her. "*We* are not doing anything. My dad is doing that. Your dad used to take you to pick peaches. Ours took us to PrepperCon. And while you were in London getting your picture taken with the Royal Guard, we were in the desert seeing how long we could survive eating barrel cactus. I don't know…how…why you're blaming me for all of this. *I* didn't marry your dad. *I* didn't make you move here."

Charles runs out of the bathroom. And backs away. Away from me. I've been yelling.

MacKenna bites down on her lower lip with an odd look I've never seen on her face.

Sadness. Or maybe fear.

My brother makes a face. "Can you guys stop fighting for five minutes?"

But I already realize I'm being a jerk. MacKenna and I might not get along, but she did just watch her dad get hauled out of our house by the cops. I try to think of what might make her happy. "Um…look on the bright side. There are plenty of phones down here. You can call Toby."

"Really?" MacKenna asks. Her shoulders relax.

"Yeah. Dad keeps a bin of burner phones. And some SAT phones too."

I go to the bunk that's usually mine and drop the yellow bag on it.

MacKenna plops herself down on a bed on the opposite side of the room. "What's a SAT phone?" She fiddles around with her suitcase.

I walk over to the corner that Dad calls the Opps Center. If we're doing the drill, the next step is to get the monitoring systems set up. I flip on the array of six monitors, and images from the surveillance cameras he's got all over the property and even on top of his house fill the screens. The monitors show empty hallways and the moon setting on a cold desert landscape.

"Um. It's a kind of phone that uses satellites instead of the cellular network. You can get service in really remote areas. It can be more secure. These days they can triangulate the position of a cell phone to within a few feet. SAT phones are much harder to track."

I turn on the console that displays the security system status and pick up the old rotary telephone sitting on the desk. There's a dial tone.

Everything is functioning normally.

"Charles, the water. And snacks," I remind my brother. Part of every drill is always to stay hydrated and fed. People can't survive without food and water.

My brother is sitting at the bunker's kitchenette table, his little legs swinging underneath his chair, picking at a half-dead houseplant. "Dad promised he'd water my *Paphiopedilum*."

Dad promised a lot of things.

"Charles."

He keeps mumbling. "Look at the stem. Even if I repot it—"

"Charles."

He lets out a dramatic sigh but does go to the refrigerator. He passes out bottles of water and protein bars. I stop him before he can return to his half-dead orchid.

It's almost morning, but still. "You have to get a couple hours of sleep."

He yawns as he says, "That's not the drill."

Even though I'm so tired I can barely move, I say, "I'll handle the rest."

I deviate again when I reach into a bin under the desk and pull out a few phones from the backups Dad keeps in stock. I toss one of the smartphones on the bed next to where MacKenna is sitting. "It's got a label on the back with the phone number. In case you need to give it to Toby."

She nods but sits there without dialing.

"You can text and everything. It should work," I say.

Charles crawls underneath his covers. I tuck him in and turn off most of the lights in the bunker, leaving just enough light for me to finish my work.

"I wish Toby were here," MacKenna mumbles.

"Me too," I say. And it was true. Toby always knew the right thing to do. "Hopefully, he'll be home tomorrow."

She nods and dials the phone, and I get back to the drill.

Next step. Get our gear ready in case we need to leave quickly.

I cross the basement, open the container full of our emergency supplies and find my utility jacket. It's the same as it was the last time I saw it. The outside is a standard black windbreaker. The inside is lined with the essentials of survival. A couple small knives. Paracord and carabiners. A personal locator beacon. Tactical flashlight. A compass. And a Taser gun. I grab my brother's jacket as well and place them both near the door.

Dad keeps a few extra backpacks in one of the supply cabinets. I fill one with burner phones, put a ruggedized orange SAT phone on the top and add the bag to the pile of stuff.

MacKenna sighs in frustration. "He isn't answering."

"He's probably asleep."

She sets her suitcase down gently on the floor, being careful not to wake Charles. "Who could sleep through all of this? Jinx, you don't think anything's happened to him, do you?"

"No." Not even we could be that unlucky. "We should get some sleep."

She pulls back the covers on her bunk. "Can I ask you a question?"

"Sure," I say, although this makes me uneasy.

"Why did you bring those books?"

Oh. The ones I stuffed in my bag so I could smuggle Jay's laptop out of the house? Yeah. Those. "I guess... I thought we might end up having time. While we wait."

"You think we're going to be waiting so long that you'll have time to read a twelve hundred–page book?" she asks me, her voice laced with incredulity.

I can't help but yawn. "I don't know anything about politics, and it seems like, with everything going on, I probably should."

"You know, your mom teaches history. She's an authority on this stuff."

I turn off the rest of the lights, leaving us with only the glow of the monitor. "I know. But she's always talking about game theory. And late-stage capitalism. And something about John Locke and Alexander the Great and Plutarch. It makes next to no sense to me."

MacKenna lies down as well. "You think you understand machines but not people."

Crossing to my bunk, I say, "Machines are predictable."

From researching that cryptic message on Jay's laptop, to checking in with Terminus, to seeing what's happening on the news, there are a lot of things I should be doing right now. Instead, I crawl into bed.

She yawns. "Machines are made by people, and people are predictable too."

I prop myself up on my elbow. "What does it say? *The Modern Guide to The Spark*?"

She sits up as well. "Seriously?"

"Seriously."

She thinks for a second. "The Spark is about making things fair for everyone. Giving everyone civil rights, a chance to live the American dream. The Spark is about doing something real. Unlike The Opposition, which is about *stopping* other people from doing things."

"The government is always saying it's gonna do things, and then things stay the same."

She lies down again. "Next, you'll be saying all politicians are the same."

"All politicians *are* the same."

MacKenna sighs. "Jinx, Ammon Carver bought his results with money, influence, bigotry and hate. Because of him, real people will suffer and die. Even if things could stay the same for us, we shouldn't look away from the fact that they won't for everyone."

My eyes won't stay open a second longer. "Everyone's for Rosenthal."

"Right."

The wolf is shaved so nice and trim. Red Riding Hood is chasing him.

I drift into a sleep with dreams filled with wolves and dark woods and red cloaks.

A world that won't be controlled by machine code.

I awaken in a panic.

Noise fills the bunker.

The *ring, ring, ringaling* of the archaic rotary phone.

But also something else.

The more electronic *bing bong* of the modern console.

The perimeter alarm.

I bolt up, sending my blankets flying toward the end of my bunk.

Running to the Opps Center, I almost fall into the desk chair on wheels and have to grab the desk to keep myself from rolling away. I pick up the heavy phone receiver and press it to my face.

"Yes?" I say. That's kind of a stupid greeting, but I'm groggy and using part of my attention to watch the sequence of security camera images flickering on the monitors for a sign of what might be setting off the alarm.

"Susan?" Mom's hollow voice comes through the phone.

Crap. She never calls me Susan.

"Mom? Are you coming home?"

The feed from the camera that my dad has mounted high

on a weather vane on the roof appears on monitor one and turns my blood to ice.

In the distance, a cop car turns onto the dirt road that heads to the house.

And then another. And another. And another.

They're coming for us.

"Jinx, there isn't much time." Mom sounds like she's calling from another planet.

Charles rustles in his bunk. "Jinx? Jinx? Is that Mom?"

I wave my arm frantically at him to be quiet.

"They're using some obscure antiterrorism law to hold Jay without arraigning him, without even arresting him. They're going to transport him somewhere within the next hour or so. I called in a big favor from one of your dad's old friends, and he was able to convince the National Police to let me go too. But I don't know where they're taking us."

Charles stands behind me now. "Jinx? Can I talk to Mom?"

"Listen to me," Mom says. "If there's any hope at all, you need to find your father."

Charles makes a grab for the phone. "Mom? Mom?"

The line of cop cars has come into view of the mailbox camera.

Oh God.

"Hope?" I repeat stupidly. Hope for what? "Find Dad? How will that help?"

Mom continues in a flat voice. "Your father knows people. People in The Opposition. He knows what to do. He might be able to negotiate. He might be able to help Jay."

"How can I... How do you think..." How do you find someone who's unfindable?

The pings of the alarm grow louder and more frequent. MacKenna sits up in her bunk. "What the hell is going on?"

"Don't get caught by the police. They'll want to hold you. Perhaps use you as leverage to force Jay to take a plea. *Find your father*," Mom repeats one last time.

The line goes dead.

We're on our own.

I can't breathe.

I scramble to my bunk and force my Cons onto my feet.

"We have to get out of here. Now!" I toss MacKenna's boots in her direction.

She stands up and rubs her eyes. "What are you talking about?"

Before I answer, her eyes widen at the images on the screen behind me.

I scoop my groggy brother off his bed, grab the bags and head up the stairs.

The last image I see on the screen is a nondescript black sedan approaching the house.

I already know.

It's Tork.

DR. DOOMSDAY'S GUIDE TO ULTIMATE SURVIVAL

DO WHAT YOU HAVE TO DO. THINGS WILL BREAK DOWN FASTER THAN EXPECTED.

RULE FOUR:

This is all my fault.

I was getting sloppy. Making mistakes.

According to the drill, someone was supposed to stay awake to keep watch.

I push my brother up the ladder and into the shed.

Thankfully, it takes less time to get out of the bunker than to get in.

And I don't bother relocking anything. Any amount of time the cops spend searching the place actually helps us. We need every second we can get.

Outside, the sun is fully up. It's probably about eight or nine.

As I drag Charles along, he's asking questions like, "What did Mom say? Where are we going? What's happening?" with MacKenna right on our heels.

"Zip it!" I whisper.

I take us to the truck with a camper shell on the back, the closest vehicle to the shed. Because Dad's nothing if not predictable, I find the keys to the truck in a magnetic holder in the wheel well of the driver's side rear tire. They jingle in my hands as I walk to my door. When I open it, I'm knocked back by the stench of gasoline. This old truck reeks.

Both MacKenna and Charles hesitate.

From in front of the house, there's a cacophony of police radios, car doors slamming and shouted instructions. We need to leave before the cops make their way to the back. I shove my bags onto the floor of the passenger seat.

I swear I hear someone shout, "Tork!"

My mouth turns dry and dusty.

"Let's go."

The two of them get their butts in gear and get into the truck. MacKenna takes the front seat while my brother shimmies through a small window into the camper.

The truck rumbles to a start. It shakes and sputters every minute or so, but it runs. I pray there's enough noise in the front that we attract no notice.

I experiment with the pressure on the gas pedal, trying to get the truck going fast but kicking up as little dust as possible. We drive out the back. Dad planted a few rows of mesquite trees, which should be enough to cover us until the road dips down and we can no longer be seen from the house. We've done plenty of drills snaking around Castle Rock on a series of dirt roads and trails. We'll do that until we hit the highway.

Once we're away from the house a little bit, MacKenna says, "It reeks in here."

"Roll down your window," I say. The truck really is ancient and has the old-fashioned hand cranks. They could use some oil, but we get them down. After a minute or so, I can only sort of smell the gas fumes.

But we're getting covered in dust.

MacKenna coughs. "I don't get it. I don't get what we're doing."

She saw the fifty cops rolling up to the house just like I did. "What do you mean?"

"You said nobody could get in the bunker. And there's about a hundred years' worth of food and a power generator. Shouldn't we stay in there? Isn't that Rule 3 of that dumb book?"

If our dad has a prime directive, this is it. *Stay safe.* Never move from a position of security into one of danger.

Except I'm stupid and I messed it up. "They were gonna figure out that we were down there. Maybe if I'd done something about the Suburban..." I should have thought to ditch it somewhere. "But it was parked right in the driveway...and I... I told that guy... Tork. I told him we were going to Dad's."

I take a deep breath to stop my voice from shaking. "The bunker can keep people out, but not indefinitely, and particularly not half the National Police. It was a matter of time before they figured out a way to open the hatch. And anyway, Mom said to..."

Charles pokes his head through the little window at the mention of Mom. "What did she say? Why didn't you let me talk to Mom?"

I repeat what Mom told me on the phone.

The road has gotten rough from recent rain. MacKenna bounces up and down in her seat. "She wants us to find Dr. Doomsday? Why?"

And how?

"I told you. She thinks he has contacts with The Opposition."

MacKenna frowns. "You've spent the last three months telling me that he doesn't."

Sigh. "I know what I said."

We arrive at the base of Castle Rock and I start to relax a little. The plan, such that it is, appears to be working. The road is clear of police. I steer the truck south.

"Did Jay tell you anything? About what they think he did?" I ask.

Or maybe what's going on with his computer.

MacKenna snorts. "You know he didn't. He treats me like I'm made of glass."

Our parents have this in common. Jay thinks MacKenna's all messed up because of her mother's death from cancer five years ago. Meanwhile, *my* mom thinks Dad's drills have driven me off the deep end. They try hard to keep anything unpleasant away from us.

Jay once struggled to tell MacKenna that the yogurt shop around the corner had run out of chocolate sprinkles.

"Anyway, what could he have possibly done?" she goes on. "All he does is run background checks and train security guards. The most exciting thing that ever happened at the bank was when one teller stole someone's ramen from the break room fridge. You know my dad. Becoming a citizen was the best day of his life. He'd wear his Silver Star with his pajamas if I let him. He's about nothing but the flag, baseball and apple pie."

She digs around in the pockets of her leggings and produces the phone I gave her.

"What are you doing?"

"Seeing if Toby called back." She presses a few buttons on the screen. "He's still not answering. Something's wrong."

I think she's right. It's *way* out of character for him not to return calls. But I find myself saying, "Maybe he just doesn't recognize the phone number...or maybe... He's nineteen and, as you keep reminding me, some kind of a genius. I'm sure he's fine. I'm sure he's still at school."

My stomach lurches. I am *not* sure he's fine.

MacKenna settles back into her seat. "We need to find him."

"I'm not sure we can."

"Not sure we can?" she repeats. "You think we *can* find Dr. Doomsday—a man with a background in counterintelligence, who can build a phone from a coconut and a cymbal-banging monkey toy, who is deliberately hiding from us—but we *can't* figure out a way to pick up my brother from college?"

I drum my fingers on the steering wheel. The tiny dash clock blinks and reads 10:14 a.m. "I think there's a good chance that we'll be caught. They'll expect us to go there."

"They? Who's 'they'? You think *they* will go after Toby?"

I glance at the yellow duffel bag resting at MacKenna's feet. "No. Mom says they're looking *for us*. That they might want to detain us, and they'll be expecting us to do something... well...stupid."

"Why do they want us?"

"I don't know. Mom didn't explain it all to me. But they do. You saw them. There were probably a hundred cops back at the house. They weren't coming to say hi."

Oh, and also, we have the laptop that triggered the explosions at the banks.

Charles leans in. "We're supposed to stay together."

"I know! But we don't know what's happening out there."

"Exactly!" MacKenna whirls around, and her ponytail smacks her in the face. "Okay. Sure. If that's how it's gonna be, fine. We're supposed to be a family. We're all in this together. Until *you* are all safe in here—" she waves her hand at me and Charles "—and my brother is stuck out there."

My dad would say to follow the drill. To get out of town. He'd tell me that going onto a densely populated college campus in the hopes of finding a single student is stupid bordering on suicidal.

But Dad is gone, and I'm not sure I want to be the kind of person who leaves my family to twist in the wind.

Anyway. Screw him.

I stop the car when the dirt road intersects with the highway. A few cars pass, but it's normal traffic. Staring at the asphalt, I try to come up with a new plan.

I face MacKenna. "Okay. If we're gonna do this, we'll have to work together."

"Okay," she says.

"Keep trying to text Toby," I say. "The challenge is going to be how to find him if we can't get ahold of him. Campus is huge, and we need to get in and out as fast as possible."

"Any ideas?"

"Well. I could track Toby's phone. Assuming it's turned on, we could get a pretty accurate read of his location. At the very least, we could determine when he last used the phone and where he was when he used it."

MacKenna nods. "You think that will work?"

I knew it would. I already had the scripts all set up. I just needed to get into Dad's server to deploy them.

Turning on to the highway, I drive in the direction of the university. "We need a quiet place to work. And network access."

It's a risk, but I decide the best thing is to go to Dad's office in the Computing Commons building. Technically speaking, Dad was on sabbatical, but he still kept an office on campus.

On one hand, it might occur to someone to watch it. On the other, I'm familiar with the parking lot and the area.

We make the turn from McCallister into the little lot behind Dad's building. I stop the car in the shadow behind one of the building's dumpsters.

"And we are...?" MacKenna asks, pausing her efforts to do something about the horrible static coming through the truck's hollow speakers.

"Finding an out-of-the-way place to park. So we can find the car later, and so no one messes with it while we're gone." I roll up my window and reach over to open the glove compartment. Standard operating procedure for Dad would be to keep a bunch of different parking passes in here to prevent the car from attracting special notice. Sure enough, there's a manila envelope with a bunch of stickers and placards inside. I grab the university permit one and put it in the front window of the truck. There's also a lone stick of beef jerky that I force my brother to eat.

MacKenna rolls up her window too. "Well, I'll say this for your dad, Dr. Doomsday really does think of everything."

"You have no idea," Charles mutters from the back. He wriggles through the window and into the space between me and MacKenna.

I don't know why, maybe out of habit, but I pull down the visor to check myself in the mirror. The prehistoric vehicle doesn't have vanity mirrors, so I slide a bit toward the center. I can see myself in the rearview. My bangs are stuck on my forehead again. I'm not sure I even combed my hair after my shower.

"Oh. For God's sake. What are you doing? You're fixing your hair? What the actual hell? We. Need. To. Find. My. Brother."

I jump as MacKenna slams her door. I know I have to pull myself together. Reaching into one of the inside pockets of my jacket, I check to make sure I've got my mini tool kit. We'll need to pick the lock to Dad's door. I grab the yellow bag.

My hand warms with guilt as I wrap my fingers around the handle.

But I don't have a choice.

Jay's laptop is the only computer I've got.

MacKenna takes Charles's hand and pulls him close to her.

We make our way out of the parking lot and toward the tall, redbrick building, passing several groups of students lounging near the fountain in the courtyard. There's chatter I can't quite make out, mumbling, the occasional burst of laughter.

Inside the CC, it's really crowded. I've been here on a weekend before, and there's usually only a couple teaching assistants stuck grading papers hanging around. Today, an odd mixture of people fill the halls. Students carrying blue protest signs. Old guys with their heads down, checking their phones.

Two security guards in blue uniforms.

Breathe.

Stay calm.

Before the security guards see us, I tug us into the stairwell. "Dad's office is on the third floor."

MacKenna's eyes are wide. She nods and we take the stairs.

We arrive on the third floor, all of us out of breath. Charles opens the door to a hallway, and it's more like I expected. Quiet and mostly deserted.

It smells like someone has been through here recently with a plate of cupcakes.

A copy machine clicks and hums on the opposite end of the hall.

I lead us through a series of turns. Dad's office is on the

windowless side of the building, the side away from the attractive courtyard, down a narrow subhall that contains three tiny workrooms.

I stop in front of the door labeled Dr. Maxwell Marshall, Data Architecture.

The locks in the building are old and crappy and mostly meant to deter students who might want to cheat on their papers. I spent fourteen hours one Sunday with my dad, who wouldn't let us get up from the kitchen table until I could pick most locks in less than thirty seconds. I pull the little tool kit from my pocket and hand it to Charles. He's done this a hundred times too, so without any discussion he passes me the tension wrench.

"You two must be really fun at parties," MacKenna mutters.

I insert it into the bottom of the keyhole and hold my hand out for the pick. I fiddle around for a few seconds, and we're in. Charles locks the door behind us.

Dad's office is dusted and deserted. There's a pen jar on one corner of a large wooden desk and a bookcase on the far wall with a bunch of computer science reference manuals. Dad's got a whole shelf of Pascal.

I take a seat behind the desk, open the yellow bag, rifle through the books and socks and dig the computer out of the concealed compartment at the bottom. The instant I have it set up on the desk, MacKenna and Charles move to stand behind me.

They lean over me while I work.

"Not helping, you guys."

"If this were your brother, you'd be sitting on my lap," she says.

I grab the computer and turn it so the screen faces away

from them. It is annoying having someone look over my shoulder. MacKenna resigns herself to sitting in one of Dad's guest chairs.

I make a few clicks to access the university's Wi-Fi network.

My pulse quickens. Accessing the network starts the clock. This laptop has a unique MAC address that I don't have the time or tools to try to conceal or spoof. If Tork really does have a partial log of the server activity of one of the banks, he'll have this MAC address too.

And he'll be watching for it.

We've got five minutes.

Maybe ten if we're lucky.

And I am a jinx.

I log in to Dad's server, open a console window and start the script running. Dad insisted that I write the basic code as part of one of our drills.

I just hope that MacKenna and Toby don't get pissed that the app labeled AZ Weather on their phones actually grabs and sideloads GPS coordinates and sends them to Dad's server.

I tap a few keys and wait.

A chat window pops open.

Terminus: Where the hell have you been?

Me: In the bunker.

Terminus: This stuff is all over the news.

Me: I know.

I hesitate for a second. But I might as well ask.

Me: I need to find my dad. Do you have any ideas?

Terminus: No and if I did I wouldn't keep them to myself.

There's something off about this.

Me: What are you talking about?

Terminus: You haven't been watching the news, have you?

Me: No.

Terminus: First Federal made an announcement an hour ago. They started trying to do a data recovery last night.

Of course they did. You'd expect that. Their data centers were destroyed. They'd make an attempt to get a provisional system set up and start a recovery from their backup. Why is Terminus spooked by standard operating procedure?

Terminus: There's no backup.

In spite of the fact that Terminus isn't with us, I find myself shaking my head.

Me: That isn't possible.

Terminus: They discovered a piece of latent malware resident in their system. It's placed all the bank data behind some kind of encryption nobody understands and corrupted five years of backup.

Me: They think my dad had something to do with it?

Terminus: Publicly no, but in the dark web...

Terminus: They're looking for him.

Terminus: I mean honestly who else could it be?

Who else could it be?

If I'd had anything to eat this morning, I'd be throwing it up.

Who was in charge of redesigning First Federal's data architecture systems five years ago? Who worked on encryption schemes the way some people did crossword puzzles?

Dad.

"Dad keeps licorice in his drawer," Charles tells MacKenna. Dad hadn't been on campus in a long time.

Finally, a map renders on the screen. I let out a long exhale. The last reading from the phone was from more than six hours ago. I zoom in on the map until I get close to the blinking dot of Toby's possible location.

"Toby's across campus in the Student Union. Or at least he was. Six hours ago." I stare at the map as messages from Terminus continue to pop up.

Terminus: Jinx?

Terminus: Jinx?

Terminus: You have to listen to me. I did some research about this guy Tork. He's a real whackjob. I mean Revelations, real end of the world type stuff. With him it's not business. It's not personal. He's some kind of vigilante.

Terminus: He's dangerous.

Terminus: And he's good.

MacKenna's shoulders slump. "What does that mean?"

It takes me a second to mean that she's talking about Toby and not the cryptic message from Terminus. "Ah. It means his phone is probably off. So all we've got is the reading from the last time his phone pinged a tower."

She thinks for a second. "Okay, but that's a starting point?" There's hope in her voice. "We can go over there. Maybe ask if anyone's seen him."

I sigh. "We can't leisurely stroll around interviewing people, MacKenna."

Charles freezes with a piece of candy rope hanging from his mouth.

"You're not supposed to be eating that!" I snap at my brother.

"I'm hungry."

God only knows how long that candy has been there. On top of everything else, I've failed to watch my brother. Or make sure he's had anything decent to eat. I keep typing.

Me: What are you saying?

Terminus: Maybe running isn't the best option.

"We can check his room," MacKenna goes on.

I shake my head. "It would take too long. The dorms are huge and you probably need an access code or a key to get in. Going there isn't smart."

We can't turn ourselves in.

We're supposed to find Dad. And stay together. And stay safe.

A bunch of directives that contradict each other.

MacKenna stands. "Well, I'm going."

We've probably used four of our five minutes.

"Wait. Wait." I close the chat window with Terminus and make a few clicks in the server window. "They have IPTV all over campus." Dad used to have a program that let him tap into the feed. He made it so that he could check which vending machines had cheese balls. If it still works, we can see into the Student Union without having to go there.

"What?" She scowls.

"They have a network of web-enabled security cameras."

Dad's program does work. It bypasses the university's security protocols and images from around campus rotate across the screen. A couple of people walking into the library. Scenes from the book stacks. I make a few more clicks until I locate the Student Union.

I rotate Jay's laptop so she can see it too.

My breath catches at the sight of Toby sitting with his fingers spread wide on a table in an otherwise empty white security office.

The images continue to change. The whole second floor is totally empty.

Which makes sense.

Because.

On the first floor, there's a riot.

And there's a knock at the door.

DR. DOOMSDAY SAYS:

CERTAIN SITUATIONS DON'T CALL FOR BRAINS. OR BRAWN. THEY TAKE NERVE. SURVIVAL IS AN ACT OF WILL.

I slam the laptop shut and shove it into the yellow bag.

Once I move from behind the desk, I open the door a crack and find one of the security officers from downstairs. "There have been some disturbances on campus. We're checking in to make sure everything is all right."

I give him what I hope is a nice, nonsuspicious smile and snatch a couple of old, dusty computer science books from the shelf. "Dr. Marshall asked me to come by and pick up some stuff for a project he's working on."

He nods twice. Slowly. "Dr. Marshall, huh?"

He knows.

Through the sliver in the open door, I see his hand travel to the radio at his belt.

I reach inside my jacket, circling my fingers around the grip of my Taser. I catch MacKenna's gaze and jerk my head in the direction of the corner farthest from the door. She gives me a small shake of her head. But she seems to get my plan and moves Charles into the corner behind the desk.

Okay. Okay.

Deep breath.

I slam the door open. Hard. Sending the radio flying through the air.

The guard covers his face with one of his hands and blood drips through his fingers.

With the door now open, in one swift motion, exactly the way we always practiced, I pull my Taser out of my inner jacket pocket, slide the safety into the armed position and press the trigger. Two blue wires and a few pieces of pink and yellow confetti shoot out from the gun. The silver probes hit the guard in the neck, just a hair above the collar of his uniform shirt.

I'll hand it to the guy. He's tough.

He does fall to the ground, but grunting and gasping, he manages to bring his hands within a couple inches of pulling out the probes.

I have to shock the guy through three cycles. A full thirty seconds.

That's what it takes to keep him down, clutching his chest and taking shallow breaths.

There's no telling how long he'll stay there.

So I move fast.

MacKenna is staring at me. "Was that really necessary?"

"Get over here and help me move this guy. We have to get him into the office. It's like he's made of poured concrete." I plant one of my feet against the hallway wall and try to leverage my body weight to make it easier to move the guard.

"He doesn't...he doesn't look that heavy," she stammers. I can tell she's scared.

"Well, he is," I shoot back.

Working together, it's all we can do to get the guard through the door and onto his stomach on the grimy floor mat just inside Dad's office.

Charles remains huddled in the corner.

I kneel, and the corrugated rubber mat digs into my knees. The lower I go to the ground, the more it smells like feet. And transmission fluid. And like someone has thrown up over and over, and another someone did a crappy mopping job with watered-down lemon cleanser.

I check the guard's utility belt until I find the plastic ties that campus security uses as handcuffs. The guy's got huge biceps and thick legs that jut out like twin tree trunks. He groans as I pull back his arms to bind his hands with the plastic tie. This can't be a comfortable position for a man with those kinds of muscles. When I'm done I also take the ring of keys hanging from his belt.

"Get the radio," I tell MacKenna.

I rip out the cord that extends from the phone on Dad's desk into the wall and stow it in my bag. When MacKenna returns with the radio, I place it on the tile floor in the office and stomp it with my foot. Bits of plastic scatter everywhere. I kick them so they're inside the small office.

"Come on." I motion to my brother. He's watching the blood run onto the mat.

"It's fine… I swear. It's fine." I'm panting. I hope my brother can't hear the drumbeat of my heart as it betrays me. He nods and runs through the door carrying the yellow bag.

When he's out, I shut the door, lock it and jam a random key in the hole, twisting it until it's firmly stuck in the knob. The guard is tied up and has no phone or radio. Plus, it'll take them a while to get him out.

Still. There isn't much time.

The instant I shut the door, MacKenna turns on me. "Have you totally lost it? I don't like the cops either, but seriously... whatever is going on...you just made things a whole lot worse. We need to think about this...consider our options..."

Mom said our only hope is to find my dad. "If you want to see Toby, we have to go now."

"I'm scared, Jinx," Charles says.

Me too. This is what I want to say.

Instead, I take his hand and squeeze. "We'll be okay."

We make it out of the CC without attracting further notice. I'm not that familiar with ASU, which means we have to follow the signs to the Student Union and stick to the main walkways. MacKenna has one of Charles's hands and I have the other, and we take the campus at a jog. We pass groups of students carrying bright blue Everyone's for Rosenthal signs. Groups of older men in red shirts with The Opposition slogan on them crisscross the campus.

Make today as good as yesterday.

By the time we arrive at the huge building that houses an assortment of restaurants, a bowling alley and a bunch of offices, MacKenna is the only one of us who isn't completely out of breath. She's on Jay's fancy treadmill every morning at six thirty. I quit jogging the day Mom filed for divorce from my dad.

The mess from inside the building has spilled onto the lawn. Clusters of kids in blue shirts wave signs. Someone is playing the drums. A woman with a torch paces in front of a man with a white beard standing on a box and shouting.

We blend into the crowd.

The man yells out, *"When I was a boy, this country was a*

*place where a man earned his keep, kept his earnings and was asked
to give only his guidance to others…"*

A few guys run out of the SU with armfuls of bags of potato chips and cases of soda.

The fire alarm begins to wail.

MacKenna can't help herself. She taps a girl with brown
braids on the shoulder. "What the hell is going on?"

The girl shrugs. "Annika Carver was supposed to speak
here a little while ago. We came to protest. I mean, first, The
Opposition basically rigs the election—"

*"The Spark emerged from the decay of old political parties, a
ghost from the ashes, a specter imposed upon us by those who want
to take—"*

The woman waves the torch, sending a blast of lemongrass
and citronella in our direction.

I put my hand on MacKenna's arm. We don't have time
for this.

From somewhere behind us, a woman's voice calls, "We
didn't rig the election. The Opposition campaign was just
smarter."

"They levied taxes, created programs hostile to the common man—"

Braid girl smacks her gum. "You got some computer weirdo
to show you how to stop people from voting. I read about
this place in Wisconsin where just by messing with the traffic
lights on the streets where people from The Spark lived, they
stopped enough people from voting to swing the district."

"That's not illegal!"

"It should be!"

MacKenna pokes the girl again. "You're saying the president's daughter is in *there*?"

The girl shakes her head. "No. The bobble-headed bleach
blonde didn't bother to show up. Typical."

"Yet it's not too late. Not too late to make today as great as yesterday—"

"Go to hell!" a boy in the crowd shouts.

"As of Monday night, The Spark is a terrorist group," a man behind MacKenna says. "They're responsible for the attacks on the banks. Rosenthal won't be satisfied until he destroys everything."

A chair is thrown from one of the windows.

This time I grab MacKenna. "We have to go."

I keep Charles as close to me as I can while we run up the handful of stairs into the SU. At the doorway, I can see all the way down McCallister. Off in the distance, the National Police have arrived and are setting up barricades. From up the block, I catch a glimpse of an angular form in a black suit.

It's Tork.

Tork is coming.

We rush in against a steady flow of people. My brother is almost knocked in the head by a girl running out with a box of paper cups. Inside, students swarm the restaurants. A kid stands on a sofa trying to pry a TV off the wall. In the bowling alley, people are throwing heavy neon balls in every direction, creating a steady series of thumps and thuds. I spot a few security guards, but they're completely overwhelmed by the chaos. A pizza oven smokes and sends the smell of burned pepperoni all through the first floor.

That explains the fire alarm.

Charles releases my hand to cover his ears. I grab the collar of his jacket.

Ahead of us, there's a loud crack. Shouting.

It's looting.

And gunfire.

"Jinx," he says.

"It's okay. We're okay."

My brother's mouth keeps moving. Mumbling. He's doing the rosebush thing again.

We are so screwed.

Somehow, in all the mess, MacKenna manages to find the emergency stairwell.

We hustle in and I close the door. We're alone. At least I can hear myself think.

Maybe it's my imagination, but the lights seem to be dimming.

MacKenna lets her breath out in a huff.

"You think we'll find Toby up here, Jinx?" Charles asks.

"I hope so." Finding him would be a relief. At least, we'd all be together again.

My Cons squeak and slide on the superclean white tile floor. The upstairs space is organized in groups of offices. We pass doorways labeled Alumni Association, Facilities Management and Student Activities before coming to one that reads Security.

There doesn't seem to be any point in being subtle about it.

We can't change what's on the other side of the door.

We'll either get Toby. Or we'll get caught.

I push the door open fast.

It feels a bit melodramatic when the room on the other side is empty.

We're in what basically looks like a reception area with a tall desk on one side and several waiting chairs on the other. Framed posters that say things like *"See Something Say Something"* and *"Keep Calm and Call Security"* cover the walls.

I check behind the desk and find a pink phone message pad, a stack of yellow lined notebooks and a box of ballpoint pens. The only noise comes from a golden French bulldog nestled on a blanket in one of the corners. It raises its head, snorts a couple of times and flops down again.

Toby must be in one of the offices behind the reception room. I get my lock pick kit out of my jacket pocket, but that winds up being unnecessary. All the doors are unlocked. The first office is empty with an unoccupied, long white table in the center of the room.

Behind the second door, we find Toby, with his hands folded neatly on the table in front of him, staring into space. He blinks a few times as if he might be imagining us.

Relief floods me. At least, whatever happens, we're all together.

He stands. "MacKenna?" He's dressed in a pair of baggy gray sweats and a maroon ASU T-shirt, looking the way he always does when he's hanging around the house studying. He's got MacKenna's same pale complexion and dark hair that always seems to be carelessly ruffled.

MacKenna rushes to him and gives her brother a huge hug. Charles runs over there as well. I find myself standing to the side of their little huddle, picking at the edge of my basic sweater.

"Come on, Jinx. Group hug," Toby says.

I shuffle over awkwardly and end up squeezed in between my brother and Toby with my face smashed into his muscular bicep. The warm hug, and Toby's always calm demeanor, is exactly what I need to keep my building hysteria from overtaking me.

Conscious of the fact that time is running out, I step back. "We need to get going."

"Go? Go where? What's going on?"

MacKenna purses her lips into a grim expression. "It's not good."

"We can fill you in later." I leave the small room, hoping they'll follow.

They don't. MacKenna stays put, telling Toby everything that's happened since we were trapped in Halliwell's last night.

"We seriously need to go."

When they ignore me again, I decide to check the last un-opened door in the little cluster of security offices. Charles goes with me, and we find ourselves in a place that's part break room and part monitoring station. There are a couple of small tables with partially eaten sandwiches on them—like someone had their lunch interrupted and had to get going in a hurry. A huge array of flat-screen monitors covers one of the walls, showing camera feeds from all over the SU.

Toby and MacKenna have moved into the hall.

"What are *you* doing in here?" she asks him.

I stare at the monitors. Downstairs, the National Police have gotten things under control. Officers in riot gear have students lined up facing the walls. Smoke, probably from tear gas, fills the bowling alley.

Toby's voice echoes off the walls. "Security came to my room this morning. Early. Maybe about two or three. At first, they said it was for my protection. Like the fact that Dad was being detained might make the news and then…well…then they took my phone. For a while, they let me stay in the lounge and watch the news. About an hour ago, they brought me up here. To be interviewed. Except they ran out of here before anyone asked me any questions."

"There's a riot downstairs," I call out.

"A riot?" he repeats. "Because of the bank systems being down?"

"What? No. Because of Annika Carver." MacKenna describes the scene downstairs while I continue to watch the screens.

"Ouch!" Charles says.

I realize I'm squeezing his shoulder. Hard. "Oh. Sorry."

The cops are clearing the SU. Like they do on TV shows when they get the crime scene ready before the important investigators show up. When a couple officers run forward to hold the door for a shadow in the entryway, I already know.

Tork is coming.

He steps into the Student Union, pausing long enough to give a blistering stare to the camera pointed at the door. Like he's staring right at me.

Tork is coming for me.

Not only that, the National Police are amassing near the stairwell.

Waiting.

I run into the hallway and skid to a stop in front of Mac-Kenna. "We have to go. Right. Now."

MacKenna frowns and steps around me. "Hey, Pumpkin Spice Latte, we haven't elected you group activity leader."

I wave my arms in her face. "Tork is coming!"

"Who's Tork?" Toby asks. His brown eyes dart back and forth from me to MacKenna.

MacKenna crosses her arms. "The guy who searched our house. Some undertaker of a cop who couldn't find his ass with both hands and a flashlight. We could go to any police station in the country and there would be ten Torks. Nine of them would have better suits. Why would *he* be here?"

"We don't have time for this," I growl at her. Had she forgotten about that guard we left in my dad's office? "I'm the one who's going to spend the next twenty years in a correctional facility if we don't get out of here. I'm the one who just Tasered and tied up a security guard and I… I…" I don't know how to finish my thought.

Toby tilts his head to look me in the eyes. "You *what*?" When I don't answer, he goes on. "Jinx, my father was arrested last night on the suspicion that he helped blow up a bunch of buildings. That security guard is the least of our problems."

MacKenna shakes her head. "There's something really, really wrong with this story."

I reach out to take Charles's hand, but he doesn't offer it to me. He's waiting for Toby to weigh in. Muttering to myself, I wrap my fingers around the ribbing of his T-shirt and pull him toward me. "Let's go."

I pull Charles toward the door. MacKenna moves to block me. Getting Toby back has restored our more normal dynamic.

"MacKenna…" Toby begins.

She brushes stray strands of dark hair away from her face. "No. No. I want some answers because this is. Not. Normal. It doesn't make sense. Even for you, Jinx. The cops already have my dad. Why are they after *us*? Why are you so freaked by this one guy? Why do you look like your eyes are gonna pop out of your head every time I ask you a question?"

"I told you, Mom said not to get caught," I say.

Toby arches his eyebrows at Charles. "How long have they been at this?"

"I don't know. Maybe since July?" my brother says.

"Right."

MacKenna's already shaking her head at me.

I consider telling her to go to hell, but Toby is watching me with an anxious expression. I can't put it off forever. They're going to find out eventually.

Reaching into the yellow bag, I take out the computer and hold it in front of MacKenna's face. "This is Jay's laptop. It triggered the explosions at the banks."

Her mouth falls open into an O. "How do you know—"

"I compared the IP address it was using to the one the cops retrieved from the bank server log. They match. And it was running something. Some kind of code object."

MacKenna's face turns red. "That's why they're chasing us? You… You… You…"

I scowl at her. "I told you. I think they screwed up when they let us go last night. Mom thinks they want to use us as leverage to force your dad to accept a plea deal. But I don't want to get caught with this—" I shake the laptop "—before I can check it out."

MacKenna opens her mouth.

Toby holds up a hand to silence her. "Over two thousand people were killed in the five explosions. You're saying that my dad actually had something to do with it?"

"No! Of course not. I'm saying, there's something going on with this machine. That's why I hid it. It was getting messages. Weird ones."

If possible, MacKenna grows ever angrier. "*Hid* it? You should have destroyed it! It's the evidence they're gonna use to frame my father!"

Toby puts his hand on her shoulder. "Mac. It could exonerate him. Think about it. If the laptop has been hacked and we can prove it, that could help."

"Can we?" she demands.

The seconds are ticking by and all I want to do is run. To get as far away as possible.

"I don't know." I'm so tired. "I haven't had time to inspect it or…"

Toby leads us back into the security break room. "You said it was getting messages?"

I nod as I follow. "The one I saw was, 'The wolf is shaved so nice and trim. Red Riding Hood is chasing him.' Does that mean anything to you?"

Toby thinks for a second and drums his index finger on his sweats. "No. Mac?"

"No."

I sigh. "Maybe it's a substitution code? Or a Caesar cipher?"

"I know what it means," Charles says.

I know my brother means well, but there's no way he could have already cracked the coded message.

The more we stand in one place, the more I want to give up. Maybe this is why my dad can't stop running. "If I could just get a few minutes to do some research, I could…"

The rest of the words catch in my throat. On one of the monitors, Tork makes his way up the staircase with a contingent of National Police.

Another screen rotates through images of the Student Union's exterior where protesters and police argue and clash. I squint and check again to make sure I'm not losing it. But it's him. The guy in the black hat. Navarro. He slips behind a barricade guarded by a distracted officer and continues on toward the Student Union. Toward us.

What the hell.

I let go of my brother's collar and use my free hand to poke MacKenna in the arm. "It's him. He's here."

She's watching Toby. "We know. You told us. *Tork is coming.*" She says that last part in an almost perfect impression of my voice.

"No. The other guy. From school. Navarro." I stare at the screens, hoping he'll reappear.

"Navarro? What are you talking about?"

Toby interrupts us and casts a sideways glance at his sister. "What are the implications of turning ourselves in?"

I dab a bit of sweat off my brow with my sleeve.

We can't turn ourselves in. Not only did Mom expressly tell us not to, if my dad drummed one thing into us, it's that you can't allow someone else to control your safety. "We'd be giving the National Police the laptop before *we* know what information it contains. If Mom is right, if my father is the only one who can help Jay, we'd be giving up our opportunity to go after him. And there's something about this guy Tork. Something wrong with him. He's—"

Terrifying.

Charles tugs the sleeve of my windbreaker. "Jinx. The message. I *know* what it means."

I turn to my brother.

And then I turn to ice.

Footsteps fill the hall.

They're coming.

DR. DOOMSDAY'S GUIDE TO ULTIMATE SURVIVAL

BE PREPARED TO LEAVE EVERYTHING YOU KNOW BEHIND.

RULE FIVE:

"Okay. We run. For now." Toby points to a small door on the left side of the break room that I hadn't noticed at first. "This is how they brought me in. I don't think they wanted anyone to see me."

It leads to a narrow service staircase. We close the door with seconds to spare before the security team enters their offices with stomping footsteps and loud conversations. Toby carries Charles and takes the stairs two at a time, leaving MacKenna and me to run behind him.

We emerge into an industrial kitchen, and I almost face plant into a stainless-steel rack full of sub-sandwich bread. Toby extends a long arm to stop me from crashing into the kitchen equipment.

I want a sub sandwich.

That thought is short-lived.

Toby lets Charles down on the floor. They stand silent and motionless, staring at the sight of a black baseball cap bobbing across the kitchen. It's Navarro and MacKenna is about to speak to him, but I clamp my hand over her mouth. Toby gives me a questioning look, which I return with a small shake of my head.

We have to hide. We don't know this guy or know what he wants, and anyway...

Trust no one.

We duck in between the rows of stainless-steel bakery racks. Toby wheels one right in front of us, concealing us from view.

I.

Hold.

My.

Breath.

I watch Navarro through the narrow slots in the rack, over the round tops of the fresh bread. He comes close enough that I finally get a good look at him. He's probably a little older than me. Tall like Toby. Handsome. With neatly cut dark hair, a sharp chin and small dark eyes. He moves with a certain amount of stiffness and precision, scanning the room as he walks. Like someone who spends all his weekends doing... well, drills.

We wait.

Navarro walks with purpose. Like he's looking for something. Or someone.

But whatever he's after, he doesn't expect to find it in the kitchen. He comes within a couple of feet of us, passing us after a couple of seconds.

I don't exhale until I hear the door on the opposite side of the kitchen click closed.

Breathe.

"Why are we hiding from him?" MacKenna asks. "You think he's chasing us too?"

I shake my head. "I don't know."

MacKenna opens her mouth but Toby interrupts.

"We can deal with this later. For now, let's just get out of here."

We take the kitchen as far as we can and eventually come to a door. Toby partially opens the door and then jerks his head for us to follow. It spits us into the main walkway. We're able to blend in with a mob of students being herded away from the Student Union. We keep our heads down and stay close to the students. I'm hopeful that there's enough chaos out here that we won't be spotted by surveillance.

Outside, in the full sun of the winter afternoon, we keep walking until we arrive at a staircase that disappears into an underground library. We go down a few steps until we are concealed from view.

"Where did you guys park?" Toby asks.

"Behind the CC," I say.

MacKenna rolls her eyes at my attempt to use college slang.

Toby's been living on campus since August, and he's able to do a much better job steering us back to the truck without being noticed. We snake through the library and make our way across a couple of deserted courtyards to find the old truck exactly where we left it.

"Interesting set of wheels you got here," Toby says.

He smiles at me. His regular smile. The one that transports me back to a place where my biggest problems were my *Republicae* guild and the book report I had to do for history class.

"You look like you haven't gotten much sleep lately. I should drive."

I get the keys out of my jacket pocket and drop them in his palm.

Toby uses the keys to open the camper in the back of the truck, and MacKenna and Charles climb in. I take the passenger seat.

The truck rumbles to a loud start. Like you'd be able to hear all the noise it makes from the moon. My face heats up. It's stupid, but I'm embarrassed. This beater is way different than the fancy cars that Jay has. There's definitely no autodrive and no built-in e-tablets. "I know this thing is really old. My dad doesn't trust cars with computers. He says a vehicle shouldn't have a problem that requires more than a set of wrenches to diagnose."

"Right." Toby shuts the truck door. He puts the truck in reverse, but hesitates. "Where to?"

We have nowhere to go.

Charles sticks his head through the camper window. "I know where to go."

I desperately want to keep my brother safe. But that doesn't mean that we should let an eight-year-old decide our next move. "Charles—"

He snorts. "Jinx. I *know* what the message means. 'The wolf is shaved so nice and trim. Red Riding Hood is chasing him.' It's from that place we used to stay with Dad. It had the loveliest installation of Queen Victoria Agave. The plants must have been quite mature, because remember how they were in bloom the last time—"

We don't have time for a three-hour lecture on desert plants. "Charles! What are you talking about?"

He frowns and sounds like our father when he continues in a know-it-all tone. "I'm *trying* to tell you. I'm talking about that little hotel. The one with the stuffed animals. That message is on the window of the barbershop. Right next to the agave."

He's right.

"The Lone Wolf Motel." I say this mostly to myself. "In Gila Bend." To Toby, I say, "It's the starting point of several of my dad's evacuation plans. He made us do drills—I mean, practice leaving the country in a hurry. In the event of an emergency. Gila Bend is a small town in the desert that's a good place to be if you need to get to Mexico."

Toby bites his lower lip. "You think that message could have been from Dr. Marshall?"

MacKenna leans into the cabin too. "That's a good reason *not* to go."

"I don't know." Truthfully, I doubt it. A message like that isn't Dad's style. Dr. Doomsday can be plenty cryptic when he wants to be, but communicating over such an unsecure channel without any control over who would see the message and how they would interpret the data doesn't seem like something he would do.

But the Lone Wolf Motel is odd and out of the way. "I think it's our best option."

"Our best option?" MacKenna repeats. "I don't think *it is* our best option."

"Of course you don't," I snap. "It's my idea. So naturally you hate it."

"Everything's not about you, Jinx."

Charles coughs. "It's my idea! I'm the one who recognized the message."

Oh, for God's sake. "Okay. It's your idea, Charles. And I can't think of a better one."

"You guys, chill," Toby says. He twists in his seat to face

his sister. "Mac, we have to find a place to regroup and decide what to do next. That sounds like as good a place as any."

"It'll be fine," Charles tells her. "We've done the Evac plan
lots of times."

The last time we did the drill was also the last time our
parents were together. The Monday after we got back from
Mexico, Dad packed a bag. A couple weeks later, we had a
new house and a completely different life. As I think about
it, I like the idea of reliving that trip less and less.

But what other options are there?

Toby puts the truck in Drive and takes off out of the parking lot. "What about money?"

"Dad always packs emergency supplies."

Speaking of which.

I turn in my seat. "Charles, you have to find the food bin
and get something to eat." To my relief he doesn't argue. He
lumbers up the main aisle of the camper, opening the cabinets until he comes across the white food bin. He passes out
protein bars and water to everyone.

As the car jiggles, I dig my brother's glucometer out of the
yellow bag and force him to stick his hand through the camper
window. I scan the little white disk on his upper arm. His
blood sugar is a little high. Hopefully, the protein bar helps.

We're quiet for a while. Toby drives casually. Not too fast.
Not too slow. My brother settles down. We *have* done this drill
a lot. There's a sense of relief that comes from the familiar.

Every once in a while, I give Toby directions.

When we make it onto Maricopa Road, my breathing
evens out.

No one appears to be following us.

For the most part, the road is deserted. It's a pain in the
ass to plan a route through a hundred old highways and back

roads. People stick to the interstate. Way off in the distance, I spot what's left of the old stadium. It's like a massive silver turtle, poking its shell out of the sand. Mom said that, before the New Depression, it used to host concerts and football games and that she even went to a taco truck party once. But now, it's abandoned.

A white car goes by us, and a gleam of light flashes over Toby's face. "You got a haircut?"

"I don't know." He sounds amused.

"What?"

"Come on. I can almost hear the gears of your mind grinding away. You want to know what I think about all of this. If it's going to be okay. If we'll be okay."

"Well, will we?"

"Yes, on the cut. I don't know about everything else."

I open my mouth…and nothing comes out. This is what we always do in our house. Avoid talking about all the things that worry us. But I have to ask.

I force the words out. "What about your dad?"

Toby's grip on the steering wheel tightens, and the skin around his lips crinkles into an expression of concern. "I have to believe that justice will prevail. Right? That they'll figure out who really did this and things will go back to normal."

It seems to me that, by the time you're on the run from the National Police, the prospect of things returning to normal is seriously diminished. Still, Toby's optimism, his feeling that anyone can be good or that things can work out okay, might be the only thing that, in the end, will keep us going.

I lean toward the rearview mirror. Charles and MacKenna are sitting at the camper's tiny table, setting up our old backgammon board.

"But I have to admit," Toby continues in a lower voice, "there's something going on here that scares the hell out of me."

My heartbeat slows to a dull thud.

"On the news, they said all of First Federal's paper records for the last five years have been destroyed. And now they can't get their computers to work either?"

I take the last bite of my protein bar and chew with a forced deliberation. "Terminus said the bank mainframe is infected with a piece of malware that's been running for a while and corrupting their backups."

"Terminus?"

"My hacker friend," I say. "But honestly, so what? Some people will have copies of their own records. It could take a while to repopulate the system, but eventually they'll get it straightened out."

Toby's shoulders slump. "*Eventually* isn't much help when your rent is due on the first of the month. Things are already really bad because of the New Depression. But, beyond that, do you understand how banks work? I mean, how money works?"

"No." I understand how bank computers probably work, but that's it.

"Banks take in money and then they loan it out, so at any given time, they can't repay everyone who has made deposits. If people become afraid that they can't get access to money when they need it, they start taking their money out of banks. It's Wednesday afternoon,. and there were already five major runs on banks. The news said that all the banks in the country are closing early. The ATM systems are down. They're saying that maybe the banks won't reopen tomorrow unless they can get emergency funds from Congress."

It's suddenly very warm in the truck. I slide out of my jacket and put it on the seat next to me. "I... I don't understand."

Toby glances at me. "First Federal is not just the oldest bank, it's the biggest. They underwrite a lot of big loans. They touch a lot of sectors of business. They underwrite almost a third of all mortgages. My economics professor says money is almost an illusion. It's the idea that the country's economy is strong. That people are productive and can pay for goods and services. Since the New Depression, that illusion is very fragile. What happens to the country if that illusion goes away? What happens if they try to blame my father for *all* of that?"

I don't know what to say. So we're quiet again.

The state route goes through the small town, carrying us directly to my dad's destination of choice. The Lone Wolf Motel. It's not the Hilton, but it's better than some of the dumps we've stayed in. They vacuum the carpet. And there are no bugs. That you can see.

Toby parks the truck on the far, hidden side of the Lone Wolf Grill, which is usually open and serving lunch to truckers and hungry interstate travelers. Now it's closed and deserted.

I reach into the glove compartment and am relieved to find a thick envelope of emergency cash. "So...uh...let's go get a room, then I'll come back out and see what my dad packed in the way of supplies."

Toby gets out of the truck. I grab the yellow bag and follow.

Before he opens the door to the camper, Toby touches my arm lightly. "Hey. Listen. What we talked about. Can we keep it between us? For now. Mac's not so great at processing too many things that are..."

Terrifying?

"Yeah. Sure. Got it."

Toby's hand freezes on the door handle. He stands there

facing the rusting metal. "You think you could really find something on that laptop? Something to help my father?"

I don't know.

That's what I should say. That's the truth. If the machine's been compromised, whoever hacked it could have messed with it and deleted the rogue files. And just as easily removed the evidence that they were ever there. Or added incriminating files in ways that would be hard to identify or track.

That's my dad's area of expertise. Maybe that's why Mom wants us to find him.

Instead. "Yeah. I think it will take some time. But yeah." Toby's lips relax as he opens the door.

Charles stretches and jumps down onto the asphalt. MacKenna comes out after him.

Toby locks the camper and we go, passing by the diner first. Through the window, I spot stacks of unwashed dishes on the counters. Like the customers got sucked up by the rapture or something. A handwritten note that reads Cash Only has been taped to the door at a hurried angle above a yellowing flip sign turned to the Sorry, We're Closed side.

"This seems really weird," I say.

"The National Police are chasing us, my dad's in some unknown jail somewhere but what bothers you is some gross Podunk diner closing early?" MacKenna asks.

I'm sick of her attitude. "Okay. First of all, the diner's not gross. They're famous for this homemade pie—"

"It's rhubarb!" Charles chimes in. "And they have real meat."

"Not synthetic?" Toby asks.

I ignore this and continue walking toward the motel office. "—and, anyway, I'm only making the point that closing in the middle of the afternoon on a Wednesday—"

MacKenna talks over to me. "*I'm* making the point that—"

"Enough. Both of you. Enough." Toby stops and puts up his hands as we arrive at the small barbershop, which is also closed.

We all face the mural in the window.

The wolf is shaved so nice and trim. Red Riding Hood is chasing him.

That message is etched in gold, swooshing script that is cracked and faded. Underneath, there's a Burma Shave logo and a picture of a blonde woman in a red cape grinning at a wolf in an elegant suit. The sign has been there so long that most of the woman's face has worn away.

Charles approaches a series of deep green succulents that sit in large terra-cotta planters. He touches one of the rounded, tipped leaves. "See. I told you. Oh. Oh dear. They really need to trim those pups. And drain the planters better, because—"

I pull my brother to the end of the sidewalk. "Okay. We have to divide up the money."

Toby squints at me. "Why?"

"In case we're jumped." *Or get separated.* "That way no one person has all the money." I pass out a few twenties to Toby and MacKenna.

"You people are really paranoid," she says, stretching her arms over her head.

"My paranoia is the reason we're not sitting in a cell right now."

"Really, you guys?" Toby mutters.

"No one gave me any money," Charles says.

"You don't need any money. You're a child."

My brother grunts. "Jinx. The rules say we all get money in case we're—"

"Here." I press two crumpled bills in his hand. I really don't want to start another argument with MacKenna about what might happen if we have to split up.

We make our way across the parking lot. There are a few sedans scattered around, a couple of 18-wheelers, and an old pickup truck parked right in front of the motel office. A blue neon Vacancy sign glows in the office window.

A bell rings as I push the door open.

"No. We ain't got no pie," a man's voice calls out.

It's been a year since I've been here with my dad.

The office is exactly the same.

Creepy.

Scratch that.

Creepier than before. Like last time, the walls are covered with deer heads, but now at least a dozen taxidermied birds hang from the ceiling. Small lamps scattered on a few tables throughout the room cast a shallow light. Only the birds' feet are visible. In the corner, I spot the form of Ol' Renegade— a massive stuffed buffalo.

My gaze darts around, but I can't find the speaker and this wasn't the greeting I was expecting. "Uh. I'm sorry. What?" I call back.

A tall, grimly thin, gray-haired man emerges from a small room at the back. His hair shoots out in every direction, and he's dressed in overalls so dirty that I was probably a small child the last time anyone washed them. Even in the low light, I can see that he's covered with spots and spills.

"I said, we're outta pie," he repeats. He hunches over a maple countertop and removes a pair of glasses from his head, then polishes them with the tail of a dingy shirt hanging out from the side of his overalls. "We ain't got no lunch neither."

"Oh now, Mernice." A woman joins us in the office. Her neat, trim, perfectly pressed slacks and blouse sharply contrast with Mernice's wild appearance. I bet she sleeps with her gray-blond hair in rollers.

She smiles. "Welcome to the Lone Wolf Motel. How can we help you?"

Mernice scowls. "They're kids. Of course they want pie. Which we ain't got."

"No rhubarb?" my brother asks.

If possible, this question puts the old man in an even worse mood. "That's what I said."

My brother shouldn't have any pie, at least not until we can check his blood sugar.

And we're not supposed to leave an impression.

The woman ushers my brother farther into the office, motioning for him to sit on a brown plaid sofa. She opens her mouth into a very wide smile and pulls the top off a candy dish with an odd amount of gusto. "Everyone loves a nice butterscotch, dear."

"Oh, for crying out loud, Maybelline," the old man mutters.

We really need to get out of here. "You got rooms?"

"Yeah. We got rooms. What we ain't got is food, flat-screen TVs, fancy little scented soaps in the bathrooms or working credit card machines. So cash only." Mernice retreats to the smaller room, muttering, "Cash only." He shuffles back and drops a heavy leather-bound book on the counter, causing a jar of pens to rattle.

Mernice peers around me through the glass door and into the parking lot. "You alone? You *kids* walk here?"

"No." My face heats up. "We parked over by the diner."

"Whaddidya do that for?"

All these questions are making me very nervous. "We're hungry. We wanted to eat. But I know. There's no food."

He nods. "There's also no checking in without an adult."

Toby steps in front of me. "Sir," he says in a voice much friendlier than mine. "I'm an adult and we're on our way to meet our parents shortly." He pats the pockets of his sweats and I can see it dawn on him that he doesn't have his wallet.

Which is our first break, really, because the last thing on earth we ought to do is show a piece of ID with a real name on it. My heartbeat picks up. This is taking too long. Arousing too much suspicion. And Toby's still wearing his ASU shirt. It's bright and loud and places us.

Breathe.

"We have cash," I say quickly.

I can tell he isn't going for it, but the woman, who must be Maybelline, has been won over by my brother.

"Oh now, Mernice."

I bet Maybelline spends a good portion of her life following her coot of a husband around and saying *Oh now, Mernice* over and over.

"We got plenty of rooms. Let the kids have one." She gives Charles another piece of candy. "Just send your parents down when they get here."

Mernice grunts and nudges the registration book in my direction. "I hate those damn computers, so we do it the old-fashioned way. Write your name on line five. It's still sixty dollars a night. You kids will be pleased to know that the Wi-Fi works."

I write my name as illegibly as possible and drop three twenties on the book.

It helps that Charles opens his mouth and a supercute yawn escapes from it.

Maybelline motions for us to follow her. "These kids are dead on their feet. I'll walk 'em over to their room."

"Interesting decor in the office," Toby says as he opens the office door.

Maybelline smiles. "Mernice's daddy was a taxidermist. West of here. In Wickenburg. That stuff came to us when he passed. There's even a stuffed penguin in there somewhere."

We follow Maybelline outside. It's colder than it was when we came in.

She leads us down the shaded sidewalk that surrounds the motel. "I hope you kids don't mind Mernice. There was quite the to-do this morning when people heard about the banks. We had some fellas walk out on their bill. And there was some fightin'. More of this business about the election. People can't put their differences aside long enough to have a patty melt. Some trucker pushed the pie case over. I ain't never seen anything like this, not anything at all. We had to close early and…" Maybelline trails off.

"I'm sorry," Toby says. He always knows what to say.

"Yes. Well." She recovers her cheerful demeanor. "Contrary to what my husband thinks, I do plan to get the kitchen open this evening." She stops in front of the last room on the end, near a row of flowering bushes.

"Here we go," she says, opening the door to room twenty-five. She gives Toby the keys. Maybelline's gaze travels over two neatly made queen beds and a clean dresser.

Charles trots by me. He grabs a couple of leaves off the bush as he passes. "Miss Maybelline. I think you're over-watering your bougainvillea. They've got chlorosis. Maybe from root rot."

"Oh, bless your heart." Maybelline's about to go when she adds, "Do come by after about five for a spot of dinner. From the looks of you, it's been a while since you had a decent meal."

"Thanks, Maybelline," I say as I close the door.

The cheap plastic clock on the nightstand between the beds reads 2:30 p.m.

"So how are we doing this?" MacKenna asks, glancing from one bed to the other. "Girls versus boys? Or Novaks versus Marshalls?"

"Charles is a total bed hog." I know what I should be doing. I should go back to the camper and do a basic inventory and then make a lap around the motel.

Charles runs into the bathroom.

I'm exhausted. And also amped up on adrenaline.

I stay near the door, heavy with fatigue. Working up the energy to continue the drill.

I need to check the room, check the property and check on my brother.

Outside, heavy footsteps scuff the cement walk.

I freeze.

Someone's coming.

I look out the door's peephole. I can't see anything, but I sense someone on the other side. The tiny hairs rise on the back of my neck.

I left the Taser in the truck.

"Get Charles and hide. In the closet."

Toby is a few feet behind me. "Oh *hell* no," he whispers back.

"It's probably the old lady coming back," MacKenna says.

"Mac. Please. Do it. Now."

I've got my fingers wrapped around the door handle. I tell myself they aren't shaking.

Okay. Okay. Just like we practiced. Just like we practiced.

Like we practiced.

DR. DOOMSDAY'S GUIDE TO ULTIMATE SURVIVAL

RULE SIX:

TRUST NO ONE.

Your adversary is likely to be male.

And to have height and weight advantages.

Do whatever you have to do to disable your attacker.

I throw open the motel room door and jump out onto the sidewalk before my brain has time to feed my body information on how totally insane of an idea this is. There, in the shadow cast by a concrete brick pillar, a dark form waits like a storm cloud.

Knee strike. This is most likely to work against someone who's surprised or who has little self-defense training. I reach out and grab what I hope is my enemy's neck. I pull down with my arms as I lift my knee to his groin.

He's mostly able to block me by pushing back on my knee with his hands. But I get enough traction to do a little damage. "Oof."

A male voice.

"Wait. Wait," he whispers.

The guy is off guard enough that I try again. *Palm strike.* Thrusting up with my hand, aiming for his chin. Again, he's pretty good at blocking me, but I'm able to knock him back into one of the pillars.

He hunches over, and that's when I see it. The black hat with the gold medallion. It's Navarro, who's obviously been following us. I grab at the smooth, satin fabric of his windbreaker, drag him into the room. This might not be the best idea, but I'm pretty sure the three of us can take him, and it's better than letting him run around without supervision.

Toby tackles Navarro and pushes him onto the bed nearest the door. The baseball cap gets knocked onto the room's cheap carpet. "You know, you could have let me do that."

I'm out of breath. "Don't…be…such…a sexist…"

Navarro is facedown on the bed, Toby sitting on top of him, but even still, he isn't making much of an effort to get away. This seems off. Like someone who's successfully tracked us almost a hundred miles should be making more of a fuss.

"What should we do with him?" Toby asks.

I resist the urge to shudder at the outline of a weapon on the inside of his jacket.

"Get the gun."

"Wait. Wait," comes a muffled reply. "I've…something… say something."

"Yeah, what's that?" I ask as Toby removes the gun from a holster and makes a disgusted face as he passes it to me. It's a Glock 22. A classic. My dad would approve.

The chamber indicator says it's unloaded.

Also weird. Who comes to a confrontation with an unloaded weapon?

"Snuhflahk."

It sounds like *snowflake*.

Dad's safe word.

"Let him turn over," I tell Toby.

Navarro rolls over slowly into a seated position. Blood runs down the side of his chiseled face. I got a pretty good shot at his nose.

"What did you say?"

"You heard me the first time," he almost growls.

"Who are you?" While I wait for an answer, I shove the gun into the waistband of my jeans and force myself to step forward and search his pockets. I'm ready with another palm strike if he decides to try anything. Instead, he stays calm and relaxed. The guy smells like a campfire and juniper and some kind of spicy aftershave.

MacKenna and Charles come out of the closet.

"I told you," MacKenna says. "His name is Gus Navarro."

Navarro doesn't resist as I search his pockets. "You don't remember me? That hurts."

It's intended to be a flippant comment, but it has a soft edge. Like his feelings really *are* hurt. Meanwhile, the things I'm pulling from his pockets cause my stomach to churn. A pocketknife. Waterproof matches. A plastic flask. A few small flares. A box of ammo.

Everything looks familiar. Like a Dr. Doomsday survival kit.

My heart fall into my stomach. "Why would I? We don't have any classes together."

"What's going on?" Toby asks, glancing from me to Mac-Kenna. "You two know this guy?"

"He goes to our school," MacKenna says.

I straighten up. Try to look as tough as possible. Stare right into the guy's dark, brooding eyes. "I want answers. And if I don't get them, I'm gonna load this Glock, and I will totally shoot you in the head. Who told you to say that?"

"Snowflake?" Toby repeats. "That's important in some way?"

"It's the safe word," Charles says.

"Who do you think, Susan?" Navarro smiles.

Like he's enjoying this.

Like he's already figured out that I won't really shoot him.

My pulse quickens at the sight of his lopsided grin.

Which sucks. I've already given up any advantage that we might have had due to superior numbers or Dad's training.

The last interior pocket of Navarro's windbreaker contains an orange SAT phone and a thin wallet. Rifling through the billfold, I find a couple hundred in cash and a driver's license.

Gustavo Navarro. That's his name. He's eighteen and on top of everything else, he actually has the nerve to look good in his driver's license photo.

"Gustavo Navarro," I say out loud, trying to make sense of this.

"I go by Gus."

My brother scoots out from around MacKenna and approaches Navarro. "*I* am Charles Maxwell III." He holds out his hand before I can stop him.

I sigh internally. Dad was never really able to cultivate a sense of distrust in Charles. My brother likes authority figures. He'll spill his deepest secrets to the mail lady. Gustavo Navarro, clad in his survivalist uniform, fits that bill. He shakes my brother's small hand.

I toss the wallet in Navarro's lap. "Why are you following us?"

His smile fades. "My job is to make sure you get on the

road. But Dr. Marshall didn't tell me there'd be anyone besides you and your brother. I don't know what's going on here, but whatever it is, it's not part of the plan."

"*You're* not part of the plan," I say.

The conversation is unnerving Toby. "You're saying Dr. Marshall sent you? Sent you to help us?"

Navarro stares at me when he answers. "To help *you*? No."

Charles plops down on the bed next to Navarro. "Did my dad *really* send you?"

MacKenna makes a face. "And do you know what's *really* in those tofu nuggets?"

A weird sort of frustration builds up inside me. Almost like riding a bike down a steep hill. I'm going too fast and the brakes won't work.

Toby wants more information. Charles wants to make new friends. Even MacKenna is relaxing and leaning against the white wall.

"Dad wouldn't send anyone, Charles. Rule number six is *trust no one*. And even if he did send somebody to help us, it wouldn't be a *boy* we've never met before."

The smirk slides off Navarro's face. "I'm a man. And we have met before. Last summer? At PrepperCon?"

PrepperCon? Great. I snort. "So you're one of those idiots who follows my dad around and hangs on his every word?"

MacKenna nods enthusiastically. This might be the first thing we've agreed on in months.

Navarro shoots me a dark look. "Yeah. I'm such an idiot. Well, I got you here, didn't I?"

Of course. It hits me then. "The messages on the laptop? That was you?"

"How did you do that?" MacKenna asks.

I already know the technical details. The real question is why.

Toby preempts me when he says, "Why would you do that? Did you have something to do with what happened at the banks?"

Navarro rolls his eyes. "All I know is that I got a call from Dr. Marshall yesterday. A little after noon. He sent me the script, told me how to run it and then said to meet you here. Except you left the bunker and you weren't headed *here*. So I followed you. Going to a college campus in the middle of a riot was stupid, by the way. Very, very stupid."

Well, that explained his presence in the Student Union kitchen.

"If we're so stupid, how did we make it past the National Police?" MacKenna returns.

Navarro stands up and we all jump. "Relax. I'm just getting my hat, okay?"

Toby shakes his head. "I'll get it." He hustles out the door and returns a second later with the hat, then drops it on the bed next to where Navarro stands.

Navarro sits again. "Thanks. And in answer to your question, you made it past the National Police because I took out the campus surveillance systems. They would have found you in about thirty seconds if they'd been able to see you on the IPTV."

This makes sense. It explains how we were able to get off campus without being spotted. But there's something off about it too. Navarro doesn't seem like a hacker.

"*You* took the security systems off-line?"

His face flushes pink. "Well, Dr. Marshall did."

My breath catches.

Navarro's saying he had contact with Dad. Today.

Charles grins. "You talked to my dad? Did he say when he's coming back?"

Navarro shifts, and a look of uncertainly falls over his face. Like he's suddenly realized he's going to have to be the one to put into words that Dad isn't coming back. He pats my brother on the shoulder. "He didn't say, little man. It was a pretty quick conversation. Susan? You want proof?" He points to the orange phone in my hand. "Redial the last number I called."

I frown. "How do I know it's not being tracked?"

He shrugs. "You know the deal. It takes about ten minutes to obtain the position of the SAT phone based on a call. You don't like what you hear? Hang up and get out of here."

Oh God. This guy sounds like he's been spending all his weekends with my dad.

Navarro twists his lips into a wry smile. "Oh sure. I know what you're thinking. How do you know I didn't make a call when I got here? I didn't. But if I did, you'd already be pretty screwed. Another twenty or thirty seconds won't change your fate."

I find myself smoothing down my hair with my sweaty fingers and then hating myself for how totally stupid this is. I have to focus. *Focus.*

I pick up the phone and redial the last number in the menu.

The call gets answered on the first ring.

"Is it done?"

Dad.

It's Dad's voice.

I have to bite down on my own tongue to keep from crying. "Is what done? Dad. Dad. We're in some—"

Charles jumps off the bed. "Dad? Is that Dad? Can I talk to him?"

I have to twist and turn to keep the phone out of my brother's grasp. "Some…um…trouble and…ah…"

"I'm being watched. My location may be compromised. I

sent someone to help. I told him all about the trip we took. The one to Snowflake. You may need to make some route modifications, but generally speaking, stick to the Evac plan. I'll meet you when I can. If I can." Dad's voice is hollow. Tired.

"Someone?" The panic I've been fighting off since the explosion at First Federal flares up. When I speak again, there's nothing tough about me. I glance at Navarro. "This guy? How will that help? And we can't follow the original plan. Mom and—"

"No details."

"Dad!" Jesus. I'm going to throw up. The remnants of the protein bar are forcing their way back up. "What the hell is going on?"

"Did you get my message? I told...uh...*the boy* everything that's safe for you to know."

Charles is making swipes in the air, grabbing for the phone. "Tell him about the riot! Tell him I solved the clue!"

I have to put my hand on Charles's forehead to keep him from taking the phone. "Message? Dad. Listen to me. J— um—my stepfather—he's in jail and Mom thinks—"

"I know." Flat. Unaffected.

He doesn't even ask about us. Or say where he is. My building anger is almost a relief. It's a relief to feel something, anything, besides complete and utter terror. "You *know*? Well, if you know, then it has to be really fu—"

"Is that language necessary?"

We were very nearly crushed by a building. We were chased out of our house in the middle of the night. And my dad's big concern is maintaining a PG vocabulary? "—obvious why the plan isn't going to work."

"You need to follow the plan. That's how you'll be safe."

"What about Mom?" I ask through clenched teeth. "She told us to find you. She wants—"

"I know what she wants. This isn't going to end the way she's hoping."

God. It's like he can never say one real thing. "I won't abandon Mom just because that's what you did."

There's a pause. "I'll meet you as soon as I can."

"Meet me? Where? How will you..." I trail off.

"Jinx. Trust no one."

The line goes dead.

I'm talking to myself and holding a silent phone to my ear.

I open up the motel room door and stumble out, falling onto the concrete, breaking one of Dad's big rules by leaving the room without determining that it's safe. MacKenna comes out too. Maybe we're on friendlier terms now, because she holds my hair while I heave into a planter. I haven't eaten since that protein bar, so next to nothing comes out and all the stomach acid stays in my throat.

That might have been the last time I'll ever speak to my father, and he didn't even tell me he loves me.

I guess I didn't tell him either.

When I stagger back into the room, MacKenna on my heels, Navarro's still sitting on the bed while Toby stands near the door. They don't say anything, and I avoid their eyes as I go into the bathroom to rinse out my mouth.

When I come out, I pull a chair in front of Navarro. Try to seem tough. Try to seem normal. "Okay. What's the message?"

He smiles. Folds his hands in his lap. Like it's already occurred to him that the best way to push my buttons is to be calm and unconcerned. I wonder what else my father told him. "You need to get some rest. We have a long drive ahead of us and plenty of time to talk."

"We'll talk now." I stand up straight, plant my feet shoulder-width apart, put one hand on my hip, smoothing my T-shirt to make sure the gun in my waistband is in Navarro's line of sight. "My father said he gave you a message for me."

Navarro smiles even wider. "Yep. I see Dr. M put you through Ludvach's How to Intimidate with Body Language seminar. Good. That stuff's important."

I bite down on my lower lip and fight the urge to take the gun and throw it at his handsome face. "Listen. If you think—"

He stands up too. He must have also done the seminar and manages to be much more intimidating than me. "Marshall gave me a job to do. I'm supposed to get you going on his Evac plan to Mexico. Once we cross the border, you get your message. We leave after dark."

MacKenna joins us and we form an odd circle. "I don't care what that crackpot Dr. Doomsday has to say. He's not in charge. Neither are you."

"I'm not here for you, princess," Navarro tells her. "So you do whatever you want. But do you really think you can go back to your McMansion and your swimming pool and your fancy clothes? By this time next week, Jay Novak will be the most hated man in the country. The Opposition is out for his blood, and The Spark is trying to deny they've ever heard of him. I don't know how you think this is going to end, but it's not with you and your dad having a nice steak dinner together."

"Screw you," she says, between clenched teeth.

Stomach acid still burns the back of my throat. "Why don't you just tell me what my dad said?"

"You know why." Navarro moves even closer, making it clear how much taller he is than I am. "That message is my ace in the hole. Otherwise, we both know that you'll ditch me the first chance you get."

I fiddle with the fraying edge of my striped sweater. I can't believe I have to ask this of a complete stranger. "Do you have any idea where Dad is?"

Navarro shrugs. "About as good of an idea as you do."

"We need to find him."

"Find Maxwell Marshall?" Navarro says, his voice laced with skepticism. "You don't find Dr. Marshall. He finds you."

Toby watches this conversation from his position in the corner near the door.

It feels stupid to keep standing around. I sit down in the chair again. There also doesn't seem to be any point in keeping basic things from Navarro. Dad obviously *did* send him, and we aren't getting rid of him anytime soon. "My mom thinks that Dad could use his influence with The Opposition to help Jay."

"Influence?" Navarro repeats, almost chewing on the word. "There's no way that The Opposition is gonna help Jay Novak. There's also no way that you're gonna find Dr. Marshall if he doesn't want to be found."

"Well, aren't you a big ray of sunshine," MacKenna snaps.

"We should find Dad," Charles says uncertainly, watching Toby for a response.

"We should figure out what's up with that laptop," Mac-Kenna says with far more conviction. But a sympathetic, motherly expression crosses her face.

Navarro's dark eyebrows travel up his forehead.

Trust no one.

Whatever is going on with the laptop isn't something we should discuss with a stranger. Particularly one who's operating according to a set of secret instructions that he got from my father.

Before he can ask questions, I say, "We have to keep going no matter what. We may as well follow the drill. The best way to find Dr. Doomsday is to follow his plan." Plus, if there's any truth to what Dad said on the phone—that he'll meet us—he will expect to find us on the Evac route.

"Good. Then we leave tonight—around seven. As planned," Navarro says.

Toby finally speaks and, when he does, he directs his remarks to Navarro. "It seems like it makes sense for us to work together."

Navarro nods. "For now."

SURVIVAL MODE IS THE ABILITY TO TUNE OUT ANYTHING UNRELATED TO ONE'S CURRENT SITUATION. DISASTER IS RARELY SUDDEN. IT BUILDS LIKE A STORM, APPARENT TO ANYONE PAYING ATTENTION TO THE WEATHER.

We settle into a tense silence. But Navarro's presence throws off the rhythm of the drill.

He leaves the room to get some ice for his nose. When he returns, he spends his time in the desk chair with a cold pack on his face while Charles peppers him with questions. My brother doesn't let me get a word in, but it's just as well. I doubt Navarro would answer any of *my* questions. Toby takes a seat on the bed near the window and turns on the news, flipping through the channels. MacKenna lies down on the opposite bed and resorts to reading the Annika Carver book. Every once in a while, she glances up when we hear Jay's name on the crappy TV.

There's never much of an update, and most of the networks are covering the situation at the bank. Discussing the implication for the economy if First Federal can't recover its records. There are executives in suits trying to be reassuring. A woman with a tearstained face tells the camera that she worries she won't be able to buy groceries if her bank card won't work. A computer expert does her best to explain the malware.

I get out the glucometer and take Charles's blood sugar reading again. He doesn't squirm like he usually does. The number is high. Which is to be expected. Because of the stress. Also because my brother probably ate a candy bar in the camper when I wasn't looking.

Digging around in the yellow bag, I find the insulin pen and give Charles his dose. After that, I hunt around for a large bag of almonds and bring them over to where Charles sits next to Toby. "Here. You need to eat these."

He makes a face. "I don't want almonds. I hate almonds. They taste like dirt and they're gross and take too long to chew. You know, the almond is not even a nut. It's a drupe. They—"

Everything is a fight. Sigh. "Charles! You have to lower your blood sugar or—"

"I'll have some," Toby says. "They sound delicious to me." He takes the bag and pours some into his palm.

"I'll have some as well," Navarro says from underneath the ice pack.

I roll my eyes, but a couple minutes later Charles is busy chewing.

According to the drill, I'm supposed to inventory the supplies in the camper. That will partially determine what we do next, since how much food and gas I find there will dictate the route we take. Then I'm supposed to do laps around the motel. Make sure we're safe and secure.

But we have only a couple hours before we have to leave, and I don't know when I'll have another opportunity to inspect the laptop. I also don't know if I can trust Navarro. I had no idea what Dad might have told him to do. So I get the computer and act casual, taking the far side of the bed away from the window and making a show of fluffing up the pillows. I sit cross-legged on the orange Southwestern patterned bedspread.

The screen powers on, and I barely get the console window open before Navarro sits up and puts the ice pack aside. "What are you doing?"

"Looking at a few things," I say. Every time Navarro moves, I have to force myself not to stare at him.

Navarro stands at the foot of the bed where I sit with MacKenna. When his gaze rests on the laptop, I add, "Don't worry. I know what I'm doing."

"Do you?" he counters. "Because you're supposed to be doing a perimeter check. No one has made any effort to ensure the safety of our positon."

MacKenna turns a page of her book. "That sounds like an excellent job for you, Captain Courageous."

Navarro opens his mouth, closes it again and finally says, "Fine."

He leaves the room, and I'm uncertain whether or not that was a good idea.

"That guy is tons of fun," MacKenna says.

"We need him to find my dad," I reply.

"I'm still not totally convinced we *need* to find Dr. Doomsday. I think it's a better idea to use whatever's on that computer to get my dad out of jail."

I turn my attention to the computer.

There are two issues.

One. Is the code that triggered the explosions at the bank still on this machine?

Two. If it is, how did it get there?

A smart hacker could easily code a piece of malware to trash itself after it executes. But if you were deliberately trying to frame someone, you wouldn't do that. The whole point would be to plant evidence.

At least, that's what I'm hoping.

It was called *Day Zero*.

This is Dad's area. But generally, a zero-day exploit is a piece of malware that's been hanging around for a while. Day Zero is the moment when the user becomes aware that they're screwed.

It's usually the start of something.

Something terrible.

I do a search and find the term in the directory. Quickly. Easily. It's in the main documents folder buried in a few folders. But I can tell.

It was meant to be found. And it was modified on Monday. Around 4:00 p.m.

Right before the explosion at the Rancho Mesa bank.

I open the program file in the console window, and code fills the screen.

I have no idea what I'm looking at.

The code calls all sorts of audio files that must have been on the bank's mainframe. I stare at the screen. It would take me months to even scratch the surface of what this program was or what it did. Worse, there's something about it. Something familiar. It's got a certain style.

It reminds me of Dad.

I shudder.

Next to me, MacKenna leans over my screen. "You found something?"

"Maybe." I rotate the laptop so that the screen is at an angle that she can't view. "I'm not sure what though."

She cocks her head and gives me a disbelieving sigh.

"I'm serious. I mean…"

On TV, an attractive woman describes the efforts to find David Rosenthal.

Toby uses the remote to turn down the volume. "You mean what?"

I have a book report due on Friday. Mom needs to add more money to my school lunch account. That's what hits me at that exact moment. That I should be home forcing myself to read my textbook and whining about not being able to play *Republicae.* I'm so tired, and reality is hitting me like an Arizona dust storm.

Our lives are gone.

I bite the inside of my cheek. "I mean, I might have found something. Terminus said that the National Police think someone used the built-in speaker systems at the banks to detonate explosive materials. I *think* that's what this program does. But you'd need a PhD in computer science to understand this thing."

Basically, you'd need to be my father.

"Can people do that? Cause explosions that way?" Toby asks.

I hate the fact that so many of these conversations keep coming back to Dad. "My dad thought so. He felt computer hardware was vulnerable to a sonic attack, and he was running experiments when he was still friendly with Carver. Dad wasn't able to get the technology to work though."

It seems risky to use the Wi-Fi to contact Terminus, but I don't see any other choice. I connect the laptop and start a chat.

Me: You there?

Terminus: Yep and for the record you're scaring the hell out of me. Where are you?

I don't have time to get into what's happened or exactly where we are.

Me: Looking for Marshall.

Terminus: You need to think about this.

Terminus: You're not gonna find him and half of the state is out looking for you.

Terminus's assumption that there's no way that I could possibly find my dad sort of pisses me off. I mean, it's probably true. But still.

Me: I spoke to him. About an hour ago.

Terminus: Uh...

Terminus: Did he say where he was?

Terminus: Or what he's doing?

Me: He said he'll meet me.

Terminus: What?

There really isn't time for this. And MacKenna is staring at me. I type faster.

Me: I need your help. Check this out.

I drop the file into a secure partition on the server.

Terminus: Whoa.

Terminus: What the hell is this?

Me: I need you to figure that out.

Me: I mean, who could possibly have written something like this?

Terminus: Other than Marshall? I don't know.

Terminus: I'll put out some feelers.

Me: I'll contact you as soon as I can.

I'm about to close the chat window when another message comes through.

Terminus: Wait. I did find out one thing.

Terminus: Jay Novak is being held at Goldwater Airfield.

Terminus: Chat in the back channel says

Terminus stops typing.

Me: Says what?

Terminus: They're going to kill him. On Friday. Carver will address Congress that morning and then

I close the chat window.

Oh. My. God.

At the same time, MacKenna slams the book shut and points at the silver computer. "We have to destroy that thing. It's obviously the evidence someone has manufactured to frame my father. We don't need to help them do it!"

It feels more critical than ever to save it.

She makes a grab for the laptop.

I shut it and jump off the bed. "I'm not finished inspecting it. And, anyway, it's not that easy to destroy a hard drive."

MacKenna gets up too and reaches again for the laptop.

"Oh, it's plenty easy. We can run over it with the car. Or smash it against the desk. Or fill the bathtub with water. Or—"

"No, we can't!" People always think it's so easy to destroy data. In reality, hardware techs hate having to retire servers. The process of truly making sure that data can't be retrieved from a drive is time-consuming and annoying. You need to secure-erase the files, populate the drive with garbage data and then physically destroy the computer. "The National Police have a crime lab where they can recover data from partially destroyed computers. They've been able to get files off disks that have been put through a shredder."

She makes another grab for the laptop.

"We should…at least see if…we can figure out how…the file got there," I tell her as I back into the corner near the bathroom to keep the laptop away from her.

"You guys," Toby says, sitting up. Charles is watching with his mouth open.

We all freeze at a light knock at the door.

Toby gets up and, after pausing at the peephole, opens the door, letting a bit of blue twilight into the room.

Navarro's back. "What the hell is going on?"

"Nothing," MacKenna and I say at the same time.

I shove the laptop into the yellow bag and leave it in the corner. "Did you find anything?"

Navarro shrugs. "Eleven out of the twenty-five rooms are occupied. There are a few truckers probably en route to the interstate. A pair of elk hunters. A family having their house in Why fumigated. A rep from Dice Pizza checking out the local store. No one seems like a threat."

We need things to calm down a bit. Toby gets MacKenna to sit on the bed, and after a while she's reading again.

"How's the book?" I ask, trying to make conversation.

MacKenna frowns. "Annika Carver is one cold, robotic bitch." She adds, "Her skin cream is good though."

Leaning over, I glance at the page she's reading from. A passage catches my eye.

Ammon Carver's operatives have largely shielded the tycoon's daughter from deep scrutiny, working to bury reports that Annika cheated on her college entrance exams and to destroy unflattering photos. Annika Carver's ethics, whatever they may be, remain mostly unknown.

MacKenna turns to me. "Did you ever meet her?"

I shake my head. "No. Dad worked with Carver, but we didn't see him much. I only met him once. He didn't seem like a family man."

MacKenna shuts her book and removes an old-fashioned pad of paper and a pen from the drawer of the nightstand. She begins scribbling notes.

"What are you doing?" I ask.

"Working," she says. "If we ever get to go home, I want to be ready to write."

Forever a journalist.

Toby manages a weak smile even as his biceps tense. He leans forward. "About our dad? You'll have one heck of an inside scoop."

Ammon Carver's face fills the TV screen. He's wearing his usual dark blue suit, but his yellowing hair and beard aren't as neatly trimmed and combed as usual.

He's standing at a podium in the presidential mansion's rose garden with his wife hovering in the background, fidgety and inconsequential.

Carver's voice grates. Like someone filing their nails.

"My fellow citizens, in a move designed to prevent further instability, I've been working with Congress to enact a series of tempo-

rary emergency measures that will include curfews, supply rations and transportation restrictions."

Oh no.

"Supply rations?" Toby repeats. "What the hell does he want to ration?"

I'm more worried about the transportation restrictions. That could mean more patrols. Or roadblocks. We now not only have to *find* Dr. Doomsday; we have to do it faster.

"It's also essential for every citizen to cooperate fully with the on-going investigation into the recent terror attacks. While I am relieved to report that The Opposition has worked with authorities to apprehend the main instigator, we do not believe that The Spark organizer, party financier and Croatian immigrant Jesen Oscar Novak, was working alone."

Jay's picture flashes on the screen.

I shiver. I should say something. Now. *Say something. Now. Now. Now.*

"Spark organizer?" MacKenna says. "He manned a voter registration table one day for three hours! I had to beg him to do it!"

"We are now in possession of critical evidence that my political adversary, David Rosenthal, masterminded the terrible violence that rocked our republic yesterday—"

Toby moves to the edge of the bed. "It makes more sense than calling Dad a Spark financier. I think he went to one pancake breakfast with Stephanie."

"I wish we would go to a pancake breakfast," Charles says.

"—with full support from The Spark leadership at the highest level—"

"I had to force him to do it!" MacKenna goes on. "Dad wanted to play golf."

Navarro remains at the desk, saying nothing.

"What critical evidence would they possibly have?" I ask.

"Any citizen with knowledge about these attacks must come forward immediately…"

Toby rubs his eyes. "No idea. But Carver is clearly neutralizing his political rivals."

At that moment, I wish I'd paid more attention to one of Mom's thousands of political lectures, because I don't understand what a lot of this means. "Why? Why would that be necessary? He won the election."

Carver continues speaking in the background while Toby says, "He won by a very narrow margin, using very questionable methods."

"Yeah, Dr. Doomsday's methods," MacKenna grumbles.

"He came into the presidency with very little political capital."

"Rosenthal's despicable acts have severely impacted First Federal's ability to provide important financial services to its customers—hardworking, everyday citizens. I had to walk away from my role at my family's bank to seek the office of the presidency, in order to do what I feel is critical work on behalf of the nation. However, I am maintaining daily contact with the First Federal team at all levels. They are doing their best to bring critical systems back online. The New Depression has crippled our great nation these past ten years, and what impact this crisis may have, I cannot say. I do say that…"

MacKenna fiddles a strand of her long hair. "He wants to hold The Spark responsible for the New Depression. For everything."

Toby agrees. "The engine of outrage will only run when there's someone to blame. Someone to hate."

Of course, MacKenna and Toby understand this stuff more than I do. They study more and they haven't spent the majority of their free time over the past few years in a Doomsday bunker. I want to ask Toby what he thinks. But he doesn't look like he wants to talk.

And MacKenna is actually shaking her fist at the television.

"…and make right the wrongs of the last few years. This is a time to focus on what unites us, not divides us. But make no mistake, I will work tirelessly to restore the fundamental values for which so many of us yearn. In our country, let each man retain for himself the fruits of his own labor. Yet, let us all harvest from a common garden of ideas, of shared ethics and morals, of well-understood social roles and responsibilities. When a man earns his keep, keeps his earnings and is asked to give only his guidance to others, our nation will once again be the land of hope and prosperity."

Light applause follows these words.

The broadcast cuts almost immediately to the local news, where a blonde woman seems to be repeating what we just heard. Toby turns down the volume.

"That shit is creepy AF," MacKenna says. She looks at me, waiting for me to agree.

I pick at the sleeve of my sweater. "Um. Yeah. But I don't get it."

MacKenna's eyes get wider and wider. "You don't get it? That crackpot Ammon Carver is gonna use those explosions to throw anyone who opposes him in prison. Starting with my dad. Then, The Opposition is gonna let rich men establish their own little fiefdom in what's left of the government."

I look at Toby.

"Carver's speech is code for cutting taxes for the rich and ending programs that help the poor and promote equality," he explains.

MacKenna's gaze turns to the heavy curtains covering the window. "It's always the same story. These guys. They think there's something wrong with the world when really there's something wrong with them."

Navarro is reading the room's Bible. "Maybe there *is* something wrong with the world."

MacKenna relaxes onto her pillows. "You mean like the fact that a bunch of old guys run it?"

What would MacKenna do if she knew what I knew? What would she do if she'd seen the message from Terminus?

They're going to kill him.

I'm so cold. I pull the edge of the cheap comforter up around my side.

"I *mean*," Navarro says, closing the book, "that the country has been on the edge of a financial collapse for almost ten years. The Spark has all this smug superiority, but what are they doing to help? What they do is make rules. And impose taxes."

MacKenna sits up again. "Society has a moral responsibility to help people who can't work or can't feed themselves."

Navarro leans forward in his chair, almost devastatingly handsome. "Because the government should enforce morality? The Opposition thinks so too. Once you accept that basic principle, all that's left to argue about is the definition of what's moral. What is the morality of marriage? Of death? Of having children? And is it really moral to take from one person to give to another?"

Toby runs a hand through his dark hair. "You wouldn't give your extra money to help a friend?"

Navarro glances at me when he says, "I'd do anything for a friend. But that would be my choice."

MacKenna purses her lips into a thin line. "I can't believe this. The Spark is trying to make sure that all people have basic human and civil rights. That everyone gets treated equally."

"The ability to take food off a stranger's plate isn't a right," Navarro says. "Anyway, nothing is ever equal. People don't work equally hard. They aren't equally enterprising. You can't treat everyone the same, because they aren't the same."

"My dad says that. He says the thing about the plate," I whisper.

I pull at a loose strand of my hair. I always used to ignore the things that Dad said.

MacKenna opens her mouth. "The problem is—"

"The problem is," Navarro interrupts, "that you can't figure out how to have a world where you believe in democracy but also in depriving people of the freedom to determine their own fates."

Tremors return to my stomach. "I think we should discuss this later."

"Of course you do," MacKenna snaps. "You've spent your whole life pretending that these kinds of problems don't exist."

Charles is on the verge of tears.

"MacKenna—" Toby says in a concerned voice.

Navarro ignores both of us. "*You've* spent *your* whole life as the daughter of a rich and successful man. What makes you think you really understand these issues?" He pauses for a second, thinking. "You know, we're not so different. My parents are immigrants too. They came from Mexico when I was a baby. My mom put herself through college. My dad started a business importing generators. But that was then. Today, The Spark taxes food. And wages. And profits. And, if Rosenthal got his way, business equipment, imports and more."

"Everyone's for Rosenthal," Charles says, through a stuffy nose.

Toby puts a hand on my brother's back.

Navarro makes an effort to relax his face. "Your father is a self-made man. A war hero. Doesn't it bother you at all that in the reality created by The Spark, it's impossible to become a man like your father? Or like mine?"

The mention of MacKenna's dad sends a new wave of horror through me.

MacKenna picks up a pillow and clutches it like she might throw it in Navarro's face. "So that's it for you, then? Let the rich exploit the poor? Let the powerful dominate the weak?"

"Let everyone do their best to become powerful."

"This isn't getting us anywhere," Toby says, with a glance at my brother's tearful face. "We should be working together."

"Maybe," Navarro says with a shrug. "But maybe our objective isn't what you think."

I'm a heartbeat away from telling everyone that Jay has been taken to Goldwater Airfield. "We should be talking about what we're going to do next."

From telling them what Terminus said.

But I'm too late.

The conversation is over.

Ammon Carver's press conference ends and a new story takes over the TV.

Underneath the headline *Wanted for Questioning*, school photos of me, Toby and MacKenna appear on the screen.

Our images are replaced with one word in large, red letters. *REWARD*.

People talk about being paralyzed with fear. It's like the biggest cliché ever. But in that moment, I become cold, immovable stone. Unable to turn. To walk. To move.

We're going to die.

It's also perfectly clear why Dad sent Navarro.

Dad's right. We can't deal with this on our own.

DR. DOOMSDAY'S GUIDE TO ULTIMATE SURVIVAL

RULE SEVEN:

YOU CAN NEVER TELL WHAT SOME PEOPLE ARE CAPABLE OF.

We're silent for a minute. But we all know.

We're so, so, so screwed.

I have to keep it together.

For my brother.

I force myself to keep breathing.

To keep a neutral expression on my face.

It's a little before 6:00 p.m.

Navarro snatches the remote from Toby's hand and turns off the TV. "We need to go."

I'm about to agree when Charles pipes up.

"Miss Maybelline said we could come by the diner," he says.

From the look on his face, Navarro clearly wants to argue.

But Charles needs to eat.

I grab the yellow bag from the corner. "I think we'll have to go over there. My brother hasn't had a decent meal since yesterday, and if he goes too long without protein or vegetables—"

Charles scrambles off the other bed. "You're not going to say it'll 'aggravate his condition' are you? I hate it when you say that."

"You need to eat," I tell him. To Navarro I say, "We also need to inventory the supplies."

He makes an impatient noise. "You didn't inventory the supplies?"

I catch Navarro's gaze and quickly look away. Despite everything, my traitorous cheeks heat up.

Getting back on track, we agree that MacKenna and Toby will take Charles to the diner while Navarro and I check the camper.

"I hope they have pancakes," Charles says.

"You can't have pancakes. You need meat and salad."

Not everyone is happy with this plan.

As we leave the room, Toby lingers with his hand on the door.

"We'll meet you in a sec," I say to reassure him. "Try to keep Charles away from the syrup, okay?"

We stay together until we reach the parking lot. A cheerful, yellow light spills from the diner window, meaning Maybelline must have been able to prove old Oh-Now-Mernice wrong. Navarro and I make our way to the rear of the restaurant, where we left Dad's truck. Toby takes everyone else around the front.

Birds chirp as Navarro and I cross the lot. It's becoming a cool night, and patches of grass scattered around the motel grounds are wet with evening dew. It feels normal. Like we're back in a world where we're not being hunted by the police.

Make.

Conversation.

"So, you're for The Opposition? You're for Carver?" It comes out like a sneer.

Navarro smiles.

I'm glad it will be dark soon since I'm sure my hot face is as red as a tomato.

He really is good-looking. With perfect white teeth. It's the first time I feel comfortable taking a long look at him. As I stare at his sharp features, I can't help but notice how the fabric of his black T-shirt stretches over his chest.

I will myself to watch the blinking neon motel sign on the edge of the parking lot.

"I'm not *for* anyone," he says. "I'm for doing what's right."

We arrive at the truck, and I'm surprised to realize that it's actually a pea-green color with grayish primer patches all over the camper.

I unlock the camper door and climb into the back. As I hoist myself up, the light catches on the metallic circle in the center of Navarro's cap. I can really see it now. It's some kind of religious symbol. A man in a flowing golden robe. An odd choice for Navarro, a guy who comes across almost as disillusioned as my dad. "What's on your hat?"

He shuffles around on the asphalt. Acting as the lookout.

We've fallen into the rhythm of one of Dad's two-person drills.

"It's…um…San Judas."

Reaching into the recesses of my memory of catechism, I ask, "Saint Jude? The patron saint of the impossible?" I take a step into the camper and realize I left my utility jacket in the cab earlier that day. Face palm.

"Not of the impossible." Navarro says this like it's a painful admission. "Of…of lost people. Of lost causes. He's my patron saint."

"Okay. Why Saint Jude?" I pop my head out in time to see Navarro's lips pucker into an embarrassed frown.

And why, exactly, am I looking at his lips?

When he doesn't answer, I ask instead, "Do you have a flashlight?"

My question restores the cynical expression to his face.

He digs in his jacket pocket and holds out his light. "You lost your flashlight?"

I reach for it and, as our hands touch, for a second, the same shock of electricity I felt in the grocery store parking lot pulses through my fingertips. But I force myself to say what's on my mind. "Is that why you're helping us? You love a lost cause?"

He sighs and lets go of the flashlight. "You think this is a lost cause?"

My stomach drops but I'm able to sound calm. "Don't you? My mom wants me to find Dad. But really, MacKenna is right. Even if we find him, what is he gonna do? If we get caught…*when* we get caught, you're going to be in the same crappy situation as the rest of us."

He thinks for a second. "San Judas is the patron saint of Mexico City. That's where my mama grew up. There's a church. Very old. Beautiful. Pilgrims go there. Some to pray. Some to give out trinkets or candy. Mama gave Judas to me as my patron and she said, if I have faith, he'll protect me. Even when everything seems lost."

"You have *faith*?" I ask, unable to keep the surprise from my voice.

He stares into the quiet parking lot. "I have faith that the world can be something more than what it is right now. That we can make it so."

I'm not sure who *we* are.

Navarro shakes off his reverie. "Anyway," he says more normally, "I believe in Dr. Marshall. I believe he knows what he's doing."

My pulse quickens. "What's he doing?"

"Nice try," Navarro says. "My turn for a question. What makes you so sure Jay Novak isn't behind the attack on the banks?"

Navarro isn't going to give me any info he has on Dad, so I make my way farther into the camper and open the doors of the cabinets one by one. "I know Jay Novak. He is the last person on earth who'd be a terrorist." Or maybe the second to the last. *Toby* Novak is the *very* last.

There's a pause, and then Navarro says, "You can never be totally sure what people are capable of."

Dad's rule. Number seven.

"My friend Terminus thinks they're going to kill him," I blurt out. I'm not really sure why I say this. I guess I need to tell someone.

"We can't worry about that," Navarro says.

"I think we have to." It hits me right then. What I'm doing. I don't want to be responsible for making any decisions.

"We can't," he says again. "We can't help Jay Novak. We can barely help ourselves."

Or maybe I want someone to blame.

I shine the flashlight into the cabinets and, in spite of everything, I'm flooded with relief. Dad left the truck very well stocked. There are several rows of colored plastic containers. White for food. Blue for my clothes. Orange for my brother's and gray for Dad's. Red is first aid. There's a smaller green box, which is money and spare SAT phones. And on one side, two rows of yellow jerry cans of gas. Five gallons each, and there are at least ten.

The truck is a gas guzzler but it probably gets about fifteen miles to the gallon. I mentally crunch the numbers. Seventy-five miles per can. Ten cans. Seven hundred and fifty miles. We can make it. All the way into Mexico.

We can make it.

Before I can really process this, the flashlight beam lands on a small, clear container that isn't coded according to Dad's system. I remove it from the cabinet and pop it open.

It's my brother's medicine.

Probably a year's worth of insulin and blood sugar testing strips. It would be impossible to get this much medication from the National Health Service.

Dad would have needed to buy it on the black market.

Dad thought about us.

Not in the abstract. Not as part of some survival checklist.

He thought about our real needs.

And I'm crying.

God. I suck.

I do my best to wipe off the tears and be normal when I come out of the camper. "We're pretty set on supplies. We've got plenty of gas. With all five of us eating, there's probably enough food for about a week. We can make it." I barely choke out that last part.

Navarro reaches out to give me a hug.

I hug him by reflex, then let go immediately. Even worse, my knees almost give out so he holds on and pats my back. "See. San Judas is helping already. It's not a lost cause," he says softly.

I want him to let me go. And keep his arms around me.

Navarro smells like the orange blossoms of the trees growing around the motel.

The world is ending, and I can't spend my last moment crushing on some guy.

Anyway, I'm most likely going to prison and not to the prom.

Navarro releases me but puts his hand on my arm. There's something reassuring about the way that he can maintain his relaxed, kind expression. Stay warm and alive. Not turn into a hollow statue filled only with adrenaline and terror. "Susan, I promise. We're going to make it."

I want to focus on something. Anything. "Why do you call me Susan? Everyone else calls me Jinx."

He shrugs. "Dr. Maxwell says you hate that nickname." Before I can ask anything else, he adds, "We need to get out of here. We've already made too many mistakes."

I'm grateful for the anger that surges through me. Navarro's being a total jackass, but at least I've got something to think about. "Mistakes? You mean the flashlight thing? Because—"

"Dr. Marshall told me that you're stubborn. What's the first order of business in an uncontrolled environment?"

Do a perimeter sweep. Check for anything strange.

"That's right," Navarro says. He takes the flashlight from my hand. "Notice anything unusual? All the lights are off in that office. Where's the old man?"

My gaze jerks over to the diner.

"Yep. Fifty bucks says that these geezers saw you on TV and are in the process of selling us out," he says.

Um.

"Stop." Navarro grabs my upper arm with a firm grip. This is the guy you want to have around when you can't get the lid off the pickle jar.

It hurts. Especially because all my muscles have tensed. I'm pushing up on the balls of my feet. Ready to run.

"Don't run."

Either Navarro has cosmic psychic powers, or my every idea reads on my face. "My brother is—"

"I know." He's still got a grip on my arm and pulls me into the camper, cornering me in the back. He reopens the cabinets I just closed, rooting around until he finds the right bin. Black.

Weapons.

I should have thought of that.

Mistake.

I realize Navarro's already got his Glock when I should have secured it earlier.

Mistake.

He needs both hands to load it safely. "If I let go of your arm, what are you gonna do?"

"Get the .22, the side holster and a roll of duct tape and—"

"No," he says with a frustrated sigh. He does release my arm but blocks the black bin with his body. As he clicks the cartridge into his gun, it's like we're doing a weird kind of two-step. Me lunging for the box of weapons. Him stopping me.

I am energy. And rage. And fear. The feeling that if I don't get my brother out of the Lone Wolf Diner safe and in one piece, the world won't be worth living in ever again.

"We need a plan."

Bouncing up and down on my heels, I make one last attempt to reach around him. "I have a plan. I'm getting a gun and then my brother."

He puts on the side holster and shrugs into his windbreaker.

"You're overreacting. We need a plan that doesn't involve you needlessly shooting little old ladies. Or yourself."

My face burns. "I would *never* shoot myself. And overreacting? Are you serious? You're the one who just said that Charles is—"

He gives me a little smile. "I said I *think* the old man and his wife are trying to turn us in." The smile vanishes. "We act only on what we know." He's now cool. Almost cold. Like he's done this drill a million times. Or like he's done it for real.

This guy must be my dad's BFF.

Navarro shoves the weapons box as far back into the camper as he can. "Plus, I'm not sure if you've noticed, but your stepsister's a bit of a hothead. That inserts an element of unpredictability. I hate unpredictability." Most of Navarro's face is in shadow, shrouded by his hat. "We'll increase our odds of survival by splitting up."

"We stick together," I say.

Navarro says the same thing he told Toby earlier. "For now."

I regain a bit of control as I lock the camper and put the keys in my pocket. Navarro still won't let me have a gun. "We stick together. We're going to find my dad and take it from there."

"Fine," he says. There's another unspoken *for now* attached to these words, but that's his problem. Navarro points to the diner. "Walk me through it."

Breathe.

Treat it like another drill. "One of us should go in the front. Act natural. Try to get everyone out of there as quickly as possible. Give me the gun. I'll go in the back and cover you."

Navarro scowls at me. "Didn't we just decide you'd be better off without a firearm?"

"I'm terrible with people. You're charming. The lady would rather talk to you."

"You must not talk to many people if you find me charming." His face softens at the compliment but he shakes off the wistful look. "Anyway, no one's seen me yet. It will definitely raise a red flag if I march in there instead of you."

He jerks his head in the direction of the restaurant. "You know what you need to do. Let's go."

He does let me keep the duct tape. I put it around my wrist like a bracelet.

Navarro remains by the truck for a minute, until I begin my walk to the diner door. I glance back to find him jogging toward the back of the building. He was trained by my dad and has been a step ahead of me so far. Chances are he's got a plan to get in and has already begun to execute it.

I walk fast around the front of the diner. The Closed sign is still in the window, but I can see Charles, Toby and MacKenna through the glass. They're sitting at the counter with their backs toward me. My brother's legs swing under his stool. Breezy. Unconcerned.

Act natural.

A little bell rings when I push open the door.

"Hey," Toby says with a nod.

Maybelline is nowhere to be seen.

"Jinnkess," Charles says, his mouth completely stuffed with food. He swallows and points to his plate. "Maybelline makes the best French toast. In the universe."

Great.

"You're having too much sugar," I say automatically. Stepping closer, I check his plate where a river of maple syrup runs down the center of two fluffy pieces of toast. "Oh, Charles."

"Wut?" His green eyes widen as he scoops up another drippy bite.

"You're going to make yourself sick."

Toby and MacKenna can never say no to Charles, but I don't have time to deal with them.

The place is empty except for the four of us. The counter is the only part of the diner that's usable, because jagged remnants of porcelain plates and coffee cups litter the main part of the restaurant. The smashed-up pie case has been dragged into the walkway, blocking access to most of the diner.

Maybelline emerges from the kitchen carrying an orange coffeepot. "A spot of homemade French toast won't hurt the boy." She props the door open with a large coffee can.

Make conversation.

I take a breath and try my best to sound normal. "He's got type 1 diabetes. Since he was a baby. He has to take medicine and watch his sugar intake."

The look on her face. A mixture of motherly concern. And guilt. Navarro called it. We're in danger, and I need to get my brother as far away from here as possible.

Keep it casual.

"Let me fix you up somethin' good, sweetie." Maybelline's wearing an apron over her olive-green polyester outfit. It's got a skeleton sitting next to the Arizona flag and the words, But It's a Dry Heat. At least the woman sending me to prison for the rest of my life has a sense of humor.

"Aw. Thanks. I'm really not hungry." I glance into the kitchen for a sign of Navarro. Even though I want to crawl out of my own skin, I will my feet to stay firmly planted. "We've had a long day and I should get my brother to bed."

"Bed? I thought we were leaving?" MacKenna mutters.

"I'll explain on the way." I tug Charles off his stool.

Toby and I exchange a tense look.

"Jinx. What are you doing? I'm not finished," Charles said.

"We've taken up too much of Miss Maybelline's time. We have to find Dad, remember?"

At the mention of our father, Charles straightens up and stops resisting. It's kind of depressing, the way we're conditioned to follow orders. Like soldiers in an undefined army. Fighting a hidden war.

"Let's go."

Toby tosses his napkin on his plate. "What do we owe you for the meal?"

The clang of metal rings out from the kitchen. A frying pan wobbles on the tile floor in the kitchen doorway.

Navarro's making mistakes too.

He's not perfect. And not as careful as Dad.

"Let's go. Now." I grab Charles by his collar.

"Come on, Mac," Toby says.

I'm one pace from the door when Mernice emerges from the kitchen, nudging Navarro forward with the barrel of a shotgun. "Well, well, Maybelline. We got ourselves a new guest checking in."

My heart nearly explodes.

Mernice has an old Remington 870 Wingmaster. Five rounds in a standard mag tube. Enough ammo to shoot all of us, including Navarro, who's wearing a very sheepish expression.

"Oh now, Mernice. This ain't the time for none of your damn jokes." Maybelline pours a cup of coffee and motions for me to sit at the counter. "These poor kids are scared to death. We can at least make them comfortable until Sheriff Dan arrives."

MacKenna's shoulders tense and her mouth falls open. "What the hell is happening?"

I tuck Charles behind my back. "They're turning us in. For the reward."

"These *poor kids*," Mernice sneers, "are wanted by every county in the state."

"Miss Maybelline?" Charles says, peeking out from behind my back.

"Try to understand," she says to my brother, pleading, her pleasant veneer disappearing for a second. "We sunk our life-savings into this place, and since the New Depression…well, the people who mighta wanted to stay in this kind of place can't afford to travel. We thought we'd be able to retire. To help our grandkids…and now this thing with the banks… Fifteen people walked outta here without payin' this morning, and on the TV they say it could get worse."

What is it that MacKenna had said? That The Opposition wanted to keep people desperate enough to do anything.

Maybelline makes a tortured face, but it passes and she smiles at me. "You've got time for a patty melt, dearie. I can whip that right up." She turns to go back into the kitchen but freezes in the doorway. She cranes her neck toward her husband. "Although. You think I oughta go change? What if Sheriff Dan wants to take pictures with that fancy camera of his?"

"You look fine, Maybelline."

"Why didn't you just call 911?" MacKenna asks with a confused look.

Toby casts a sideways look in her direction. One thing we don't need is *more* cops coming for us.

Mernice scowls. "I don't trust those Rural Metro units. Sheriff Dan will make sure I get my money."

"How much is the reward?" I ask.

"I'm guessin' it'll be enough so my wife won't be scrubbin' toilets most afternoons," Mernice says. He keeps Navarro on the opposite side of the counter.

"We didn't do *anything*," I say, as calmly as I can. *Breathe.*

"Sure." Mernice snorts. "Because the jails are full of innocent people. The government wouldn't be lookin' for you if they didn't have to."

"I don't want to be in the newspaper in my house dress, Mernice," Maybelline says, frowning down at her Hush Puppies shoes.

"Dammit. You look fine, Maybelline."

"This would be the same government that can't end the depression," MacKenna says.

The color drains from the old man's face. He bares his teeth. "Don't you talk about things you don't understand. You. You. Kids like you in your copper houses. Sitting in coffee shops drinking ten-dollar, almond-milk-caramel-mocha-whatevers. Talkin' about whether monkeys have rights and how we all need self-driving cars. And we're out here…"

Mernice is panting, and the fingers wrapped around the butt of the shotgun are turning white. He's unstable.

You can never really know what someone is capable of.

Toby's leaning closer to MacKenna, the muscles in his arms tense and taut, ready to spring into action if anything happens. He wants to do something. He's on the verge of doing something. *I* need to do something first, because Toby didn't sit through fifty hours of *How to Disarm Your Enemy* with Dr. Doomsday.

"Why don't you drink your coffee, sweetie?" Maybelline almost yells this. Her husband is making her nervous too. She comes out from behind the counter and extends her arm to draw me to the cup of steaming coffee.

This is a mistake.

Their first mistake.

I don't dare look at Navarro. But if he's spent a significant amount of time with my dad, he'll know this is the opening we've been waiting for.

One more step.

I need Maybelline to take one more step. I try to keep my face soft even as my body is getting ready to spring into action. I bend my knees ever so slightly.

One more step.

Focus. Behind me, Charles huddles closer to my back. My father always says that the way to overcome fear is to imagine the worst-case scenario. Picture yourself overcoming it. Imagine what will happen if you don't. These people. They're going to sell my eight-year-old, diabetic brother to the highest bidder. My fear burns away.

I will beat this old lady to a pulp if I have to in order to save Charles.

Then. She puts one tattered brown velcro walking shoe in front of the other. Because I don't breathe, I hear them squeak against the clean linoleum. One. Two.

Go.

DR. DOOMSDAY'S GUIDE TO ULTIMATE SURVIVAL

RULE EIGHT:

IT IS ESSENTIAL TO ESTABLISH A CHAIN OF COMMAND.

Leg. Sweep. Kick.

I hook my foot around Maybelline's ankle and sweep my leg toward me. It works like I've practiced. She falls flat against the hard floor, landing with a sickening *crack*. Charles jumps back as Maybelline screams. Her hip is probably broken.

While I throw myself on the ground and use the duct tape to bind Maybelline's hands and feet, Toby's already scrambling over the top of the counter to the opposite side, where I can hear Navarro wrestling with Mernice. There's a bang and my ears ring.

I jump up in time to see a pile of drywall and plaster fall onto MacKenna's head. It doesn't hurt her. Charles wraps his arms around her, and the two of them stand locked in a terrified embrace.

Navarro has the gun.

"Susan. Tape," he yells.

I take one last strip for Maybelline's mouth and toss him the roll. Things seem calmer after I gingerly cover her mouth. At least it's quieter without her screaming bloody murder.

Mernice may be scrawny and gaunt, but he's strong as a horse and gives Toby and Navarro the fight of their lives as they subdue him. It takes the two of them working together for several minutes to get the motel man's hands secured behind his back and a thick band of tape wrapped around his ankles.

Navarro wipes a few drops of blood off his top lip.

I force myself to look at the ceiling.

"God… I am tired…of getting decked…in the mouth," he says, struggling to catch his breath. "Okay. Okay. Get her." He shrugs in Maybelline's direction. "There's a walk-in freezer in the back."

"You're going to freeze them to death?" MacKenna shrieks.

"Of course not," Toby says as he grabs Mernice's upper body. "Calm down. We'll unplug it or something."

Navarro takes Mernice's feet, and together he and Toby go into the kitchen.

Maybelline moans as I drag her petite form behind me.

"Aren't you guys a pair of regular badasses?" Mernice says. "Beatin' up an old man and his wife. They're gonna find you. They're gonna—"

Navarro fishes the roll of tape from his jacket pocket and slaps a strip over the old man's mouth. We never hear what *they're gonna* do. Mernice's prophecy remains in the air. One more thing for me to be worried about.

Maybelline whimpers. Blackened pots swing from a rack hanging from the ceiling.

We push them into the freezer. Navarro reaches into Mer-

nice's jacket pocket for a set of keys, and then we leave the man
and his wife sitting on the floor between two empty metal
shelves. I lock the door, and Navarro gets Toby to help him
move a heavy stainless-steel worktable in front of the freezer.
Toby fiddles with the controls, turning the cooling feature off.

It's over.

Sort of.

Navarro has a better sense of the ticking clock than I do,
because he's still in full-on, mission-critical role. He leads us
out the back door. Once we're outside he turns to me. "Move
one of the trash dumpsters in front of the door. Then pull the
truck around front."

"What are we doing that for?" MacKenna asks.

"Mac, take Charles and wait in the truck," Toby tells her.

Either Toby is keyed in to Navarro's plan or he's prepared
to roll with it. We push one of the half-full dumpsters behind
the café flush up against the back door.

I run around to the back of the truck and let Toby, Charles
and MacKenna into the camper. As I slam the door, I see
Navarro jump out of Mernice's old Ford pickup.

It continues on without him, smashing through the café's
glass doors and demolishing most of the counter area where
Charles was eating French toast only minutes before.

Glass cracks, crashes and explodes.

I climb into the driver's seat and move the truck in
Navarro's direction.

MacKenna opens the window that divides the truck from
the camper and pokes me on the shoulder. "Care to fill me
in on what's going on?"

"It's a diversion tactic," I tell her.

In the back, Toby takes over the explanation. "Right. It'll
take the cops a while to even get in that building to figure

out if we're inside. By the time they get on the road, we'll be long gone. That's smart. Mercenary. But smart."

I roll down my window.

Glass crunches under Navarro's boots as he makes his way to the driver's side of the truck. He pulls something small and black from his pocket. One of my Dad's programmable key chains. He presses a button, and there's another explosion in the motel office. Thick, black smoke fills the parking lot.

When Navarro did his laps around the motel, he was busier than I thought.

"Jesus," MacKenna says.

Navarro opens my door. "Susan. I'll take it from here."

I'm tempted to argue, but fighting about who gets to drive seems like a waste of very precious time. I move to the passenger seat.

Scattered glass sparkles against the asphalt in the glow cast by the motel's neon sign, and the smoke from Mernice's burning truck rises into the evening sky.

Navarro steers the truck onto a street behind the motel.

MacKenna pushes as much of her head and shoulders that will fit in through the small window, bringing her face very near to mine. "I'm not on board with this," she says. "Do you hear me? We need to destroy that computer and…and…"

"And what?" Navarro snaps. "Pray for the invention of a time machine to go back to Thursday when Jay Novak wasn't the most hated man in the country?"

Behind her, Toby tries to be reassuring. "MacKenna. Let's talk about this later."

She returns to the camper. "Toby Oscar Novak! Don't you *MacKenna* me. Jinx and Major Manic just stuffed two geezers in a freezer and destroyed a diner."

It's getting dark. Toby and MacKenna are two silhouettes

facing each other. Charles is huddled at the camper's table. MacKenna waves a rectangle in the air while Toby matches her movements, the two of them stepping from side to side.

MacKenna has the laptop.

A new, frantic anger surges through me. I turn around, shoving my face into the camper. "Do not break that! Mac-Kenna! Seriously!"

"You had your chance to look at it," she says. "What did you find that could help us? Nothing!"

I make another grab for the computer while Toby tries to reason with his sister. "Mac, come on," he says.

Navarro somehow manages to ignore all this and turns on to Gila Bend's main drag. Ours is the only car on the road.

Putting my entire upper body through the window, I wave my arms around. I'm desperate to stop MacKenna from destroying what I think is our only chance to figure out what's happening. I have to do something, I have to say something. "I found out one thing. I know where they're keeping Jay," I blurt out. Like if I can tell her something useful, she'll understand why we can't destroy the laptop.

Navarro makes a disgruntled noise.

He thinks I've said the wrong thing.

I've said the wrong thing.

But it works. She looks like she wants to murder me but she hands the laptop off to Toby who promptly puts it in one of the storage bins.

"Well," she says. "You have your damn computer. Where is my dad?"

I turn around and face front even as MacKenna leans in to get my attention. "Um…Goldwater Airfield. I guess. According to Terminus."

"Terminus? What? Where is that?" she asks.

"I don't know," I say.

She clucks her tongue and shakes her head. Behind her, Toby is saying something I can't make out. He might be talking to Charles.

"I don't!" I say with more force. "I don't remember seeing it on any of Dad's maps. It could be a lone airstrip or something. They don't mark those."

I wipe my sweaty hands on the truck's grimy, velour upholstery. We pass by Gila Bend's now-closed Slam Burger and a small park. Everything is vacant. The streetlights switch on.

MacKenna's face is very close to mine, and she's breathing hard. "They're not gonna hold a suspected terrorist at a lone airstrip, stupid! We should be able to figure out where he is!"

Navarro's hands tighten on the steering wheel. "It doesn't matter. We aren't going there."

My hot anger gives way to a cold, growing panic.

Navarro knows.

He knows how to find Goldwater Airfield.

"It isn't up to you, jerkface! We make decisions together," MacKenna tells him.

I realize that this is what I've been avoiding all along. I don't want to make a decision. I follow the drills.

And now.

If we know where Jay is, we'll have to decide what to do with that knowledge.

The destruction of the motel grows smaller and darker in my side-view mirror.

Navarro stares straight ahead. "We'll discuss this later. Right now, we stick to the plan."

Spoken exactly like Dr. Doomsday.

Except the plan should be to stay on the backroads and

make our way south to the border. Navarro is driving on the town's main road, through its small business district.

I glance at him. "Where are we going?"

He grips the wheel even harder. "We have to ditch this vehicle. Those wrinkled old prunes have seen it and probably got the license plate. I hid my truck behind a billboard at the gas station."

MacKenna moves to the back of the camper where she and Toby continue to argue.

We stop at a gas station. It's got a sandwich board sign in front at the edge of the curb.

Floyd's Fuel.

The windows of the minimart attached to the station are almost completely covered with ads for different kinds of beer. The lights are on inside, but it's impossible to tell who or what might be in there. The place is generally in a state of disrepair. White paint peels off the walls in long strips. The concrete surrounding the gas pumps is cracked, and there are gouges in the parking lot asphalt.

There's a low billboard for Burma-Shave where the weathered image of a clean-shaven man smiles down on us on one side of the parking lot, about fifteen feet or so from the minimart. Navarro parks the truck in front of it.

Navarro points to the billboard. "My truck is on the opposite side. Everything in here needs to go in there. Except we leave a few cans of the fuel."

He plans to destroy the truck.

Um. Yay.

I shrug into my jacket and slide out of my seat. Navarro is clearly trying to take charge, and I'm not sure if I should let him. But this stuff is also Dr. Doomsday 101. Getting rid of the old truck is necessary.

I meet Navarro at the back of the camper, and he opens the door.

Charles jumps out and runs by me. "I have to go to the bathroom."

Making a grab for the collar of his jacket, I hiss, "No. Charles. Wait. Why didn't you go in the room before we left?"

"Let him go," Navarro says, shining his flashlight into the camper, where MacKenna and Toby are arguing in whispers.

I turn and watch Charles trot across the parking lot and open the door to the minimart, spilling bright light into the darkening parking lot. "I should go after him."

Navarro grabs my arm. "It's safer for him to go alone. His picture wasn't on the news and anyway, people are less suspicious of little kids." He gets into the camper, opens the first set of cabinets and passes me one of the yellow jerry cans full of gas.

It might be *safer*, but it's not safe. I watch Charles go.

Navarro takes two gas cans for himself as he addresses Toby. "You guys unload the bins from the cabinets while we start hauling stuff over."

MacKenna stays put. "You're not listening. I said—"

"We're on a schedule here," Navarro says with a curt nod. "Sheriff Dan lives in Smurr. Best-case scenario is we have ten or fifteen minutes before he shows up. Worst-case is that an officer on patrol shows up at the motel even sooner than that."

Toby comes over to where Navarro is standing in front of the cabinet. A little bit of my internal panic registers in the high pitch of his voice. "Look. My sister's right. We need to slow down, talk this over. Talk about if we might be able to help my dad. I believe in the power of the truth and in justice. Maybe we have other options here."

"Other options?" MacKenna repeats, turning her anger toward him. "We need to rescue Dad. Now."

"There's no rescuing Jay Novak." Navarro has his back to me. "You want to stay here?" He drops the gas cans and his voice is hard. "You want to go turn yourself in? I don't care. I'm here to do one thing. Make sure that Dr. Marshall's children make it across the border in one piece. Dealing with the two of you adds a layer of complexity to this that I just don't need. Or want." His ramrod posture is pretty intense.

MacKenna leans around him. Even in the semidarkness of the flashlight, I can read the horror and betrayal that define every feature of her face.

I stare at the door to the minimart, trying to figure out how long Charles has been in there. Trying to make myself breathe normally.

"Jinx!" MacKenna says. "Are you gonna stand there looking stupid?"

"Let's get to somewhere safe and then…and then…" I stammer.

"You mean somewhere *you* are safe?" she says through clenched teeth. "What about my dad?"

"We agreed that we'd try to find my dad. If anyone—"

"No, *we* didn't agree," MacKenna says. "We agreed to leave the house when the police came to search it. We agreed to find Toby, and that's the last time we've agreed on anything. We both know that Marshall probably *can't* help and, even if he can, he probably *won't*. We need to *agree* to stop somewhere and think about what is really going on, because none of this makes any sense. Of all the advice Stephanie could have given us, why did she send us on a wild-goose chase after Dr. Doomsday?"

"I don't know, Mac," Toby says. His gaze darts from Mac-

Kenna to the minimart and back to me. His face scrunches up like he's trying to solve a math problem that has no known solution. "Dr. Marshall is a computer expert, and the only evidence we have that might help Dad is—"

"Enough of this," Navarro says. He picks up the cans and hops out of the camper. I take one more look at MacKenna before I follow him. We have to do something, and what I'm going to do is struggle with a gas can, I guess. I'm not sure how much the can weighs, but it feels like about a zillion pounds. I have to stop once to rest.

Meanwhile, Navarro carries one in each arm with ease.

He leads me behind the billboard and shines his flashlight over a Chevy pickup that's very similar to the one we've been driving, except this one is a sandy, desert brown. It's got a slightly smaller but similar camper on the back. I have to hunch over to climb inside.

I get my own flashlight out of my jacket pocket and point it all over. This gives me a chance to catch my breath and check out the truck. Navarro's camper is cleaner and more nicely decorated than Dad's. He's even got cute little curtains on the windows.

"It came with those," he says as I run my light over the ruffles.

I don't answer. I don't want him to see how wiped I am.

He leans into the cab, inserts the keys into the ignition and turns on the dome light, which makes it a little easier to see.

We put the gas cans away. As I climb down out of the new camper, a truck engine rumbles to a start.

Navarro left the keys in the other truck.

We run back around the billboard in time to almost be crushed by Dad's truck, squealing forward with MacKenna behind the wheel. Toby is nowhere in sight. He must still be in the camper.

She slows down long enough to roll down the window and call out, "Families help each other but all you want to do is help yourselves. I can't lose my dad too. I'm gonna see what I can do to help and I don't give a damn what you have to say about it."

My heart drops into my stomach at these words.

While Navarro and I stand there with our mouths open, she circles the minimart and speeds out of the parking lot, up the main street in the direction of town.

Toby's form is in the back, and I can hear him arguing with her through the window as they drive away. Without Navarro, I don't even know how they'd find Jay Novak, let alone rescue him. But MacKenna is desperate.

And desperate people…well…they can be unpredictable.

I'm more scared than I've ever been. The only thing keeping me upright is that I'm becoming stiff and numb. This is not a drill, and the conditions aren't controlled or ideal. Dad always says to be prepared for anything, but this was not anything I was prepared to prepare for. We have only three cans of the gas. Between my brother and me, we've got around eighty dollars of the emergency money. We don't have the food or the phones or my brother's meds.

MacKenna and Toby left us.

And Charles is still in the store.

I'm going to lose my brother.

I'm going to lose everything.

MacKenna will probably destroy the laptop as soon as she can.

I'm waiting and hoping and praying for Navarro to say something.

He doesn't.

He stares in the direction of the vanishing truck. His mask of horror perfectly mirrors how I feel inside.

Safety critical system failure. That's what we're experiencing. When I was a little girl, Dad did some consulting for firms that made life-support systems. He worked on software for defibrillators and dialysis machines. Those kinds of systems couldn't fail.

When they did, people died.

My light jacket isn't enough to protect me from the cold, cold terror.

"It could be worse, I guess," Navarro murmurs.

Another engine starts, and a bland, dark sedan emerges from a hidden spot behind the minimart. It rolls to a stop in front of us, its headlights nearly blinding me.

A long, thin leg emerges from the driver's side, making the hairs on my arms stand up at the sound of asphalt grinding underneath the heel of a shoe.

I wait to see what I already know.

It's Tork.

THERE'S NO SUCH THING AS A WORTHY ADVERSARY. OPPONENTS WHOSE SKILLS MATCH OR EXCEED YOUR OWN ARE TERRIBLE, EXISTENTIAL THREATS. IF THEY MUST BE DEALT WITH, UNDERSTAND YOU'LL NEVER EXPERIENCE A SENSE OF TRIUMPH AND MAYBE NEVER FIND ANY RELIEF.

"It's Tork," I whisper.

By then, I'm quite sure. His bony figure and the way his suit sort of hangs off his frame. I remember it. I recognize it.

I feel like I have to explain this new threat to Navarro. "He's this cop who—"

"I know who he is." Navarro's voice is thick with tension.

"How did he find us?" I say, mostly to myself.

"Why is he here alone?" Navarro adds.

We both glance in the direction from where Tork's car appeared behind the minimart. We should have noticed the car before. We should have done a perimeter check.

I wonder what my dad would do if he were here. He'd probably ditch Navarro. The keys are in the truck. The path of least resistance would be go save my brother and leave Gus to deal with Tork. Dad often said bravery is for suckers. He'd watch hours and hours of old war documentaries. *The best of us didn't come home.*

That's what he said.

But Dad's not here.

"Go get your brother," Navarro whispers.

"That's not a good idea, Jinx," Tork calls. He's a silhouette. A shadow created by the car's headlights. "We can settle this right now. Just the two of us."

In one smooth motion, Navarro withdraws the Glock from his side holster.

In all the confusion, he got his gun back from Mernice.

Dad would be proud.

"Go. Now."

I make a run for it as I hear Tork withdraw his own gun.

The inside of the minimart is bright but dingy. No one has mopped the floors in quite a while. A Slurpee machine chugs along from its position nestled in between a rack of burned nachos and a grill full of greenish hot dogs. The tops of the racks are lined with electronic billboards that look like they haven't worked properly in a long time. One blinks occasionally, showing half of a model's smiling face.

I don't immediately see Charles, and only the fact that we'd probably end up in even more trouble keeps me from screaming his name. That, and I'm out of breath again.

What if Tork sent someone in here to hurt my brother?

What if he's dead?

My throat tightens.

But I hear Charles.

I force myself to step beyond a rack of potato chips.

My brother. I see him.

I want to hug him and simultaneously kill him.

Charles leans up against the counter. Casually. Snacking

on a long rope of red licorice. More sugar. Perfect. He's talking to an old man with a long white beard who nods along
while restocking a container full of scratch-off lottery tickets.

"The thing is," my brother says, "you really have to deep
water roses at least once a week. Soil temperature is the issue.
You could get a water probe but if you don't keep the root
area generally moist—"

"Hey! We need to go."

His face flushes a bit pink at the sight of me. It would honestly be kind of cute were it not for the fact that we were on
the run from a bunch of people who wanted to kill us.

"Okay, okay," he says, walking quick in my direction. "Bye,
Mr. Nick. And don't forget what I said about the mulch."

The shopkeeper's response is lost in the sound of gunfire.

A single shot.

I grab Charles by the sleeve and race out the door.

Navarro's on the ground. Clutching his stomach.

Oh God.

What if he's been shot?

I can't even exactly work out why this is such a cold, dark
stab to my heart. I mean, I've known Navarro less than twelve
hours and I've always tried not to be sentimental. The more
things you love, the more you have to lose. Somehow, though,
I hate the thought of losing Gus.

When Navarro hobbles to his feet, I'm momentarily
flooded with relief. I don't see any blood and Tork no longer
appears to have his gun. Navarro hasn't been shot and more
or less is okay.

He's alive.

But maybe not for long.

Tork circles him like a vulture patrolling the open desert.

Charles hugs my side. He's about to scream, *Gus!* I cover his mouth with my hand before he can.

A calm settles over me. I'm so drained and empty. If I stay here on the pavement, I could sink into the darkness. Fall away into nothing. Then I remember.

Charles.

I can't let Tork decide what will become of my brother.

I have to try something.

Do something.

I come up with a stupid, probably beyond-idiotic plan.

I bend down so that I'm eye level with my brother and drop my hand. "Don't scream, okay? I'm going to have to ask you to do something really dangerous. I'm sorry… I…"

His green eyes open wide and his cheeks have a yellow glow from the light from the minimart. "I can do it, Jinx. It's okay. I can do it."

His eagerness to risk his life makes my heart drop.

But it's the only plan I can think of.

I take my brother's hand. "Okay. Navarro's truck is on the other side of the billboard. We have to make a run for it. Fast. I'll go up front. You get in the camper. On the count of three."

One.

Two.

Three.

We run.

Fast.

Behind where Tork has Navarro in a headlock.

We fly around the corner of the billboard, out of eyeshot of the smiling, well-shaved man in the picture. When we're right up on the truck, I let go of my brother's hand. I hear the camper door flap open as I get behind the wheel.

"The can of fuel," I shout through the camper window. "Take the lid off and knock it over."

Charles grunts a couple of time but he's able to push the large container on its side. The whole place instantly reeks of gasoline. I start the truck, rev the engine a couple of times and put it in gear. I remove the emergency flare and water-proof matches from my inside jacket pocket and pass them to my brother.

Deep breath.

"Okay. Go to the very back of the camper. Right by the door. When I say 'now,' light the flare, toss it toward the front of the camper, then jump out. Jump out and run, Charles. If anything happens to me, keep running. Okay?"

It's too dark to make out his face.

"Okay?" I repeat.

"Okay," he says in a small voice.

"Promise me you'll run. You have to promise."

He sounds like he's about to cry. "I promise."

I put my foot on the gas. The truck is going to have to go slow enough that my brother can jump out but fast enough to hit Tork's car with a decent amount of force.

Okay.

Here we go.

I pull the truck out from behind the billboard. In the parking lot, Tork and Navarro's fight continues and I narrowly miss them on the way to Tork's car. I make a small loop, positioning the truck to rear-end the sedan.

When we're about ten feet away, I yell.

"Now!"

Charles lights the flare and tosses it forward.

He launches himself out of the back of the truck with all his might as flames fill the camper.

I lean into the center to watch him disappear into the brush surrounding the gas station.

But this is a mistake.

The hot, mounting flames push through the small open window and I have to duck to avoid a face full of fire. My jacket is fire resistant but my hair and ear are not.

I can't take the time to scream at my hot flesh.

I hit the gas harder.

Every muscle in my body tenses and my heart hammers away in my chest. It takes all my resolve to open the door and fall onto the asphalt as I send the flaming volcano of a truck forward. As I skid backward along the asphalt, tiny rocks rip open the skin inside the palms of my hands.

But the plan is working as intended.

The impact of the accident is enough to propel both vehicles forward, sending them creeping toward Tork and Navarro.

I roll up and make myself stand. I'm surprised to find my bloody hands don't hurt. Then again, I'm nothing right now except pure adrenaline.

Navarro's truck explodes with a loud boom, creating a fire large enough that it spreads to Tork's car. The two vehicles move together, a giant torch in the small town night. The low rumble sends tremors through the asphalt. My ears ring as I scramble off the ground.

It's enough of a disruption for Navarro to get back on his feet and separate from Tork. Navarro wobbles like a top running out of momentum. Like one more blow might finish him.

But he's gotten his second wind.

He charges Tork and is finally able to force the tall, thin man to the ground.

I get closer.

"Susan…get the…guns," Navarro says.

The procession of flaming cars hits the Burma-Shave billboard just then. It catches fire, making the parking lot plenty bright. I spot Navarro's Glock midway between the sign and the minimart.

The cashier emerges from the store. "What the hell are you people doing?"

"Call 911," Tork responds.

The skinny Santa looks from me to Tork to the burning billboard and returns inside.

Navarro has gotten Tork's handcuffs and is towing the vigilante cop toward the minimart door. "Get…the other…gun."

I need to find Tork's gun.

There isn't much time.

Charles leaps out of the bushes. "I see it."

A second later he runs up to me, gingerly carrying a Sig Sauer P226. Nine-millimeter. Short reset trigger. Once upon a time, a gun only for badass military types like the navy SEALs. These days, the authorities were supposed to use more modern guns that recorded the DNA and the fingerprint of the user. But when you were on a questionable, covert government mission you wouldn't want to leave that kind of footprint. Of course, Tork would choose an old gun.

I hate the sight of the Sig Sauer in my brother's tiny fingers.

Once I have both weapons, Tork stops resisting.

I give the Glock to Navarro and I can see his plan.

Together, we back the cop up against the minimart door. Navarro has put Tork's handcuffs around one of his wrists. I thread them through the curved, metal door handle and cuff his other wrist. He won't be going anywhere for a while.

In the light of the store, I get a better look at Navarro's face. He's been beat all to hell. One of his eyes is bruised and bloodied. Small jagged cuts, probably from the asphalt, are etched into his neck and cheeks. His lips are swollen and blue.

At least he hasn't been shot.

My brother's face puckers into a worried frown.

Tork has a black eye, but he must've had the upper hand in the fight. He manages to smile. "Ah, I would have expected nothing less from the daughter of the infamous Maxwell Marshall. I'll hand it to you. This is brave. Stupid. But brave."

"Screw off, you mouth breather," I say.

Charles makes a disapproving noise.

As I'm backing away, Tork sighs.

"Listen to me, Jinx. Listen. I'll make you the deal of the century right now. Come in with me. I'll let your brother and your boyfriend here go and I'll do my best to ensure your safety. That's a hell of a lot better than you'll get when I catch you with a division of the National Police in tow."

I glance at Navarro. His dark expression gives nothing away. Clearly this is a stupid offer and I don't understand why Tork would make it.

Charles takes my hand and squeezes it. "Don't send me away, Jinx."

I would never.

"I can't leave my brother. And anyway. How stupid do you think I am? We both know that you're going to kill me."

He looks at me like he's imagining me as a giant turkey leg. "Maybe. But not for the reason you think. Despite what Marshall may have told you, the *reason* does matter, Susan. Why do we do the things we do? The answers matter. Even to him."

Navarro lifts his gun. "Who sent you? Who told you to look for us here?"

Tork smiles even wider. His eyes are a piercing blue.

Part of me thinks he's right. Why is this happening? Why is this all happening?

"Fine. Then why do we do the things we do? Why are you doing this?"

His eyes narrow. "I'm doing what's right. We're living in an era of chaos. Ammon Carver will set things right. I'll do what I have to do to help him. If that includes killing you, then so be it. But I'm giving you a chance to be part of the solution here, Susan."

"She isn't going anywhere with you," Navarro says. He plants a punch on Tork's square jaw. The hit opens a small cut on the cop's lip and a couple drops of blood drip onto his chin.

"Why are you doing this, Jinx? You fix computers because that's what Marshall taught you to do. You run because that's what Dr. Doomsday told you to do. But who are *you*? What's gonna happen to you when you realize that you don't have the first damn clue?"

Navarro turns to me. "We should kill him," he says in a voice devoid of any emotion.

"We can't," I whisper. I don't want to become a killer. There are still limits to what I will do to survive.

Navarro lifts his gun. "Last chance. Who sent you?"

I pull on the sleeve of his jacket. "Gus. We have to go."

They're coming.

At least a dozen cop cars off in the distance, lights and sirens blaring.

We have to run.

DR. DOOMSDAY'S GUIDE TO ULTIMATE SURVIVAL

RULE NINE:

COVER YOUR TRACKS. LET YOUR PLANS BE DARK AS NIGHT.

We jog behind the minimart, where Tork can't see which direction we choose, and set off down a residential street. Navarro keeps his head down. The people in the first few houses come out into their yards, watching the flashing red and blue lights that rise into the night. We pass a house where I see a nice normal family through their living room window. They're sitting together and watching a game show.

Someone is grilling hamburgers. Fire. Charcoal. Browning meat. The aroma is enough to overpower the smell of mothballs that seeped into my sweater. It makes me think of Jay and the first time we met. He came to our house, fired up the grill and seemed like he was made to throw backyard pool parties. I want, more than anything, to get back to my backyard and find a bacon cheeseburger waiting.

The rest of the houses are quiet, and I imagine them filled with people living ordinary lives.

Like the one I had until Monday.

After about fifteen minutes, the paved road turns to dirt. My stiff, tired legs drag and kick up dust. After another fifteen, we reach the end of the small town and head into the open landscape.

Police sirens blare in the background.

We enter the desert on foot.

At night.

With no food or water.

The rising crescent moon provides a little light, but not much. Even if I could see, what would I be looking at? Flat. Open. Dry. Nothing but short, squat cactus and yellow brush as far as the eye can see.

It gets cold in the desert at night. Sometimes close to freezing in the winter.

Our only advantage is that they'll probably wait until daylight to come and find us.

Navarro is hurt.

He tries to keep us at a quick trot.

Every few steps, my pant leg catches on something and I almost trip.

I hold the flashlight. It's impossible to keep it steady.

Navarro detaches a compass from a carabiner hanging on the inside of his jacket. "There's a butte a few miles north of town. It should provide a little bit of cover. Maybe we can rest."

This feels like an exercise in futility.

"I miss Mom," Charles says with a sniffle.

I lean over and plant a kiss on his forehead. "Me too."

"Do you miss your mom?" Charles asks Navarro.

"Sort of," he answers. "I mean, don't get me wrong. My mom is amazing and I'd give anything to sleep in my own bed tonight. Wake up to a nice, hot breakfast." Navarro pauses for a second, clutching his side. "We always eat together. As a family."

"Maybe we should rest for a minute," I say.

He shakes his head and goes on as if he hasn't heard me. "But if my mom saw me looking like this, if she knew what I'd been doing, I'm not sure she'd be able to come up with a punishment bad enough... I think I'd rather be arrested."

I point the flashlight at Navarro to get a good look at his face. "Where do your parents think you are, anyway?"

He turns away from me. "Visiting my uncle."

"They don't approve of Dr. Doomsday?"

He sighs. "Oh, my dad could give Dr. Marshall a run for his money in the prepping department. Why do you think I was at PrepperCon? I think I've done as much drilling as you. My parents might approve of Marshall's politics. But not of me getting involved."

I point the light back at the ground in time to avoid tripping over another rock. "Why are you doing it, then?" I desperately hope he'll answer this question. Like maybe if I understand him, I could also understand myself.

"You really don't remember me?"

It's cold and every part of my body aches and it's hard to even think about the summer. We were busy moving and Dad did a bunch of appearances at conventions.

Navarro hesitates. "You were working the Doomsday booth and you sold me a copy of Dr. Marshall's book. The expression on your face. It was like the world was gonna end and you just found that idea so damn boring."

Before I can think much more about this, Charles reaches out and squeezes my hand. "Jinx, why did they leave us?"

I still can't believe Toby and MacKenna took off like that. Except.

Part of me knew MacKenna was right.

"It's my fault. I thought... I didn't..." I didn't take her feelings seriously, or try to be particularly understanding of the fact that it's Jay who's in the most desperate situation. MacKenna is always so tough. She seems so sure of everything and everyone. Still, she should have been given much more say in what we decided to do.

"It's not your fault," Navarro tells me.

"Yes. It is," I say flatly.

Charles sniffs again, and my throat tightens. He's crying. "Don't they love me?"

I stop for a second. "Yes. Of course they do. Sometimes people get pushed to their breaking point. I pushed MacKenna. I should have..." My breath catches. I should have listened to her. I should have realized how much having her dad gone would hurt. Especially after she'd already lost her mom.

"Will we see them again?" Charles asks.

"Yes," I say. "We will." I hope we will.

We continue walking in silence.

We walk on.

And on.

I make out a darkish mount. It's still way off in the distance.

Navarro hitches his step every couple of minutes.

He's getting worse.

My teeth chatter. This is bad. We can't lose Navarro.

Because he's the best with directions and because...

A bit of warmth returns to my bloodstream.

"How bad are you hurt?" I ask.

"I'm fine," he says.

"Navarro. Gus. Seriously, you need to—"

He puts his arm in front of me to stop me from taking a step.

A rumble echoes and fills the wide desert. A car engine.

It's getting louder.

My shoulders fall.

We're done.

I wrap my arms around my brother.

Charles collapses against my shoulder, and I cry out as I catch him.

The licorice. The French toast. All the stress. His blood sugar has probably gone through the roof. "Charles! Charles!" I shriek. I shake his little arm. It's clammy and limp. I lower him to the dusty, desert ground.

"What? What is it?" Navarro asks.

"He fainted! He...he..." I burst into tears.

I press my face to my brother's and can hear small, shallow breaths. The air from his lungs smells sweet, like synthetic strawberry flavoring.

We don't have his medicine.

It's too dark to make out the exact features of my brother's little face. Gus is hurt. There's no way to get Charles more meds. We're going to die out here. We followed Dad's drills, but the drills always acknowledged that there could be casualties. What Dad called the human cost. My shitty decision making was going to cost my brother his life.

"Susan," Navarro says with an edge of panic. "We have to get ready."

For what? We're all going to die.

A pair of headlights appears. Some kind of vehicle bobs up and down as it makes its way across the low brush. It comes to a stop in front of us.

Navarro gets out his gun.

At a loss for what to do, I lower Charles's head gently to the ground and drop the flashlight. I take the Sig Sauer from my jacket pocket.

We wait.

A door creaks open.

"Honey, I'm home."

My breath lets out in a rush. It's MacKenna's voice.

MacKenna gets out of the driver's side, and I spot Toby's figure a second later.

I consider killing my stepsister, but there isn't time. I run by her into the camper. Inside, I wildly toss things from the cabinet until I arrive at the bin full of meds. I grab a glucometer and an insulin pen.

"What's happening? What's wrong?" MacKenna is saying outside. Navarro says something to her but I can't hear what.

I slide around in the rocky dirt as I make my way back to Charles. MacKenna is holding him now and saying, "Charles, Charles," over and over. I push her out of the way and hold the meter up to the sensor on my brother's arm. An insanely high number glows in blue on the display.

I mentally calculate an insulin dose and go to measure it with the syringe. But it's too dark. I frantically pat the ground looking for the flashlight that doesn't seem to be there. Navarro seems like he's about to pass out.

"I can't see! I can't see!" I basically scream this right in MacKenna's face.

"Is he gonna be okay?" MacKenna asks.

I can't answer her. I can barely breathe.

Toby carries Charles to the front of the truck so that we can use the headlights. He holds my brother, and we both kneel again. My fingers shake as I twist the insulin pen to the correct dose and plunge the needle in the fatty part of his arm.

Then we wait.

Is it a few minutes? An hour? It's a space that feels like all of eternity. Tiny rocks poke into my legs. I stare at a small grouping of beehive cactus. Force myself to focus on the geometric patterns of their spiny needles.

My brother's eyes flutter open.

Thank God.

Navarro must be feeling a bit better. He hands me a bottle of water. I raise Charles to a sitting position and press the bottle to his lips. He takes a couple of gulps.

"Jinx. I'm sorry. I'm sorry I ate the French toast." His crackly whisper is the sweetest sound I've ever heard.

I burst into tears again.

I'm still crying when Charles spots MacKenna and Toby. "You're back," he says in relief. "Jinx said you'd come back." Toby helps my brother to his feet.

MacKenna has backed a few paces away. She has found the flashlight and watches the whole scene with a kind of stiff horror.

I get up off the ground and round on her. "You…you… could have killed Charles. He could have died!"

She kicks the dirt sheepishly. "Well. You could have listened to me. You could have—"

I don't care what she thinks I could have done. "You could have stayed and worked things out. You could have stopped Charles from eating all the maple syrup south of Phoenix!"

All of this is true, but I realize that I'm also racked with a terrible guilt. I could have gone into the gas station and stopped Charles from eating candy. I could have done more to help manage his stress. He must be scared out of his mind.

It's my job to take care of my brother.

Toby stands between us like he fears he might need to break up a fight. "We wanted to come back right away," he said. "But we don't know the area. Luckily, we saw you make a break for it so we knew where to look for you, but we had to wait and find our way around all the cops."

Charles gets up and runs over to hug MacKenna. Clearly, he's already forgiven her.

"The two of you need to stop trying to destroy everything in your path," she says, jerking her head first at Navarro and then at me. "You're like a pair of Tasmanian Devils."

I open my mouth in fury.

"Mac, do you have something *else* you'd like to say?" Toby asks his sister.

MacKenna is still hugging Charles.

"I shouldn't have left you," she says, squeezing my brother. "I'm sorry." From the crestfallen expression on her face as she hugs my brother, I can tell MacKenna really means it.

"We have to stay together, okay? Okay? Right?" Charles asks.

"Right," Toby says firmly. "We're staying together."

Navarro steps forward. He's doing a good job concealing the extent of his injuries. "Well, now that the band is back together, we need to get on the road. We're stuck with our original problem. This truck is recognizable. We'll have to ditch it tomorrow. We need to make some major headway tonight."

MacKenna puts her hands on her hips.

"We should discuss what we're going to do," I say. If there's any hope of avoiding more arguing we have to come up with a plan together.

Navarro sighs. "Okay. Dr. Marshall has a man on the other side of Why. It's a straight shot south from here. He'll help us. That's where I think we should go." He holds his hand up to cut off MacKenna's objection. "But Goldwater Airfield is southeast. Let's go twenty-five miles or so south tonight. We'll camp there. Tomorrow, we decide what to do. If we go to Goldwater, we just have to cut over east. If we continue on to Why, we keep going south."

"We decide together?" MacKenna clarifies.

"Yes. Together," I say.

Toby nods. He extends his hand to Navarro. There's a brief pause, but Navarro shakes it.

Navarro and Toby get into the cab, leaving MacKenna, me and Charles in the camper. The truck jerks to a start. Even though Navarro must have the four-wheel drive turned on, the ride is bumpy as hell.

There's a little clock in the camper. It's nine thirty.

I'm getting more tired by the second, so even though it's hard to keep from falling over, I unpack the supplies we'll need. I pull out all the sleeping bags from underneath the bed, get out a meal ration for each of us and find the first-aid bin. I clean and bandage my hands. Charles has a few minor cuts and scrapes that I'm able to dress while we're moving.

Navarro wants to stay off-road, so progress is slow. It takes us till a little after eleven to make it the twenty-five miles he wanted. When we stop, I climb out of the camper.

I have to hand it to Navarro.

We are in the absolute middle of nowhere.

We can see every star that's ever been in the sky. They hang over us like a glittery blanket.

Navarro goes into the camper. He comes back out with battery-operated lanterns and distributes them to me and MacKenna. "Keep it on the lowest setting. And keep it close to you. You can never tell who, or what, is out here in the desert. We don't want to be seen if we can avoid it."

"It's cold," MacKenna says with a shiver.

"Yeah. It's January," I say. She's right though. Even for wintertime, it seems worse than normal. Charles stands, frozen in place, staring out into the abyss. I make a mental note to scan his blood sugar again before bed.

Navarro and Toby get lighter fluid and matches from the camper and build a fire using dried brush and a couple of pieces of deadwood.

"Charles. You need food and some water." I bring out the rations and hand him a self-heating, foil bag of beef stew and a bottle of water.

We bring out the sleeping bags and take seats around the fire. I start to feel sleepy and warm.

I open up my own meal. It's cheese tortellini, and it's not too bad. After I eat, I usher my brother into the camper. Because we're so cramped for space, I make a bed for him on the bench at the tiny kitchen table. I kiss my brother on the forehead and snuggle him into his sleeping bag. His blood sugar has come down closer to normal. He kind of stretches and gives a tiny yawn.

After MacKenna and I change into fresh leggings and sweaters from the supply bins, Navarro comes in and stows the weapons.

Toby puts his sleeping bag down in the aisle that runs down the center of the camper, leaving the bed in the back for me and MacKenna to share.

Navarro moves to sleep in the cabin of the truck.

I grab a few supplies from the first-aid bin and follow him over there. If Tork did any real damage, there won't be anything I can do. But I can check out the cuts and scrapes.

The night is quiet and unbroken by the sound of a passing car or a plane overhead. I find Navarro hunched over behind the steering wheel.

"Is anything broken?" I ask.

"I'm fine." He keeps his face turned forward. The dome light from overhead casts long shadows across his face.

I finally get a decent look at him. A blue-black circle surrounds his eye. There are patches of dried blood on his lips.

"That isn't what I asked you," I say. When it seems like he won't say anything else, I add, "First aid is part of the drill."

Navarro picks at the scab forming on his lower lip. "Nothing's broken. I've got some bruising. Cuts and scrapes. I've had worse."

I glance at a deep gash on his forearm. "Really? When?"

"Get some sleep, Susan—"

I'm already ripping open an alcohol wipe.

"Wait. What are you doing? Hey—"

He tries to dodge me, but I'm able to land the wipe on the open wound. The muscles in his arm tense as I clean and bandage the wound.

And I notice he's hunched over. Forward. Leaning away from the seat.

"I need to see your back."

He flashes me a wide grin. "Oh. Do you?"

In spite of everything, my face heats up. "Maybe I should have let Tork keep dragging you across the parking lot."

Navarro's smile fades, and he raises his shirt. His muscular back looks like someone drove a truck across it. I tend to the scrapes and burns as best I can. Navarro flinches the first time I touch him.

I tell myself it's because the alcohol wipes are so cold.

After a few minutes, I pack up my stuff.

He gives me a small smile. "Good night, Susan."

I smile a little too. "Good night."

And.

And.

"And thanks," I say. "For, uh, not letting Tork shoot me."

Navarro laughs. "Well, thank you, I guess. For not letting him drag me across the parking lot."

"Yeah. Uh. Good night." I shiver. From the cold.

Charles and MacKenna are already snoring when I return to the camper. I climb in bed, toss a few times and finally drift off.

A sharp pain jabs through my ribs. MacKenna is poking me and saying, "Jinx. Jinx."

My eyes flutter open.

It's barely morning, and still mostly dark. The first thing I see is MacKenna's frantic face. "There's someone out there," she says.

I blink stupidly.

"Out there," she repeats, jabbing her finger toward the narrow window next to the bed.

I sit up, scoot over and press my eyes to the glass.

Fight off the cold panic on the verge of overtaking me.

She's right.

Outside, a few feet from the camper, there's a hulking male figure in a black hoodie sitting on a red camping pack with his back to our camper.

MacKenna wraps her arms around herself. She's terrified.

All right.

I slide off the bed.

Slowly.

Trying not to shake the camper with my movements.

Making as little noise as I can.

I don't even dare breathe.

I shove my feet into my shoes. There's no choice but to creep out and jump the guy. I'm not sure if it will help or hurt the situation.

I tiptoe around Charles.

Over to the cabinets.

Which creak so loud.

A sound to deafen everything in the desert.

I open the bin that contains the weapons.

Luckily, the Glock is right on top along with a couple of preloaded magazines. I take the gun, pull the slide back until it catches and insert the magazine. *Index finger always on the frame*, I tell myself, following Dad's step-by-step instructions.

All right.

I meet MacKenna's wide, horrified eyes as I put my hand on the camper door.

Okay.

Go.

Slow. Slow. Slow.

I push the door open.

One foot goes down to the dirt.

Then the other.

The man doesn't move.

I take a slow step.

Then another.

"Trying to sneak up on your old man, eh?" says a familiar voice, and my knees seem to turn to water.

My father.

I remember all the times I would race home on my bike to see what he was doing. What we could work on together.

Everything hits me.

The hope that he'll fix this mess we're in.

The fear that he can't.

The gnawing sensation in my stomach every time I think of Dad's work. The Spark. The Opposition. *The Guide to Ultimate Survival.*

It's all there.

Dr. Doomsday has come to camp.

IF YOU CAN'T OUTRUN THE PAST, YOU CAN HIDE FROM IT.

"Dad?" I ask.

What are you doing here?

Where have you been?

What is happening?

WHAT THE HELL ARE WE GOING TO DO?

These questions don't come out.

Instead, Charles bounds out of the camper. "Dad? Dad!" My brother wears a massive grin on his face as he runs by my frozen form and jumps into our father's arms.

Dad musses Charles's reddish-brown hair. "Hello, sonny boy," he says.

It's dawn in the desert with the sun creeping up and sending first light over the yellowing brush. From the horizon, the golds of the sunrise burst over the low cholla into the early morning sky. Nearer to us, scattered saguaros are rendered in cool violet and indigo hues.

Navarro has taken us to a pretty good position, nestled in between two buttes, keeping us out of sight of anyone traveling across the open landscape.

I take slow steps toward my father. He appears to be clean, well fed and well rested. He's even trimmed his beard. I'm covered in dirt and grime and splotches of blood, and look like I've been sleeping under the Adams Street Bridge for the past week. Dad looks like he just returned from free waffles at the Ramada Inn.

He's sitting in front of a cheerful fire made of wood he must have brought with him.

I've got a thousand questions. "What…how did you find us?" is the one that comes out.

Dad eyes the distance between us. "Hello to you too," he says. "Gustavo has a geolocation device. He gave me the coordinates."

Navarro has a way to get in contact with my dad and I don't. There's something about it that feels like a betrayal. I glance around looking for the traitor but don't find him. "Dad…" I say.

He smiles. "Jinx. Get some breakfast. Sit down. We have a lot to discuss and we need to get moving as soon as we can."

"Like the fact that Mom thinks you can get Jay away from The Opposition," I say.

His smiles fades. "Yes. Like that. After we eat."

The fire crackles and pops.

MacKenna slowly steps out of the camper, putting her hair in a ponytail while she walks. As she approaches, she clears her throat. In addition to everything else, I've got bad man-

ners, because it doesn't immediately occur to me to introduce her. Dad's book didn't cover remote campsite etiquette.

It's Charles who plops down next to Dad on the camping
pack and says, "Hey! Dad! Did you ever meet MacKenna?"

The answer is no.

The fact that Mom got remarried so soon after the divorce
really messed him up. He never made an effort to meet Jay.
Or MacKenna and Toby.

"She's awesome," Charles goes on. "She knows everything.
She reads everything. She writes for the newspaper."

"The school newspaper," MacKenna says quietly.

Charles grins. "She knows everything about The Spark.
She was the teen volunteer coordinator for Rosenthal. Everyone's for Rosenthal."

I shake my head at my brother. "Dad is for The Opposition."

"I'm not for anyone," Dad says in a low tone. "Not anymore."

But Dad doesn't seem surprised to see them.

My anger builds as I realize Dad's spoken to Navarro.

Toby comes out of the camper, a yawn breaking through
his surprise at the odd new scene. "That's my stepbrother,
Toby." I point at Dad. "My dad, Max Marshall."

"That's Toby," Charles begins. "He's—"

"My father isn't a terrorist," MacKenna blurts out. Loud.
Forceful. Her voice carries across the open desert.

"I know," Dad says with a finality that doesn't invite more
questions.

Behind me, a horse whinnies.

A horse.

I turn, and there are two of them. About twenty feet from
the camper. Navarro is doing his best to get them to drink
from a silver bucket. He gives me a sheepish wave.

MacKenna smiles. A real, genuine smile. I haven't seen

that in so long that I'm caught off guard. She glances from the large dark reddish mare to the slightly smaller, creamy-blonde one. Dad rode out here. On horseback.

So he has to have some kind of base of operations nearby.

I move away from Dad, toward MacKenna and the horses.

"Quarter horses," she says. Her mouth widens into a grin. "Stock type?" she asks.

I shake my head. I have no idea what kind of horses these are, and I'm kind of surprised that she does. We're both from big cities, not ranch towns.

MacKenna shrugs. "My dad sent me to Crossogue." When I continue to stare blankly, she continues, "Some bougie equestrian camp. In Ireland."

I squint at her.

She sighs. "Right after my mom died, Toby studied all the time, but I don't think Dad knew what to do with me. Anyway, the camp did this whole unit on the different kinds of horses." She joins Navarro and helps him with the water bucket. A couple of seconds later, they're actually laughing as one of the horses snorts and sneezes right in Navarro's face.

I want to sneeze in his face.

From all our weekend drills, I know that arguing with my dad when he's got a big master plan going is a pointless waste of time. Nothing's gonna happen until we have *breakfast*. So, I return to the camper and get busy pulling food out. I locate several rations, mostly of maple-flavored oatmeal and what looks like the last of our remaining water bottles. From inside, I can still hear Charles giving Dad a detailed list of every plant he's seen since leaving the house on Tuesday.

MacKenna comes in and kneels alongside me. "You know, he's surprisingly handsome. For an old guy."

"What? My dad?" I ask, nearly dropping one of the bottles of water.

She stands up and looks out the camper window. "He's actually kind of hot. In an over-the-hill action hero kind of way. Like an aging movie star. The kind of guy who looks great but everyone says they paint on his abs in the makeup trailer, you know?"

No, I don't. I think MacKenna needs to stop reading so many celebrity blogs. I roll my eyes and hand her the bags of oatmeal. I bundle up the sleeping bags and bring them outside so we'll all have something to sit on.

I toss Dad some oatmeal.

It rebounds off his chest. He's staring into the open desert, unusually unalert.

I drop the sleeping bags at intervals around the campfire and take a seat on mine. Toby and MacKenna join me. They regard my father with unnerved faces, staring at him the way someone might stare at a spaceman. Or a ghost.

Something odd and unreal.

Toby starts with a softball. "What exactly are you a doctor of?"

Charles pipes up. "Computer science and cryptography. Dad did his undergraduate work at Stanford University. He has a master's degree in computer simulation from Cornell and a PhD in data science from—"

"I don't think they need my whole résumé, son," Dad interrupts, reaching out to ruffle my brother's hair. "I used to teach computer science at Arizona State until I decided to…"

Build a bunker in your backyard and drive your family nuts with disaster drills?

"Write your book," Charles says with enthusiasm.

I glance sideways at my stepsister. "MacKenna knows all about this. She did a report on Dad for school."

Her lips pucker in an embarrassed grimace.

It's silent again except for the occasional scuff of horses' hooves in the dirt.

We all watch Dad open his oatmeal. Eat a few bites. Stare into space some more.

Sit there while his bearded chin moves up and down.

It's excruciating.

I check my brother's blood sugar and give him a small dose of insulin. Then I can't take it anymore.

"Dad, can you do anything to help Jay?" I say.

He stops. "There's nothing I, or anyone else, can do at this point."

MacKenna folds her arms over her chest.

This is exactly what she thought would happen.

I continue on. "Mom thinks you know people."

Dad continues to stare out into the creosote bush. "She knows better than anyone that I've burned my bridges with The Opposition."

My sweater smells like the mothballs Dad must have put in the supply bins. "But you know Ammon Carver."

"Yes. I do." The way he says this. Like it settles the whole matter.

Beads of sweat break out on my forehead. I have to believe that he's just not getting it. I get up, go back to the camper and return with the laptop. I hand it to Dad, who reluctantly accepts it.

"You in need of tech support?" he asks with a wan smile.

"You have to listen to me. Terminus said—"

Dad snorts. "Terminus? You mean Harold? My old student? That's where you're getting your information from?"

My face heats up. "He hacked into the Rancho Mesa PD mainframe and——"

Dad shakes his head. "Of course he did."

"Dad, the explosions at the banks were triggered remotely. By a software program that used the built-in speaker systems to detonate explosive materials that had been——"

"Jinx," Dad says, his lips pressing into a thin frown. But he's thinking.

"You were doing research along those lines," MacKenna says, in a blend of a question, a statement and an accusation.

"I could never work out the details," Dad says, stroking his dark beard absently. "In my tests, the sonic device had to be too close to the explosives for the whole thing to be of any value. It would have been less conspicuous to detonate a conventional bomb."

"——previously placed there by——"

"Somebody must have gotten it to work," Toby says.

"Maybe," Dad says, unconvinced.

Navarro's head swivels back and forth from me to my dad, like a spectator at a tennis match. He heads toward the horses.

I sigh in frustration. "It *does* work, because the code is on that laptop. Jay's laptop. And if we could figure out who put it there and when and why...well, maybe we could help Jay."

Dad holds the laptop in front of his face, as if he's contemplating opening it.

"We know where my dad is being held," MacKenna says. "At Goldwater Airfield."

"Mom is there too," I add.

Dad shifts uncomfortably on the red pack. "Jinx..." His voice is full of warning.

I find myself trying to fight off a mounting sense of dread by brushing dust off the knees of my jeans. MacKenna continues to observe my father the way an anthropologist might regard a stranger from an undiscovered country.

I point at the laptop. "Dad, we can—"

Dr. Doomsday shakes his head. "What could we do? Surely you must know that any programmer good enough to create the kind of code you're describing is also capable of altering file dates, editing logs, covering their tracks. We could check a few things, but it wouldn't accomplish anything."

I don't know what is worse—Dad's apathy, or the fact that MacKenna totally called it.

"There are logs that might have been autogenerated while the hacker was placing the file or running the code. And you could create a user model based on Jay's profile. Show that two different people were utilizing the computer." A fire builds up in my belly. "This is what you do! You create these kinds of models. Can't you look at the laptop? Can't you at least check it out?"

"It wouldn't prove anything," Dad says. His voice. Dry. Bland.

"It might prove that someone else besides Jay Novak is responsible," I say, slapping my knees in frustration.

Dad drops the laptop into the dirt. "Someone else *is* responsible. Don't you understand? Who stands to benefit from the explosions at the bank? Who wanted more power than the election was going to deliver? It's an old systems model. You create a little chaos. Blame your enemy. Demand a power transfer to help you restore civilization."

Toby leans forward. "You think Ammon Carver blew up his own banks and killed thousands of people just to disrupt The Spark?" He says this fast. Like he's been thinking about this idea for a while.

Dad's expression darkens. "Carver doesn't want to disrupt

The Spark. He wants to destroy it." The sun is beginning to rise directly behind him, creating an odd halo around his dark hair. "I left The Opposition when it…it became clear that Carver didn't want to beat Rosenthal, he wanted to annihilate him. That Carver regarded The Spark as an existential threat and believed the only way the world would survive was if he eliminated that threat."

MacKenna frowns. "And he also messed up the data at the banks? Why would he do that?"

Dad says nothing and fills the silence by crumpling up the empty bag of oatmeal.

Oh my God.

My breath catches in my throat.

Terminus called it.

"It's not him. It's *you*. You wrote the malware. Terminus said it was installed at the bank five years ago, back when you were consulting at the bank. *You* put it there. You've known… You've known…" I can't breathe. My dad knew this was going to happen.

He'd known for years.

Charles scowls at me. "That's not true, Jinx."

MacKenna jumps to a stand. She looks like she's about to charge through the fire. "You don't *think* Ammon Carver blew up the banks. You know it. Don't you? You *knew* that's what they were planning. Did you know they planned to frame my dad? Did you?"

"MacKenna, how can you say that?" Charles asks. "Dad would never hurt Jay."

Navarro returns from feeding the horses and pulls another sleeping bag up to the fire and sits. "We should think about getting on the road."

Toby glares at him. "I want an answer to the question."

Dad shakes his head. "No. No, I did not. It was clear from the discussions happening that they would need to find someone to pin this mess on. There has to be someone to blame. Why they chose him specifically, I can't say."

I have to do something. Scooping up the laptop near Dad's feet, I get up and pace around in the dirt, kicking up a small storm with my shoes. He knows more than he's saying. "I think you could say!"

Dad ignores this.

MacKenna frowns in confusion and sits down again. "You mean the explosion and your…um…malware aren't related? Then…why…why would you want to delete the bank data?"

When my dad doesn't respond, I answer. "Not delete. Encrypt. It's like putting the files in a lockbox. The key is a password. Or a piece of code." I nod at Dad. "*He* has the key. Usually the point of these kinds of things is to get the bank to pay you a ransom or something, but…"

It makes perfect sense that someone as paranoid as Dad would program in a back door when working on a large system, but…

There was something else.

I freeze. "Wait. Is this why Mom wanted us to find you? She thinks you can trade the key for Jay?"

"I don't know what your mother thinks," Dad says tersely.

MacKenna cocks her head, a look of surprise overtaking her features. "But the New Depression. You can't delete or encrypt or whatever…you can't mess with all the files at the country's largest bank without there being terrible consequences…for my father…and The Spark. You have to help him. You *have* to give them the key."

"The New Depression," Dad repeats in a tone laced with dark cynicism. He shakes his head. "I created that program as an insurance policy of sorts. One, I must admit, that hasn't functioned as well as I intended. But I can't give up the encryption key. That key is the only card I have left to play. It might be the only thing that ensures our survival."

MacKenna's mouth falls open. "But—but—but…"

Dad turns to me. "Susan. Listen to me. When I first knew him, Ammon Carver was like a brother to me. He was smart. Enterprising. Charismatic. I thought he was the very best this country could produce. Then the New Depression hit. Carver had ideas about how to end it. Good ideas. Until that point, The Opposition had mainly existed as a way to stop The Spark from going too far. Pushing the world to places that were too extreme. Carver thought it could be different. This world had begun to spin out of control, and it was about to come off its axis. Carver believed The Opposition could set things right again—and I believed in Carver."

"The Spark is not responsible for the New Depression," MacKenna says.

It's Navarro who answers. "Who created the mortgage program that led to the housing crisis? Who proposed the government bailout of people who didn't pay their bills? Who had to levy massive new taxes to pay for these programs?"

MacKenna stands up too. "Those programs were designed to help people who'd been exploited and preyed upon by the super rich. You can't spend half of modern history locking people out of an economic system and then act surprised when—"

Navarro shakes his head. "Your dad has a good job. You live in a nice house, but have you looked around recently? Seen all the foreclosure signs? All the empty storefronts? The Spark put us on this path. The path of continually sabotaging the engine of prosperity."

The engine of prosperity. Another one of my dad's favorite talking points.

MacKenna has also taken to pacing around. "The Spark only exists because the old political parties weren't working. Do you remember life before The Spark?"

The Spark has been in power more than ten years. I don't remember much from before and I'm surprised that MacKenna thinks she does.

"People died without food. People died waiting for medicine," she tells Navarro.

Navarro snorts. "And now people who *can* afford to pay for medicine *can't* get it. People like Charles. Who could get a SNAP tomorrow if it weren't for the doctor shortage, and all the pharmaceutical companies that went out of business because of price regulations—"

Toby glances at Charles. "Those companies were charging thousands of dollars an ounce for insulin. I suppose you think that's fine."

"Sometimes it *is* fine," Navarro tells her. "If you have thousands of dollars, why should The Spark get to decide you can't use it for medicine? How can one person tell another what to charge for their work? Or what they can buy with money that's been rightfully earned? My parents came to this country with nothing and made a good life. They should decide how the proceeds of their labor are spent."

Dad nods and strokes his beard. "Yes. There it is. The dilemma. The Spark created a world where everyone can have only a little. The Opposition offers a world with the opportunity for some people to have it all."

My brother could have an artificial pancreas.

And someone else might get nothing.

"And anyway—" Navarro says.

"And anyway," Toby cuts through him. His voice is loud and echoes off the two buttes. "You're conveniently forgetting that *Everyone's for Rosenthal*. David Rosenthal was going to really help people. The Opposition had to cheat to win."

Navarro rolls his eyes. "The Spark created a bunch of voters hopelessly dependent on government assistance. Rosenthal had to *buy* votes with other people's tax money."

"Yeah, but Carver is trying to have us all killed," I say.

Dad clears his throat. "The point is this. When I realized that Carver didn't want to fix this world, that he wanted to remake it in his own image, I left. But it was too late."

"I'm sure that will come as a big consolation to my father," Toby says.

"But you know what's happening," MacKenna says. "You could come forward."

"Did you say this stuff to Mom? Is that why she left you?" I ask.

Dad's face falls. The answer must be yes.

My father stands, picks up his pack and leans toward Mac-Kenna. "I'm sorry about your father, young lady. But there's nothing I can do. Nothing any of us can do. Ammon Carver is in control of the government. He isn't going to cooperate with attempts to prove that his own people are behind all this. I'm here for one reason. To get you back on track. If your father is the kind of man you say he is, then he'd agree with me. Your father would agree that your safety is what matters." Dad points south. "We're headed off toward Why, but we'll bypass the town. A buddy of mine owns a ranch over there. We'll leave the truck and we can take turns on the horses, but we need to get going. Carver's people are putting up roadblocks all over the place. It's only a matter of time before they implement curfews. I don't want to be on *this* side of the border when that happens."

A light, cold breeze moves over me as I stay very still.

Dad swings the red bag over his shoulder. "We've got a long walk ahead of us. Let's pack up what we can."

Navarro gets up and takes a few steps toward the camper.

MacKenna shakes her head. "I'm going after my father."

Toby nods. "Me too."

Charles bites his lower lip.

So much for making a group decision. But my dad has a way of making democracy impossible.

He stops. "On foot? With minimal supplies? That's suicide."

The hot energy that has been building up inside me settles down.

I find a certain sense of calm. Of peace.

Maybe Dad is comfortable becoming the destroyer of worlds.

But I'm not.

I have to do what I can to fix this.

Even if what I can do is futile.

I stand, opposing my father. "She's not going on foot. She's taking the truck and whatever supplies aren't essential to get you across the desert."

And.

"I'm going with her."

DR. DOOMSDAY'S GUIDE TO ULTIMATE SURVIVAL

RULE TEN:

IT'S BETTER TO AVOID TROUBLE THAN BEAT TROUBLE.

Dad frowns. "Absolutely not."

This only increases my resolve. "I'm. Going."

I pick the laptop up off the ground. Dad might think it's worthless, but I'm still going to check it out. He follows me into the camper, where I dig around in the cabinets, searching for a spare backpack.

I find an old, camo green military-style bag and stuff it full of supplies for my brother, including his meds and glucometer. "Um. Charles had his medicine this morning. But you do need to check his blood sugar at least twice a day. A couple of hours or so after a meal."

Keep going.

I have to keep going or I'll cry or come to my senses or run away.

"I know that," Dad snaps. "I'm his father. In case you've forgotten, I'm *your* father too. You can't disobey me like this."

I haven't forgotten. That's why I have to go. "You haven't been around in a while. I need to make sure you have Charles's routine under control."

"I can't stop your friends from marching into certain death. But I can stop *you*."

Bottled water. Protein bars. Beef jerky. I keep going until the bag is full.

"How?" I ask him.

I catch a glimpse of MacKenna through the camper window. She has her arm around my brother's shoulders. Toby and Navarro stand outside, watching me argue with Dad.

Dad yanks the bag out of my grip "How? What do you mean, *how?*"

"How are you gonna stop me?"

Dad's face pales. "Jinx. This is serious. It's been daylight for about twenty minutes. I guarantee you that every sheriff's unit from Gila Bend to Why is out on patrol. Looking for…" He shakes his head. "It may take an hour or so, but they'll be organizing air patrols out of Phoenix and Tucson. You'll be caught. There won't be anything I can do to help."

I hold up my hand to silence him. In spite of my efforts to stay tough, little tears squirt from the corners of my eyes. "You've made that perfectly clear."

"Don't you understand—"

I wipe away the angry tears with my sweater sleeve. "Don't *you* understand that all of this disaster drilling is its own kind of disaster? You focused on how bad things were, and you made them worse. You were expecting the end of the world, and you've caused it. I have to do something about it, even if you won't."

Dad steps back, his face unreadable.

"Don't you even care about Mom?"

And then he looks like I've slapped him.

Charles comes in. "Jinx. You said you wouldn't leave me."

He's about to cry too.

I kneel down. "Charles. I don't want to and I don't know if we'll be able to help Mom and Jay. But we have to try."

My brother hugs me so tight. "I can help. I want to come too."

"No," Dad and I say in unison.

I kiss him on the forehead. "It will help us to know that you're safe."

"You'll be back, right? You'll come back for me, won't you?" Uncertainty fills my brother's green eyes.

"I will always come back for you." At least I'll always try.

I take Charles by the hand. Navarro helps me get my brother situated on the yellow horse.

MacKenna and Toby wait near the truck, talking among themselves.

My hand once again meets Navarro's on the horse's reins. My pulse jumps.

He looks away.

I'm cold again.

"You didn't tell me all that stuff about the laptop," he says.

"You didn't tell me you had spoken to my father. That you had some idea where he was."

He runs a hand through his thick dark hair. He's wearing a fresh shirt in dark green. "I told him I wouldn't say anything. I gave Dr. Marshall my word."

Navarro puts a light hand on my arm. "You'd prefer it if I were the kind of person who didn't keep my word?"

I'd prefer it if he were coming with us.

My stomach is churning as I pull my arm away. "You're going with my dad?" It's an accusation.

His dark eyes avoid mine. "I don't have a choice."

The deer grass rustles. I shake my head. "There's always a choice."

Navarro climbs up behind Charles.

Dad mounts his horse. "If you come to your senses, head due south. I'll be on the watch."

This might be the last time I ever see Dad. It seems like I should say something.

I could say anything. I could tell him to be safe. I could tell him that I love him. For some reason, I remember summers spent on the beach in Rocky Point. I was so warm and happy there in the sun. Talking, facing the ocean, watching the waves. Playing in the sand.

I could tell him that we used to be happy.

Then I remember something else.

Even then, we didn't build sand castles.

We built fortresses.

I ask my father for the one thing he can give. Advice on how to survive.

"You ever hear of a guy called Tork?" I ask.

For a moment his careful composure slips away. I see it. He's terrified.

Which scares the hell out of me.

"*That's* who Carver sent? Marcus Tork?"

My heart thuds away and I nod in response.

"Jinx. If you see him coming, you do what I would do."

"What's that?" I ask. A tiny little part of me can't believe he's actually leaving me here.

"Run." Dad jerks on the reins and turns his horse south.

I stand there for a few minutes watching them ride off.

For a second thinking, or maybe hoping, Dad will have a change of heart.

Only Navarro looks back.

Toby, MacKenna and I form a tiny circle.

She takes a sharp breath. "So, we're doing this?" she says.

I head toward the truck. "I'll drive."

MacKenna twists her fingers. "I don't suppose your dad had some kind of big plan for something like this. Some kind of a big-time prison escape?"

We trained only to run away. "No."

Toby steps forward. "The way to handle this is step-by-step. Let's see if we can get to the airfield. If we do, we'll try to find Dad. Then, we'll try to get ourselves out."

"Okay," MacKenna says.

Right. Okay. "We did a bunch of the drills out here and there's a bunch of old roads back here. Mostly dirt roads used by the locals. We'll drive along them. Follow the highway. Navarro said if we head east, we should hit the airfield."

This time last week, I was in English helping Mrs. Germaine fix her laptop. The lady clicks on anything that blinks, and her machine is always one big malware mess. Now I've got a bunch of problems that can't be solved by rebooting in safe mode. There has to be some set of options that would put me anywhere but here.

At the very least, I would have paid some amount of attention to what Mom was always talking about. The world is coming apart and I can barely understand why.

And now we're trying to sneak onto a military base.

MacKenna and Toby head into the camper. I don't really want to be alone. But I don't want to talk either. I know what I have to do. Watch the compass. Stay east.

I get in the cab and drive into the desert. When I can find

something that looks like a path or trail or a worn spot of earth, I steer the truck that way. Most of the time, we're off road, bumping up and down.

The oatmeal rises up and down in my throat. From the motion. Or the stupidity of what we're planning to do.

I check the clock. We progress across the landscape slowly. At the rate we're going, it'll be nine or ten before we get near the base. All we have to do is figure out a way to sneak in.

Lost in these thoughts, I don't immediately notice the noise.

Then there's no mistaking it.

A helicopter cruises overhead. Low. Loud.

Right overhead.

Dad was right. We're going to be caught.

I rap on the window. MacKenna and Toby have heard it.

MacKenna's already sliding the panels of the window behind me. Her head comes into the cab. "Jinx. What are we going to do?"

"I... I..." I have absolutely no idea.

After a minute or so, I glace to the left.

A half a mile or so away, I see a sheriff's unit in a black Suburban.

And then another. And another.

We're being herded.

On the other side, there's a low, short hill. I could break that way. It would put something between us and the cops. But it would do nothing about the helicopter.

In the rearview mirror, back a ways but approaching fast... more cops.

My blood runs cold.

No going forward. No going back.

A chaotic swarm of motion surrounds us, coming down from all sides.

"Stay calm," Toby says "We're fine. Everything's fine."
That's Toby. Always the one to stay calm. To help.

The helicopter has circled around and is facing us. Flying low.

"Get down!" I shout. There aren't any seat belts back there.
The helicopter. Too low. Too erratic.

The cops behind us have closed most of the distance between them and the truck.

Toby shouts something but it's overpowered by the noise.

There's a loud *boom* and the road ahead bursts into flames.

Oh God.

They're going to kill us. Right now.

"Jinx!" MacKenna screams.

I hear Toby slam into the cabinets in the camper.

Time freezes.

The helicopter. *The helicopter crashed.*

Whatever's left of it, a burning, hulking mess, emerges from a cloud of dust and skids across the brush, coming fast, directly at the truck.

I slam on the breaks and steer to the right in a desperate attempt to avoid the inevitable crash. As I turn the wheel, I really wish I understood what *turn into the skid* actually means. The truck makes a full circle and collides with a piece of misshapen metal, maybe part of an engine.

I'm on the verge of passing out.

MacKenna screams again.

The trucks rocks back and forth and shimmies to a stop. Fire rises against the passenger side window.

Breathe.

Just breathe.

We have to get out of here.

Run. We have to run.

Focus on your immediate goal. Screw having some big master plan. That's the drill. What Dad always told us to do.

I push my door open with more force than necessary. If I stop to think too much about what I'm doing, I'll lose my nerve.

Okay.

Here I go.

MacKenna yells something at me. But it's lost.

Lost to the sound of gunfire and chaotic screaming.

I force myself out of the seat and into the dirty air. The dust and smoke is so thick, I shield my face with my jacket to keep from choking. *You can't run if you can't breathe,* as my dad always says. I stay low and keep my body pressed to the car's metal.

A shoulder-fired missile cruises by about ten feet or so above the ground and hits another patrol car up ahead.

We are so out of my league here.

The brush up ahead sizzles and burns, sending even more thick, black smoke into the sky. But the explosion does what it was meant to. It calms the scene. The gunfire stops...and it's quiet.

Unnaturally, deathly quiet.

I creep around the back of the truck, intending to open the camper door, and almost run into an oversize man in desert fatigues.

"I've got one here," he shouts.

I spin, hoping to take off in the other direction, but lose traction and fall to my knees on the dry, cold earth. Before I can recover, a pair of dress shoes shuffle into my field of view.

And.

A voice that's becoming all too familiar.

"Hello, Jinx."

Tork.

Of course, it's Tork.

I fall all the way to the ground and the instant my butt hits the dirt, I hear a popping noise. Pain sizzles through every nerve in my body. For a second, I have the impossible idea that I've been struck by lightning. I groan and collapse onto my back.

There's something just underneath my chin. Like a fork. Like someone stabbing me with a fork over and over. It takes everything I've got—every bit of energy, every bit of willpower—to swat at my neck. Two blue wires curl around my fingers and I trace them to where Tork stands a few feet away.

He's shot me with a Taser.

"What's a nice girl like you doing in a place like this?"

I can't answer him. Or even think what I would say if I could answer him. I clutch my pounding head and roll onto my side, my nerves overloaded with spasms and shocks.

Everything that's happened is so pointless. I want to give up, to go back to Start again. Not to just before the explosion at the bank, but long before that. To some memory that's just out of reach. Of when my family was whole, when the world was unbroken and we could live those days at the beach, over and over, watching starfish, collecting shells.

Tork is talking again. At least, he's making a series of sounds. But my headache is worse and I hear only distorted trombone tones as the upside-down sight of Tork and the other man pacing around fills my vision.

I try again to say something, but only a disgusting gurgle, like water bubbling in a clogged drain, comes out. It's just as well. I think I would say, *I want my mom.*

Tork laughs as he hauls me up. In one swift movement,

he hoists me over his shoulder and carries me away from the truck.

My whole body fills with a useless rage. I still can't move my legs. I can't kick Tork. I want to kick him in his smug face. And this guy. He's not even slightly out of breath. He could probably carry me all the way to Mexico.

We arrive at a large matte beige truck, the kind that SWAT teams use in the movies. This one is completely unmarked though. Tork carries me around the back, where two double doors are thrown open. He plops me down like a sack of potatoes on one of the long metal benches that line both sides of the truck.

Two soldiers with M4 assault rifles guard the inside of the truck. As Tork exits, the soldier from earlier enters. He carries zip ties and restrains my hands behind my back. I'm in there alone for a couple of minutes until, one by one, the soldier drags in MacKenna and Toby. They get placed on the opposite bench a few feet away from each other. Their hands are already cuffed when they're brought in.

My head is still pounding and I realize that my face is covered in drool—that I've been drooling all over myself. I do my best to wipe my mouth using my shoulder. I don't want anyone to see me with spit covering my face. And then I want to kick myself because that's a stupid thing to be worried about at a time like this.

I hate myself and everything else.

Don't cry. Don't cry.

Cliché as it is, our capture proceeds with military precision. The guards leave the truck, locking the truck doors behind them. We're on the road in a matter of minutes. For a while, we listen to the tires roll across the rough asphalt and the indistinct sounds of the conversation coming from the cab.

"I saw it," Toby says finally. "They took out their own helicopter with one of those missiles. They killed their own people." Disgust fills his voice.

"They were willing to do whatever they had to do to stop us," I whisper.

"But why?" MacKenna whispers back. "Why us?"

We're silent for a while, until Toby breaks the tension with an out-of-the-blue question.

"So you met him? Ammon Carver?" he asks.

"Yes," I say slowly. "Just the one time."

"Isn't that kind of strange?" MacKenna asks. "I thought he was like a brother to your dad?"

I shrug. "Maybe. But I told you, Carver's not really family friendly. Plus, Dad says he doesn't like to leave Manhattan."

MacKenna coughs a couple times and nods. "That's true. The guy has barely left his big gold building since we were in elementary school. He's been a hermit for a decade. Supposedly his campaign staff had a hell of a time even getting him to go to his campaign rallies. A newspaper in New York put a full-time reporter in the lobby of Carver Commons, and he took note of the politicians and world leaders who came and went at all hours. Everyone said Carver hates to leave his fortified tower. What happened when you met him?"

Those days felt like a dream. Or another lifetime. "It was a long time ago. Before Charles was even born. Dad worked as a consultant at the bank. I don't know what he was working on at the time. We got invited to this retreat. All expenses paid to this lodge in the Rockies. Carver looked the way he always used to in the magazines. Like he'd just gotten back from being on a safari or something."

"What was he like?" Toby asks.

I sigh. "He only came around once. The first night, after

we set up camp. He sat with us a little…by the fire. The conversation got around to the old times. Before the New Depression. To how people lived before there was so much technology. Carver leaned back against a stump and said, 'Life is a gift. Survival is earned. It's the triumph of the mind.'"

MacKenna crosses and then uncrosses her legs. "Great. That sounds like something Dr. Doomsday would say."

Yes. Yes, it does.

We slow down. I wonder what will become of Dad's truck. If they search it, they'll find the laptop.

Then we won't even have that.

I bite my lip to keep myself from crying pathetic tears.

Toby leans closer to me. "Listen to me. We'll be okay. Let's just stay calm. I'm sure it will all work out."

Toby is always like this. Calm.

But it doesn't make him right.

We come to a stop, and the back door swings open.

The soldier from earlier scowls at me. "Okay, kiddos. Welcome to Goldwater Airfield."

STAY FOCUSED ON WHAT'S IN FRONT OF YOU. WORRYING ABOUT THE BIG PICTURE WILL GET YOU KILLED.

Goldwater Airfield.

The smell.

Someone is grilling steaks.

Goal: find Jay and escape.

"Mmm. Dinner," the soldier says with a grin. "For us, anyway."

New goal: escape, punch that guy in the face and steal his steak.

The Opposition has taken what seems to be an old air force base and modernized it. It's a large complex, surrounded by a tall, barbed-wire fence. A helicopter lands on the opposite side of the campus while we get out of the truck.

We're in the center of at least fifteen soldiers. As we're prodded along, I try to identify the various buildings. One must be some kind of communications center. There's a large white, S-band antenna off to one side, a VHF mast antenna and several more modern satellite dishes on the roof. Whoever is in that building can probably monitor most types of transmission.

We're pulled into a wide alley between two buildings. Straight ahead, I spot the grill—or grills—where several khaki-clad guys stand with oversize spatulas. This must be the commissary. Two more soldiers are unloading a truck, carrying box after box of canned beans, fruit cocktail and potato salad.

Tork emerges from somewhere behind us. "Dietrich. Take these kids into holding. I'm waiting for some instructions from HQ. Then I'll start the interviews. Around 14:00."

Dietrich. That's the giant soldier.

"You're the boss," Dietrich says.

I take one last look in the direction of the flaming grills. Tork opens an unmarked door to the building on our right. He leaves us there with Dietrich in charge. Several more soldiers in desert fatigue uniforms line the wall I'm suddenly struck by how young everyone is. Most of these guys are barely older than me or Toby. Tork and Dietrich are some kind of senior management, and they can't be much over thirty.

Inside, we find a narrow, fluorescent-lit hallway lined with identical plain doors. Toby, MacKenna and I file in. Toby is in front and as he comes to the first door, one of the soldiers pushes him through it. The door is quickly shut. Dietrich locks the door with a ring of keys he produces from his pocket.

I guess knowing that she's about to be trapped in a tiny room produces a burst of energy in MacKenna. A soldier has her by the elbow. "Hey. Who the damn hell do you think you are? And why do you think—" She's shoved into the room and the door is closed before she can finish her questions.

I'm alone in the hall with Dietrich and at least a dozen soldiers. *Okay. Stand up straight. Stay calm. Eyes straight ahead. Lips relaxed.*

Breathe in.

Breathe out.

Dietrich gives me a small smile. "I'm sure your father would be glad to know you've retained so much of your training. Hell. You even gave *me* a bit of a run for my money. Take heart in that." He nods to one of the soldiers standing at attention. "Search her."

All these guys seem to know a lot about Dad.

The cold reality hits me.

They know *him*.

Dad was one of them.

I recall the plans, the blueprints we came across back in Dad's kitchen. They were strikingly similar to this place.

I'm forced to the ground. My lips grow cold as they're pressed against the concrete floor. They take my jacket, socks and shoes and cut the pockets out of my jeans with a knife. They take all my emergency supplies and even the spare paperclip from my pocket.

"Tork wants to interview you. Until then, we wait," Dietrich says as they drag me into what will now be my room.

One of the soldiers cuts the zip tie binding my hands with a small pocket knife and then leaves the room.

The door closes.

I'm alone.

Alone in a five-by-five cell with a low bunk in one corner and a toilet and sink in the opposite. This room is lit by large fluorescent lights too, but they're not as bright as in the hall.

I take a seat on my bunk.

There's no TV, radio or books. Just four brown walls.

Dietrich is right about one thing.

There's nothing to do but wait.

Wait and think about the situation that I've somehow found myself in. At least Charles is okay. And Navarro. That's something.

Picking at the rough covering of the mattress, I'm out of feelings. Out of plans. Out of ideas. I have nothing. Except. Maybe. The drills.

Don't stand around waiting to die.

I glance around from empty wall to wall to wall.

Sigh.

Escape the Room.

That's the drill.

Great.

My dad was never a big fan of Escape the Room. We hardly ever did that drill. Or talked about it. *Think about it*, he said, *really think about it.* Think about the rooms you've been in. How many ways out are there really? The windows and the doors. Oh sure. In the movies, they love to show people crawling through gigantic air vents or creeping through human-size tunnels. But the reality is, there are windows and doors. If you're being held somewhere you don't want to be, there are probably not even going to be windows. You're going out one way.

The way you came in.

The door.

I move to the door. There's no way to slide anything underneath it. There's only a tiny sliver of space between the door and the concrete. The lock is intense and there are continuous security hinges. It would take a professional locksmith to get past this door.

Yes. *And that brings me to sunny point number two*, Dad said.

You'll have to wait for whoever put you in the room to come back and open *the door.*

Which is why we train not to be captured.

Dad's not here because, of course, he saved himself.

Sigh.

This sucks. This sucks so bad. I want to tuck my brother into bed. Heat up a chicken potpie and get behind my terminal with my pro controller and suit up for my *Republicae* mission. I should be having an Extra Jolt cola right now.

I beat on the door a few times with my fists. It's stupid and a waste of energy. But I pound again and again and again. Until I'm out of rage and adrenaline. Until I collapse. I fall down with my back to the door and slump over into the fetal position.

Never mind that the floor smells like rubber and insecticide.

I'm going to die in here. I'm never going to see my mom or my brother or my house or spend the night in my own bed. Life will go on at school. There will be parties and tests and people making out behind the bleachers at football games. Toby won't take me to senior prom the way I always hoped he might.

Whatever we were, whatever we were going to be, is vanishing right before my eyes.

My whole body aches from the crash. I put my hand on my neck and massage it a few times, realizing I must look like one of those posters for chiropractors who treat whiplash.

I let my whole body sink all the way onto the floor.

I lie there and cry and cry and cry.

"Jinx? Is that you?"

A quiet voice comes from somewhere near my head. I realize there's a tiny vent on the wall near the floor. It's Mac-Kenna's voice coming from her cell to mine.

I wipe the boogers off my face using the tail of my sweater and try to sound normal. "Um, yeah. It's me. I'm here."

"Have you been crying?" she asks in a tone that perfectly expresses her usual eye roll. "We've been in here, like, maybe thirty minutes. You need to pace your breakdowns. We might be here for a while. If anyone should be crying, it should be me. I'm the one who's going to die in these awful leggings."

Oh God. We were wearing identical leggings from the supply bins. "You look fine," I say.

On one hand, it seems ridiculous to be talking about our clothes at a time like this. On the other, I was grateful to be able to have something to think about besides bombs and dead bodies and infected laptops and fire.

I should keep things light. Instead, I blurt, "I miss my mom."

There's a pause and I'm sort of expecting MacKenna to ridicule me or something. Because she's tough and always has it together.

"Me too," she says in a small voice.

This is a surprise.

It occurs to me that MacKenna hardly ever talks about her mother and I never ask. It occurs to me that I've been kind of a self-centered brat. All I know is that Marissa Novac died five years ago from an inoperable brain tumor. It was the kind of thing that people so young aren't supposed to get and that doctors are supposed to be able to cure.

"What was she like?" I ask.

There's another pause, and when MacKenna speaks again, it sounds almost like she's smiling. "She was the best. The kind of mom who made all the costumes for the school play. The kind who always asked how your day was. She ran a bakery in Boulder. It was famous for its *fritule*."

"What's *fritule*?" I ask.

"Um…they're like little Croatian doughnuts, but they're puffy. A bit like beignets. But with rum. And raisins. She used the recipe that Grandma Novac brought from Labin."

My mouth waters.

"Mom volunteered a couple of days a week at a soup kitchen. She was so busy. That's why she kept putting off going to the doctor," MacKenna sniffles. "She wanted to…"

Feed everyone. MacKenna's mom wanted to make sure everyone had enough food. MacKenna's interest in The Spark was more personal than I thought.

She wanted to finish her mother's work. To make sure everyone had enough.

"I'm sorry." I don't know what else to say.

"Me too."

We're there, silent for a few minutes.

Until footsteps.

I hear MacKenna's door open and then shut again. A couple of seconds later, my door opens. A brown paper bag is tossed inside. I open it. There's a smooshed peanut butter sandwich, a bag of fruit snacks and a bottle of water.

"Bon appétit," MacKenna says through the vent.

I sit up near the vent with my back against the wall. It's not the best lunch I've ever had but at least it's something.

"Can you talk to Toby too?" I ask.

"No," she says. "He's in the room next to me, but there's no opening between."

After I eat a few bites of the disgusting peanut butter sandwich, I say, "We've got to get out of here." I wipe my mouth on the sleeve of my shirt.

We're silent until MacKenna says, "Why did you decide to come with us?"

"Because I had to try to help my mom." And I had to try to atone. "And because I love Jay too, you know."

She must be sitting very close to the vent on her side, because her voice has a quiet, soft girlish sound but I can hear her perfectly. "I know."

It's weird that our relationship is the best it's ever been and we have a literal wall between us.

"How could I not see that my father was really involved in all this stuff?" I say, mostly to myself.

MacKenna answers. "You didn't want to see. None of us really want to see things that are unpleasant. But, Jinx, it's better this way. If we don't have the truth, there isn't much of a point in surviving. There isn't anything worth surviving for."

The fluorescent lights flicker twice.

"If we're going to survive, we'll need some sort of a plan," I say.

"Yeah."

But I don't say anything else. I don't know if the room is under audio or video surveillance. And there can be only one plan anyway.

Try to escape when they come to get us for the interviews.

I take the sheet from my bed and sit near the door. In case anyone is watching, I attempt to make my movements seem like a nervous habit. I twist the sheet as tight as I can, forming a makeshift rope. Twist and twist and twist. My idea is to wedge the bottom into the door the instant it opens and then do my best to face punch whomever Tork sends to interview us. Either we can escape or we can't and we might as well find out one way or the other.

It's not a great plan.

MacKenna tells stories through the wall. About how her mom would boil cabbage and make sauerkraut and how you

could smell it from the driveway at their old house in Boulder.
How they had a scarlet oak tree in the corner of their yard.
Every year, the leaves would turn as red as fire, then brown
until they'd be carried off by the wind, dancing past her win-
dow. In the end, I want to get out even more, if only to visit
Colorado someday.

We wait.

And wait.

And wait.

I'm losing all feeling in my butt and I have to keep doing
little circles with my feet and ankles to keep them from falling asleep.

But it happens.

There's some loud talking in the hall.

I'm on my feet.

Fast.

Dad always says, *Stay focused on what's in front of you.*

The door.

The door.

It opens.

I've got the sheet wrapped so tight around my hand that
my fingers tingle and the tips have grown numb.

The door. The door. The door.

I chant this in sync with my heartbeat.

I'm ready.

DR. DOOMSDAY SAYS:

KEEP YOUR FRIENDS CLOSE.
KEEP YOUR ENEMIES IN THE MORGUE.

The first part goes okay. I'm able to use the sheet to jam the door. I grab an arm by the sleeve of a desert camo jacket. It's the fight of my life to get the makeshift rope wrapped around the soldier's arm but I do.

I slam the door on the arm.

Slam.

Slam.

Slam.

Until I'm pretty sure I've broken it.

Whoever is out in the hall is screaming bloody murder and I can hear MacKenna shouting my name through the wall. All this racket is bound to attract unwanted attention. I need to get a move on it.

Now.

I drag the soldier inside my room. In what feels like our first lucky break so far, he's not that much bigger than I am.

And he's surprised. My dad always told me that the one advantage I'd have in a fight is that my opponent would be unlikely to take me seriously.

He's thin and blond and boyish.

He goes for my nose.

I'm mostly able to block it but the punch lands hard enough that I see electric stars in my peripheral vision. I'm pretty sure my nose isn't broken. Thank God for small favors.

I ground myself and get ready for a kick. I have to give this everything I've got. Every. Last. Thing. I've. Got.

Groin kick.

I will survive.

The guy is down on the floor. I scramble over, forcing him in a face-down position. I take an elbow to the face and I know I'll have a black eye later, but I see it. A ring of keys dangling from a utility belt. I rip them off and jump up.

I kick the soldier once in the ribs to make sure he stays down.

And then I'm in the beige hall.

And it's quiet. Way too quiet.

Considering how blond boy was screaming bloody murder, I'm waiting for half the damn base to storm the building. And anyway, there's no choice.

Keep going.

I lean against the door, using my body weight to keep it closed because the soldier won't stay down forever. Sure enough, as I'm trying keys on the ring, he starts tugging on the door. There are at least thirty keys and if I have to test all of them, I'm really, really screwed. There's just no getting around that the soldier in the room is stronger than I am.

The sixth key locks the door and I breathe a sigh of relief.

The soldier continues to yell and beat on the metal door

as I move down to MacKenna's cell. Luckily the same key opens her door as well, so I don't have to waste a lot of time.

Her mouth is frozen in a shocked O as I swing the door open. "Jinx, what the hell? You took out the guard?"

"Let's go," I tell her.

"You actually think we can escape?" she says, still sitting on the floor near her vent.

"Not if you don't get a move on it."

She's up and with me in the hall. "You look like shit, you know."

Of course, this is what she says. I use the key to open Toby's door. He's as surprised as his sister but gets going right away. "What's the plan?" he asks.

"Find Jay. Get the hell out of here," I tell him as we run toward the double doors where we came in.

"Simple," MacKenna says. "Also. Probably insane."

Before I can push open the door, a loud alarm rings out and keeps going, over and over. The lights flicker again and then go out.

Well. This is probably going to be the world's shortest escape attempt.

Toby shrugs. His face says, *We have nothing to lose.*

I push open the door, expecting to find the infantry just outside the door. But that's not what I see.

Instead, the base is in total disarray. A fuel truck has crashed through the barbed-wire fencing in the distance. There's screaming and gunfire and the alarm blaring from every building.

Goldwater Airfield is under attack.

The gas truck explodes, sending a mass of black smoke into the sunset and the smell of burning plastic and rotten eggs everywhere.

It's scary as all hell.

And it's an opportunity.

To escape.

Gunfire rings out from the opposite side of the base where the sun is setting behind the communications building. It hits me. Everything we need to know is over there.

MacKenna pokes my arm. "What? What are you looking at?"

"That has to be the comm center," I say, pointing toward the rows of satellite dishes and antennae. "If we can access a terminal, we can find out where they're keeping Jay."

We exchange a look and I know.

We're going.

I turn to Toby. "We should split up." I point in the direction that had Tork vanished the last time we saw him.

Toby looks at me like I've lost my mind. "Oh hell no," he says. "We're gonna stay together."

This was Toby. Always wanting to take care of everyone. But would good would it do us if we all got killed?

"No, we need to increase our chances of survival," I tell him, shaking my head. "If we split up, we double our odds that one team can find Jay or get out of here. Worst-case scenario, we all get recaptured."

Toby scowls. "Worst-case scenario is one of us gets killed while we're out here prowling through the next world war."

"No," I say with a firmness I don't really feel. "No more arguing. We increase our chances of finding Jay."

Of course, this is all false bravado. Toby wouldn't have to do much to talk me out of what, even I must admit, is a pretty dumb plan. I have to get moving before I lose my nerve. MacKenna takes off as well.

"I'll wait fifteen minutes," Toby calls. "That's it."

I wish I'd thought to take the soldier's boots when I tackled him because running along the rocky desert soil without shoes on really, really hurts. Tiny rocks get stuck in my skin and dig in deeper with each step.

I don't know why Toby and MacKenna got to keep their shoes.

We hug the barracks and cross into the open only when there's no other option. No one notices anyway. Whatever's going on must require all hands on deck, and we don't attract any attention as we make our way to the communications building. And it's loud on that side of the base. A long row of power generators hums in the pauses between the gunfire and explosions.

The door is locked.

My heart drops.

MacKenna's eyes are wide with horror.

I shift my weight from foot to foot, trying to get some relief from the pebbles breaking my skin. I have to hope and pray that one of the three billion keys on the ring I stole from the soldier will open this door. My hands shake as I try to insert the first one into the lock.

It doesn't fit.

This idea was really, really stupid.

I'm about to say as much when two things happen.

First, there's another explosion from somewhere by the barracks, and then the comm center door is thrown open. I'm barely able to catch it by the door handle to keep from getting hit in the face. Two soldiers exit. MacKenna and I share a terrified look as we huddle together, trying to shield ourselves as much as possible with the now open door. I brace myself to be caught.

But the soldiers continue on, walking forward at a brisk pace, talking to each other.

Man 1: Finally. We get to see some fucking action.

Man 2: For all you know this is another drill. I'm tired of drills.

Man 1: We have to prepare for deployment somehow.

Man 2: We're ready to roll. We just need Carver to give the order.

Man 1: It won't be long now. This world isn't ready for us.

Their conversation trails off. I grab MacKenna's arm and drag her inside the comm building. I shut the door behind us. Slowly. With a soft click.

MacKenna's eyes are so big, bigger than I've ever seen, like saucers or the moon or some other childhood cliché. We stare at each other, and I wonder if she's realizing the same thing I am. They're preparing for an invasion. They're using this base to get ready.

We don't have any time for this terrifying new reality. We have to keep moving.

Focus.

It's *way* more quiet in here. The alarm isn't blaring.

We're in another long beige hallway. We hear voices. Chatter. The indistinct mumbling of people talking quietly.

We creep down the hall. I don't know when it happened, but I've got my hand wrapped around MacKenna's upper arm. If it hurts, she doesn't say anything.

We come to a set of double doors that are thrown open. I peek around the corner. There are more soldiers, sitting at terminals and watching an array of screens mounted on every wall. They're relaying tense instructions into microphones mounted on the desks. "There's a fence breach in northwest four," one guy says. "Tell the jerk who's firing at Red 6 to cut it out. They're hitting the Doppler."

I hop past the door, and then MacKenna does the same.

As we near the center of the building, we come to what looks like a series of office doors. I notice that the doors are reinforced and fireproof. The floor underneath my feet gets cold. MacKenna shivers.

The only reason to keep this building that cold is if there's a ton of computers in here and they're using a cold aisle containment system.

I stop in front of one of the doors and pull.

My pulse races as I wrap my hand around the cold handle. Almost dizzy.

The door is unlocked and it swings open.

My weak legs take two jerky steps.

And.

We're inside.

It's almost like going to Disneyland. I forget for an instant that the base is filled with people who want us dead or tossed in the bastille. I see only rack after rack of neatly installed servers. Perfectly networked and maintained with their blinking blue lights pulsing through the dimly lit space. Carver has taken every precaution. The racks are lined up with precision on raised flooring. Overhead power distribution. Perfectly cooled.

"What is this?" MacKenna asks.

"It's a data center," I say over the hum of the servers as I gaze around in awe. A place like this just shouldn't exist way out here in the middle of the desert. "A massive one."

"God. What I wouldn't do for a camera phone right now. Can you imagine if The Spark knew about this place? Or the media? How do we access these things?" MacKenna asks, gesturing at a server rack.

"We need to find a terminal that's networked in," I say. We move across the wide room to a door on the opposite side. *"This doesn't make any sense."*

I'm not really conscious that I've said this out loud until MacKenna answers. "Why not? This *is* a military base."

The cool cement floor feels good against my raw feet. "Yeah. I guess." But's it's a small one, and this is a major computer data center. It isn't smart to keep all this stuff in such a warm, remote area where you have to cool it and bring people in to maintain it. "This place. It's probably got fifteen, twenty petabytes of storage. There's no reason they should need this much storage. Unless..." I trail off.

Backup.

This place is for backup.

Oh God.

"Hello?" she says when I don't answer.

"I think this is the proof. The proof that Carver planned the attacks on his own banks."

"What?" she exclaims.

I can't put it into words. How I just sense that this is the base of operations for The Opposition's plan. The Opposition created this data center as one last safety measure after they planned the explosions at the banks. It's one big backup plan.

But the bank data hadn't been restored yet.

Something must have gone wrong.

Something that probably has to do with Dad.

MacKenna wants more answers, but we have no time.

We have to keep going.

We arrive at the door on the opposite side of the room. We go through it and find ourselves in another beige hallway.

This side of the building is lined with more offices, and they have windows. Through one, I spot the back of a small man with neon purple hair facing three large, glowing monitors.

His terminal is our way in.

I motion for MacKenna to join me at the door to the office. She pushes down the handle. Slow. Slow. Slow. And then opens the door silently.

Breathe.

The room is divided into twenty or so empty cubicles. On the far side of the room, a couple of the overhead fluorescent lights are on, but on our side, we've got only the glow coming from the one guy's monitors.

We really don't need to bother being so quiet. Even from across the room, I can hear screamo music blaring through the dude's oversize headphones.

But still. We creep.

I glance around. On a table near the door, I see a box of orange extension cords. MacKenna frowns at me as I grab one. Wrapping the edges of the cord around my hands as I walk, I skulk across the industrial carpet. My bare feet are silent.

Soft.

Quiet.

Steps.

I position myself directly behind the guy's head of greasy, bright violet hair, hold the plastic cord so tight that it cuts into my fingers. As fast as I can, I reach my arms over the man's head and wrap the extension cord around his neck. He wriggles under my grip, gasping for breath and clawing at the cord. His headphones get knocked off his head, with one of the speakers blasting music into his cheek.

"You're choking him," MacKenna says in a panicked voice. "You're gonna kill him."

I pull him back, tipping his chair. He knocks over a wire mesh pencil holder full of all different colored highlighters and several pens as he crashes to the ground.

My mouth falls open at the sight of the face falling onto the cheap blue, military carpet.

I release the cord, letting it drop down to the floor as well.

What's left of my heart might break.

It's Terminus.

DR. DOOMSDAY'S GUIDE TO ULTIMATE SURVIVAL

SAVE YOURSELF. IN THE END, THAT MIGHT BE ALL YOU CAN DO.

RULE ELEVEN:

Terminus gets up and puts his hands in the air. "Okay, Jinx. Okay. Let's not do anything we're both going to regret here."

He looks a lot different than the last time I saw him. It's been a year since he graduated and we used to see each other in real life. He's thinner, dyed his hair and has completely lost the tan he got while working summers for his dad's landscaping company. He's white as a ghost.

I eye the cord on the ground. "I should kill you."

MacKenna is shocked. "You two know each other?"

"Terminus," he says with a nod as he sinks in his chair. He makes a couple of clicks with the mouse and the music goes quiet.

"Your *name* is Terminus?" MacKenna asks. She side-eyes me.

"As far as you're concerned it is," he says. "Terminus was a Roman god who—"

"His name is Harold Partridge," I say through clenched teeth. "He's a hacker who's known for—"

"Do *not* call me Harold." Terminus scowls.

Everything that's happened.

Everything makes perfect sense now.

Everything.

A hatred is building, creeping through my skin and into my bones. I pick up the phone cord and grab his office chair, sending him spinning a few feet past MacKenna and onto the carpet again.

"I'm going to call you an undertaker, you backstabbing piece of garbage."

He gets up but stays on his knees.

All I see is red. Blood. Fire. Rage.

My knees tense and I prepare to lunge at my old friend.

MacKenna steps in front of me. "Jinx! What are you doing? We have to find my dad. And you can't just go around killing people."

Out of breath, I huff. "Oh really? Well...let me introduce you to the guy...who framed Jay Novak."

"Who...what...?" MacKenna asks, dumbfounded.

I'm such a fool. I should have seen it. From the very beginning.

Terminus wrote the Day Zero exploit.

Trust no one.

I jab my finger in the air. "It's him. He's the one who hacked Jay's laptop. He wrote the code that caused the explosions at the bank. Then he told me where to find it, probably thinking I'd destroy the evidence."

Teminus tries to look charming. "That would have been helpful."

Tightening the cord between my fingers, I make an attempt to step around MacKenna. She blocks me again.

I have to make her understand. "He told me where Jay was being held. He all but dared me to show up here." I truly hate myself. I should have seen all of this coming. The reason that they brought Jay here of all places was probably because of Terminus. My dad's old student knew enough about our adventures in the desert to be able to make an educated guess as to where we'd go. And he knew he'd be able to use Jay to lure us here with the evidence.

I duck around her to look Terminus right in the face. "Why?"

"When Marshall backed out, they called me. I'm his best student," he says. "Who else would they choose?"

"I'm asking," I say through clenched teeth, "why you did it. You're for The Opposition?"

There's a pause before he speaks. "I'm for cryptocurrency. There's a war coming, Jinx, and when it gets here. I want to be on my own private atoll in the Maldives. They would have found someone. If not me, then someone."

"Screw you. Where'd you get Jay's security credentials?" I ask.

"Tork," Terminus answers. "He keeps saying they've got someone on the inside."

"On the inside of what?" MacKenna demands.

"I don't know. I mean, he's not exactly a real chatty fellow, you know."

"You killed *two thousand people*!"

Terminus rises to his feet and takes a small step toward his computer. "I wrote a piece of code. What I did was nothing more than ones and zeroes. Characters on a screen."

"Don't you dare touch that keyboard, you human slug. You disgust me."

Terminus squints at me with what I now see as his beady little weasel eyes. "Oh, you think you're so morally superior? Deep down in places you don't want to talk about, The Opposition appeals to you too. You just can't admit it. Why do you think you like playing *Republicae* so much? What is that game really? A simulator with an all-powerful person in charge. You control everything from life and death to economics and morality with absolute impunity. Because some part of you believes the world would be better if one person ran things. As long as it was the *right* person. Marshall thinks the same. He put all his faith in one man. Except maybe he chose wrong."

I scowl at him. "If Carver is the wrong man, why are you helping him?"

Terminus slouches. "I told you. My services are available to the highest bidder."

For a minute, I can't speak. Terminus doesn't realize, or care, that he's sold out our friendship too. This is oddly devastating.

He mistakes me and continues on. "What? You think this makes me worse than your father? You'd be happier if I was a true believer in Carver's neo-fascist bull?"

I shake my head. "Say what you want about my dad. He refused to help Carver blow up those banks."

Terminus turns red and waves his hand in the air. "Right. All he did was set up this place. Carver is starting a revolution and Maxwell Marshall is its IT department."

This isn't getting us anywhere. The clock is ticking, and I want to get as far from Terminus as possible. To MacKenna, I say, "We need to get on with it. They'll be coming for us any moment now. We have to find Toby and Jay and get out of here."

Terminus runs his fingers through his curly purple hair. "The base is under attack, so you may have more time than you think. Jinx. Listen to me. I did what I did. You don't have to like it, but I can help you out now."

MacKenna eyes him uncertainly. "How can you help?"

My hands ball up into fists. "He won't help."

MacKenna gives me a look of warning. Part of me knows she's right. If we can help Jay and Mom, we have to focus on that.

Terminus has the nerve to look almost hurt or offended. "Yes. I can. I need to get to my computer." He picks up his office chair.

I glance at MacKenna and she nods.

I hate Harold Partridge.

But we're desperate.

"Fine, *Harold*, but so you know, I can kill you before anyone can get in here to help."

He pushes his chair behind his desk and sits down.

MacKenna and I stand directly behind him.

Terminus jiggles his mouse and the screens power to life. His hands hover over the keyboard and he speaks to us like a professor giving a lecture. "The first thing I'm gonna do is report a situation normal over here to buy some time."

He types in his username and password, unplugs his headphones and pulls a USB microphone toward him.

I'm ready with the phone cord.

"Blue 1 reporting. Building clear. Situation normal."

"*Roger.*" A voice comes over the computer speakers.

"Okay," Terminus says. He fills the monitors with images from the base's CCTV system. He makes a few taps until we see an image of Jay in a cell, sitting on a bunk and reading a book, another one of Mom in some kind of a waiting area staring out a large window, and finally we see Toby, crouching behind a desert-camo Jeep.

"All right. Here we go," Terminus says.

The building where Jay is being held has computerized locks, which Terminus releases with a few clicks. It must make some kind of a noise, because Jay looks up in surprise, gets up and approaches the door. Next Terminus accesses Goldwater's lighting system. He flashes the floodlights repeatedly on a large beige building until it attracts Toby's attention.

Toby ducks out from behind the Jeep and makes a run for it.

MacKenna watches all this. She taps Terminus on the shoulder. "Why did they choose my dad? The bank has dozens of people working in security. Why *my* dad?"

"No idea, sweetheart," Terminus says without looking up from his console. "That information is need-to-know, and I guess I don't need to know."

He opens what looks like the camera admin systems.

I fight off the urge to yank Terminus's rotten eggplant hair. But I'm wondering...

"Why are you still here?" I ask him. "Your code worked. They've got Jay. What do they need you for?"

Terminus's face turns red. "Marshall's little piece of malware has crawled through all of the bank systems, including this server farm right here, which was supposed to be the backup of the backup. They've got me trying to figure it out."

He's looking for Dad's encryption key. He won't find it.

"You won't beat my dad."

His face flushes red. "I got Day Zero to work. He couldn't."

I snort. "You probably just took Dad's old work and tweaked it like some script kiddie. And Dad clearly saw something like this coming. That's why he wrote the malware. He says your code looks like shit, Harold."

MacKenna stares at the image of Toby running across the base.

Terminus is suddenly sincere. "When you saw Marshall, did he say why he did it? Why he took out the bank data?" It occurs to me just then that my dad was like a father figure to him. That he wanted a way to preserve that connection.

"No," I say flatly.

Terminus makes a few more clicks with his mouse and the screens go blank, replaced by frantic static.

"What happened?" MacKenna asks, still watching where Toby was a moment before.

"He took out the camera system," I say.

Her lips press into a thin line. "Now we can't see what's going on."

"But neither can anyone else."

Terminus turns to me with a bit of hope in his face, like we just finished a game of counterstrike at computer camp or something. "Okay. If you take a right out of this office and go to the end of the hall, it's a straight shot to the citadel where they're holding Novak."

We have to go.

MacKenna is thinking hard. "Can you get a message out of here?" she asks Terminus.

"A message?" he repeats.

"We need to warn the country. Tell them what's going on."

Terminus shakes his head. "What's going on is that all communication from this base is monitored. What's going on is that Ammon Carver declared martial law last night. This base is a perfectly legal use of his emergency powers. There's nothing to warn people about."

"Except the end of the world," she shoots back.

A voice comes across the intercom. *"Is the video feed running over there?"*

"Negative," Terminus says into his microphone.

There is no time. "Give me your shoes," I tell him.

He frowns but does toss me his high-tops. I stuff my feet into them. They're a size or so too big, but better than nothing.

MacKenna bounces up and down on her heels a couple of times.

Getting ready.

To run.

We make our way to the office door. When I open it, we can hear shouts from outside. "They're never gonna stop coming after us, are they?"

Terminus swivels in his chair. "They're not after you at all. They want Marshall."

I turn to go.

"Jinx. I hope you make it," Terminus calls.

"I hope I never see you again," I call back.

They want Marshall.

That phrase sticks with me as we go.

We leave the room and run toward the double doors at the end of the hall. MacKenna throws one open, and we keep running out onto the base. We're near the edge, up against the chain-link fence that forms the perimeter.

Mud squishes under the high-tops. I glance over my shoulder to see water running out through a plastic pipe coming from the roof. Probably condensation from the massive AC needed to keep the data center so cold.

Running as fast as we can, we head along the data center building toward the citadel that Terminus showed us on the screen. He left the floodlights on, so it's easy to spot. Mac-

Kenna's a much better runner than I am, and she overtakes me after a few paces.

There isn't much time to think about that. Or formulate much of a plan.

More gunfire erupts and there's another *boom*. More smoke rises from a position on the opposite side of the base.

"What the hell is going on out here?" MacKenna shouts.

We stop at the end of the data center, waiting for a moment of calm in the chaos to make a break for the detention center.

But then.

I see Toby.

He and Jay and Mom are peeking around the corner of a building opposite ours. I don't know how they got out of the citadel at the center of the base, but there they are. They run in our direction and I'm flooded with intense relief. Jay and Mom look basically okay. Toby is alive.

This feeling. Maybe this is why Dad always said to focus on survival. The search for the truth is cold. Survival is like fire; the desire for it ignites and explodes inside you.

I have a thousand more questions but I don't get to ask.

I say "Mom" and MacKenna shouts "Dad!" at the same time.

There's hugging and crying.

"What the hell is *she* doing here?" MacKenna asks.

"Mac," Jay says, shaking his head.

For an instant I think MacKenna must be talking about Mom.

But my gaze darts up, and I see what she means. Toby has someone with him. *She* is a girl. A little bit older than me. Tall. Blonde. Perfect. There's something very familiar about her ultrahigh cheekbones and anime-big blue eyes. She's got this look about her. Like she's an actress who's been cast in an action movie. She's wearing perfectly pressed khaki shorts with rolled up cuffs and a camo-green T-shirt that's knotted to show off a little bit of abs.

I'm conscious of the fact that I'm bloody and filthy and probably look like I haven't changed my clothes in two days.

MacKenna scowls. "Toby! I asked you a question. What—"

Things happen fast.

More gunfire.

Shouts from inside the comm building.

A green supply truck backs through the fence, knocking down a section of chain links right in front of us.

We're caught.

I clutch my sweater, trying to pretend it's a piece of armor that might protect me.

Breathe.

I screw everything up.

I let Terminus lead me into a trap.

I decided to go ogle a bunch of Nutanix servers and totally screwed up the one chance I had to get us out of here. And for what? To find out my one friend murdered a lot of people? I could have maybe lived happily ever after without that intel.

Breathe.

I prepare to surrender.

MacKenna grabs my hand.

And then I almost fall over when the canvas flap covering the back of the truck's cargo area is thrown open.

Navarro's head pops out.

"Ah…oh…crap…" I gasp as I fall backward onto the hard ground.

"Real happy to see me, I guess," Navarro says.

I scramble up and can't fight off a grin. "You came back."

All the tension suddenly releases from my body and I'm light as air.

Oh and.

Navarro's eyes really are a gorgeous shade of brown. Like new copper pennies.

"Obviously," he says. It's meant to be brisk, but he's smiling too.

Another voice comes from the front of the truck. "Yeah, yeah. We're all thrilled. We can have a big party when we're far, far away from here."

Dad.

It's Dad's voice.

Dad came back for us.

Navarro holds the canvas flap open and I can see Dad's arm waving and pointing to the troops in fatigues coming toward us, emerging from every building. "My guys can't hold them off forever. We have to go. Now."

Dad has guys.

Some kind of resistance.

MacKenna reaches for Navarro's hand. She disappears behind the canvas flap.

Navarro pulls me in. I wish I could count the dark brown freckles on his nose.

He draws me forward toward the cab of the truck. Most of the inside is filled with plastic containers, but a series of oversize backpacks line one side. MacKenna crouches, looking more disgruntled than scared.

Mom and Jay get in next.

I spot Charles wedged between a large bin and the truck's side wall.

I turn to see Toby pushing himself up and over the gate.

He's probably reaching for the girl when the doors to the comm building are thrown open.

"Go," Navarro screams. He jerks me and MacKenna down so that we're sitting in the bed of the truck and then he hits the metal sidewall.

"No. No!" Toby says. He's still got his arms outside the truck.

Three shots.

High-pitched pops.

Navarro crawls over toward Toby. Charles tries to do the same but I force him down. Dad is taking the terrain at top speed, and we're knocked back as we run over bushes and brush. Through a gap where the tarp covering is attached to the truck, I see military grade vehicles leaving in all directions.

The attack on the airfield is our escape.

Navarro and Toby finally succeed in tugging the girl into the back. From the looks of her now-dusty and filthy boots, she's been dragged along for the past minute or so. Toby places her down very gently so that she lies on the only stretch of the truck not covered with containers.

And then the blood.

Red. Running. Blood everywhere.

The girl's leg is covered in it, and she's heaving and crying. Taking shallow, asthmatic breaths and groaning in pain.

And.

The.

Blood.

"Mom! Mom!" I shout. Mom has tucked Charles onto her lap. Her mouth has fallen open and it looks like she's in some kind of shock.

"Help!" Toby almost screams this at me. "Jinx. Help!"

I glance from side to side helplessly. I don't know what

Toby expects me to do. I'm not a doctor, and I have nothing to work with.

MacKenna gets onto her knees. "Oh *hell* no. Toby Oscar Novak. We are tossing her snotty blonde ass right out the back!"

"Jinx!" he screams again.

"Toby, I'm talking to you!"

"Mac! Now is not the time for this."

Jay gets up and makes his way to his children. "Calm down. Both of you," he says.

Charles tries to get up too, but we're all thrown down by what feels like the truck going over a huge speedbump.

"Charles! No!" Mom shouts over all the noise. She pulls him into a tighter hug.

I make another attempt to crawl over to the center of the truck where Toby is bracing himself. MacKenna reaches out and grabs my shirt.

The expression on her face is almost deranged. "Do you know who that is? Do you even know?"

It's hard to stay calm. I shake my head.

We roll over another bump, and I crash into MacKenna.

"It's Annika! Fucking! Carver!" she screams.

DR. DOOMSDAY SAYS:

IF YOU'RE GOING THROUGH HELL, KEEP GOING.

Annika Carver.

Of course, MacKenna would recognize her before I would. She reads more news than I do and follows all the coolest celebrities online.

Annika Carver. Ammon's teenage daughter from his brief marriage to supermodel Paulina Hertzogovitch. She's a National Merit Scholar, a championship tennis player and has her own line of skin care products. She's a living dream doll who might have been created in a lab and is designed to show us the perfect future that awaits with Ammon Carver as our savior.

"Stop the truck," MacKenna tells Navarro. "Miss America is getting off."

"We're not stopping," Navarro says. He's already busy moving the packs away from the pool of Annika's blood. "If you wanna toss her, why don't you do it before she bleeds all over the food?"

For some reason, the two of them finally agreeing on something scares the crap out of me.

Mom moves Charles closer to where Dad is driving the truck.

"MacKenna. She helped me. I'm not sure I would have found Dad without her help." Toby is on the verge of breaking into tears.

"She would know her way around. Because she's one of them," MacKenna says.

"That's why they shot her?" Toby demands.

We go over another large bump and Annika screams.

"It's okay, Charles," Mom consoles my brother.

MacKenna uses one of the bins to steady herself. "They were shooting at *you*, stupid!"

"Jinx! Don't just sit there," Toby yells.

I crawl forward toward where Toby kneels alongside Annika. The kneecaps of his jeans are stained with dark red blood. The truth is that MacKenna is right. We don't know Annika Carver or know what her agenda is. Plus, traveling with an injured person makes our situation worse. "I… I don't know, Toby. Even if we can dress the wound—"

"Jinx!" Toby shrieks. "Don't try to tell me that your nutcase dad taught you to use every kind of gun, drive every kind of vehicle, and fight soldiers twice your size, but didn't teach you first aid. I *know* you know what to do. Get over here and *help me*."

The motion of the truck has calmed down somewhat. Jay stands and assumes control of the situation. "Enough. All of you. We're not tossing anyone, and we won't let a human being bleed to death if we can help it. Jinx, we'll do this to-gether."

MacKenna folds her arms over her chest.

I exchange a look with Navarro. He places a metal box with a handle in my arms.

A first-aid kit.

Okay. Okay. Okay.

It's a real mess over where Toby is, and I can't even tell where Annika was shot. "Where?"

He points to her right calf, which I guess makes sense considering she was shot as Toby was dragging her into the truck.

Okay. Leg wound. Right.

I open up the first-aid kit. There are some gauze sponges and a few bleedstop bandages but not nearly enough to stop the bleeding *and* dress the wound. There are two pairs of latex gloves. I squeeze my hands into one of the sets.

"I need a—" Before I can finish with the word *shirt*, Navarro has opened a bin and tossed a white undershirt onto my hand.

"MacKenna," I say. "Find a bottle of water."

Okay. Step one. Triage the wound.

Breathe.

I spot small entrance and exit wounds. So no need to worry about the bullet.

Taking the shirt in my hand, I press hard on the spot Toby pointed to. Annika's eyes open for the first time as she writhes and screams.

"Here," I tell Toby. "Keep the pressure on. And stop her from moving."

I'm so grossed out. I want to throw up. Or maybe jump out of the back of the truck myself. My blue gloves are al-ready covered with red blood. And Navarro is watching me with a vacant expression. I can't tell whether he approves of this plan of action or not.

Okay. Step two. Stop the bleeding.

I need to elevate Annika's leg.

"Have you…uh…done this before?" Toby asks. He looks like he's about to pass out.

"Yes," I say.

Turning to Toby, I add, "More pressure. If you're doing it right, she should be screaming her head off." I move one of the plastic bins underneath Annika's perfectly shaped leg. "Um. Yeah. The weirdo at the How to Suture Your Own Wounds seminar actually had someone shoot him in the arm. We had to dress the wound."

Toby doesn't have the stomach for this kind of thing. Luckily, Jay is there and kneels down alongside us. I should have thought of that anyway. Jay was in the army before doing security. Between the two jobs, he must've had some first-aid training.

I fall back onto my butt as the truck goes over what feels like a dune. This would be a whole lot easier if Dad wasn't trying to turn the ride into a rip-roaring theme park attraction.

Jay applies more pressure to the wound. "Hang on, sweetheart."

Annika whimpers.

"MacKenna," I call. Her arm reaches out from behind a bin with a water bottle in her palm.

Okay. Step three. Bandage the wound.

"Yeah. Okay," I say. "There's only one package of Quik-Clot in the kit. Jay, we're going to have to do this fast." I open up the gauze pads and bandage tape. "You remove the pressure. I'll pour water on the wound. Clean it with the alcohol pad. Then the QuikClot. Then I need you to press hard with the gauze pads while I do the tape."

"Got it," Jay says.

Toby fidgets with his shirt.

"What's QuikClot?" MacKenna asks Navarro.

"It's in first-aid kits," Navarro says. "Some kind of mineral that makes the blood clot faster. Stops bleeding quicker than it might stop on its own."

"Now!" I say. I don't have time to repeat myself and the longer I wait the more likely it gets that I'll chicken out or give up.

Jay moves the shirt to reveal a bullet hole in the fleshy part of Annika's calf. I pour water on it. "This is going to hurt," I say as I put the alcohol swab in place. She's still yelling as I pour the QuikClot.

Toby has a horrified expression on his face and doesn't reach for the gauze. He's scooted back and looks one heartbeat away from retching. If anyone gets to puke, it should be me.

"Okay. The bandage."

Jay places it on the wound. By some minor miracle, things stay calm in the truck long enough for me to wrap Annika's leg tight with tape.

Navarro tosses me another shirt to put over the blood on the floor of the truck. "Relatively clean entry and exit wounds," he says. "That's a break."

"Yeah," I say with a confidence I don't really feel. "And a nine mil. Could be worse."

Navarro nods. "Looked like a Beretta M9."

"That would make sense." The government probably has a ton of old guns, like Berettas, in surplus.

Okay. Focus. Keep calm. *Keep calm.* I remove the gloves

and toss them on a bloody shirt. "She…uh…needs stitches though. Unless you have some Steri-Strips or glue…"

He glances at the suture supplies. "Unless *I* have Steri-Strips? You're hoping to push this off on me?"

"No." My face heats up. "Um…no. I'm only saying…the exit wound is still bleeding… And anyway…um… I can't do it now. While we're driving…the bumps…and…"

Navarro purses his lips into a thin line. "Well, *you* can do it when we stop." He waves his hand in Annika's direction. "Because *this* is not my problem."

Great. Just great.

MacKenna nods. "*We* shouldn't be doing *this* at all. What happened to *this is a democracy?*"

At this, some color returns to Toby's face. "You know what, Mac? We're not gonna vote on whether or not we murder people, okay?"

"You know what, Toby? We weren't gonna murder her. Just leave her where her friends could come and pick her up."

"No…" Annika pants. "Not friends…no."

Toby glares at his sister. "They were holding her prisoner too. She helped us escape."

Jay draws in a deep breath. This is the first opportunity I've had to really get a good look at him. He's wearing a pair of army-green sweats and a T-shirt. In the last couple of days, he's grown a short, scraggly beard. "Excuse me, son, but I will be in charge of the important decisions from here on out. Mac, Toby is right. We couldn't just leave her there."

Annika has settled down and Toby moves closer to her. He picks up her hand but quickly drops it at the glares of Mac-Kenna and Navarro.

Jay squeezes my hand as I move toward the back of the truck to sit alongside Charles and Mom, resting my head back so I get a glimpse of the scenery through the narrow gap between the tarp and the truck. Yellow brush blurs by under the blue, cloudless sky. The ride gets slightly less bumpy and our speed evens out. Dad must have gotten us safely away from the airfield.

Jay, Toby and MacKenna continue to talk.

Mom smiles at me. A sense of calm fills me. Mom's here. She'll take care of Charles. And me. And everything. Still, a bit of awkwardness eats at me. A little bit of unease, I can't quite get rid of. Yes, here we all are. My mom, dad and brother, just like we used to be. But everything is different now.

Oh, Mom. How does her hair always look so neat and smooth and flawless? "Not the way you thought you'd be spending your afternoon, huh?" she asks.

I manage a small smile.

Her brown eyes, which are the exact same color as mine, darken as her face settles into a more serious expression. "I'm proud of you. You kept Charles safe. You found your father like I asked. You even rescued us."

I want to tell her about everything that's happened, but I can't. I can't relive it or make it more real.

Mom pats my leg and tries to be reassuring. "We'll be all right."

Charles puts his head on her shoulder.

As I relax, I realize that I'm beat. I stand up to find the first-aid kit, bouncing up and down as we hit the occasional rough spot of terrain. I sit on the side opposite Mom and Charles on a large supply bin.

Navarro takes a seat next to me. My stomach does a somersault.

I'm sure that's because of Dad's driving.

"You look like hell," Navarro says.

"Thanks," I say as I open the kit.

He glances at my feet. "What happened to your shoes?"

"They took them. Maybe they thought I'd hidden something in them. I stole these."

Navarro's eyebrows arch. "Ah. Hiding something in our shoes. I wish I'd thought of that."

Me too.

"Your dad stashed some of your spare clothes." He opens a bin and returns with a pair of Cons and some clean socks.

I take a few alcohol wipes from the first-aid kit. My feet burn and sting as I dab them with the wipes. And then, it's like I feel everything. The marks on my hands where the plastic cord cut into them as I choked Terminus. My puffy swollen nose. I can tell without checking that a bruise is forming on my left side where the guard checked me with his elbow.

Navarro shifts on the bin. "Look. About earlier. I should have… It was stupid to…"

"I understand," I tell him. "Thank you for coming back for us."

He smiles and a warmth rushes through my chest. My dad always says *Trust no one.* But what if Navarro is someone I can trust?

I put my own shoes on and make my way into the cab, which is separated from the rest of the truck by a beige canvas partition, and slide into the passenger seat. We're in some kind of hilly desert area. Mostly low brush and cholla. Once in a while, Dad has to steer around a tall saguaro or a lonely mesquite tree. I can see the horizon, and there's nothing but rolling hills in front of us—no buildings or telephone lines or even anything that looks like a road anywhere. I have no idea how Dad even knows where we're going.

I wonder if it's weird for him to be traveling in a band of fugitives with his ex-wife and her new husband.

"You came back for us," I say. I want to stay detached, cool, calm. Like him.

But I find myself smiling.

Dad continues to watch the road, but he smiles too. "Your brother and Gustavo were quite persuasive."

"We couldn't have escaped without you." I'm feeling better. Even more relieved. We can follow the Evac plan. Maybe our old lives are gone, but we can start new ones on the other side of the border.

"Jinx," my father says. "You have to understand. I haven't always done what's right. But I've always done what I thought was right for you. And Charles. I wish I'd done some things differently. But what I did was for you."

We're quiet as we come to a butte.

As we near the large mound, a cloud of dust builds up behind it. My pulse quickens, but I notice my dad isn't at all alarmed. A few seconds later, a large truck emerges from behind the hill. Dad brings our army surplus truck to a stop.

The sun has shifted to the west, beginning its descent into night.

The other truck stops in front of us. A man who would be right at home on the cover of one of Dad's old Western paperbacks unfolds from the driver's side door. He's clad in a paisley printed Western shirt that was probably red right around the time I was born but has since faded to a salmon pink. Coarse gray hair pokes out from under a weathered, beige Stetson.

We get out of the cab. I wait by the headlights as Dad strides forward to meet the cowboy.

He gives Dad a curt nod. "Well, well. Here you are. I gotta

say, when Ramona told me you'd run off to storm the bastille, I didn't think we'd be seeing you anytime in the near future."

Dad smiles. "I told her I'd be back today. I'm a man of my word."

"I know you are, old friend. But these are strange times."

This guy and my dad might be brothers from another mother.

Led by Navarro, everyone else clambers out of the back of the truck. Annika Carver has her arm around Toby and the two of them hobble along slowly.

MacKenna glares at them and so do I.

Dad points to each of us and says our names. He finishes with, "Kids, this is Bob Healy. He owns Brown Canyon Ranch right up ahead."

Healy's gaze travels from face to face, lingering on Mom before finally settling on Annika. "Does my wife know you're bringing…extra guests?" he asks Dad.

He keeps his back to Healy and says, "No."

"You know, Max, if you find yourself in a hole, the best thing to do is stop digging."

"It's like you said, Bob. These are strange times."

"Right."

Dad tells us to get busy taking what we need from the supplies. Toby stays with Annika while we transfer the backpacks and bins into the back of Healy's truck.

I'm not sure what the etiquette is for traveling with a person with a gunshot wound, but if it exists, my dad doesn't observe it. He picks up my brother, drops him into the bed of Healy's truck and climbs into the cab alongside Healy. Dad leaves Toby to help Annika. I get in and take a seat on the opposite side of the two of them. To my surprise, MacKenna plops down next to me. Mom and Jay get in last.

"That old guy doesn't seem too happy to see me and Toby," she whispers.

"I don't think it's you," I whisper back. "He keeps staring at Annika."

She snorts. "Doesn't everybody?"

Healy revs the engine and takes off. The dust keeps us from talking any further.

He takes the brushy, desert terrain at a much faster clip than I would have expected given that he's got a bunch of kids in the back. We all bounce around and struggle to stay steady. Toby does his best to keep Annika's leg still.

We come to a stop in front of an old green ranch house that looks like it's been abandoned for at least a decade. Green paint curls off its wooden siding in thick, spiral strips. It's encircled by a low, river rock fence and a dirt drive gutted with deep potholes.

If you didn't know someone lived there, you wouldn't know someone lived there.

The instant Mr. Healy opens his door, a tall thin woman rushes out from under the dark covered patio that surrounds the house.

I'm pretty sure this is Ramona.

Her long, silver hair is tied in two neat braids on either side of her weathered but pleasant face. Like Healy, she's wearing a faded Pendleton shirt and a pair of jeans.

I stare at her, puzzled. There's something really, really familiar about Ramona.

"Well, Bob, you sure took your time in getting here. As usual. I bet those kids are starved to death. But no matter. I've got a whole pan of—"

She doesn't finish her sentence. Her mouth stays open as her eyes find us in the back of the truck.

For a beat, I worry that maybe MacKenna was right.

Then, with Toby's help, Annika stands up in the truck, casting a long shadow over the old woman.

Annika breaks the silence. "Gramms?"

DR. DOOMSDAY'S GUIDE TO ULTIMATE SURVIVAL

RULE TWELVE:

DON'T GET COMFORTABLE.

Without answering or finishing her sentence, Ramona goes into her house, leaving us with no option other than to follow her.

So we learn that Ramona Healy is Annika's grandmother.

But this new piece of intel raises more questions than it answers. How does my dad know Annika's grandma? Why didn't Annika recognize Mr. Healy? Why did we end up here of all places?

Before any of those questions get answered, I learn something else.

Navarro can cook.

Really cook.

Which comes in handy, because Ramona Healy's consciousness has been beamed to another dimension. She's left a pan of fried chicken sizzling on the stove, potatoes on the verge of boiling over and a bowl of dough on the counter waiting to be pressed into biscuits. Navarro smells it the instant that the green screen door slams behind our backs and asks Healy to point him toward the kitchen. Charles goes with him.

I linger in the Healys' living room where burlap sacks, tools and work clothes rest on unkempt but expensive furnishings. A bunch of dusty copies of *National Geographic* clutter a low table with ornate, curved legs.

Ramona sinks onto a fancy, French-looking sofa that looks like it's had its blue upholstery clawed off by a large dog. She stares vacantly out the wide window.

Healy ushers Annika into an oversize leather armchair. My dad kneels alongside her to check out her wounded leg. "Well, well, Annika. Here you are. It has been quite some time. I wish we were seeing each other under better circumstances."

It occurs to me that Dad used to make occasional trips to Carver's vacation home in Kennebunkport. He's met Annika.

"Indeed," she says, composed in spite of everything. "It's nice to see you again."

Forever the political princess.

Toby remains with them in the living room.

Healy went out front almost immediately, like he can't stand to be indoors or something. Mom and Jay go out there too. I don't blame them. Jay's been locked in a cell since Tuesday night. He needs the open space.

MacKenna and I join Navarro in the kitchen.

I find him in the cramped space behind the Healys' old stove, flipping drumsticks with a pair of tongs. "Why don't you get going on the biscuits?" he says.

I either use too much flour or not enough flour or don't press the biscuits into a shape that's small enough or big enough or round enough for him. He makes Charles take over. I have to admit that my brother does a better job.

Navarro finishes the chicken, makes gravy, somehow throws together a green bean casserole and watches the biscuits as they rise in the oven. After almost three days without a decent meal, it takes every ounce of willpower I've got not to rip the plate of chicken out of his hands.

"Your mom teach you to cook?" MacKenna asks.

Navarro shakes his head. "My dad is actually the cook in our house. My mom works with food all day at the school nutrition office. And no, I won't tell you anything about the tofu."

MacKenna smiles, jumps in and works on the potatoes, dropping a mound of butter and a splash of cream into the pot that Navarro took off the stove. She gets started mashing.

As I creep toward the potatoes, Navarro makes conversation.

"You cook?" he asks MacKenna.

"Um, my mom owned a restaurant," she says as she stirs. "The Kastel Pineta. It had the best sarma in the country."

"*Had* the best sarma?" Navarro asks.

"My mom died. Five years ago."

Navarro nods.

Maybe I should say something but I'm so distracted by the pots of steaming food the two of them are conjuring up. It's such a horrible cliché to say that something smells like heaven, but if anything could smell that way, it's this meal. I'm two seconds away from scooping a bit of potatoes into my fingers when MacKenna slaps my hand with a wooden spoon.

"*You* can eat when we all eat," she snaps. "If you wanna do something, set the table."

I roll my eyes. We don't know where *the table* is, or if *the table* even exists.

But there's no point in arguing, and if it weren't for Navarro and MacKenna, not only would we have no food, but the kitchen would probably be on fire right now.

I return to the living room. Dad, Toby and Annika are gone. Ramona hasn't moved a muscle. She sits there like a living statue. I hover for a second, hoping she'll acknowledge me.

She doesn't.

"Um, excuse me? Um, Mrs. Healy? Where would you like us to set up the food?" I ask.

She doesn't answer. I come closer. She has a very old sunbleached copy of *Life* magazine on her lap. The face of a glamorous woman with a haunted expression rests underneath the headline of "The Curious Case of Ramona Carver."

This is Ammon Carver's mother.

Everyone has a mother.

I have to remind myself to breathe.

Healy's been sitting in a rocking chair on the porch, just on the other side of the open window. He comes back inside the house. "The dining room is thisaway," he tells me, drawing open a rickety set of bifold doors directly behind Ramona's sofa.

The dining room is tiny with a small, scuffed up table that has only six chairs. A china cabinet crowds one of the corners. Inside, I find place settings for twelve with red palm trees and flowers on all the plates. I can tell the china is expensive and old. Inside a drawer, there's silverware and it's real silver. I put a plate in front of each of the chairs.

"Hey there, friend," Healy calls in the direction of the open window. "Can I get a hand?" Jay steps through the screen door. He and Healy drag a card table and several chairs out of a closet in the hall. They set it up in the living room in front of the blue sofa. When they're done, I set that table too.

I return to the kitchen where Navarro, MacKenna and Charles have piled the food into serving dishes. At MacKenna's direction, we set up a buffet line on the edge of the dining table. Someone's put several lit jar candles on each table, and Charles arranges them neatly in the center. My dad reappears with Toby and Annika in tow. She's limping less, which probably means that Dad did a much better job dressing her wound than I did.

While we were dealing with dinner, Annika clearly took a shower. She's clean, smells like lavender and is wearing a spare set of *my* clothes. My black yoga pants fit her like baggy capris and my gray sweater hangs off her thin frame.

It must be really, really nice to be able to focus on grooming yourself while everyone has to work. I open my mouth to rip into her. Toby gives me a look of warning. That's not what stops me though. *The expression on her face.* It's absolutely the most pathetic thing I have ever seen. Her big blue eyes are frozen wide-open and her mouth is a stiff white line that twitches every few seconds. She wants to cry.

And run.

Instead, she picks up a serving spoon and doles a dainty portion of green beans onto her fancy china plate.

Healy ushers his wife into a chair at the dining room table. She still doesn't look away from the window where the sun is sinking lower by the second.

"Guess who's coming to dinner," Toby mutters.

We all take turns piling chicken on our plates. Healy, Dad, Mom and Jay join Ramona at the dining room table. The rest of us squeeze into the card table. It leaves me feeling like a kid at a wedding.

Toby helps Annika into a seat on the side of the table that faces away from the dining room and slides into the chair next to her. I sit on the opposite side and I have a perfect view of Ramona's aristocratic profile. MacKenna is to my right. Charles inserts himself into the corner between Navarro and Toby.

I pick up a warm biscuit. Butter drips onto my fingertips. The biscuit is inches away from my watering mouth when, from the other table, Healy clears his throat.

"We need to say grace," he says gruffly.

Dad nods. I drop the biscuit.

"Bless us, O Lord..."

It's been so long since we had real food.

"...and these, Thy gifts, which we are about to receive..."

Navarro must have done something to the chicken batter. It's better than how we found it. Many of the pieces are redder and are filling the dining room with a spiced aroma.

"...from Thy bounty..."

I think it's paprika.

"...through Christ, our Lord."

The butter keeps my fingertips warm.

"Amen."

I make the sign of the cross as fast as humanly possible and then shove the entire biscuit in my mouth before anyone can say or do anything else. I haven't finished chewing before I load my fork with mashed potatoes.

MacKenna side-eyes me. "Girl. Pace yourself. That chicken won't taste nearly as good coming back up as it does going down."

I bite into a piece of chicken without slowing down. "I don't care wut yoo say," I say with my mouth full. "Hmm. This is the best food I've ever had. Ever."

Navarro smiles.

"Is this *real* meat?" I ask. It's been years since I had anything besides meat grown in the lab.

"This is a real farm," Healy calls from the next table. "We got real chickens."

Charles watches Annika pick at her own plate. "Miss Annika, do you know that old lady?" he asks her.

"I used to," she whispers. Her shoulders sink and she's somehow smaller and sadder.

I kick Charles under the table to stop him from asking more questions. He scowls at me. But it's silent for a while. A grandfather clock in the hall ticks. Cows moo in the distance.

Suddenly, Annika lifts her gaze from her plate. In a voice barely above a whisper, she goes on. "They said she was dead. For ten years...my father said..." She turns to Toby. "She took a cruise. New York to Rome. They never found a body... They thought..."

"They thought your dad had her killed," MacKenna finishes.

Toby reaches out and pats Annika's hand, a move that earns him yet another glare from his sister. "I'm sure there's an explanation," he says, his voice calm and reassuring.

Annika's left eye twitches. "There is." In a louder, more normal voice, she says, "She ran. Away. From *him*. She left me. Left me there."

At that, Ramona comes alive, twisting in Annika's direction. What's left of the color in her face runs to ash. She and her granddaughter wear identical masks of sorrow.

The sky outside explodes into a sunset of bright pinks with streaks of purple. Silhouettes of cattle pass across the window.

For a second, Annika's polished facade is replaced by a hard look. "My own grandmother would rather hide out in the godforsaken desert outside some tiny crap town called Why, Arizona, than face my father." She drops her fork. "My father terrifies everyone. Especially those who know him best."

I shiver. But Annika is again elegantly scooping small bites of mashed potatoes into her rose-red lips.

Ramona speaks for the first time since we came into the house. Shadows cross her face as the candle on the table flickers. "I expect you know, Max, this changes a lot of things."

"We can talk about it, Ramona. In the short term though, the girl needs a doctor," Dad says. "I should get supplies as soon as I can. We need food that travels well. Sunscreen. Whatever medicine we can scrounge up. There's no telling how long we have. Things are moving faster than I expected."

"Now that we're all together, there are different considerations," Mom says. "A lot of things to be taken into account."

"There are things to discuss," Dad says in his usual bland way. "After dinner."

Jay scratches his new beard. "I agree. There's time enough for a meal."

The old woman watches the cattle outside. "There ain't gonna be that much to talk about. This can only end the one way."

Charles relaxes in his chair, and I find myself doing the same. The majority of Dad's conversations have this cryptic quality. This is familiar, and it's reassuring that he's got some kind of plan. There's an edge to his voice though. Like he's trying to solve an equation with too many undefined variables.

I tense again and fight off another shiver.

"We can go into town after dinner," Healy says.

Dad shakes his head. "We shouldn't do anything out of the ordinary. We should ride in tomorrow. Like usual."

Ramona sighs. "This thing with the banks has people spooked, Max. Bill Collins is guarding the general store with a shotgun. There ain't no more ordinary."

"This is what he wants, you know," Annika whispers. "My father. He wants this kind of control over people and their lives."

MacKenna snorts. "Power that benefits *you* enormously."

Annika stares right at me and says, "If you're lucky, you'll live long enough to understand that there's no upside to being the daughter of the devil."

Toby nods, and it takes all my resolve not to kick him under the table too.

The conversation at the other table continues. "...and it's too late to turn back," Healy adds, stabbing at the dish of butter on their table.

"We'll go tonight, then," Dad agrees. "Bob and I can—"

"Bob's got the damn cows to deal with," Ramona interrupts. "Even way out here, we get cable news. We were all staring at your handsome face for hours on end before you got here. I'll go. With your girl. We won't attract much notice and if we do, I bet she knows how to handle herself. We'll ride by Doc Truman's place on the way back." I'm surprised by this plan, and also surprised that the lady even knows I exist. She's been doing a great imitation of a person in a coma since we pulled up in the truck.

At our table, Navarro squirms in his chair and clears his throat. "Mrs. Healy, I'm not sure that's such a great idea... I think I should... I mean..."

I lean back into my chair to catch his gaze for an instant. His face turns red. Does he think I can't handle myself? I almost broke his nose and kept Tork from beating him to death. I'm torn between pangs of anger and gratitude. He *is* trying to keep me from getting stuck with Ammon Carver's mom. And maybe something else too.

Ramona cocks her head. "Son, I grew up on a ranch with a thousand head of Brahman cattle. I am well acquainted with Messrs. Remington and Winchester. Of this there is no doubt." She reaches up to fiddle with one of her braids. "Before you were a figment of your grandparents' imagination, I was riding to and fro across this desert all by my lonesome."

My dad says nothing and this silences Navarro.

"I should go," Mom says. "I don't like the idea of Jinx being out after dark, things being what they are."

Dad shakes his head. "Someone needs to deal with Charles's medication and monitor Miss Carver. Plus, I can use all the help I can get loading up the truck."

Annika straightens her shoulders at the sound of her name.

Mom continues to shake her head.

But Dad doesn't budge. "Jinx will be fine. I trained her myself."

Even though I'm not in love with this plan, the truth is that going to get supplies myself is a good idea. Dad likes to think that he thinks of everything. He doesn't.

Refocusing on my plate, I eat several more pieces of chicken. I can't remember the last time I ate so much. Or when green beans tasted quite so good. After dinner, I'm slow and sluggish. I thank Navarro and MacKenna and begin stacking the plates at our table. It seems fair that I should clean up when they did all the cooking.

Ramona is growing more animated by the minute. "Bob, it'll be dark soon. Time to see about the cattle."

He nods and exits through the front door. My dad goes too.

Ramona grabs the candles off her table and moves into the kitchen. I bring a stack of plates in and take a place in front of the kitchen sink. Toby and Charles carry in dirty dishes as I rinse.

She stands next to me. "You probably want to go get yourself cleaned up a bit. We'll get on the trail in thirty minutes or so. The bathroom is up the hall. Second door on the left. I had Max put your bags in the spare room. That's the first door." She's dismissing me from the kitchen. I take the hint and move up the hall.

MacKenna's already in the spare room when I get there. She's sitting on the edge of the room's double bed and waving a candle across a short bookshelf against the wall opposite the door. She pulls out a beat-up hardcover. It's a Larry McMurtry Western. *"Comanche Moon,"* she reads off the cover. "It figures."

"I have to take a shower," I say. "And then I'm riding into town."

She turns to me. "So, you're leaving me here to babysit your brother and the beauty queen?"

"You can come if you want to," I say. I'm not totally sure if this is true. I assume that the ranch has more than two horses, but who knows. "Navarro can keep an eye on Charles."

MacKenna scowls. She's holding the candle under her chin like she's about to tell spooky ghost stories. "*I* don't want to go. I want to know why you're so eager to ride off to the OK Corral with that creepy old woman."

I spot my pack in one of the corners and dig out the last clean set of clothes. "I'm not *so eager*," I tell her. "Look, sooner or later one of us is going to have a period. Do you think my dad and Mr. Healy will be packing those kinds of supplies?"

She pauses and then nods slowly. "Okay. Point taken," she says. "Get me some deodorant. And lip balm."

I'm back in the hall in the doorway of the bathroom when she adds, "And cold cream."

I poke my head back in the door. "Will you…do me a favor? While I'm gone? Maybe…um…keep an eye on things?"

"Things?" she repeats with an expression on her face that makes me regret asking.

"Never mind," I mutter as I step into the hallway again.

She comes to the door. "What things are you talking about?"

"You don't think that conversation at the dinner table was a little weird?"

MacKenna snorts. "Every conversation I've been in since Monday has been a little weird."

"Forget it."

The instant I close and lock the bathroom door, the room's overhead light pops on. The yellowish globe fades in and out. Like the rest of the house, the bathroom and shower are small. An odd aquamarine wallpaper with funny sketches of people in the shower covers the walls. I run my fingers over a drawing of a woman with a mermaid's tail.

I glance at my reflection in the mirror. I look like complete crap. The area around my eye, where that soldier elbowed me, has swollen and is surrounded by a purplish black ring. I've got scratches all over my chest from rolling through the asphalt. I. Am. A. Mess.

My appearance makes Ramona Healy's rationale for our ride all the more ridiculous. On what planet are an old woman and a teenage girl, who looks like she's been beat all to hell, horseback riding at night not going to attract a lot of attention?

Sigh.

It's Thursday night.

I leave my dirty clothes on the tile floor, step into the porcelain claw-foot tub and pull the blue curtain closed. The silver shower knobs could stand some grease.

Warm water runs over my body. It stings a bit when it gets to my feet. I've got some deep gashes down there. I do my best to clean them up with soap but I'll have to break out the first-aid kit later.

After I dry myself off, I find a comb in one of the bathroom drawers and do the best I can with my hair. Dressed in black leggings and a blue sweatshirt, I return to the spare room and dig around in my pack. My windbreaker is so filthy that I don't want to wear it, so I shove what I can into my pockets. Dad's stashed most of the good stuff someplace else, so all I end up with is a miniature flashlight, a pocketknife, a bit of twine and a book of matches. MacKenna is no longer in the room. I set off to find her.

Ramona Healy waits right outside the door. "Take the path straight. Go out the house gate and turn right. You'll hit the stables. Can't miss it. I'll meet you there directly."

I go through the living room. Toby and Annika are gone again. My dad and MacKenna sit on the couch, both reading cowboy novels from the spare room. It's an odd sight. My dad's gaze travels along the page like he's really interested in his book, which hilariously is called *The Lonely Men*. Next to him on the sofa, MacKenna shakes her head and frowns at *Comanche Moon*.

"I'm going," I say. They both sort of nod.

I let the screen door slam behind me and pass Mom and Jay on the porch.

"Be careful," Jay says, patting me on the back as I pass.

Outside, it's not quite dark but it will be soon. The lights on inside the Healys' house stand in stark contrast to the barren, brushy landscape.

I turn on my flashlight and kick up dust as I walk down the path.

The stables are easy to find. The building is much larger than the house. It's probably painted some shade of green as well, but it's tough to tell exactly. Daylight is almost gone and the outside of the stables is lit by a single yellow light attached to the wall.

I put my flashlight in my pocket and duck inside the door.

These people sure love their horses. Rustic lights hang from the high ceiling and soft piano music plays from a radio sitting on a bench. On either side of me, I find wide gated stalls. I count six on each side.

The first two stalls are labeled Goldilocks and Jesse's Girl. The other stalls are also full. A black horse pokes its head over the door of the third stall, revealing an interesting pattern of white spots on its neck. These are not all the same kind of horse, and I wish MacKenna was here to identify them.

It's pretty clean in the stable. I move through slowly. On the side opposite the door, I find bundles of hay, stacks of feed bags and some plastic containers. Saddles hang from pegs on the wall.

My heart stops at the sound of shuffling behind me.

Crap.

I was so mesmerized by the horses that I didn't check out the room. Or the ranch, for that matter. Something about it feels safe. But it's not. I should have done some recon. That would have been smart.

Unlike my best plan right now, which is to use the flashlight as some kind of weapon and fist fight as best I can. Which is really stupid. I brace myself.

"Relax," a voice says.

It's Navarro.

I can't relax though. "You scared the hell out of me."

He steps out of an unlit corner. "Shh!" he says. "I'm sorry. I should have said something but you looked...almost happy."

Before I can say anything, he continues, "She'll be here any second." He slips out of his own windbreaker and hands it to me. "If there's one thing I know, it's that you can never trust women like Ramona Carver."

He leans in very close, his brown eyes only inches from mine.

For a second it's like he's going to...

My heart races. I close my eyes.

Light footsteps approach the door.

Ramona is coming.

I open my eyes in time to see Navarro step back into the darkness.

I put the jacket on. It's still warm and smells of whatever kind of musky cologne Navarro must wear. Where is he getting cologne from?

As the door swings open, I realize why he gave me this thing.

It's got a knife in one pocket and the SAT phone in the other.

DR. DOOMSDAY SAYS:

YOU CAN LIE TO EVERYONE BUT YOURSELF.

The spotted horse is an Appaloosa named Freckles. He steps back from the stall door when I approach him.

"You've got the jitters," Ramona says.

I look at her blankly.

"That's what my daddy always used to say." She smiles. "City folk have the jitters. The animals can tell. You can't let 'em get the upper hand though."

She throws open the wide gate doors to the stable and then saddles Freckles while I watch, feeling very out of my element. "Your sister says to tell you that she'd prefer *cherry* lip balm, but between you and me that is *very* optimistic. Bill Collins don't keep a real good selection of toiletries in the best of times. And these are not the best of times."

I'm startled by her mention of MacKenna. She's been paying more attention than I thought. There's also something really off about her demeanor. It's like she belongs on this ranch. Not at Carver Commons in New York. "But aren't *you* city folk?" I ask her.

Ramona disappears for a second and returns with another saddle. She draws a gorgeous reddish-brown horse from the stall next to Freckles's. "No, ma'am. I am from Wilcox, Arizona. My daddy had a ranch up in those parts. Back in the days before man-made meat. He was a good man but not a good *business*man. To make a bit of extra money…well, see, we had a few cabins on the property, and my daddy had this idea to rent them out to out-of-towners. Let 'em see what it's really like to work a ranch. That's how I met my husband. Not Bob. My first husband. The Carvers came to our place one summer. I don't think my daddy ever really cared for Cornelius, but he wanted me provided for. The feeling was, I suppose, quite mutual, as the Carvers did not care for me much either. I was too unrefined for them. I think Cornelius meant to make some kind of a point by getting hitched to a working-class girl and not a duchess. But it's always unwise to do things that run contrary to your deepest nature. It's like riding against the wind. My husband found out the hard way. You can take the girl off the ranch but…"

She draws her horse toward the open gate and clearly expects me to do the same. It takes a couple of tries because Freckles doesn't like me and because I haven't ridden a horse since sixth grade summer camp.

Ramona calls out, "Come on now, Freckles!" and this gets the horse going.

Outside in the cool night, the moon rises. It's not as hard to see as I thought it would be.

Ramona shuts the stable doors and mounts her horse. I awkwardly do the same, almost falling back on my first try.

"You fall a lot? Is that how you got your nickname?" she asks.

"No," I say shortly as my face heats up.

We ride in silence for a bit. Freckles is familiar with the terrain and I don't have to do too much other than trot alongside Ramona. This would be a nice experience were it not for the fact that civilization is about to collapse and I'm in the middle of nowhere with a loony old lady.

"It's hard to explain," Ramona says as if she's replying to a question I haven't asked.

"What?" I ask.

"I faked my own death and ran away from my family. You want to know what kind of person does that. And why. Those are natural questions. With complicated answers."

"Are you afraid of your own son?" I ask. She's right. I have a million questions, but this one seems the most pressing.

For a minute or so, there's no response other than the soft tread of the horses' hooves against the dirt path. "In the beginning," Ramona says, "I told myself that was the reason. That I was afraid. Afraid I would never have a life outside of my son's control. He can be very domineering. And dangerous, like his daddy. Also like his daddy, Ammon's got the idea that a man's family should be, on the main, very loyal servants. Before I left, my son wasn't yet in politics, but he was already so ruthless. He caused the mortgage crisis. Made a fortune making bad loans. Then again from insurance payments when people defaulted. Then again when he evicted them and sold their houses out from under them."

Ramona turns her profile up toward the white moon. "My husband died. I was a well-to-do, privileged lady. All I had to do was show up in my white gloves and fancy hat whenever my boy wanted to cut a red ribbon with a giant pair of scissors. Yet I couldn't stop thinking about those summers back on the ranch. How I'd get up before dawn. The feeling of the smooth leather of the saddles when I polished them. The way I'd be so tired at the end of the day from bailing hay or helping Momma in the kitchen. It's not the same kind of tired that you get from tryin' to sit all day long with your legs crossed just so or keepin' a smile on your face."

Okay. Life as a Park Avenue socialite totally sucked. But. So what? "That's why you did it? You let everyone think you were dead? You wanted to come home?"

The old woman focuses her attention on her horse, patting its neck softly. "When he was six years old, my son pushed a neighbor boy out the second-story window of our house in Nantucket. They were arguing over a game of backgammon. We covered it up, of course. Even in those days, people were starting to ask questions." She turns to me, mostly silhouetted in the moonlight, with long shadows falling across her face. I can't make out her expression.

I pull the windbreaker tighter around me. There's nothing left of Navarro's warmth. The desert temperature continues to drop, and it's like the ghosts of Ramona Carver's past are riding alongside us.

"It took me a long time to understand. I'm not running from my son. I'm running from myself," she finishes. "From the guilt I feel. The role I played."

Up ahead, I can make out a series of red lights, possibly flares or emergency lanterns, placed in a pattern on the ground. "What about Annika?" I ask.

Ramona stares at the red lights as well. "When I was a girl, I had two kittens. Both calicos. Beautiful animals. They found a litter of baby rats in the barn. Raised 'em as their own. Got them food and water. Kept 'em in a warm spot, covered in hay. Away from the goats."

I fight off the urge to sigh dramatically. We're getting closer to a square, isolated building that's pretty much a minimart for the zombie apocalypse, and Ramona Healy is telling pointless stories from a million years ago in a tone of voice usually reserved for the eulogy at a funeral. "I don't understand. What does that mean? What…what…"

Freckles snorts and her gait slows.

"The point, Miss Marshall, is this. What happens when a predator tries to raise its own prey? It's a question we all must have an answer to. Given what lies ahead."

What lies ahead. Tork had said this too. A bit of dust catches in my throat.

Also. "What happened to the rats?"

Ramona tightens her hold on her reins. "What always happens. The cats got hungry and ate 'em."

Okay.

The details of the scene ahead become clearer. It's a long, low building that we must be approaching from the rear because there's only a single, narrow door. It's lit by a lone yellow lightbulb on the right. A couple of four-wheel ATVs are parked haphazardly near the side farthest from the door.

"So now you're for The Spark?" I ask her.

She makes an impatient noise. "I think I'm too old to be for The Spark, girlie. They think they can use *the laws* to make everything fair for everybody. To put a chicken in every pot. Except their laws don't often account for the fact that somebody has to feed the chickens and someone has to manufacture the pots. They want to change the world. Well, when you get to be my age, you stop believin' the world *can* change. Most people won't even change their haircut."

A gunshot rings out.

Ramona reaches out and grabs my reins, keeping a tight

grip on both horses and muttering, "Whoa…whoa now," a few times. They come to a stop.

I wonder if Freckles can hear my heart.

The desert is so vast and empty that it's hard to tell where the sound came from. Before I can register the acid flooding my stomach, a hooded figure ducks around the corner of the market and climbs onto one of the ATVs. I jump at the sound of its motor turning to a start.

Another shot. A low blast. Probably some kind of shotgun.

I fight back my panic.

The engine fades as the ATV makes good time away from us.

"Let's go!" Ramona tells me. She drops my reins.

This is the first sensible thing the lady's said all day. I'm hoping she'll help me get Freckles turned around as I can't see the horse taking that kind of direction from me. Instead, my mouth falls open in horror as Ramona urges her own horse forward.

Toward the gunfire.

"Get a move on it, girl!" she says.

I try to do what I saw her do. Pull up and down quickly on the reins. Freckles shakes her spotted head a couple of times and whinnies. Her body shimmies underneath me. It's as if she'd like nothing better than to be rid of me and away from here. She doesn't want to go either.

Smart horse.

This is going to be okay. Great even. Me and Freckles will just hang here.

When Ramona is midway between me and the store when she shouts back, "Aw. Come on now, Freckles!"

With one last snort, Freckles takes off at a pace slightly faster than Ramona's horse. Ramona slides gracefully out of her saddle as I pass through the perimeter of red lanterns. She reaches out, stops Freckles and waits as I pretty much fall down, kicking up a cloud of dust. Ramona sighs as she leads both horses toward one of the red lanterns. There's not really anywhere to tie the horses, so she stands there holding both sets of reins.

Ammon Carver's mother glows completely red, like the sanctuary candle at church back home. I blink a few times. It's almost like the old woman flickers.

She motions for me to follow her. "Have your weapon ready," she says.

"What are you talking about?" I whisper, I step closer to her. Close enough that I can see her lips pressed in a thin, white line.

She moves into the shadows near the market wall. "Come on, now. Between your daddy and that Spanish fella who's madly in love with you, I know one of them woulda set you up with a gun or something," she says. "If ever there was a time to have one handy, this would be it."

I have a knife.

I also have a phone.

Ramona kneels down to mess with a potted plant in the ground. She returns with a key, holding it up and out of the shadows. She nods toward the door. "Okay. You go in the back. I'll go in the front and…"

Even though I approach the door, I'm already shaking my head. That's a terrible idea. Not only is it an almost exact repeat of what Navarro and I already tried back at the Lone Wolf Diner, I'm not interested in charging into unfamiliar terrain with Annika Carver's grandma. "No. No," I say. "We'll call my dad. He'll know what to do."

"There ain't no cell phone service way out here, girl," Ramona says, unable to keep the impatience out of her voice.

"I have a SAT phone." I remove the phone from my jacket pocket. My index finger hovers over the menu button.

She moves back into the red light, a cold look settling over her face.

Both of us jump at the sound of another shot. A loud, close, higher-pitched shot.

The backdoor swings open, hitting me hard on the side and knocking me to the ground. The phone slides away from me and lands between two lanterns.

I roll onto my back and get my knife ready.

I'm facing a second large figure in a black hoodie.

Cold. Dark. Panic. *Breathe.*

My fingers reach into the jacket pocket and find the knife. I remove it from its holster.

But I needn't have bothered.

The figure falls back against the wall and slumps over, tumbling to the ground.

DR. DOOMSDAY'S GUIDE TO ULTIMATE SURVIVAL

RULE THIRTEEN:

PEOPLE WHO PANIC DON'T SURVIVE.

As I get my bearings, I find myself facing a guy about my age. Streaks of greasy brown hair poke out from the edges of his black hood. He's on his knees, clutching his shoulder.

A terrified, lanky, bug-eyed boy.

He's dropped something on the ground. It's an old gun. Like it should be in a Wild West museum or something. It's silver and perfectly suited to train robbery. I kick it away from the howling guy.

"He...shot me! That...stupid idiot...shot me!"

He gets these words out in between screeches and pants.

I want to run away and hide somewhere. I try to remember the drills. Try to think about what Dad would do. Only I can't imagine my dad would be stuck in *this* stupid situation. I force myself not to shake and move a step closer. "Who...

who shot you? Who are you with? The Opposition?" I say with as much confidence as I can gather.

"Oh good Lord, no," Ramona says. "That's just Derek Dinges. His folks have a place on the other side of Why." She's relaxed quite a bit and seems strangely at ease considering all the blood running out of the kid's arm.

Oh God. More blood.

Don't throw up.

"He shot me… Leelo…fu—" Dinges says again.

"Watch your language, boy," a deep male voice says. An old man emerges from the back door and props it open with a potted plant. He stands next to Ramona.

"Howdy, Bill," she says with a nod. This must be the store owner.

"Ma'am," he says, tipping his cattleman hat.

"This is my great-niece Susan, visiting from Flagstaff," Ramona says, pointing to me.

"My language?" Derek moans, disrupting these pleasantries. "Watch my goddamn language? Your dumbass clerk shot me!"

"That's what you get," Collins says. "You and your brother come in here, tryin' to rob me. And look what happened. You got your ass shot. That's what."

"Stow your weapon, miss," Collins tells me.

I put my knife away and get a better look at him. The deep lines in his face. The Wranglers. This guy probably sleeps in his cowboy hat.

Ramona tosses the horses' reins to Collins, shrugs out of her flannel shirt and approaches Dinges, coming to kneel beside him.

"You…you…stay away from me, woman. I want…the doctor. Not some damn…damn witch tryinta take care of me," he says.

"I have to stop the bleeding," she tells him tersely.

"I want the damn doctor," Dinges says again.

A second male voice responds. "What makes you think *I* want you?" It's coming from around the corner. A second later, a tall, slim man rounds the side of the building. He too is clad in a felt cowboy hat and jeans.

"Ah. Doc Truman. Ain't this convenient," Ramona says.

I'm not sure if she means convenient because of Annika or because of Dinges.

"You know where to find me," the doctor responds. "I'm here most nights. Typically, this fine establishment *does* manage to have some beer on hand."

Collins snorts. "You been watchin' the news same as me. Deliveries are delayed on account of all the roadblocks. And it ain't my fault that anyone with a bit of cash in their pocket is hell-bent on hoarding supplies."

"Would you mind tellin' me who's hoarding the beer?" the doctor asks.

Collins opens his mouth to answer but is cut off by another wail.

Dinges slumps down with his back to the store wall. "You gotta fix me up."

"You need to go to the hospital, son," Truman responds.

"In Ajo? Oh come on!" Dinges answers. He's taking shallow breaths. I have to give it to the guy. His tolerance for pain must be high. Most people would be screaming their heads off or would have passed out by now. "It's just a shoulder wound. Can't you fix me up here?"

"Hell's bells." Truman puts his hands on his hips. "Just a shoulder wound? Just like on TV, right? Oh sure. I'll dig out the bullet with my goddamn fingers, put your arm in a sling and we'll all live happily ever after. Son, that ain't real life. If you don't get to a damn hospital within the next few hours or so, worst-case scenario is you'll bleed to death, best-case scenario is you'll lose the use of your right arm."

"Will your brother come back for you?" Collins asks.

"Andy'll wait for me over by where Gunn Loop breaks off into the trail," Dinges says.

The doctor motions for Dinges to scoot into the light coming through the doorway. He takes the shirt from Ramona and kneels down beside the boy, being careful to stay out of the light. Dinges groans as Truman wraps the shirt tight around his arm. "Hard to tell just by looking whether or not the brachial artery's been hit. You need a surgeon."

I'm supposed to be getting supplies but, more than anything, right now, I want to get out of here.

"Aren't you at least gonna call the cops?" Dinges asks through clenched teeth.

"What cops?" Collins growls. Freckles snorts and backs up. "Ain't it such that the whole reason you felt so damn comfortable with the idea of helping yourself to the contents of my cash register is the fact that there're no cops anywhere near here?"

"I said I was sorry!" Dinges says. "Anyway. Leelo shot me!"

Collins pays no attention to this. "After what went down on the backroads today, what law enforcement we *did* have is either dead or laid up at County General."

He's talking about our wreck in the desert. I turn my face away.

"You can say hi to 'em when you get there." Doc Truman stands up and takes a couple of steps back from the door.

Ramona rises as well and casts me an uneasy look. I wish she'd say something about the supplies. Or do something to move things along.

Dinges pleads with Collins. "On the radio, they're sayin' the banks might not reopen this week. Some people are sayin' they might not reopen…at all."

"They'll fix the computers, son. The banks will reopen," the doctor says.

He's trying to be reassuring, but the combination of the odd shadows falling across his face and the fact that he has no idea what my dad has done to the bank computers makes my blood run even colder.

"I'll get Leelo to ride you out to the trail," Collins says.

"Susan? Susan?"

Ramona's calling out this name. I snap to attention. "Um. Yeah? Yes?"

She's holding out a couple of large canvas sacks for me to take. "Run inside and send Leelo out. Then pick up what we need."

Desperate to get away from Derek Dinges, I don't hang around.

The conversation continues as I walk into a small supply room. "I don't want to go nowhere with Leelo," Dinges says.

Ramona and Collins ignore him.

There are shelves on either side of me. Collins has extra toilet paper back here, along with bags of charcoal and supplies like toothpaste and mouthwash. There's one whole shelf full of mayonnaise, mustard and ketchup bottles of various sizes, which strikes me as odd given the small size of the stockroom.

"I guess you're robbin' me too, huh?" Collins asks Ramona.

Her voice grows faint as I approach a doorway covered by a set of plastic strip curtains. "You know I'm good for it. Anyhow, I don't think it's gonna come as much of a shock that the free market economy has largely been suspended around here."

I glance behind me to find I've left a set of dusty footprints on the concrete floor.

Collins chuckling softly is the last thing I hear before I duck through the plastic strips.

A typical minimart is on the opposite side of the plastic. Many of the shelves desperately need to be restocked. To my right, the wall is lined with a near-empty refrigerator. There's one lone gallon of milk. The shelves underneath the BEER! sign are totally empty.

I creep around in between shelves half-full of Donettes and Twinkies and almost fall over when a voice says, "We're closed."

This must be Leelo.

Moving with more purpose, I follow the direction of the sound to a counter in the front where a guy sits cross-legged on top of an old-fashioned glass case full of cigarettes.

"We're closed," he repeats, not looking up from the *Dirt Bike* magazine he's reading. He's wearing a maroon T-shirt with the words PHILOSOPHIZE WITH A HAMMER printed in white block letters on it.

I spend a split second wondering what that statement could possibly even mean.

"We're gonna start closing at dark," he continues, reaching up to press a stray brown lock into place with the rest of his slicked back hair. "Until things get back to normal. By the way, you can't just sneak in the back when the front door is locked."

The guy is pretty calm considering he shot somebody about two minutes ago. "Are you Leelo?"

His eyes snap up. "I'm Lee. *Lee.* How many times do I have to tell that old coot cowboy I don't go by Leelo anymore? Who are you?"

His intensity renews my nervousness. "I'm…uh. They told me that they need you outside. They need you to give some guy named Derek Dinges a ride."

Lee hops off the counter. "Can't Double Dee get home the same way he got here?"

"Well, you did shoot him." I'm distracted by what looks like an e-tablet on the counter where Lee was seated. I approach cautiously.

"We have a stand-your-ground law in this state, you know."

When I don't answer, Lee adds, "This ain't New York City. Where someone can rob you and then send you a bill for the gas for their getaway car. He had a gun, you know."

I'm at the counter and I rest my arm on the e-tablet, the *Southern Arizona Tribune* displays on the screen. The main headline is about the bombs at the bank.

I can't stop myself from snorting. "That old Colt. I doubt that thing even works. It belongs in a museum."

He squints at me the way you do at someone you think you ought to recognize. It occurs to me that this guy might have seen my face on the news.

I should have stayed by the Twinkies.

And kept my mouth shut.

I decide to cut my losses. "Well. Anyway. They want you outside."

"Right." He gives me a skeptical glance and heads toward the plastic curtain.

"Wait," I say. Something inside me makes me stop him. Everything is such an unresolved mess. Maybe I can figure out one thing. Just one.

"Your shirt. What does it mean?"

He freezes in the doorway. "It's a quote. By Nietzsche," he says with finality. As if this pronouncement not only has explained his shirt but somehow also unlocked all the secrets of the universe.

I frown. "Okay…"

Lee drops the piece of the plastic curtain he's holding and faces me, getting an even better look at my face. "We need to be both intelligent and brutal. Like Caesar. Or Napoleon. The world should be a meritocracy dominated by those who can control it." He sighs. "To put it in a way you can understand, it's the idea that you need to be brainy and brawny. Because only the strong will survive."

This guy hasn't spent his entire life with the world's foremost expert on disaster drilling. Otherwise he'd know that's not how things work.

God. I can't even get one small victory. Even this one thing can't be explained. Whatever the hell that quote means, I'm pretty sure Lee's monologue has nothing to do with it. "Napoleon was defeated by the Duke of Wellington. Caesar was assassinated and caused a civil war. My mom says no one really understands Nietzsche."

Lee's cheeks flush pink. "Your mom is wrong."

He turns to leave again.

"If you think only the strong should survive, why go out there?" I ask, making one last desperate attempt to get a straight answer. "That guy isn't strong. He came in to rob a store with a weapon that barely works, got himself shot and can't make it to a hospital. But you're going to help him?"

There's a pause. "You're one of them, aren't you?"

Just like that, my rage is gone. Replaced again by cold panic. "Who?" I've probably wasted so much time with this guy that he's recognized me.

"*Them*. You're for Rosenthal," he says with a scowl.

"Everyone's for Rosenthal," I say out of habit.

Lee's already on the other side of the curtain when he says, "No, we're not."

That conversation was a mistake.

It gave too much away. Made me too memorable.

I really have to get going.

Given that we need supplies now more than we did before, I start collecting what I can. Ramona is right. It doesn't look like there was ever much of a selection, but even what was there is mostly gone. I pack one bag full of all the sundries I can. I'm able to get a couple of boxes of tampons, a jar of face lotion, three plain lip balms and a couple sticks of male deodorant. Dad always says to get whatever medicine you can find which, in this case, is a bottle of cough syrup, a few of rolls of antacids and tube of hydrocortisone cream.

I move on to the food, going for things that have a long shelf life and don't need to be refrigerated. I end up with a bunch of beef jerky, cereal bars, semi-stale cookies and as many bags of salted pretzels as I can fit in the large burlap sack. The minimart is totally out of bottled water, so I'll have to hope that Dad has that covered with enough canteens to get by.

As I pass back through the plastic curtain, traces of a hushed conversation drift in from outside. Ramona is speaking in a tone barely above a whisper, and I catch only a few phrases. Generic things like, "you know what" and "too many years" and "he doesn't know."

I glance around the shelves in the stockroom for anything useful but don't find much beyond condiments and paper products. Then it hits me.

Nobody is answering Ramona.

I pat the pockets of my windbreaker.

I dropped the phone and didn't pick it up.

The overhead lightbulb flickers.

Without taking another breath, I hustle out the back door.

Ramona Healy is alone, cradling the SAT phone face-down in her left hand.

But the darkness the of desert night gives her away.

The phone's screen gives her away.

Her palm glows orange from its lit screen.

She called someone, and I have to find out who.

DR. DOOMSDAY SAYS:

IN A DISASTER SITUATION, YOUR PRINCIPLES WILL ALWAYS BE PITTED AGAINST YOUR ODDS OF SURVIVAL.

"Who were you talking to?" I demand.

I glance around. The ATV is gone and, in fact, its engine grumbles off in the distance. Lee and Derek have left for town. The doctor is gone too.

Ramona shuffles closer to her horse. "You dropped this," she says, shaking the phone a couple of times. She doesn't give it back to me though.

"I heard you talking to someone," I say, struggling to stay calm. "I don't know why you're bothering to deny it. The SAT phone keeps a log of incoming and outgoing calls. I'll be able to see the number you dialed."

My open hand hovers in the space between us.

A heavy car door slams and Bill Collins rounds the corner of the building. "The Opposition knows Marshall is here. Trouble is coming sooner than we thought."

Ramona still doesn't give me the phone.

The ATV's engine dies down. In the moonlight, I spot two small silhouettes about half a mile away. One is seated on the vehicle and the other, probably Lee, is pacing around it. There's another engine surge and the loud bang of a misfire.

The noise is enough to startle the horses. Ramona's horse whinnies, bucks and knocks into the old woman's shoulder. She makes no effort to stop the phone from falling from her light grasp. Once again, it falls and slides through the dirt.

Right on cue, Freckles steps forward and crushes the phone under her black hoof.

She did that on purpose so I wouldn't be able to see who she called.

"I'm guessing *this* is why they call you Jinx," Ramona says, almost chewing on the words as she spits them out.

"You...you...you..." I sputter. I don't know what makes me angrier. The fact that Ramona destroyed the phone. Or the fact that she's blaming me.

She rubs her arm and grimaces. "*You* better think very carefully how you plan to finish that sentence, girl," Ramona says, her voice icy and stern. She's drawn herself up to her full height and the pleasant, folksy veneer falls from her long face. A cold, hard statue casts a shadow over me. *This* is the woman who gave birth to Ammon Carver.

Collins steps between the two of us. "Carver's people are already in town. It won't be long until they show up here." He glances disapprovingly at me. "You need to get on the road as quick as possible. When they get here, I'll give 'em something to worry about. I'll buy you as much time as I can. I reckon it won't be much though."

He reaches inside the back door, pulls out a folded-up lawn chair and turns the lights inside the minimart off, leaving us with only the red lanterns.

Ramona tries to steady her horse, which never quite calmed

down after the noise. She takes the bags from me, ties them to her saddle and mounts the horse. "Don't do anything stupid."

I'm tempted to keep on arguing with her, but the sight of Collins unfolding his lawn chair stops me. He has the air of a man who knows what's coming for him and has decided to greet the inevitable with a defiant dignity. He sinks into his seat and tugs the brim of his hat, pulling it farther down his forehead.

Collins shrugs, his face shrouded in darkness. "You oughta consider takin' your own advice."

I get into Freckles's saddle as best I can, eyeing the phone's smashed circuit board on the ground as I climb up. Something makes me remember what Lee said and I turn back. "Mr. Collins? Are you for Rosenthal?"

He snorts. "I'm for runnin' my store, keepin' my own house in order and doin' right by anyone who crosses my path. I leave everything else to a higher authority."

This sounds like something I would have said a few days ago. But now, that kind of detachment feels off. I said all politicians are the same. Well. Carver and Rosenthal no longer seem the same.

At all.

"Well. If you don't care what happens, why are you helping us?" I ask.

"I didn't say I don't care," Collins says. "I said I'm for doing what's right. And what Ramona's boy is doing ain't right."

Ramona urges her horse forward, leaving Collins behind in his lawn chair.

The ATV is gone and the desert has fallen into silence again. Lee and Dinges are tiny dots, barely distinguishable from the brush. We ride toward the ranch. I'm about to ask about the phone again when Ramona speaks.

"This conflict is bigger than you, girl. I hope you understand that," Ramona says. "If my son becomes the ruler of this world, any number of people will suffer a terrible fate. Max Marshall may be the only man alive who represents a serious challenge to my son."

My shoulders fall slack and sullen. "My dad helped Ammon Carver get elected. What makes you think he can stop him? Or that he even wants to?" Usually, all Dad wanted to do was run. Or hide. But he came for us at Goldwater Airfield.

And he seemed to have his own army.

My blood runs as cold as the winter desert night.

Ramona doesn't answer my question. She quickens the pace of her horse, putting some space between us and making things tougher on me because Freckles knows who's boss. And it's not me.

There's clearly not going to be any more discussion about the phone. Plus, if Ramona was out to make me feel freaked out, she succeeded.

Yet there's no denying that Ramona called someone. But seriously. Who? Maybe my dad? But how would she have gotten his number? Why wouldn't she just tell me she called him? No. It was someone else. It had to be.

We can't trust Ramona Carver. She gave birth to the most dangerous man alive. Faked her own death. Lied to her family. Who knows what kind of resources she has? She must know people. Rich and powerful people.

She's Ammon Carver's mother.

I spend the rest of the ride back trying to goad Freckles into catching up with Ramona. It doesn't work. She's got the horse too well trained.

The clip-clop of Freckles's steady pace creates a falsely comfortable lull.

Ramona bypasses the stable and rides directly to the house. By the time I pass through the gate, she's tied her horse to a post and gone inside. I do the same.

There's a Jeep in front of the brightly lit house.

Through the large window, I see Dr. Truman examining Annika's leg while Toby watches from a nearby chair. Ramona must have spoken to the doctor while I was in the store. My dad moves in front of the window, in deep conversation with the doctor.

For some weird reason, all the concern for Carver's daughter stings. I expected Toby or at least my dad to come out to meet me and ask how things went. Instead, everyone's top priority is Annika Carver's bullet wound.

I don't immediately see MacKenna, who launches herself off the porch and meets me in the center of the yard.

"We have a problem," she says.

Oh God. Here we go. "I know," I say. It's so lame that I want to cry.

She blocks me. "What are you talking about?"

I sigh way too melodramatically. "I totally screwed up. I let that old lady get ahold of the phone and I'm pretty sure the doofus in the minimart recognized me." I move to side-step her and go into the house. I have to talk to Dad. The Opposition is coming.

"Really?" she asks, becoming interested. But then she shakes her head. "No, nevermind that now. Look. Navarro's gone."

"What?" Gus *cannot* be gone.

"You heard me," she says. But she comes a bit closer and lowers her voice. "After you left, I followed Dr. Doomsday—"

"You did?" I ask.

"You asked me to. You asked me to keep an eye on things," she says, scowling. "He went over behind the barn—"

"Since when do you ever do what I *ask*?" I say, stuck on that point.

"If and *when* you ask me to do things that make sense, I will do them. Anyway—"

"The barn?" I glance around. Another chill settles over me. I'm stalling. She's trying to tell me something I don't want to know.

Navarro cannot be gone.

"Do you want to hear this or not?" She points to a large structure behind the stables. "That's the barn. Anyway. Dr. Doomsday went over there. Then Stephanie and my dad show up and they're talking for a while—"

Where they couldn't be seen from the house.

"—and I couldn't get that close but it sounded like my dad was saying something like, 'the only thing that matters is that the kids are safe,' and Stephanie was crying and your dad was standing there looking like a cyborg the way he always does. Then Doomsday goes back in the house and there's more crying and my dad patting Stephanie on the back—"

Something creeps across my arm and I instinctively smack it, leaving the remains of a fire ant in my palm. I begin to itch. "Okay! But what does this have to do with Navarro?"

"I'm getting to that. After a while, *my* dad goes back to the house too. Then it was like someone flipped a switch. Stephanie starts talking on the phone—"

"Ramona said there's no cell service out here."

Mom has a SAT phone?

"You think she was talking to Ramona Healy?"

MacKenna's expression shifts into worry. This is what she looks like most of the time now. "Ramona? Why?"

"I told you. Ramona Healy used the phone when we were

at the minimart. I had one of the SAT phones. Navarro gave it to me."

"*Had* the phone?" MacKenna asks, momentarily distracted.

"Yeah. I *had* it. Then, Ramona got ahold of it. Now…now, well, it's gone. Ramona got the horse to crush it. Otherwise, I would have been able to see who she called." I can't explain what happened in some way that doesn't sound ridiculous.

MacKenna's reached the point where her impatience overpowers her curiosity. "Yeah. Whatever. Sorry I asked. Anyway. Stephanie was out there pacing around and talking into the phone. She said something like, 'You have no appreciation of the reality on the ground.' Does that mean anything to you?"

I shake my head. That doesn't sound like Mom. Why would she say that kind of thing to Ramona Healy? "No. But what does any of this have to do with Navarro?" I crane my neck around, expecting to see him any second.

"He came out here after Stephanie got off the phone. They got into it. But they kept it down so, no, I don't know what they said." She kicks a small rock with the toe of her shoe.

My mouth falls open. "Navarro got into an argument with *my mom*?"

MacKenna glances in the direction of the barn. "All I know is that a couple of minutes later Navarro went inside the house, packed up his stuff and took off."

"On foot?"

"Yeah," she says, suddenly small and quiet.

My coldness is replaced by a much warmer panic. Navarro left the ranch. On foot. When The Opposition is on the way. I walk to the wooden fence and scan the landscape. It's absolutely silent, dark and empty. I can't see The Opposition out there yet.

I can't see Gus either.

"I have to find Mom."

I go to the porch. I've got my hand on the screen door when it knocks into me and I find myself face-to-face with my father.

"Have you seen Mom?" I ask, through the screen.

"She's in the barn," he says, pushing the door forward again, clearly trying to signal me to move. "In case you haven't noticed, I'm dealing with a few time-sensitive situations here."

Ever droll. Ever devoid of any human emotions. My father.

"Dad! Navarro is gone and Mom was the last person to see him."

"At least let us out of the door," he says with a sigh.

I scoot back, clearing the way for him. Ramona follows right behind.

Doctor Truman is the last out of the house. "I did the best I could with what I have to work with, Ramona. You know my opinion. The girl should go to the hospital." He tips his hat at us and shakes Dad's hand.

"I wish you luck, Max. You're gonna need it." The doctor gets into the Jeep. It kicks up a cloud of dust as it speeds away.

MacKenna, Ramona, Dad and I form a tight, cramped circle on the porch.

"This discussion is not over, Max," Ramona says.

Dad sidesteps all of us and Ramona is first in line in trailing after him. I'm yet again assigned a low priority.

"You heard what the doctor said, Ramona. It isn't safe for the girl to travel," Dad says as he takes off at a quick walk. I'm about to follow when he says, "The two of you need to get your personal packs organized and bring them out to the truck. We leave in twenty."

MacKenna and I exchange a glance. What truck? We left Dad's truck back in the desert.

"Dad. What about Mom?"

My father runs a hand through his hair. "Jinx, Carver's people are coming and I don't want to be hanging around when they get here. I'm sorry about Navarro, but believe me when I tell you that he can take care of himself. All other conversation will have to wait."

Ramona ignores all of this. "Now, you listen to me you SOB. The doctor says if she travels she might get an infection. If she stays here she'll be killed. Sick beats dead, Max."

Ramona jogs after Dad, who's making a beeline for the barn. Their conversation continues as I head inside the house. MacKenna remains in the doorway, looking unsure of whether to follow me or them.

She follows me.

I ignore Toby and Annika over in the corner on the side of the room farthest from the door, but MacKenna stops. I'm already in the hall when I hear her say, "Doomsday says to get our packs together. We're leaving in twenty."

"I'm not leaving without Annika," Toby tells her.

MacKenna scowls at him. "Your butt is gonna be in that truck if I have to drag you out there by your—"

Their conversation fades as I enter the guest bedroom, being careful not to disturb Charles, who is sprawled out diagonally across the bed, reading a book.

Ramona has tossed the supplies from the minimart onto the floor alongside the row of our disheveled backpacks. I pack for me and Charles. Since MacKenna hasn't come back, I get her stuff together as well, divvying up the tampons, deodorant and lip balm between our bags. This, too, is part of the drill. Never let one person carry all the supplies.

I follow the drills. I do what I'm told. Step by step.

I grab all three packs and hobble down the hall to where Annika is watching Toby and MacKenna argue. Her perfect blond head moves side to side, following the action. As if she'd like nothing better than to grab a bowl of popcorn and enjoy the show.

"The bottom line here is that you don't get to decide—" Toby is saying.

I toss MacKenna's backpack at her feet and sling Charles's over my shoulder. "MacKenna is right. The bottom line *here* is that if Miss Universe can't manage to stuff a pair of pants and a shirt in a bag, she shouldn't be coming with us. We're leaving in fifteen minutes."

Toby's anger shifts toward me. But I don't care. Losing Navarro and getting stuck with Ammon Carver's daughter feels like the worst of all worlds.

I leave the house.

MacKenna stays close to me. It's like she wants to find my mom as much as I do. Her survival skills are getting better. She busts out her flashlight and shines it over the trail. Together, we jog toward the barn.

Light streams from a couple doors that have been propped open by Folgers coffee cans. The large building is made of the same green wood siding as the stables. Dad and Ramona are inside and in the middle of a heated conversation.

"This wasn't part of the deal, Ramona," my dad says. He is in the process of loading supplies into Healy's old truck. He's also got a couple of laptops set up on a worktable. One is connected to a long flight drone. Military grade. I fight off the temptation to ask where he could have possibly gotten it.

Ramona puts her hands on her hips. "I'm changing the deal. You want your kin safe. I want the same."

"You didn't give a damn about that girl until she walked through your front door a few hours ago," Dad says gruffly. He grabs two-gallon jugs of water in each hand and carries them into the horse trailer.

When he comes out, Ramona rounds on him. "I thought she was safe. That she'd be safe. Now I know she's not. It changes things."

Dad sighs.

I come into the center of the barn, near the truck.

Mom and Jay are carrying supplies to the horse trailer.

I jump in front of Mom's path. "I have to talk to you."

Mom looks weird. Like she's dressed up in Ramona Healy's clothes. She's wearing a fancy blue sweater with an old-fashioned white collar. She's styled her hair.

"This isn't the best time, Jinx," she says, looking around me at Dad, who continues to argue with Ramona.

"Mom, what happened with Gus? He's gone. Did you tell him to go?"

MacKenna stands a few paces away but she's watching what's going on.

Mom's brown eyes snap to mine. She hesitates for a second. Thinking hard. When she speaks, it's in a whisper. "You have to listen to me. Your father is a great man. But he doesn't know everything, and one of the things he doesn't know is how to take his own advice. *Trust no one*. Let me tell you, Jinx. That boy *cannot* be trusted."

DR. DOOMSDAY'S GUIDE TO ULTIMATE SURVIVAL

NEVER SURRENDER. DON'T PUT YOUR FATE IN THE HANDS OF YOUR ENEMY.

RULE FOURTEEN:

My heart falls.

She has to be wrong. "Mom, we can't let him wander around in the desert—" Before I can tell her how Navarro got his butt kicked to save me and Charles at the gas station, she puts her hand up.

"I'll explain more when there's time." She puts her arms around me and with a reassuring squeeze says, "I can see why you like him. Sweetheart, sometimes the things we like aren't good for us. We need to focus on getting out of here."

In a louder voice, one meant for MacKenna, she says, "We need to focus on getting *Jay* out of here."

My gaze travels to Jay, who is making trips back and forth between several maple wood cabinets along the wall behind us and a pickup truck with a trailer attached. It's the truck Healy was driving when he picked us up earlier today.

Mom walks past me. I look to MacKenna to make sense of all this, but she too appears to be thinking hard.

Bob Healy enters the barn with a sense of purpose. "They're coming. Just got off the radio with Collins. A few units, probably from Goldwater, were at his store a couple of minutes ago. He said they're using his parking lot as a makeshift command center and are sending patrols to scout things out. One or two vehicles at a time. The good news is we have enough firepower to take 'em. Bad news is, you won't get much of a head start." He joins Jay at the wall and opens the last cabinet in the row.

Guns.

Lots and lots of guns.

Bob Healy begins clicking ammo clips into AKs with speed and precision that would put my dad to shame.

Jay comes to stand in front of the cabinet. "I can't believe this. Carver has been president for three days and he's somehow managed to declare martial law."

Mom puts her hand on his back. "I've been lecturing on this for years. How the military is operating with way too little oversight. Carver clearly got key people to cooperate with him even before he had the legal authority to order action."

Dad shrugs. "Ultimately this manhunt is good for Carver. It will increase fear and panic. What he wants is total control, and there's an astonishing number of people willing to trade freedom for the perception of safety."

Determined to get back to the task at hand, Dad says, "Miss Novak, I need to ask you to go inside and get my son. Ramona, the horses, if you don't mind. Jinx, deal with the drone. I mean the code. Don't touch anything but the laptop."

MacKenna heads for the door.

Before I can ask what the hell my dad is talking about, Ramona cuts in. "Maxwell Marshall, you aren't leaving here in *my* truck with *my* damn horses unless you take the girl."

Dad throws up his hands in exasperation. "Fine. But I make no promises. Our chances for survival are dwindling by the second and Annika Carver isn't ready for this kind of life."

At that moment, Toby brings Annika into the barn. She's an out-of-place princess in the barn full of hay bales and truck parts and machine guns, but she comes to life and stands up a bit straighter. "No disrespect to you, Dr. Marshall, but I know my father a great deal better than you do. I understand better than anyone what he's capable of."

She clearly thinks what Ammon Carver is capable of includes killing his own daughter.

A serene calm has settled over Ramona Healy. "My son sees himself as the salvation of this world. A Moses for modern times, delivering mankind from evils of the heart and of the flesh. 'If I whet my glittering sword, and mine hand take hold on judgment; I will render vengeance to mine enemies, and will reward them that hate me.' Deuteronomy 32:41. Ammon will almost certainly exact vengeance on those who commit the sin of defying him." There's an awkward pause and she finishes with, "I'll see to the horses." Ramona walks, straight and tall, out of the barn.

"Ammon's gone nuts," Dad mutters. "Jinx. The drone." He joins Bob Healy at the gun cabinet. They load guns into the passenger side of the truck.

"Yeah. What do you want me to do with it?" I ask, watching Ramona go.

His shoulders slump in a do-I-have-to-do-everything-myself kind of way. "I figured The Opposition would set up somewhere in town. They're probably going from place to place looking for anyone who might have seen us. So I jotted down the geo-coordinates for a few spots. I've got the code ready to go. All you have to do is enter the coordinates for Collin's market in the right place."

I take slow, heavy footsteps to the worktable on the other

side of the barn but frown in confusion at Dad's setup. There doesn't appear to be a controller. "How are you even going to pilot the thing?"

Dad actually groans. Like he thinks we've had this conversation a million times already or something. "It's a static program. Compile it and then copy it to the SD card I've got in the laptop." He looks up. "I'll insert it in the drone. Don't want you to touch the C-4."

I jump back from the table. "That thing's a bomb? And you won't be able to communicate with it once you launch it?"

"I'll launch it. Just deal with the code. Coordinates and compile."

Okay.

Breathe. Breathe. Breathe.

The drone is long and thin, with elegantly curved edges. Dad has painted it black to attract little attention at night. It's like a fancy little rocket for tiny space people.

Oh. Also. A bomb that could kill us all.

I tap the trackpad on the laptop, and the screen powers on. I see Dad's code.

```
if ((mDeviceController != null) &&
(ARCONTROLLER_DEVICE_STATE_ENUM.ARCONTROLLER_DEVICE_
STATE_STOPPED.equals(mState))) {
    ARCONTROLLER_ERROR_ENUM error = mDeviceController.
    start();
        if (error == ARCONTROLLER_ERROR_ENUM.ARCON-
        TROLLER_OK) {
            success = true;
        }
}
List<Pair<Long, GpsCoord>> waypoints = loadWaypoints();
mDeviceController.queueWaypoints(waypoints);
```

I find the geolocation coordinates that Dad has scribbled out on a notepad he tossed onto the worktable. I scroll down and replace the placeholder data in the code, compile the program and copy it onto the SD card.

MacKenna returns with Charles. My brother is smiling. He doesn't quite grasp that this isn't a family reunion. It's not a drill either. He's holding a small bouquet of wildflowers.

He gives them to Annika.

My brother was out picking flowers for Annika Carver.

Terrific.

MacKenna joins me at the worktable and squints at the laptop screen. "And this is?"

"A drone," I explain. "My dad wrote a program that will send it over to the minimart, where The Opposition has set up a command center. It's got some explosives attached. He's hoping to take out some of their communication equipment. Maybe some of their vehicles..."

MacKenna's mouth falls open. "So...we're gonna launch a bomb without any concrete knowledge of who it might really hit?"

Dad walks by the table, overhearing part of the conversation. "If Jinx enters the coordinates correctly, I have concrete knowledge that it will hit the minimart."

"I entered the coordinates the way you wrote them!" I say.

But my pulse picks up. I don't want to be responsible for hurting innocent people.

Seeing MacKenna's face, Dad adds, "We have to do whatever we can to get whatever head start we can."

Bob Healy speaks. "I gotta get in position." He grabs several black duffel bags that he's filled with guns and ammo in the time I've been working on the laptop. "Between the AKs and the Stinger, I'm fairly confident that I can take out the first patrol. The rest depends on how long it takes 'em to get reinforcements organized."

Dad extends his hand to Healy. "I understand. And thanks."

They shake, and then Dad goes over to the far side of the barn where he throws open the wide double doors, clearing the way for the truck.

"Dad, just so you know. Ramona used the phone. She wouldn't tell me who she called."

When he ignores me as usual, I repeat myself. "I said—"

Ramona reenters the barn then, leading Goldilocks from the stables into the horse trailer. She leaves a moment later to get the second horse.

"I heard you the first time," Dad says once she's out of earshot. He puts his hand on my shoulder. "We have limited bandwidth. We'll have to address the situation with Ramona and Miss Carver later."

Later.

Ramona. Annika. Navarro. Everything has to be dealt with later.

"All right. You kids in the trailer," Jay says, making his way around the truck, slamming the doors, one by one.

"We moved the old love seat inside," Mom says to nobody in particular. "It'll be cramped. But you'll live."

"We won't all fit back there," I say. "Not all of us and both of the horses."

MacKenna casts death glares at Annika. "Can't we ride in the back of the truck?"

Mom fidgets with a strand of her long brown hair. "I don't know. I think it might be safer to have all of you in the back."

"It'll be fine, Stephanie," Jay says.

"We need to get on the road," Dad says.

Mom's face is red, and it strikes me that it must be so awk-

ward to be in a three-way debate with your old husband and
your new one.

Ramona is back with Jessie's Girl. She approaches Annika.
"I'm sorry I can't do more for you, girl."

Annika is doing her movie-star limp to the trailer when
Ramona calls out, "I wish it could have been different. I used
to dream that someday I'd bring you here. I think you would
have liked it. But this world, well, it sometimes won't let us
live in peace with the ones we love."

"I'm not sure this world is the problem," Annika answers.

It's not much of a final farewell, and I don't know if it's because the Carvers lack genuine feelings or if superrich people
are just weird.

Annika disappears into the trailer. A second later, Ammon
Carver's mother vanishes into the darkness of the night, into
obscurity once again.

Toby holds hands with Charles and leads him into the
trailer.

Once they're in, Dad adds Jessie's Girl and slams the trailer
door. The horse doesn't appear to be too happy and sniffs and
snorts a few times.

Dad tosses the keys to Jay. "I need someone to pull the
truck out while I launch the drone. Right out there. Ten feet
or so ought to do it."

"I'm on it," Jay tells him.

I climb into the bed of the truck and flop down next to a
mound of stuff covered by a tarp.

Dad reaches into the driver's side and pulls out a black bag.
I take it and realize it's full of weapons.

"If you use the AK, be sure to brace yourself. Don't put
me in the position of having to leave you here because you
get thrown from the goddamn truck."

"Got it." I scoot over in the bed so that my back is against the cab and the bag is next to me. I unzip it and get ready. MacKenna climbs in next to me.

Everyone's accounted for.

Except Navarro.

I'm surprised when Mom gets into the back of the truck with me and MacKenna. She does her best to smile. "I thought you guys might want some company." That's code for *you need adult supervision.*

Jay slides behind the wheel. He cranks the old truck engine to a start and moves us out of the barn so that we're outside in the moonlight facing a dirt road that must cut through the ranch. A cow moos.

The truck's diesel engine percolates and sputters, but even it can't conceal the sound of the AK fire that breaks out on the other side of the ranch.

The Opposition is already here.

My dad is almost strolling away from us. Yeah. That's the word I'd use. He's *strolling* in the opposite direction, drone in hand, as if everything is going according to his master plan. I stare at the back of his Wranglers, wishing he would get a move on.

More gunfire.

And some screaming.

Whoever is out there, Healy is really letting them have it.

"That guy Healy thinks he can take out Carver's whole army," MacKenna whispers.

I can see Jay through the window, clutching the steering wheel so tightly that his knuckles are turning white. I wonder if Charles is okay in the trailer.

"Who would you rather run into in the desert at night?

One of those soldiers from Goldwater or Healy with his five hundred guns?" I whisper back.

"Good point," she says.

Healy has a face that's as weathered as a saddlebag and he is tough as nails. If anyone can give a patrol from The Opposition a run for its money, it's Healy.

With a soft whir, Dad releases the drone into the air and makes a break for the truck.

The instant Dad is in the passenger side of the truck, Jay slams on the gas, sending me crashing into MacKenna. Mom is able to steady herself in the bed of the truck. We skid forward in a haze of dust, pieces of hay and some kind of grass that smells like cow dung.

Jay drives pretty similarly to my dad, taking the dirt road at a fairly fast pace.

I reach into my bag to get one of the AKs ready.

There's something next to me. An odd, misshapen mound under the black tarp.

I don't remember seeing anyone load supplies in the back of the truck, and anyway Dad always keeps everything ultra-organized in waterproof bins.

Even though a little voice in my head tells me not to, my pulse races as I find myself pulling at the edge of the tarp.

Revealing a pale, white hand.

A hand the size of a baseball mitt.

I simultaneously fight the urge to panic, scream and throw up. Every muscle in my body pulses and one of my legs sort of twitches.

The hand yanks the bag of guns away from me and pulls it under the tarp. Then it uncovers enough of a face so that only I can see it. A man's face.

Tork.

I can't breathe.

Tork sits up with the tarp around him like a cloak, with his back to the cab so he can't be seen. From the rearview mirror, it probably looks like the same lump of stuff that was in the back all along.

Mom and MacKenna recoil in horror, both about to scream.

He has the AK from my bag. "Shh!" he says. "Listen. Just listen."

Considering we've already established that Tork can kick my ass with minimal difficulty and he's also got the bag full of guns, I don't know what choice we really have.

I take a deep breath and try to sound confident when I whisper, "My father's going to kill you." But it sounds high-pitched and shrill and childish. I should have said, *I'm going to kill you.* I can't though. I can't say it and I can't kill him. It would be like trying to shoot the devil.

I'm not sure I have what it takes to survive.

Because you have to be able to do whatever it takes to survive.

Tork rolls his eyes. My dad is pretty much the ultimate badass, yet somehow Tork finds him nonthreatening and ridiculous.

"Even if he does," Tork says in a low tone. "There's a hundred more of me right behind me and a hundred more behind them. What you're doing is pointless. Surely you can see that. Like swimming against the tide. Come in now. If we get what we need from Marshall, we'll let you go. I give you my word."

They want the encryption key.

I should have thought of this. All along I should have thought of this. The real threat to The Opposition wasn't Jay

Novak. Or me. Or my brother. It was Dad's malware and the chaos it would unleash on the world.

A chaos that The Opposition didn't have a plan to use or control.

Dad's malware is the real zero-day exploit.

"Your word?" I echo. "You want me to hand over my father?"

Mom puts her hands up and makes a few panicked pants. "Okay…okay…okay…let's not do anything stupid here," she says.

Tork glances at her. "Maxwell Marshall is leading an insurrection against the government. But Carver's got a soft spot for his old buddy. If Marshall comes in voluntarily, he might not be executed. Help me bring him in."

"Ammon Carver isn't the government," I say.

"Yes, he is," Tork answers. "You just don't realize it yet."

"Everybody just stay calm," Mom says.

Stay calm. Stay calm.

The calm survive.

"If this is so pointless, what difference does it make if we surrender or not?"

His blue eyes are unexpectedly earnest. He glances again at Mom. "Believe it or not, we don't enjoy hunting women and children. There are people at the top who want to see you survive."

"What about my dad?" MacKenna asks. She's pushed herself against the wall of the truck and is stiff with tension and terror.

Tork shakes his head. "Jay Novak is a dead man. I won't lie and pretend there's anything I can do."

"Screw you," she tells him.

Mom watches Tork with terrified eyes. "I guess you didn't read my husband's book. Max won't surrender."

"Of course, I've read it," Tork whispers. "You need to convince him that coming in falls under Rule Number Eleven—"

He's cut off by a low rumble in the distance.

I turn my head to see yellow orange flames burst into the sky.

From where we are, Collins's burning store might be a campfire. In some other version of reality, there'd be charming people clustered around it, melting marshmallows and making s'mores. The black smoke gives it away though. It rises into the deep blue night, floating in front of the yellow moon.

I let out a terrible scream but the sound is lost amid the backdrop of the explosion, Healy's gunfire and the noise of the truck.

"Typical," Tork mutters.

He places his other hand on my upper arm. "Don't you see what's happening? To this country? To this world? People are desperate. We're one catastrophe away from another civil war. A strong leader like Carver is the only hope we have for *real* survival. Not running away from disaster like your father talks about in his book. But setting the world right. Restoring it to its rightful orbit. Ammon Carver is a new Atlas for a new era."

Like Terminus said, Tork is a true believer and not a soldier of fortune.

Tork sighs. "Okay, here's what we're going to do…"

Before Tork starts to reveal his little plan, I realize I know what I'm going to do. I'm going to kick him as hard as I can in the nuts. Then I'm going to pound on the truck's window as hard as I can. This should attract Dad's attention. Hopefully, he can do something before Tork can shoot us with my bag full of guns.

Get ready.

Okay.

Go.

Pumping the muscles in my hands a couple of times, I force my body into a crab position, flex the muscle in my foot and kick Tork.

At least I try to kick him. He catches my foot midswing.

"Like father like daughter. Stubborn. Fine. We'll do this the hard way," he says.

But he's given me an important piece of intel. He's not supposed to shoot me.

I suck in a deep breath and ready my most bloodcurdling scream. Before I can make a sound, Tork scrambles forward and clamps a thick hand over my mouth. I bite down hard.

He tastes like salt, gasoline and menthol cigarettes.

I gag. Tork doesn't let go.

But it's enough of an opening.

MacKenna pushes herself off the sidewall of the truck bed. She's got a fierce expression on her face.

Tork pushes me back as MacKenna takes a swing at him. My head hits the sidewall of the truck with a *bong*. Throbbing pain bursts through my temples and bright spots flicker in my peripheral vision. The wind is knocked out of me but the duffel bag is within my reach. I grip it tightly even as I struggle to breathe. I hear a thud.

As I sit up, my gaze falls on Mom. She is hugging her chest and breathing hard. She hasn't drilled in a long time, and she must be having some kind of panic attack.

MacKenna has fallen down too. Tork hit her. Blood oozes from her forehead. She stumbles up, intent on taking another swing at Tork. I can't let her do this alone, so I crawl forward and charge his knees.

Tork blocks us both, crowding us to the side of the truck.

He shoves me hard, and I knock into MacKenna. At that moment, Jay takes a dip in the dirt road without slowing. The weight of the horse trailer acts almost like a catapult, sending us bouncing into the air.

I make a grab for Tork's jacket collar to stabilize us. That doesn't go the way I hope.

Instead of keeping *us* in the back of the truck, I take Tork with us as we fall from the bed and skid into the dirt.

The truck is probably only doing fifteen or twenty miles an hour, but the landing still hurts like hell. MacKenna grunts as we roll along the rocky earth. I'm able to keep the bag of guns with me and come to a stop in some kind of prickly bush.

I sit up.

If there's any consolation, it's that the horse trailer clips Tork as it passes. He screams and is sent flying farther ahead, falling into the center of the dirt road before crawling into the bushes on the other side.

I'm about to force myself up when I realize.

No brake lights.

They aren't stopping.

I see Mom on all fours in the back of the truck, trying to get a look at what's happened.

She knows we aren't back there.

She doesn't do anything at all to try to get them to stop.

The truck gets smaller and smaller and smaller.

They aren't stopping.

WE OFTEN GIVE OUR ENEMY THE MEANS OF OUR OWN DESTRUCTION.

Well, this is it.

Dust to dust, I suppose.

I release the bag of guns. My hair is tangled up in what smells like creosote, but since Charles isn't here, I can't be sure.

There's nothing left to do but sit here and wait for the inevitable. The Opposition will find us. According to Tork, they won't kill us.

Some things are worse than death.

I want to cry but I can't.

I feel dead. I understand Collins now. That look he had on his face. When you know your fate, the only thing you can do is to accept it. Wait for it. Embrace it.

Somewhere behind me, MacKenna shuffles around, the tiny rocks sliding and crunching under the soles of her Cons. Coming closer, she whispers over my shoulder, "Okay. Okay. What do we do?"

What do we do?

When I don't answer, she crawls even closer and nudges me on the arm. "Come on. What's the plan? Jinx? Jinx?"

"There is no plan," I say. I fight off a cold shiver.

"What? They're coming back, right?" She stands and faces the direction the truck went. Like she might spot them out there somewhere. "Did they see that we fell out?"

"My mom saw." And she didn't do anything.

I try to reason with myself. Tell myself that Mom panicked and that there was probably nothing she could do. Tork really seemed to scare the hell out of her. She probably hasn't seen him since he came to the house. But…however it had happened, we were out here.

Alone.

"Okay, okay." MacKenna's breathing heavy. On the verge of a panic attack. "What about those famous drills? Maybe—"

"No, we didn't practice what to do if we were ever out in the middle of nowhere, surrounded by lunatics with guns and our whole family drove off with Ammon Carver's daughter." I want to face MacKenna, but I can't muster up the energy to get my hair out of the bush.

MacKenna sinks into a cross-legged position next to me and pulls strands of my hair from the bush. She sighs. "Well, we have to *do* something, Jinx. We can't just sit here and wait for The Opposition to come pick us up."

I'm able to turn my head, so she must've gotten my hair out of the creosote. "We have no car. No food. No water. No supplies. My dad is gone." For a minute, I think I've managed to make MacKenna as dejected as I am.

Instead her face fixes into a hard resolve. "We got out of Phoenix and halfway to Mexico by ourselves. We escaped from Goldwater Airfield. We can do this."

I blink hard to stop the tears.

"Come on. What are we gonna do?" MacKenna asks.

Before I can answer, there's a low moan from across the dirt trail.

Oh my god.

It's Tork.

He's not dead.

I'm on my feet in a second. "It's impossible to kill that guy," I whisper.

"He's like the walking dead," MacKenna answers.

"Come on," I say, taking her arm.

I come alive the way I do when I'm groggy in the morning and take that first sip of coffee. "We have to get out of here. We'll go back to the barn. Maybe we can find Healy. Or maybe there will be something in there we can use. If not, we'll get to the stables."

"Okay. Let's go," MacKenna agrees. "Don't forget the guns."

It takes about twenty minutes at a pretty fast jog to get back to the barn.

When we get inside, I throw open each door of the supply cabinets, but we don't find much. They've been picked clean. There's two really old cans of Mexican beer and a box of 9mm ammo, but not much else. "We'll have to go to the house," I say.

I jump at the sound of more gunfire coming from the direction of the house.

We are so totally screwed.

"I don't want to go back in there," MacKenna whispers.

Neither do I. But traveling without supplies is risky. "If we go without food and water…and we don't catch up with my dad…we'll have to ride all the way to Ajo…"

"If we go back into the house, we could get our heads blown off," she says.

"Can you use a gun?" I ask.

MacKenna shakes her head.

I hand her one of the Glocks and do a quick demonstration. "Hold it with both hands. Fire it at anything that moves. Anything that isn't me," I add. I keep the other Glock ready for myself.

We're about to take off for the house when we hear boots scrape against the rocks.

MacKenna and I both freeze and duck behind the barn doors.

I raise my gun and put my finger on the cold trigger, stabilizing it against the metal door.

Whatever's left of my heart barely beats.

A figure emerges.

It's Bob Healy.

MacKenna gasps and I don't blame her.

Healy takes the corner slow, almost dragging one of his legs as he shuffles like he's doing a bad impersonation of Frankenstein's monster at Halloween. He's covered in blood, probably wounded.

His shoulders slump when he spots us.

"What the hell happened?" MacKenna asks.

"Let me get the first-aid kit," I say, watching the blood soak the legs of his jeans.

We hear some indistinct shouts coming from behind the house. I jump as a few engines roar to life.

"I don't want no first aid," Healy says gruffly. "And what happened is that the damn patrol from Goldwater stormed in here, looking for the lot of you, of course."

"You fought off a whole patrol?" I ask. That's typically a couple of Humvees with four to six soldiers in each.

He takes a deep breath. His gruff mask slips away. "I woulda. I gave a couple of those young guys a bit of hell. In the end though, it was Ramona. She went out and surrendered herself. Exactly the way we'd agreed she wasn't gonna do and..." He stops hobbling for a second and braces himself against the barn door. "Once they had her, that settled it. They had their prize. Ammon Carver's missing mother apparently trumps the hunt for Max Marshall." He looks at me. "You...you...didn't make it?" he asks.

"My dad did. And Annika. So I guess it wasn't totally for nothing." I'm unable to keep the bitterness out of my voice.

He huffs and resumes his slow pace up the trail. "Of course it's for nothing. It's all for nothing."

"Then why did you help us?" I ask.

"Ramona," Healy says, through clenched teeth. "She's always felt guilty. Always felt like she musta done something wrong. She wanted to atone. Maybe now she has."

"Well, then..." I don't really know what to say.

He catches my eye. "The ranch is clear. But they'll be back. If you're making a run for it, you better get on it. I keep a couple emergency packs in the stable."

I take a breath of relief that we won't need to go into the house.

We leave him on the trail and go faster than before, jogging as fast as we can without slipping in the dirt. Other than the sounds of our shoes, it's dead quiet.

The lights are on inside the stables. I file that under *thank God for small favors*. Freckles and Ramona's horse are in their stalls, but they're uneasy. I bet all the screaming and gunfire has gotten to them too.

I pull one of the saddles off its hook on the wall and try to remember what Ramona did to get these things on the horses.

"Oh here. Let me," MacKenna says, snatching the saddle from my grip. "Whoa, Cuddles. Whoa." *Cuddles*. According to a nameplate on the stall door, the golden horse answers to Cuddles. My stepsister saddles up both horses almost as quickly as Ramona did.

While she does that, I find the supply packs Healy talked about in a plastic bin. I relax a bit at the sight of several bottles of water, a bunch of granola bars, a compass, flashlights, emergency flares and a couple of Swiss army knives.

When the horses are ready, I do my best to climb back up onto Freckles, who's even more jittery than before. The bag of guns makes me clumsier than usual, but I figure we have to take them. I position the bag in front of me and wrap the handle around the saddle horn.

The ranch itself stays quiet, but as we ride from the stable I can start to make out the dull rumble of car engines echoing across the desert. Maybe The Opposition leaving.

Or coming back.

To avoid Tork, I use the compass to steer us east for a half mile or so, circling around the ranch, cutting a path through cows that are milling around, unconcerned by our affairs. After about thirty minutes, we end up back on the trail in the spot where we last saw the truck.

We're lucky that the moon is nice and bright.

"Well. Here we go," MacKenna says.

"See that hill over there," I say, pointing at a darkish blob in front of us. "We should ride that way. If I know my dad, he'll take cover behind it."

"That seems a ways off," she answers. "You really think they'd go that far without waiting for us?"

My pulse drops. "My dad would want to wait in the safest spot."

Plus. We don't know when they found out we're missing.

I decide I don't like horseback riding. It makes me nervous. My pulse flutters and I sort of suspect that Freckles would like nothing better than to be rid of me.

"I think I really am a jinx," I mutter.

"I don't believe in stuff like that," MacKenna says. "Luck. Chance. Whatever."

"Why?" I ask. "Don't you sort of wish that your dad had never run into my mom at that golf tournament? You could be back in Boulder right now eating sarma."

"That's what I mean. Dad probably would have gotten that job at the bank anyway. They were really going out of their way to recruit vets." There's a pause filled by the clip-clop of the horses. "And...and I've always thought that Stephanie meeting my dad was no accident."

She's got her face turned to the moon, so I can't read her. "What do you mean? They literally ran into each other in the line to rent golf carts."

MacKenna snorts. "Your mom doesn't even like golf. And she just happened to be there? A high school teacher at this fancy VIP event? She's hot and single and here comes a whole parade of rich men? Husband hunting is a thing, Jinx."

I want to roll my eyes but nobody would see. "My mom's not like that. And if she was, she's way too disorganized to pull a plan like that together. It's a minor miracle when she shows up to her classes with the right set of papers graded."

She sighs again. "It just always seemed to me that Stephanie was out for him. From the very beginning. She's exactly his type. Like almost deliberately. From the long, shiny hair to that uniform of designer jeans and fancy sweaters. You remember that first day we met?"

"Sure," I say, although I'm not really sure where this conversation is headed. "They took us to brunch over at the Phoenician."

"Yep. Your mom's there arranging shrimp on her tiny plate. It was like, perfect for my dad. Like he could have ordered her from his dream catalog of uppity suburban women who make ideal wives for snobby executives."

I bite down on my lip and try not to sound defensive. "My mom is not uppity."

Not uppity at all.

Part of me wishes MacKenna would stop talking. There's so much happening. The whole world is so messed up. I know life is full of shades of gray. That Mom can be a good person and an imperfect stepparent. But not now. Right now, I need to believe in her.

MacKenna keeps going. "And then they're running marathons together. Watching old movies on TV. Golfing every Saturday. I find out that she never used to do those things. Ever. Like, she'd been playing Survivor Sue in the desert with Dr. Doomsday and then, all of a sudden, she meets my dad and she's the top student at the Rancho Mesa Country Club."

My heart flutters with unease, but I try hard not to let it show. I shrug. "My mom's got one of those personality types. She goes with the flow. Plus, people will do anything for love."

"They'll also do anything for power. And money."

Even though some part of me knows what her point is, I can't allow myself to think about it. I know that my mom was a schoolteacher who was spending hours staring at her laptop, trying to figure out how to keep making mortgage payments after she and Dad divorced. Still, I find myself asking, "MacKenna. What is your point?"

"My point is that there's no such thing as luck," she says. "We're here because of a series of choices. We can't get out of it by pretending it's all up to chance."

"I didn't make a choice to be here," I tell her. All I wanted was to finish my video game.

"We're always making choices. Even when we choose to do nothing."

I hug myself. This reminds me of what I told Navarro. *There's always a choice.*

The two of us ride in silence for a while. When we can't stand the thirst any longer, we crack the bottled water.

As we approach the dark mound, MacKenna brings Cuddles to a halt. "Do you hear that?"

I strain to listen, but's she right. There are voices just around the corner of the hulking rocks ahead. Someone is on the other side of the hill. I try to be quiet as I dismount from Freckles. "Stay here," I tell her.

I toss her Freckles's reins, but she throws them right back. "No way!" she whispers. "I am not staying back here by myself."

I guess we'll have to hope that the horses stay put, because there's nothing to tie them to. I sling the bag of guns over my shoulder and get my Glock ready. MacKenna gingerly holds hers out. I pray she doesn't need to use it.

Together, we stick as close as possible to the rocky hill, coming to a point where it's possible to peer around. I can make out my dad's tall figure and my brother's much shorter one. Toby is standing off to one side. The horses are tied to one of the truck's side mirrors.

"It's them," MacKenna says.

We grin at each other, and a sense of relief washes over me.

Our excitement is short-lived. We've clearly stumbled upon some kind of confrontation. A beige Humvee is parked in front of Healy's truck and trailer. My dad stands with his hands up, facing Annika's statuesque form. She's flanked by two soldiers with AKs.

Mom is huddled up with Jay and Charles close to the rocks.

"That must be who the old lady called," I whisper.

"Maybe," MacKenna says, in a tone laced with some skepticism. "But how would they know to find us here of all places?"

I shrug. "I'm sure Ramona knew we planned to go toward Ajo."

The old woman had surrendered to The Opposition. "What if this was her plan to be reunited with her granddaughter?" I suggest.

"What kind of sense does that make?" MacKenna asks in a whisper.

I don't know how to answer her question, but it's too much of a coincidence that Ramona went rogue with the SAT phone and then we ran into The Opposition.

We creep closer.

The moon is sinking into the western horizon. It must be early in the morning. If those How to Tell Time Using the Moon charts that Dad made us memorize are accurate, it's probably around three or four in the morning.

We keep moving slowly.

Until we can make out the conversation.

"The point is we can take you or we can kill you right now," one of the men says.

I dart out from our hiding place and come close to the man in desert fatigues, placing the barrel of the gun close to the side of his skull. "Counterpoint. I blow *your* brains out right now." Taking advantage of his startled reaction, I pull the AK from his grip.

"You should listen to her," MacKenna says, doing a good impression of someone holding a gun with intent. "She's having a really bad hair day."

Nice.

"Glad you could make it, Jinx," Dad says in an almost jovial voice.

"Thanks for waiting," I say, unable to look at Mom.

"We were waiting *here*," Dad says.

"You won't shoot us," the other guy tells me.

He's so sexist and derisive that I wish I could shoot him. But he's probably right to think that I don't have the nerve.

Without turning away from Mr. Crew Cut, I place the bag of guns on the ground and slide them in Dad's direction. A second later he's got his own AK.

"She might not shoot you. But I will. Drop your weapon, Bruce."

Of course, Dad would know these guys.

I think Dad must know everyone in The Opposition.

None of them seems to like him very much.

Bruce is the shorter of the two soldiers. He places his gun on the ground. Dad motions for me to pick it up.

He jerks his head toward Jay.

I hand Jay the gun.

At first I don't quite get it, but then I realize. That's a smart move. Jay's in security. He was in the army. Better he has a gun than me.

Jay steps forward to cover the second man.

"Okay," Dad says. "Let's try this again."

His brusque manner gives nothing away. Why is he not

more surprised to see these renegade soldiers in the middle of nowhere? He didn't seem to believe me or to care when I told him about Ramona using the phone.

"At least let us take the girl, Max," Bruce says. "There's a reward. You know I've got two kids I can't afford to send to college. And don't get me started on my mother-in-law."

"She can go if she wants," Dad says. "But you're not taking our supplies. If I see either of you again, I'll kill you." He surprises me when he nods at Annika. "If you go, that includes you, princess."

Dad has positioned a few battery-operated lanterns around the makeshift camp. It's too bad for Annika Carver that there's not more light, because I suspect a great performance is going to waste. Her eyes are probably brimming with tears and her gaze darts around uncertainly. All we can see of her internal agony is her hands as she clasps them together melodramatically.

She takes a step toward Toby. "Come with us," she says, extending one elegant arm for him to hold. "I know people. I could help you."

MacKenna puts her hands on her hips. "If you think my brother's going anywhere—"

"I can talk for myself, Mac," Toby says. "Annika, you don't know what you're saying," he responds slowly. "My place is here with my family."

I can sense the tension rolling off MacKenna. "We saved you," she says. "And you're going off with them?"

I scowl at Annika too. "They're a sure thing. We might not make it."

Charles tries to run forward but Mom stops him. "Don't go, Annika!"

"All right, everyone. Stay calm," Jay says.

Dad smiles. A thin, sad smile. "Last Monday evening, Miss

Carver left her suite at the Four Seasons in Scottsdale where she was staying before her Wednesday speech on behalf of her father at ASU. I believe she intended to liaise with someone capable of securing something akin to witness protection to Central America."

"That's why you didn't show up at the Student Union?" Toby asks momentarily distracted. "You wanted to get away from your father?" He shoots MacKenna an accusatory look.

Dad nods. "However, this person was an employee of Mr. Carver, and she was swiftly transported to Goldwater Airfield. Annika was being held pending further orders from her father when she escaped with all of you. Leaving with Bruce presents an opportunity to get back into her father's good graces. She can blame what happened on Ramona. Or me."

Annika steps closer to Bruce. "You're well-informed as usual, Dr. Marshall." Her damsel-in-distress demeanor falls away. What's left is a sad, almost frail little girl. "I wanted to get away but now...I think my father will be so relieved that I'm back and that Gramms is still alive that he'll... I'm not like you. I understand that now. I don't even know what I'm running for or where I'm running to. I... I have to go back."

Toby's face falls into a stricken expression.

I almost feel sorry for Annika. Almost.

She draws in a deep breath. "Toby. You should think about what you're doing. My father always has great regard for capable men. I can make sure you not only survive what's about to happen but that you end up in a position of power. The path you're on is certain death."

Jay watches this scene with an unreadable expression.

Toby shakes his head. "I'll take my chances."

The second soldier drops the pack he's holding at Dad's feet. "Come on, Max. No hard feelings, okay? What can I say? The reward is up to a quarter million dollars. You'd do the same thing if you were in our shoes."

"Don't you go telling me what I would do," Dad says, his usual cold self again. "You don't know what *I* would do. Get the hell out of here. Don't look back."

"Good luck, Annika," Toby says in a tone that matches my father's.

MacKenna stands up a little straighter.

Mr. Crew Cut tosses the rest of our packs out of the back of the Humvee.

Annika limps to the vehicle. She twists toward us for a minute. A sharp gust of wind blows her shirt tight against her and stray tendrils of her hair whip around like well-trained snakes.

"Toby," she says. "I hope you survive."

"You too," Toby answers. "I hope you survive too."

A soldier holds the door open as she climbs into the backseat of the Humvee.

Bruce gets behind the wheel and revs the engine. It takes off, kicking up a cloud of dust as it heads west, away from the rising sun.

"That was The Opposition?" I ask, when the men are gone.

Dad shakes his head. "Mercenaries," he corrects. "When The Opposition comes for us, they'll send a lot more than two guys."

When The Opposition comes. I bite my lower lip.

I'm about to ask if Dad agrees that Ramona must have sent them, but he surprises me by giving Toby a reassuring pat on the back.

"Don't blame yourself, son," he says, leaning down to pick up one of the lanterns. "She's a Carver, first and foremost. Maybe even more lethal than her father."

MacKenna nods, agreeing with my dad for the first time. "She's only thinking of herself."

I'm not sure that's totally true. I think Annika Carver is… me. She wants to hide behind her mask of perfection just like I want to run away into my video games.

"She thinks if she doesn't pick any battles, there's no way she can lose," I whisper.

Of course, we're both wrong.

This conflict is coming for us all, whether we want to pick a side or not.

Annika Carver has as much to lose as any of us, and I wonder how long it will be before she realizes that.

Toby stares after the disappearing vehicle. "It's all over now, isn't it? I'm never gonna graduate from college. Never gonna be a teacher. It's done."

"You don't know that," Jay tells him.

Mom clears her throat. She releases Charles and she too looks into the desert. "Max. I hope you know what you're doing."

DR. DOOMSDAY SAYS:

**VIOLENCE IS NOT ONLY AN ACCEPTABLE SOLUTION.
SOMETIMES IT'S THE ONLY SOLUTION.**

The instant that the Humvee is a safe distance away in the early morning darkness, Mom rushes forward, bursts into tears and drags MacKenna and me into a tight hug. "Oh, you girls! Thank God! Thank God you're safe. I'm so sorry. I panicked, and by the time I got them to stop the truck we didn't know… Oh, Max, thank God you taught them so well." Mom lets us go but keeps crying into Jay's shoulder. He folds an arm around her.

"Thank God MacKenna knew how to put saddles on the horses," I say.

I'm still kind of pissed at Mom. I think she could have done more to help us. I try to be logical. Mom was in shock and she was terrified. Plus, Charles grins at me and my anger fades.

I hug my brother for at least a full minute, so long that he starts to squirm and say things like, "Blargh!" and "Seriously, that's enough."

Jay and MacKenna and Toby hug as well.

We all even hug Dad, who looks like he'd rather throw up than be hugged again.

I should be glad Annika's gone.

She was a nuisance and kind of unpleasant.

For some reason, I'm uneasy. Annika's gone. Navarro's gone.

Tork is out there somewhere.

And then there's Toby.

He shoves his hands in the pockets of his baggy sweats.

MacKenna casts an *I told you so* look in her brother's direction and then returns her attention to Dad. "FYI," she says, putting her hands on her hips. "That guy Tork. He got hit by the trailer. Then popped right up. Like a spring daisy."

Dad turns to her. "Tork," he half groans. "How many times am I going to have to kill him?"

MacKenna puckers her lips. "How many times have you tried?"

Dad never answers that question.

There are still a lot of things bothering me. "How did Tork get in the back of the truck anyway? Wasn't someone watching the barn? Or at least doing laps around the property?"

Dad opens his mouth, but Mom speaks first. "Your little friend *Gus* was watching the barn. When I went out there to look for him, he was gone. I found him with the SAT phone on the porch. When I confronted him, he left."

My chest aches.

Mom's inference is clear. Navarro let Tork into the barn.

I know Gus would never do that.

But then I remember.

Terminus.

Trust no one.

Toby and I share a look. The pressure around my heart

continues to build. We're feeling the same way. Conflicted. Hurt. Confused.

Dad sighs. "Stephanie, Gus Navarro isn't working for The Opposition. I chose him for this mission. I trained him myself."

"He's only eighteen years old, Max. He might not know what he's doing."

MacKenna's forehead wrinkles. She must be thinking about Mom's story. It doesn't match what MacKenna actually saw. I can't shake the feeling that Mom is keeping something from us. That *all* the adults are keeping things from us.

"You kids have some water and some breakfast," Mom says.

The sun isn't even up yet.

And anyway…breakfast? Is that what you call your meal when you don't know what time it is and you're eating Donettes and beef jerky? Charles bounces up and down with enthusiasm. He hasn't done nearly as much drilling with Dad as I have, and I'm not sure how much he understands. Civilization is on the verge of collapse, but my brother is camping with his father.

While I dig the food I got from Collins's store out of the packs, Mom draws Jay and Dad toward the rocks. She tries to talk quietly, but the sound carries across the empty desert.

"We need to talk about what just happened," she says. "These escapes are getting more and more narrow. We need to at least discuss the possibility of giving The Opposition the encryption key. That police officer said—"

"Tork is a liar," Dad says. "I won't put my fate, and the fate of my children, in someone else's hands."

"The fate of *our* children isn't up to only you, Max."

I give my brother a granola bar. He chews slowly, watching our parents argue.

In a nod to the conversation MacKenna witnessed, Dad

says, "We already agreed on what we'd do. We're going to Mexico."

Mom frowns. "We did not agree. You told all of us that you won't give up the key without any further discussion."

Jay steps in front of her. He's wearing a kind of nerdy denim jacket. "Stephanie. We *did* agree that the safety of the children is our top priority. Our bargaining position improves only if we make it across the border. We need to focus on that."

Dad checks his watch and rubs his chin. "It's Friday. Carver's been president for less than a week and he's already declared full-on martial law. The longer we wait, the more danger we're in."

I shiver.

"I'm going to turn myself in," Jay says suddenly. "Once the kids are safe."

Dad snorts. "Don't be ridiculous. They'll kill you."

Mom starts to cry again.

Jay draws himself up to his full height. "You're the one who keeps saying that we're powerless to change our fate. If that's the case, then I accept mine. I came here from the old country because I believe in democracy. I believe the republic is far more resilient than you're making it out to be."

Dad moves closer to Jay. "I'm sorry to be the one who kills your faith in mom, apple pie and baseball, but here's the deal. Democracy doesn't always yield the right results. We *voted* to create slavery, reservations and internment camps. We vote *for* war but *against* giving poor people food and medicine."

"Is that why you did it?" Jay asks, his expression becoming cloudy. "Why you helped Carver? You concluded that human nature is always bad?"

Dad rubs his eyes with one hand. "I concluded that this

world was becoming something dark. A world without opportunity, hope, stability."

Jay stares out into the yellow desert. "This world," he repeats. "Maybe the world we loved was built off the backs of oppressed people. They held up our world. What we're feeling now, that sense of instability, is those people as they shudder and shrug, no longer wanting to carry our world on their shoulders. We mourn the loss of something that was never ours to begin with."

There's a pause. "You may be right. But I can't take back what I did. There's no going back. Only going forward to survive. We have to stay together. Whether you like it or not."

Jay puts his hands on his hips. "We should stay together because Carver's most dangerous attacks will be against our ideas, against our hope for the future, against our faith in each other. He's going to *destroy* anyone with a shred of credibility or integrity, anyone willing to stand up to him, anyone willing to do what's right. Until all that's left is a version of reality he creates and controls."

Dad can't think of much of a reply to that.

Charles sniffles. I glance over to find him wiping his face on the sleeve of his windbreaker. All the arguing and fighting is getting to him.

Dad turns to Mom. "You remember Joe Halverson?"

Mom's forehead creases. "That sociology professor you were always getting into arguments with? Last I heard he was working for The Spark as Rosenthal's speech writer."

MacKenna has been sitting on the ground popping small Donettes in her mouth. At the mention of Rosenthal, she snaps to alertness.

"A lot of Rosenthal's people bought real estate in Rocky Point before the election." Dad stares at the horizon like someone waiting for the sunrise. "I think they were worried about what would happen if Carver was elected. Joe has a place in Rocky Point. We can stay there tonight and then make some decisions about what to do next."

Jay cocks his head and moves closer to Dad. "Carver *was* elected. What makes you think this Halverson guy won't be there?"

There's a pause.

"Halverson is dead."

Another pause.

"The Opposition said he resisted arrest."

There's no more arguing after that.

Dad leaves the little group and comes over to ruffle Charles's hair. "Let's get on the road."

"How are we getting across the border?" I ask.

Surprisingly, Dad actually answers. "We'll cross into the Tohono O'odham Nation. I've got a buddy who can get us through the gate at San Miguel. My people are saying that Carver can't put any troops on the reservation. Yet."

"We're going to see Antone?" Mom asks, sounding surprised.

Dad nods.

One thing that really sucks about being in the desert is having to go to the bathroom. Without toilet paper.

We take turns finding various bushes to act as toilets.

So gross.

Mom fiddles with her pack as the rest of us load the supplies that the mercenaries tried to steal into the back of the truck. This time, Charles wants to ride in the back, so Dad makes a point of checking the bed for any unwanted stowaways. When it's all clear, MacKenna, Toby and I join my brother, leaving the adults to ride in the cab.

Toby takes a seat next to me on one side. Charles snuggles up against MacKenna on the other. The sun has risen and at least it's a little warmer.

Dad drives the truck and trailer around to the other side of the hill, returning to where MacKenna and I left Cuddles and Freckles. I'm relieved to find the horses still standing there, unbothered by what's happened. Dad already had Jessie's Girl and Goldilocks in the trailer so now we have all four of Ramona Healy's horses.

"On the bright side, this doubles our number of available animals," Dad says.

"How far are we going?" I ask.

"Ten miles south. Give or take. My buddy works at the casino down there. Hopefully, it's still standing," Dad says.

MacKenna and I exchange a glance. I can tell that we both want to ask why he thinks that the casino might no longer be standing. But neither of us does.

We load the horses in the trailer and put the packs and bag of guns into the back of the truck. We have to dump a lot of the extra stuff we'd packed in the trailer to make room for the extra two horses. We leave the love seat there in the desert.

I wonder if anyone will ever sit on it again.

As the truck takes off, Charles goes on and on and on about every plant he saw while they were waiting for us. "…I'm almost sure that it was *Argemone arizonica*. The Roaring Springs Prickly Poppy. Hard to tell precisely, since it's January, so it was not flowering, but I'd bet my subscription to *Southwest Gardener* that…"

I tune out the rest of his botany lecture.

It feels almost normal to be sitting next to Toby.

Except things aren't normal. Toby folds his arms over his

chest and won't look at anyone. He just said goodbye to a girl he's probably in love with.

I think Annika is pretty awful, but I do understand what Toby saw in her. Sort of. She represents that part of his character that wants or needs to see the good in everyone. His faith. His optimism. His belief that things will always turn out okay. Annika was like a stray kitten that could be brought inside and cared for. Someone to be rescued and saved and then exist as proof that you could make the world a better place.

I pat his arm as we drive on.

By the time the sun is directly overhead, we can see the casino. It's a long, white building that looks kind of like a permanent circus tent with the words DESERT JEWEL CASINO printed in huge letters that span the whole width of the building.

"Where are we?" MacKenna asks.

"The Tohono O'odham Reservation," I say.

Even from a distance, it's easy to see that something has gone really wrong at the Desert Jewel. Cars litter the parking lot, all askew. One is on fire. An RV has been turned onto its side. A police car with every window broken out rests nearby. A sign that must have said BINGO has been cut in half, right down the middle, leaving only *BI* and part of an *N*.

Coming closer, I can see that the building's glass doors have been torn off. A truck with its front end completely smashed in lies abandoned in front of a dented metal part of the building.

Dad brings the truck to a stop in a corner of the parking lot.

"What the hell is going on here?" MacKenna asks.

Toby pushes himself onto his knees to get a better look. Studying the postapocalyptic parking lot, he says, "I'm guessing the banks didn't open today and that the credit card systems are still down. This is what happens when people get desperate."

Dad gets out of the truck and says, "Wait here. I'll see if Louis is inside." He leaves us two Glocks and one of the AKs.

Staying out here is a dumb idea, but going into the flaming casino of death is an even worse one.

So we wait.

Toby sighs dramatically.

"Oh, for God's sake!" MacKenna snaps loud enough that the horses in the trailer whinny in disapproval. "There's more than one big-boobed, six-foot-tall, blond-headed girl in the world. You only met Annika Carver yesterday, Toby."

"You don't get it," he snaps back.

"You mean the feeling that you put your faith in someone because you think they're one kind of person and then they turn out to be another? Yeah. We get that, Toby," I say, hoping I sound sympathetic.

His frozen exterior melts a little and he's more like his usual self. The one who used to read Ralph Ellison by the pool. The one preoccupied with Sociology and Psych 101.

"It's gonna be okay," MacKenna says.

"We're a family and we'll stick together," I say and MacKenna doesn't argue.

We sit in silence for a minute and I find myself thinking of the minimart and Lee and wondering if this is the feudal world he's imagining. "'*Philosophy with a hammer.*'"

"What?" Toby asks.

I said that last part out loud, I guess. "Somebody told me that's what Ammon Carver represents. Philosophy with a hammer."

Toby laughs for the first time in ages. "Some grad student was trying to pick you up by misquoting Nietzsche?"

MacKenna laughs.

Before I can answer, Toby continues. "Well, definitely don't go out with that loser. Nietzsche would *not* like Ammon Carver. 'Philosophize with a hammer' means that you take a tough look at what you believe, at who you believe in. You challenge every preconceived idea, take a hammer to all your systems of thought, until you end up with ideas that can stand up. Blindly following the son of a son of a rich man because you think that doing so is your best shot at being rich too is bullshit. If you take a hammer to The Opposition, all you get is the broken pieces of old idols."

"What about The Spark?" I ask.

"The Spark wants to create systems that are fair and that will last. But ones where the people will always have a voice. That's what Rosenthal is doing."

I envy Toby and MacKenna. They have a hero. I have a survival instinct.

Toby goes on, "That's why he's so dangerous to The Opposition. In my poly sci class—"

He doesn't get to finish his thought. A Jeep whizzes by us at top speed and crashes through the double door area into the center of the casino.

Gunfire erupts.

A woman screams.

My chest tightens and my palms break into a sweat. But I have to pull it together.

I grab the guns and scramble out of the back of the truck.

Dad.

I just got my dad back and I can't lose him again.

"Jinx! Stop!" Mom shouts through the open truck window.

From behind me, I hear MacKenna say, "Charles, wait here."

I make a run for it across the parking lot toward the casino building.

To my surprise, MacKenna comes with me.

She quickly catches up. "Am I the only one who thinks we should be running away from the sound of guns and not toward it?" MacKenna asks, in between her paces.

I'm too out of breath to answer.

We stop at what's left of the doorway, which is now more of a wide hole. Toby arrives on our heels. He takes the AK, leaving MacKenna and me with a Glock each. I load them both and pass her one.

"Ah. Okay. Well…" I want to say something but I'm out of words.

Toby motions for us to stay behind him as we enter the casino. He always wants to save everyone, protect everyone. But he has no practice handling a gun. Stepping around him, I enter the doorway first.

I've never been in a casino before, so I don't know what they ought to look like. I'm sure it's nothing like this. Most of the slot machines in the place have been flipped over and torn apart. We have to tiptoe around dropped ashtrays and pieces of cocktail glasses. A gooey pile of nachos squishes under the toe of one of my Cons. Mixed nuts, maraschino cherries and cigarette butts cover the purple carpet.

The three of us duck behind an overturned slot machine a few feet from the door. I stare at the shiny plastic graphics that cover the side, advertising some kind of game show. A smiling model fans out a wad of cash while two other grinning women look on.

I scan the room and spot my dad.

I exhale in relief.

He's on the far side of the casino, ducking behind what I think is a bar or a small service counter of some sort. He's in a firefight in front of a counter underneath a large Cashier sign, exchanging shots with a gun on the opposite side of the room.

"What. The. Hell," MacKenna mutters, surveying the room.

She's right. It's total chaos.

The Jeep is inside making a ton of noise, weaving around the slot machines, heading in the direction of the cashier counter. There are people everywhere. Most of them have some kind of weapon. I flinch each time the low *boom* of a Remington sounds.

A gray-haired man attacks the iron bars that cover the cashier counter with a crowbar.

There's a pause as the shotgun guy has to reload.

Chances are Dad's got way more ammo than every other person in this place combined. This is a waiting game. That's all.

I move closer to Toby. "It's okay. We'll be okay," I tell myself.

As I say this, a figure forms on the glassy blue surface in front of me.

A reflection.

MacKenna turns and screams.

It's one of the soldiers from earlier. Bruce. He reaches for MacKenna, bring the barrel of his gun only inches from her forehead. "Screw Tork. I hate loose ends," he says.

In that moment, I find out exactly what kind of person I am.

I don't think.

I don't hesitate.

I fire two shots.

DR. DOOMSDAY SAYS:

SURVIVAL IS RELATIVE.

I become someone else.

The me who keeps stuffed animals under my bed. Who sometimes eats so much chocolate chip ice cream that I make myself sick. The girl who still gets scared of thunderstorms even though I deny it. She disappears.

I am gone.

I am something else.

MacKenna screams again.

I take her hand and pull her away. Before she can see the blood. Or the body drop. Or the disgusting mess you make when you blow someone's brains out. When you take their humanity and reduce it to a pile of guts.

The shock on Bruce's face. That's something I will never forget. He clearly didn't think I had it in me to shoot him.

I guess now we both know that I did.

I drag MacKenna toward the wall and push her behind a row of video poker machines—basically the only things standing upright in the whole place. I scoop up a few ashtrays.

And I run.

I'm cool. Cold. Adrenaline running all through me.

The element of surprise is all I have going for me, so I need to take out the guy with the shotgun as quick as possible. I don't stop running until I get to the Sugar and Spice slot machine. The barrel pokes out over its side.

Moving farther from the door, I take off fast and round the corner between a small bar and the main casino floor. I spot the man crouched behind the machine, resting the barrel of his gun on the Plexiglas panel. I'm surprised to find that it's not really a man. It's a boy. Someone around my age. A teenager robbing a casino. In one of those god-awful red Opposition hats.

I throw the ashtray at him before he has time to react. The heavy glass hits his arm with a crack.

The boy groans and drops the shotgun. As he cradles his hurt arm, he says, "What the—"

I come close enough to snatch up the shotgun. Before he can finish his sentence, I point the Glock in his direction and say, "Get out of here or I'll shoot your face off," through clenched teeth.

He hesitates for only a second and then scrambles up off the ground.

"Don't look back," I say.

All the screaming and shooting and the dead bodies have been enough to drive most of the opportunists from the casino floor. Only the Jeep is left. Its three passengers, two middle-aged men and a woman, have climbed out and are pacing around their vehicle. The wheel is wedged on one of the slot machines.

"It will work," one of the men is saying to the other. "Just help me move this shit out of the way. We need to clear a path so we can build up enough speed to really ram the counter."

"I still think this is a stupid idea," the woman tells him. She's clad in a red Team Carver sweatshirt and her brown hair is pushed up into a messy ponytail. "They've probably put all the cash in a safe or a vault or something."

"If you're not gonna help, get your butt outside," the second man says.

"But don't think you're gonna get a share of the money though." The first man grunts as the two of them successfully move the slot machine over a couple of feet.

I walk fast. With purpose and deliberation. The three of them are busy planning the world's dumbest robbery and don't pay much attention to me.

Until I arrive at the woman. Coming up behind her, I yank sharply on her ponytail and shove the muzzle of the Glock right up against her temple. "Get out of here. Now. Or I will kill you."

I sense Toby moving behind me, and Dad is making his way over from the other side of the casino. The two men drop the slot machine they're moving and stand up.

"Girl, you ain't gonna do shit," the shorter man says. But he bites his lower lip.

"There's a man up by the door who might say otherwise. But he can't. Because I shot him in the head," I say with a hint of a growl.

The woman squirms. "You're gonna shoot me? Why? What the hell do you care whether we take the money? Do you have any idea what's going on? There ain't no way to get money. And there might not be for a long time."

"I'd like to blow your brains out for wearing that sweat-shirt," I say.

It occurs to me that this is how killing works. It gets easier and easier. The chasm between what I am and what I used to be will get wider and wider. Until I can't see or even re-member the old me.

"You're one of *them*," she gasps. "You're The Spark. You're for Rosenthal."

"Everyone's for Rosenthal." I tug harder on her ponytail.

The two men exchange a look, and the tall one gets behind the wheel of the Jeep. He backs it out the way he came in. I drag the woman with me toward the door. Toby follows be-hind me, clutching the AK tightly. At the sight of Toby, the man drives a little faster.

I spot MacKenna poking her head out from behind the video poker machines.

Her eyes are filled with terror.

I push the woman out the door. She casts a hateful glance at me as she hustles into the backseat of the Jeep. It screeches into the parking lot, leaving us alone in the casino.

MacKenna comes out from behind the video poker. "Wow," she almost yells. Her face is stuck in a mixture of shock and awe, and I fired the Glock so close to her face that it'll be a few minutes before her hearing returns to normal. "I really… My life basically flashed before my eyes. I thought we were—"

"Thanks for coming in with me," I tell her, not really want-ing to listen to what we almost were. As my body calms down, I become aware of how sweaty I am. I tuck my gun into my waistband and rub my dewy palms on my jeans.

"What?" MacKenna yells.

"Thank you," I say louder.

She nods.

Toby's whole body almost shakes as he comes closer. He bends over, putting his hands on his knees and, for a second, I think he might throw up. "Next time," he says between pants, "how about filling us in on the plan before you decide to become a one-woman army ranger unit?" More heavy breathing. "I'm not...here only to...look good in...this T-shirt."

"I know."

"I can help, you know."

I killed someone.

I. Am. A killer.

Toby must be thinking the same thing because he says, "Jinx. Are you okay? You just—"

I can't think about that. Or about that guard I beat the hell out of at Goldwater Airfield. I can't think about it.

"I'm fine. Why don't you help me move a couple of these?" I ask Toby, waving a hand over the damaged slot machines.

I killed someone.

My hands shake and don't work the way I want them to. Toby doesn't want to show it, but I can tell he's having a tough time keeping his end up too.

When we drop it in front of the door/hole, I say, "In case that Jeep comes back," as loud as I can.

Dad joins us near the doorway. He checks out what used to be Bruce.

Goes through his pockets.

We all move that way but keep a bit of distance between us and the body.

Dad comes to stand next to me. For the first time possibly ever, he's worried, his expression a bit stricken. "Bruce must have sent Annika away with that other soldier and then doubled back for us. Whoever brings us in will receive a huge reward and probably a medal. So the question isn't *why*, it's *how*. How could he know we were coming here?"

I lean in closer to Dad. I'm not sure if anyone else should hear what I'm about to say. There's no reason to scare everyone more than I already have. "He mentioned Tork. Dad, about that guy, I... I thought he was going to..." My voice tremors as I whisper. I thought he was going to kill us. But I don't think what I did was right. And I'm scared.

For some reason, these words don't leave my lips.

Dad sizes me up. "You did what you had to do to survive."

He straightens himself up but continues in a low voice. "I should have killed him myself. Back there. That would have been the more prudent move."

My mouth runs dry. "I thought you said those guys were mercenaries. But if they're working with Tork, it means..." I'm barely keeping myself together. I don't know what it means.

Dad shrugs. "They're working for the highest bidder, and all it means is that The Opposition is using all the methods at their disposal to find us." He doesn't seem frightened by this new information, nor does he acknowledge that Bruce was willing to kill us. I remember what Terminus said. *They want Marshall.* For The Opposition, the rest of us were expendable.

Dad glances at the slot machines in front of the door and says in a more normal voice, "If you guys have this under control, I'll try to find Louis."

"What makes you think he's even here?" I ask, jerking my head at the completely destroyed casino interior.

"He's here. That was his car on fire in the parking lot," Dad answers.

"Well, then," Toby says, fumbling with the tail of his shirt. MacKenna yells another, "What?" as Dad walks off.

Toby pulls a warm pack of beef jerky from his pocket and the three of us each take a small piece. I sit on one of the slot machines and MacKenna flops down on the floor. She kicks at the broken glass of one of the broken screens, trying to see inside.

Dad returns a few minutes later with a larger, brown-skinned man in a rumpled black suit.

The man scans the casino floor. "Well, well, Max. Five years gone and you show up just in time to trash my place."

"You know, I did just stop a Jeep from ramming its way into your damn office," Dad answers gruffly.

"From what I could tell on the CCTV, your kid did most of the heavy lifting on that one. You're a real chip off the old block, huh, girl?" The man's bolo tie swings as he talks. I can tell he's not paying me a compliment.

"I guess you're Louis?" Toby asks. His face is still a mask of shock.

"Louis Antone."

We go outside to the truck, where Mom greets Antone and Dad introduces the rest of us. Louis shakes hands with Jay, but the only one of us he has much affinity for is my brother, who puts his hands on his hips and says, "I think it was a mistake to plant tamarisk so close to your building. It's invasive and attracts insects."

Antone says, "We didn't plant it there, boy. It's spreading across the desert on its own. Your people brought it here," he finishes pointedly. But he smiles at Charles.

MacKenna says, "What happened?" But I'm not sure if enough of her hearing has returned. Her mouth falls into a confused O as Antone answers.

"We get a lot of old, retired white guys in here," Antone answers with a scowl. "So they keep the news going 24-7 in the bar. When that report came on about the banks, people went nuts. Started swiping anything light enough to cart off. Whatever money there was in the slot machines, of course, but also the food in the kitchen. The toilet paper. Anything not nailed down. We were fixing to close. I got all the money loaded in the vault, but a few of us got stuck back there in the cage."

His eyes wander over the chaotic scene in the parking lot and his face sinks into a sad frown. "Non-res law enforcement will show up at some point." He nods at Dad and Jay. "As the two of you are the most wanted men in the country, we should get a move on."

"We're leaving the truck here," Dad says.

MacKenna shows us how to lead the horses out of the trailer.

Antone nods approvingly. "Beautiful animals," he says.

"They belong to Ramona Healy," Dad tells him.

Antone leans on the hood of the truck. "Ah. Ramona. She called last night to say you might be comin' by." He pauses. "She said you'd have the girl with you."

If Ramona called Antone, she probably didn't give our location to Bruce.

But then…who did?

I try to get MacKenna's attention to get her help in making some sense of what's going on. But she's watching a flaming station wagon with her mouth open.

Dad answers Antone. "Miss Carver decided she wasn't cut out for this life."

Toby's face falls.

Antone's lips pucker. "And Ramona?"

"She surrendered to The Opposition," I say.

Antone draws in a deep breath. "She had a good run of it. Most people don't last nearly so long with Ammon Carver out to get 'em."

"She was an interesting lady," Jay comments diplomatically.

We stand there in silence for a couple of minutes, all of us unsure of what to say.

Dad kicks the gravel a couple of times and says, "I suppose we ought to get on the road."

"Yep," Antone agrees.

"Jinx, get the packs," Dad says.

MacKenna helps me get the packs out of the back of the truck while Toby fills Mom and Jay in on what happened. When he starts whispering, I know what he's saying.

I am a killer.

And he's telling them.

There are eight of us but only four horses. Mom and Charles ride together. Dad, Jay and Toby insist on walking.

"It won't be too bad. I'm only a couple of miles south of here," Antone says as he gets into the saddle of Jessie's Girl.

I'm sure the guys think they're being chivalrous but honestly, the situation sort of sucks. Freckles hates me and I'm pretty sure would like nothing better than to buck me off. The motion of the ride upsets my stomach, which is already in knots from the violence back at the casino. In front of me, Goldilocks keeps kicking up dust that gets stuck in my dry mouth. I'd much rather be walking.

We ride.

After an hour or so, right about 9:00 a.m., we arrive at Antone's modest redbrick house. He has a small barn, where we find an alpaca and a white goat. We're able to leave the horses there and to set them up with hay and water.

Antone leads us into his house and tosses his jacket onto an easy chair by the door then heads into his kitchen, pulls a bunch of tamales from his fridge and sets a large pot of water on the stove.

I'm not sure if I should take a seat in the living room, which is cramped with red plaid furniture. The house almost looks like no one has been in it since my dad was a kid. There's what I think might be an antique computer on a small desk in the corner opposite the front door. I move closer. "Oh my God," I say. "Is this a Model 5140?" I love these old-timey computers. I run my fingers across the old beige plastic and marvel at the tiny screen. "Does it work?"

"Yes," Antone says.

"You know my dad has this idea about using three-inch floppy disks to conceal data," I say, feeling excited. Like normal excited. Not I-might-have-to-murder-someone-soon excited. "He thinks that you can…" I trail off, deterred by the look on his face.

"Your *dad* left that thing here," Antone replies.

I'm tempted to power on the old 5140 and see what happens, but Antone tells us that the food is ready. He has set out the tamales and some beans in mismatched dishes. We all go into the kitchen and crowd around the small table.

"This is delicious," I say, taking a bite of a green chili tamale. It's a huge improvement over the minimart snacks we had earlier.

My brother must agree because he's stuffed half of his in his mouth and is having trouble chewing and swallowing.

"So here we are," Dad says.

Antone nods. "You were about to ask for my help in getting across the border."

"Your people still have transports going back and forth, I assume," Dad says.

"For now," Antone replies in a glum tone. "But, as you know, militarization on the res is a growing problem."

"You're just going to let that happen?" I ask.

MacKenna glares at me and Dad gives me a tiny shake of his head. I've obviously said something really stupid.

"Well," Antone says, scooping up another bite of his own tamale, "native people have tried negotiations, demonstrations and war without much luck. How do *you* suggest that my tribe of around twenty thousand deal with the world's most dominant superpower?"

My face heats and I sink back in my chair.

Dad's conversation with Antone continues.

Toby leans over. "We studied this in my national history class. The Tohono O'odham Nation has land on both the American and Mexican sides of the border," he whispers, "and it causes problems because—"

"Because," Antone cuts in, "my people need to move hay and feed and livestock and equipment around our farms on both sides of the border. But we've got the Federales watching us on one side and the National Police on the other. It's a matter of time before they want to start inspecting everything. Telling us what we can and cannot move across lands we have inhabited for centuries. They have no respect for indigenous people." He glances at me. "Hell, you white people can't even get along with each other."

"All we need is passage in one of the transports, Louis. A ride. That's it," Dad says.

He returns his attention to Dad. "This is risky for the tribe, Max. I can't decide this on my own. I'd have to go to the Chairwoman. I don't know how much pull I've got with her these days. Do you want me to do that? Do you want me to go to the Chairwoman?" Antone's face flushes and his shoulders slump forward. It's clear he'd much rather *not* have to go to the Chairwoman.

"Well," Dad says, "how bad could it be? She is your mother."

MAINTAINING A CONSTANT STATE OF AWARENESS IS DRAINING. YET, THE TIME YOU THINK YOU CAN RELAX IS THE EXACT MOMENT DISASTER WILL TYPICALLY STRIKE.

Even though the tribe has its own police force and should be running an autonomous government, Antone tells us we need to stay inside. He says the Border Patrol can and does come by—if and when they want to.

Mom insists that we all take a nap.

When I wake up, I find Charles watering Antone's plants. I do the dishes. Jay and Mom play cards. MacKenna and Toby get in another fight about Annika but Dad shuts it down because God forbid anyone might express themselves or that any issue might be resolved.

Dad makes use of his time by taking apart the Glock I used to kill Bruce. He dumps the pieces in a plastic bucket filled with some kind of an acid solution.

He's concealing evidence of the fact that I killed someone.

Like we'll just destroy the gun and then I won't be a killer anymore.

I sit alone on the sofa in the living room for a while until Mom comes and takes the seat next to me. She hands me a mug of cocoa. It's warm underneath my fingertips.

"I heard what happened. You okay?" she asks.

I am not okay.

"I'm fine," I tell her.

She gives my shoulder a reassuring pat. "You've really been through something."

I take a sip of the cocoa. We all have. But like Dad always says:

If you're going through hell, keep going.

"I'm here if you want to talk," Mom says.

After about an hour, Antone returns, his face expressionless. He sinks into his red plaid recliner chair. Dad strokes his scruffy beard and takes a seat in a rickety wooden chair across from his old friend.

They say nothing for a minute.

"And?" Dad finally breaks the silence.

"The Chairwoman believes that it's not to the tribe's benefit to get involved. She said this fight is not our fight."

Dad scratches the top of his head and chews his cheek.

I don't know how he's staying so calm. Toby stands in the doorway between the living room and the kitchen and he puts his arm around Charles and MacKenna. A nervous, sick feeling settles in my stomach. If there's no way out through the reservation, there's no way out at all.

"I'm supposed to escort you off the reservation," Antone finishes.

Dad breaks out into a smile. "Sometimes you really are a shit, you know."

Antone laughs.

Toby, MacKenna and I exchange a look. *What is going on?*

"We'll go through the gate at San Miguel?" Dad asks.

"No," Antone says, shaking his head. "Through Papago Farms. The National Police have a checkpoint set up at San Miguel. And Nogales. I'm taking some animal feed, a few horses and a few people through the Papago gate. It shouldn't attract too much attention."

"Good," Dad says.

When I realize Antone is helping us get one step closer to safety, my lungs inflate a little more. A bit of weight falls off my shoulders.

Antone gets up, stretches and yawns. He freezes with his hands in the air. "One thing though, Max. No guns. You've got to ditch them here. On this point, the Chairwoman left no doubt. She won't have any more bloodshed on our land."

Dad stands up as well and reaches out to shake Antone's hand. "I understand. And thank you, Louis. Thank you." He surrenders the duffel bag of guns to Antone. I have no idea what Antone plans to do with them.

Dad gives us thirty minutes.

Antone gives us everything he has to spare. He helps us reload our packs with food and water. We even get a couple of rolls of toilet paper.

Mom makes Charles take a shower while the rest of us get the truck ready.

MacKenna spends her last minutes in the barn saying goodbye to Ramona's horses.

We'll never see them again.

We'll probably never see the old woman either.

Ramona Healy sacrificed herself for us. I misjudged her. And Terminus.

I get everything wrong.

I can't shake this thought as I climb into the bed of Antone's beat-up white pickup.

I catch Antone's eyes.

"Thank you," I tell him. "For everything. I'm… I'm sorry about what I said. That was stupid."

He smiles. Or at least it's not a frown. "I won't hold it against you." Antone slides behind the wheel and starts the truck.

We all ride in the back except Dad, who is in the front seat. I'm getting kind of comfortable with these truck rides. Occasionally, Dad says something or Antone gestures at the scenery. It's cold outside, and I wish I had something warmer than my jeans and windbreaker. Charles snuggles up against me. The desert with its low brush as far as the eye can see and its far-off mountains is both beautiful as the sunrise and also becoming monotonous.

Mom's hair, the same reddish-brown shade as my brother's, is swept to the side by the wind and the motion of the truck. With the bright, midmorning sky behind her, she looks like an ad for an adventure travel company. Jay takes her hand.

I have a random piece of my dull brown hair stuck on my mouth.

After about twenty minutes, we arrive at another cattle ranch and a house very similar to the Healys'. We climb out of the truck and follow Antone around the back to the barn, where a few kids our age are loading bales of hay into a re-painted U-Haul truck.

"Grab a couple of bales to sit on," Antone says. He tells us to go to the very back of the cargo area while they stack hay in front of us. It's a sort of claustrophobic safe space. With little couches made of hay.

"It's about thirty minutes to the border," Dad says quietly. "And another hour or so to Rocky Point. Antone says he keeps an old car in a shed on the other side. It will be a very tight fit with all of us, but we'll have to make it work."

We don't talk much on the drive. All the hay is finally getting to me and I sneeze and cough. "It's actually alfalfa," Charles tells me, in between sneezes. "For horses."

It's hot and bumpy and sort of miserable in the back, and yet we're traveling more comfortably than we have in a while. Charles hums a song. We're in pretty good spirits.

The truck comes to a stop. A door slams and we hear the sound of creaking metal. "They're opening the gate," Dad says. We take off again and stop a moment later.

One of the guys from the farm removes enough bales of alfalfa that we can climb through an opening and exit the truck. *"Bienvenido a México!"* he says.

I exit the truck and I'm surprised at the view. We're on the opposite side of what I assume is the Papago Farms gate. Pretty much in the middle of nowhere, standing underneath a group of large mesquite trees next to a building that sort of looks like a barn.

The border is totally different than what I pictured. It's not like the big inspection station in Nogales, which is full of cops and cars and parking lots. This is nothing more than a metal gate secured with a standard padlock. "You know, the O'odham don't have a word for *wall*," the guy says, scowling at the metal bars.

He stares at MacKenna as she leaves the back of the truck. I'm not exactly sure how she manages to look so good in a pair of my old leggings and a beige sweater, but she does.

"Thanks, Fernando," Dad says. "Give your father my regards."

Someday I plan to ask Dad how he knows all these people.

Fernando shakes Dad's hand. "No problem, Dr. M. As I'm not supposed to help you, I definitely won't mention that Louis keeps his old station wagon covered by a tarp in the shed over there," he says, pointing behind us. "Or that the spare key is in one of those little magnetic boxes under the driver's side front wheel well." His face lights up. "Oh! One more thing." He trots to the front of the truck and returns with a plastic red fuel container. "I definitely won't leave this gas can here, in case you need it."

"Thanks, son," my dad says.

Fernando casts one more look at MacKenna before getting back in the truck. The alfalfa continues up the dirt road, leaving us alone in Mexico.

We find Louis's station wagon with little difficulty. Dad fills the gas tank and puts the container in the trunk. Dad wasn't kidding when he said we'd be smooshed. Dad drives. Jay is in the passenger seat with Mom on his lap. MacKenna, Toby and I take the backseat and Charles squeezes into the cargo area of the wagon.

But after what we've been through, being smooshed in the backseat of the beige Taurus with Toby and MacKenna is better than riding in a limo.

"We made it," I whisper to MacKenna with a smile.

She smiles back. "We made it."

The farther we get across the border, the more I relax. The tension releases from my shoulders. Dad sticks to the dirt roads and side streets. Even still, the city emerges. We pass taco stands for tourists. A few bars. A guy selling shrimp on the street corner from the back of his truck. We're getting close to Puerto Peñasco. Closer to Rocky Point.

Occasionally, I steal a look at Toby and MacKenna.

Our old lives are gone. What will our new ones be like?

The Taurus comes to a stop in an alley littered with trash cans. Dad points to a cream-colored, Spanish-style ranch house beyond a concrete block wall. "This is it." *This* is more of a mansion. We might be in hiding, but we're hiding in style.

Dad parks the car in the shadow of a palm tree. We all get out.

"A lot of these houses should be empty," Dad comments. "They're owned by Americans. As vacation properties."

We've arrived at a postcard. A sandy beach darted with colorful umbrellas. A blue sea stretches out into infinity. A light breeze drifts over us, carrying an aroma of coconut sunscreen, salt water and grilled shrimp.

"Or hideouts for The Spark," MacKenna murmurs. She frowns at the idyllic beach scene.

"That too." Dad points to the house we're facing. "Halverson used to keep a spare key under a potted plant by the back door."

We all exit the car. After Charles climbs out of the back, Dad lifts up the covering over the spare tire and produces a shotgun and a box of ammo. "Louis always keeps a gun in here. Just in case."

Approaching the luxurious house from the back, we soon arrive at the gray concrete wall. Dad gives me a boost over it. MacKenna follows me, and the two of us catch Charles as Toby lifts him up. Jay helps Mom. Dad is the last to land in the yard.

Two things immediately become clear.

One, going over the wall was stupid and pointless. The house opens to the shoreline and we could have walked right up from the beach.

Two, there is something very, very off about the scene.

My gaze travels across the yard. To a sparkling blue, walk-in pool with an inflated rubber ducky–shaped raft bobbing around in the breeze. A hot tub and a full-size basketball court. A stack of red, green and yellow kayaks leaning against the wall.

Finally, to a silver grill with smoke rising from its closed hood.

Either Halverson is *not* dead, or someone else is here.

A figure approaches the sliding glass door.

I hold my breath.

And wait.

With his arm in a sling, a man steps into the light.

Every kind of terror fills MacKenna's face.

She screams.

Openmouthed. High-pitched. The kind of scream from horror movies.

Tork.

With a smile on his face.

DR. DOOMSDAY'S GUIDE TO ULTIMATE SURVIVAL

RULE FIFTEEN:

THERE WILL ALWAYS BE CASUALTIES.

Tork comes onto the patio and leans on a foosball table. He's dressed like a tourist in a pair of khaki shorts and a red Rocky Point T-shirt. He has a weapon holstered at his side.

I guess the horse trailer didn't kill him. He has a broken arm, but we didn't even take out the hand he needs for his gun.

Dad places the shotgun on his shoulder.

Jay does his best to tuck us kids behind his back and takes one step toward Tork with his hands up. "I'll surrender peacefully but I must insist you don't harm my family."

Tork laughs. "Bringing you in is not my job, pal." He turns his attention to Dad and his smile fades. "You know, Max, I should kick your ass just for making me chase you all the way to Mexico."

"You could certainly try, Marcus." Dad's index finger

hovers over the trigger. "But since when were you ever able to beat me in a fair fight?" I can't figure out why he doesn't just shoot Tork and get it over with.

"Let's talk about the encryption key."

Dad smiles too. A fake sort of smile. "I'm afraid you lack a proper theoretical foundation to understand my work."

I push Charles behind me. I feel his hot breath on the back of my arm. "Dad. Shoot him."

Next to me, MacKenna nods, her face wide-eyed and frozen.

"That's gratitude for you. I've trailed you for more than three hundred miles making sure The Opposition didn't kill you by accident. Or on purpose. The only reason you're still in an upright position, princess, is that I've been stopping them from blowing your brains out."

"Screw you," Dad says.

Tork glances at my mom, holsters his weapon and walks to the grill. He opens it and steps back to avoid getting hit in the face with steam and smoke, then removes shrimp kebabs from the grill and places them on a platter. "Well, what are we going to do now, Max? I could kill the kids one by one until you give me the encryption key."

Tork doesn't even have his gun ready.

Why the hell doesn't Dad just shoot him?

Jay slowly shifts to the side. He's scanning the yard. Checking for anything that could be used as a weapon?

I glance at Mom, who has moved a bit away from us and is watching the scene unfold with a calm, contemplative expression.

And it hits me.

What was it that Terminus had said?

They have someone on the inside.

My blood is turning to crystal ice in my veins and my lungs

seem to seize. Who had access to both Jay's passwords *and* his computer? Who sent us on the goose chase to find Dad? Why was Tork able to track us so easily?

The reason they could find us no matter where we went... is because *Mom* told them where we would be.

It's like trying to steady myself from inside a tornado. I stab my finger stupidly in the air in Mom's direction. "Oh my God. It was you. From the very beginning. You initiated the explosions at the bank. You...you didn't leave Dad because you hated the drills. You joined The Opposition." I'm in free fall.

"What?" MacKenna asks. "What are you talking about?"

"I told you before," Mom says in a hard voice. "Come next week, the world will be a very different place."

"In...in Halliwell's...we almost died...we could have..." I sputter.

I clutch at my chest, like there's a way to physically protect my heart.

She gives me one of her *Mom* looks. Like I'm out of line. "That was your mistake. I told you to go straight home. You disobeyed me. Afterward, I sent Tork to watch out for you. Make sure you didn't truly get hurt. I would *never* let anyone kill you."

The way she says this. Like she's settled the score. Like we're all evened up.

Okay. Okay. Breathe.

"You didn't let them kill us because you knew we were pressure points you could use to manipulate Dad," I say through clenched teeth.

Mom continues with her lips pressed into a thin line. "All you had to do was follow a simple set of instructions. Find your father and stay in one place long enough for Tork to come pick you up. But no. You had to go on the run with that *boy*. You had to storm the airfield."

"What did you do to Navarro?" I say, feeling even colder inside.

"Nothing," Mom says with an indignant snort. "He doesn't matter enough for me to bother with."

"Mom?" Charles asks.

"We'll discuss this later, sweetie," Mom tells him. In her sugary sweet voice.

Everything about my world is falling apart. "You… You… You murdered thousands of people. And framed your own husband," I say. My heart continues to sink in my chest. The woman who supposedly loved me, who was always there for me, is one of the biggest mass murderers in history. Not only is everything MacKenna said true, but my mom has handed Jay Novak a death sentence and ruined our family forever.

Jay puts his hand on his gut as if he's been punched. "Stephanie… Stephanie…"

"I regret it," Mom says coldly. "But as you know, there will always be casualties." She watches my father carefully. "I can offer you a way out of this, Max."

"There was never any way out of this. Not for me," Dad says.

I turn to Dad. "Did you know?" I demand.

His face falls, ashen and sad. His beard has gotten grayer in the last two minutes. "No. I mean…it seemed like the only explanation…and yet… I hoped… I wanted…"

You hoped it wasn't true.

Oh God.

And I realize. "This is why you left us. Why you left town. You thought we'd be safer if they couldn't find you. If Mom couldn't find you."

Dad bites his lower lip. "You can never tell what people are capable of."

Tork takes a bite of shrimp. "Well, time to cash in that insurance policy, Max," he says pleasantly.

"Don't tell them anything, Dad," I say.

I glance at MacKenna whose mouth is frozen in an O. She blinks repeatedly.

Mom shakes her head. "Don't you understand what will happen if we can't get those computers back online? It could take years to fix things. The paper records are gone—"

My anger surges again. "You destroyed them!"

Mom's arms fall flat against her sides. "Listen to me. If the economy collapses...the whole system could... We've run models but..."

In the distance, two children sit at the end of a private, narrow wood dock with a couple boats tied to it. They've set up fishing poles and are playing with a beach ball while they wait for something to bite.

"Max. It's not too late," my mom pleads. She wrings her elegant hands. "There's still time. Ammon would welcome you back as a brother. It would be you and me. Saving the world from itself. As it should be. Max, please. For our family. For me."

"*Ammon?* Carver's lost it. He's a complete and utter madman," Dad says. "Stephanie, you have to listen to me. I made a terrible mistake in involving myself with him."

"You're wrong. You—" Mom says in a sharper tone.

"Stephanie! Listen! I've loved you as much as a man could love a woman. I still do. But you're talking about... I can't be a part of it. Let me leave here with the kids. When I get somewhere safe, I will give you the encryption key. You have my word."

I realize that the reason Dad can't shoot Tork is that it

would be pointless. He's got one gun. And two potential
hostiles. Obviously Tork is armed, but Mom probably is too.
She ran drills with Dad. And.

Always be prepared.

Rule number one.

Dad probably couldn't kill Mom no matter what. He's put
his life in jeopardy to be here. Cold adrenaline shoots into
my legs. I don't allow myself to stop and think. I act.

I rip the shotgun from Dad's hands. If he won't shoot Tork,
I will.

"I'm going to kill you," I say, lifting the gun onto my own
shoulder.

Mom pulls a Glock from behind her back. "Put the gun
down, Jinx."

Tork tosses down his kebab and withdraws his weapon.

Dad puts his hands in the air defensively. Jay remains frozen in shock.

"Fuck you," I tell her. "If you're going to shoot me, get
on with it."

"Mom!" Charles shrieks.

"No one is shooting anyone," Mom says. "Tork, stand
down."

"Stephanie—"

"I'm in command here. Stand down."

That's right. My mother is the fucking commander of the evil army.

Tork stows his weapon inside his holster and puts his back
against the backyard wall. "You want to shoot someone, Jinx?
Your father is the most dangerous man here. Whose data
models got Carver elected? Who has basically sabotaged the
entire economic system of the country? Who recruited me?
Where do you think Carver got his ideas from?"

Dad's face turns red. "Carver told me we were building a

system to ensure a better world. Then he joined The Opposition. When I got out, I tried to take you with me, Marcus."

"I don't want out," Tork says. "In the new world order, I want a place in the front."

"Oh, Max, you were so busy preparing for the end of the world, you didn't see that we should actually be working to create a different world," Mom tells Dad.

Dad glances at me, and the look in his eyes seems to pierce my heart. "I was so busy preparing for the end of the world that I may have caused it."

Jay inches away from us, moving very slowly, trying to attract no notice, inching toward the corner of the yard where a couple of abandoned croquet mallets lean against the wall.

Mom sighs. "Please don't make me kill you, Jay. Originally, Ammon wanted a public execution. But our current polling says that The Opposition is better off with you on the run. Having you at large is helping us neutralize The Spark in the Senate. It could be years before we can capture and extradite you. Years you'd have with your children."

This, too, makes sense. The Opposition has turned Jay Novak into a specter that can be conjured to scare people anytime Carver needs money or troops or power. That's why they didn't try very hard to recapture him or stop him from escaping.

What they really need is Dad's encryption key.

Jay stares at her with a mixture of rage and grief.

I've had enough of this. I'll shoot Tork. And then Mom can decide if she has the guts to shoot me. If she's really prepared to do anything to survive.

My heart pounds in my chest.

Get ready.

Ready.

I'm about to move when, from on the opposite side of the yard's wall, I hear approaching footsteps.

Someone is coming.

It occurs to me that this is probably a pretty odd scene for a tourist or beach-bound family to stumble upon. I move to the other side of a palm tree. Mom lowers the Glock. Tork backs into the shadow created by the grill.

We wait.

A head of dark hair pokes around the corner.

It's *Navarro.*

Something warm and giddy rises through my body. *Navarro came back for us.*

Mom sees him too. From the expression on her face, this is something she wasn't expecting. For the first time, she looks afraid. Not in total control. She sucks in a deep breath, gets her own gun out and backs up toward the wall.

Tork's gun is out.

"We can work this out. All I want to do is leave here with the kids," Dad tells her. He approaches her slowly.

Navarro rounds with corner with a shotgun tucked under his arm.

Dad creeps closer to Mom. He's one step away.

At the beach, the children's beach ball hits a fishing pole and pops.

Mom flinches.

And pulls the trigger.

DR. DOOMSDAY SAYS:

IT'S ALWAYS A SURPRISE WHEN YOU REALIZE THAT LOVE CAN DO MORE DAMAGE THAN HATE.

The bang echoes off the patio's walls and travels toward the beach.

The children stare in our direction.

Dad drops to the ground and blood gushes from his gut.

No. No. No. No. No. No.

I fall to my knees and take Dad's hand.

I barely notice when I drop the shotgun or when Tork scoops it up.

Charles bursts into tears.

This is my fault. This is my fault.

I convinced Dad to come with us. Practically dared him to go to Goldwater Airfield.

My ears ring.

Everything I see is red with rage.

"Dad. Dad," I say. "You'll be okay. You'll be fine."

Except this is a total lie. I have no idea where the nearest hospital is or how we would get him there. Blood covers Dad's shirt and spills onto the terra-cotta tile.

Dad is going to die.

I have no air. I'm drowning right out in the open.

Mom is suddenly kneeling next to me. "Max? Max? Listen to me—"

I swat at her arms. "Get away from him! Get away. *Get away!*" I scream. "I hate you. Do you hear me? I hate you!"

Dad opens his mouth. A strangled gurgle comes out.

There will be no last words.

No final instructions.

No closure.

"Jinx? Susan? Dad's going to be okay, right? Susan?" Charles cries out.

I grip Dad's hand, which is already growing cold. There's a single moment that separates life from death. We're in that space. Maxwell Marshall is drawing the last of his breaths. And I can't believe it. My dad. An infallible rock that everything else broke itself against.

I gaze around, as if help will magically appear. Behind me, Tork is pacing.

Tork's athletic shoes squeak with each step. "All right. All right. We need to think. What we need is a plausible story. We'll take the kids in. Come up with something. We'll figure out the thing with the computer. We need to make this look right."

Mom sits up, the tail of her white cotton T-shirt stained red with Dad's blood.

She wipes a few tears off her pale face and stands tall and straight.

"I agree," she says.

Without another word, she shoots Tork.

Once.

Right in the head.

Tork's lifeless body falls with a smack onto the tile floor.

Before he even lands.

I can already see it. Mom's going to run.

There are five of us and Navarro has a shotgun.

She's going to run.

I scramble up from the floor and throw myself in her path. I've got several inches and at least thirty pounds on Mom, yet she round kicks my legs out from under me with ease. I land hard on my back.

Out of breath.

Vision blurred.

Dad's warm blood runs underneath me.

Mom's been drilling again. Or maybe she never stopped. Her Krav Maga is much better than mine. By the time my brain processes this thought, she is halfway gone.

It's Navarro who leans over me.

I'm quickly flooded with intense relief.

I reach up and touch his rough face.

The sensation doesn't last. He barely has time to pull me to my feet before I hear the screams. Mom is already on the beach.

Charles is calling my name.

Over and over.

She's taken him.

She's taken my brother.

As I get to my feet, Jay makes a grab for me. "Jinx! Wait! It's not safe—"

I shake free of his grasp and take off at a run. Behind me, I hear him yell at Toby and MacKenna to stay in the yard.

I make it to the edge of the property where I have a good view of the beach. Mom has already made it halfway to the dock. Charles struggles against her and she hoists him over her shoulder to pick up speed. She jogs toward one of the speedboats at the end of the dock. That must be how Tork arrived and how the two of them planned to leave after they'd completed their mission.

Charles struggles against her, yelling, "Mom! No! Jinx!"

The sound is already growing more distant and I know, I mean really know, that I'll hear these screams. Always. Forever. In my nightmares. In my dreams. Anytime a room falls silent.

"Jinx! Jinx!" Charles calls again.

I can't let her take my brother.

I can't.

I become an extension of this thought and my body takes off on its own. I bolt down the beach, running as fast as I can in the way-too-bright sunlight.

The breeze. The swaying palm trees. The waves. This is a scene set in the wrong location.

It's too late.

Mom climbs in the speedboat at the end of the dock and fiddles with the rope. I'm still at least a hundred feet away from her. A second later Navarro is at my side with the shotgun. But there's no way he can hit her at this distance.

He fires into the ocean. Not even really in the direction of the boat. It's an act of frustration. And defiance.

It's a loud *boom* that goes nowhere and hits nothing.

Jay runs up a second later. "Son, that's enough."

Leaving the two of them behind, I continue to run after Mom even after she cranks the boat's engine on and steers it away from the dock. I run to the very edge of the wood with the tips of my Cons poking over the ends of the planks.

I stand there alone, soaked in my father's blood, facing the vast blue ocean and the tiny boat vanishing into it.

If it's the last thing I do.
If it takes everything I've got.
I'll get my brother back.
I will find you and kill you.

NO MORE RULES

I'm so angry. At my parents. At Gus for leaving us. Or not coming back in time. At MacKenna for always being right. But mostly at myself. For refusing to see what was there all along.

At first, Navarro does everything.

We wait in the house.

He wraps Dad's body in plastic.

Staying pissed keeps the pain at bay.

Toby looks angrier than I feel. He sits on the suede sofa with his fists balled up. Like he wants to tear the world apart. Jay joins his son, tries to be reassuring. But what do you say to someone when your wife has wrecked the whole world?

I'm sitting by myself at a table in the kitchen.

MacKenna comes in and pulls up another chair.

"I know," I tell her.

"What?" she asks. She hugs herself.

"You tried to tell me. About my mom."

"Jinx," MacKenna says. "I thought she was a gold-digging husband hunter. Not some kind of evil, neo-Nazi superwoman. There's no way I could have seen *that* coming."

After a pause, she says, "What are we going to do?"

My stomach turns over with unease.

I've been thinking about this myself. "I'll help you all get packed up. You should go as far south as you can. To somewhere without an extradition treaty."

"*We* should go?" MacKenna repeats. "What about you?"

My face flushes. "I don't care what happens to me," I say. "The cops will show up here sooner or later. Dying in a Mexican jail is as good as anywhere else."

"Oh, I see," she says. "You're giving up. And leaving us to fend for ourselves."

It hadn't occurred to me that the Novaks would want anything to do with me after what happened. Jay's going to be a fugitive thanks to Mom, and they'll probably be on the run for the rest of their lives.

"Well, I just assumed that… I mean…" I swallow the lump in my throat. "You've lost everything. Because of her." I realize that I can't just blame *everything* on my mother. I've had plenty of opportunities to listen. To pay attention to what's been going on. "Because of me."

"Now you have to decide—are you going to run? Or are you going to help?" She catches and holds my gaze, and I think it might be the first time we've ever really looked at each other in this way. "Jinx. I mean, however it happened, we're a family now. I love Charles too, you know. Whatever we're going to do, we'll do it together."

"Thanks, MacKenna," I say, feeling tears burn my eyes.

She nods. "You can call me Mac."

She leaves the kitchen, I assume to return to the living room to sit with Toby and her dad.

A while later, Navarro comes into the kitchen. He glances around the richly furnished house. "We can't stay here you know."

"I know."

I can see the beach through the window.

The tide. Coming and going.

"You should have told me, about my mom," I say, staring at the blue sky.

"I didn't know anything for sure, and you wouldn't have believed me," he answers. "Plus, it wouldn't have changed what your dad was gonna do. He knew more than I did."

He held out hope. Right to the very end.

"Why did you go?" I ask, unable to conceal my bitterness.

He covers my hand with his and, in spite of everything, there's a little jolt.

"You know how your dad always told us to have a backup plan? I realized I needed to *be* the backup plan, you know?"

I sigh. "Why him?" I ask. "Of all people, why Jay?"

Navarro shrugs. "It had to be someone who worked in Carver's organization. They probably wanted someone who supported The Spark. To be able to argue that Rosenthal targeted The Opposition. Jay is an immigrant. With military training."

In spite of my best efforts, I begin to cry, choking out a sob that sounds like a hiccup. Navarro puts his arm around my shoulders. "She doesn't care," I say. "Whether we live or die. If Dad died. She just didn't care."

Navarro sighs. "Would you feel better if she did? Your mom is responsible for a series of attacks that killed more than two thousand people. Including a group of toddlers at a day care center. Would you be happier if she wanted you to live but them to die?"

No, I wouldn't.

"You should have shot her," I say.

"I might have hit your brother."

His dark gaze darts around. "You can have your message now," he says.

My message?

"From Dad?" For an instant, my heart soars.

Until I realize, it's a message from the grave.

All these emotions must flash over my face, because Navarro hesitates.

"What is it?" I ask, prompting him.

He gets up from the table and returns with a pencil and a take-out menu from one of the kitchen drawers. He scratches something on the paper.

18.266735, -87.835484

I squint at the number. It's a set of DDM coordinates. Degrees decimal minutes. It's a location. "It's a map? That's what Dad left me?"

The fancy house has a working computer and Wi-Fi, so we resolve the coordinates.

They point to a remote place called Xcalak. It's south. Right above Guatemala.

We have to leave.

Navarro says what I'm thinking. "Once it's dark, we have to go."

For the next few hours, we go through the motions. There's a computer in a small room decorated like an office. I do a search for Mom and Charles. I don't know what I hope to find, but I don't find anything. Jay keeps the TV on in the living room. Partially to monitor the news and partially to fill the silent void. Navarro is the only one of us who speaks any Spanish. Occasionally, there's a news report about The Spark or about Rosenthal's disappearance, but mainly the Mexican media is covering what they're calling *Caos en la Frontera*.

Navarro translates: Chaos at the Border.

The screen shows thousands of Americans lining up at border stations in places like Nogales and Tijuana. There's a huge mess in El Paso as people try to flood Juárez. Mexican politicians appear on TV and argue about sending their army or closing the entry points.

If Dad were around, he'd probably say that this benefits us.

But Dad isn't around.

Around dinnertime, MacKenna cobbles together a meal from stuff she finds in the house's pantry. I don't even know what's in a tuna casserole, but she manages to make one. Later, I see she's found a yellow legal pad and is making notes. I'm glad she's keeping a record of what's happened. Someone needs to.

After sunset, when the beach is deserted, Navarro goes outside.

He looks almost guilty when I follow him and catch him with a shovel.

"You need to get some rest, Susan," he says.

"You're digging Dad's grave?" I ask.

There's a long pause filled with the sound of the tide.

"I want to dig."

"Susan—" Navarro objects.

"I want to dig. Please."

The *please* gets him.

We choose a spot in the middle of several palm trees, where

the earth is as dry and firm as it's going to get. You'd think digging would be easy. It's basically just moving sand from one spot to another, but it's hard, backbreaking work. The deeper the hole gets, the more it occurs to me that I'm standing in my father's resting place.

The Novaks come out and help dig. When it's totally dark, Navarro and Jay lower Dad into the hole we've created. The sand is soft and beachy and sounds like crackling leaves when it hits my father's body.

Dad is gone.

Forever.

We bury Tork too. I insist on it. I don't think he deserves a funeral. But I need it to be done. I need it to be over.

Then.

We have to leave my father's body behind.

We have to go.

I will follow Dad's plan to its final step.

And then.

There will be no more rules.

EVERYONE'S FOR ROSENTHAL

Navarro has a moldy, dirty RV. We clean it up as best we can and load all the supplies that will fit. We have to take the shotgun and the AK. Jay scowls as we load them. But he doesn't stop us.

Before we leave, Jay draws us into a huddle. I find myself sandwiched between Navarro's cool, steely control and Toby's simmering, seething anger. "We leave here together. We'll stay together. Come what may. And that's what matters," Jay says. He kisses MacKenna on the forehead and ruffles my hair.

Beyond the vast desert, over the highest mountains, through fields of corn and wheat, past icy lakes and into the heart of America's greatest city, I imagine that Ammon Carver waits in his tower of gold believing he controls the universe from his penthouse and leather chair.

Navarro gets behind the wheel of the RV and hits the gas hard, propelling us onto the street. A red-hatted gnome crunches under one of the tires.

And we drive.

In Hermosillo, Jay trades the Suburban for an old truck with a camper.

In Mazatlan, Navarro ditches the camper and steals a smelly VW bus.

Three days later, Navarro steers us toward a large, white church. We arrive at night. Inside, it's lit mainly by candles placed all over the silent sanctuary. A priest clad in customary black sits on a pew in the first row, facing the altar.

Without turning to face us, he calls out, "You're late. Marshall said you'd be here yesterday."

An invisible knife pierces my heart.

The priest continues. "Now you'll really have to make it quick. The Legion of Mary meeting starts in a little over an hour. If you're still here when Mrs. Vega arrives, she'll tell half the town about you before you can lace up your shoes."

"Something's happened to Marshall," Navarro says.

The priest rises and turns to face us. It's like staring into the face of a much older Navarro. "I see," he says.

Navarro makes a sheepish face and gestures at the man. "My uncle, Estevan."

Father Estevan scans our group. "And the boy?"

The tears come. Not like a few little droplets that I can wipe away with my sleeve. They run down my face. Mac-Kenna pats my back.

The priest hesitates for a second and then says, "Well, we can at least get you some dinner." He motions for us to follow him. I'm still sniffling as we walk through a series of cramped cream-colored stucco hallways to a little cheerful kitchen.

Navarro helps Father Estevan put out the food, which, in spite of everything, is delicious. It's the most amazing posole I've ever tasted, along with some kind of shrimp in a creamy sauce. They talk among themselves, keeping the chatter light. Navarro makes a worried face at the mention of his mother.

Father Estevan goes in and out, helping with the meeting that's being held in one of the halls. He keeps us in the small kitchen until everyone leaves. Jay, Toby and Navarro get out the map and trace our route. Every once in a while, Father Estevan points out a safe stopping point.

After everyone is gone, Father Estevan holds a service for Dad in the sanctuary.

I sit on a pew and stare at the huge stained glass window at the front of the chapel. It shows the Virgin Mary.

"As Christ went through the deep waters of death for us, so may he bring Maxwell Marshall to the fullness of resurrection and life with all the redeemed."

Mary is seated on a throne, holding baby Jesus and flanked by the three wise men. It's hard to look away.

"Maxwell Marshall, rest eternal and let light perpetual shine upon you."

The window is almost radiating a golden aura. Almost glowing.

After the mass, Father Estevan comes to sit alongside me while everyone else gets ready to leave. I try to make conversation. "So. Can you put in a good word for us? With the man upstairs?"

Father Estevan follows my gaze and regards the stained glass too. "What's upstairs isn't a man," he murmurs. "This conflict isn't of heaven. It's of earth."

In a louder voice, he says, "*Converte gladium tuum in locum suum. Omnes enim, qui acceperint gladium, gladio peribunt.* Put your sword back in its place. For all who take up the sword shall perish by the sword. So says the word of the Lord." He rests his upper arms on the pew in front of him. "Miss Marshall, God's role in this struggle might not be what we hope. I fear things will get worse before they get better."

I nod and get up, going to the back of the sanctuary and leaving him there alone in thought. It's a grim pronouncement from somebody who ought to have more, well, *faith*. Somehow, I feel more on edge than I did before.

Walking around to the back, I find Navarro repacking our gear.

It's a dark, cool night.

The sky so full of stars.

Navarro comes out of the back and stands near me, the only light coming from a lone streetlamp and the glow of the small bulb in the VW Bus. It seems like I ought to say something.

"What happened to your hat?" I blurt out. For the first time, it strikes me that he's no longer wearing his black baseball cap.

"You don't want to know," he says darkly.

It's quiet again.

After a moment, he speaks slowly. "You asked me why I came. Why I agreed to do this." He leans against the Bus. It's silent again for a second. "I came here for you. Because. Well, because... From the first time I saw you. That day at Prepper-Con. You were supposed to be giving lectures on how to jar cactus jelly but instead you hacked that digital billboard to say *Cactus Jelly Tastes Like Papaya Vomit*. It took your dad ten minutes to figure out how to turn the thing off."

Oh, Dad.

"I knew. I've always known that I...that I... I need you to know that I'll do whatever it takes to keep you safe. I think your dad could tell. He told me a lot about you."

He's leaning in.

Slowly. So. So. Slowly.

I can smell the chocolate mint he had after dinner.

Our lips are about to meet and it occurs to me that I've been wanting this and hoping for this and everything that's horrible and wrong with the world could disappear for one moment.

For one kiss.

Except.

Someone kicks open the church's back door, and I jerk my head around and see MacKenna. "Father Estevan is asking if we need any bottled—" She stops at the sight of the two of us so close together.

We exchange a tense look.

When I turn back to Navarro, he's gone.

Ten minutes later, we're all in the RV and we press on.

For the next couple of days, we take turns driving. It's forty hours of eating gas station food and barely stopping to use the bathroom.

Occasionally, we come across a café with internet access. I search for information about Charles.

I don't find anything.

MacKenna's getting more comfortable wearing the lame T-shirts and leggings we pick up in tourist shops. When we stop, she uses the computer too. Searching for details about The Spark. Trying to locate Rosenthal. His whereabouts are still unknown.

At first I can't understand why she's still looking. Rosenthal, wherever he is, can't help us. But one day I catch MacKenna staring at this quote.

People need a reason to live just as much as they need a way to live.

It's from one of David Rosenthal's last speeches from the campaign trail.

Dad tried to teach me how to survive. But in the end, survival takes more than guns or protein bars or fighting skills. People need something worth surviving *for*.

We need hope.

This is what The Spark is for MacKenna. It's about more than just abstract politics. It represents our own ability to save ourselves. For MacKenna, The Spark is hope.

Maybe The Spark could give me hope too.

We arrive at Xcalak, a blue beach that takes my breath away. It's evening as we pull in, the sky a pastel painting beginning to shift from blues into the reds and pinks of sunset.

Navarro parks next to the only thing around—a tiny, dilapidated wooden shack.

We all lean forward and stare.

"And we've arrived at…an outhouse?" MacKenna squints at the shack.

But she doesn't know my father the way I do.

It's not a shack.

"It's a bunker."

Inside, the shack is cramped, with boxes of books and old furniture, just like the shed back home. We move stuff around until we come across a hatch on the floor. It uses the same lock combinations as the bunker back home.

The stairs descend to almost an exact duplicate of Dad's basement.

There's a comm center. A tiny kitchen. A massive amount of stored food and supplies.

And bunks.

A bunk for Dad. A bunk for Charles.

They're gone.

I find myself putting a few books on Charles's bed, like if I put them there, he might suddenly materialize.

Navarro runs the drill. He turns the comm center equipment on and is soon monitoring blowing palm trees and a calm sea. The radar sweeps an empty landscape. He scoots the bin of burner phones in my direction.

Jay keeps making comments about Mom. Looking for signs that his life with her wasn't a lie. "She took Charles. She clearly cares about him. Somewhere, deep down inside, she loves him…and us."

I don't have the heart to tell him that Mom took Charles for leverage. I think this might be Jay's drill. His plan to keep going. His way of pressing forward.

I remember Ramona Carver. *What happens when a predator tries to raise its own prey?*

At least Mom needs Charles. Hopefully that will be enough to keep him safe for now.

When everything is set up, MacKenna and Navarro turn their attention to making something edible for lunch out of the buckets of dried food.

I'm supposed to get a cell phone set up for everyone, but instead I take a shower.

When I come out, I notice Dad's got an old PC pushed into the corner of his desk. Desperate to feel some kind of connection to him, I press the power button. The screen powers on, showing a blinking command prompt.

I turn my head…and that's when I see it.

Tall stacks of three-inch floppy disks. In various colors.

My heart stops as I realize what this is.

The encryption key.

Before I can examine them, MacKenna calls my name. She

and Navarro have managed to turn a bucket of dried fiesta enchiladas into dinner. I almost wolf them down.

Afterward, MacKenna goes up to the surface and sits by the water. I find her under the palm trees with one of the books from the shed. She must be desperate for reading material, because she's resorted to raiding Dad's bookshelf. I don't know how she can stand to read a boring Western.

I sit as close to the water as I can without letting the cold waves touch my bare feet. "Listen, I have to talk to you."

She looks up from her book and kind of smiles. "About you and Navarro? About kissing?"

"*What?* No!" My face heats up.

She makes a face. "Right. Whatever."

I force myself to take a deep breath. "I think I found something. The encryption key. Or at least I found the way to get it."

She drops the copy of *Showdown at Yellow Butte* into the sand. I can see she's not really reading it so much as using it as writing paper. It's also got bunches of folded, yellow notes inside. The inside is covered with her loopy script. "How?" she asks.

"My dad." I choke on the words. "One of his ideas was using old-timey floppy disks as a way to hide data. Basically, what you do is, you copy the data to the disk and then make a small nick at a certain place in the plastic. It can be read back once and then it breaks. There's a ton of old disks down there, and an old PC. We just need to put each one into the PC, copy its data and put the program back together."

She picks at one of her fingernails. "I don't know what that means. But you're telling me we could fix the computers at the bank?"

I look into her brown eyes. "Or not."

She turns to watch the tide.

"We could use the program as leverage to get my brother back. Or help Jay. Or maybe both. Or maybe access the bank computer to get money. To get help."

The edge of a wave rolls over my big toes.

The sun crashes into the horizon, creating a spectacular sunset. Oranges and reds blend into violets and blues. Soon, the stars will sparkle above.

I think of everything that we've lost. That we'll never get back.

It's all there. Like a weight on my chest.

I watch her profile.

She stares at the horizon. "Or…have you ever thought that all the wrong people end up with all the money? What would you do if you could change that? If we can access the bank data, that means we can change it, right?"

"Right," I say.

Her gaze snaps back to mine. "You want to start a revolution?"

I face the ocean again, put my feet into the cold water as the tide creeps up the sand. "Not really," I say. "What I really want is my brother back."

And revenge. Lots of revenge.

I watch the blue sea and fidget with the rough sand under my fingertips. "But I also want my brother to have a life worth living. A world worth living in." That might mean doing something revolutionary.

Right at that moment, I understand.

I am not what I once was.

We're always making choices, and it's no longer possible to choose to do nothing.

I am The Spark.

I face MacKenna again.

"What do you want to do?"

★ ★ ★ ★ ★

Thank you for reading Day Zero.

Will Jinx and MacKenna start their own revolution?
Will they ever see Charles again?

Don't miss Day One!
Only from Kelly deVos and Inkyard Press.

AUTHOR'S NOTE

While I have made my best efforts to ensure that the technical information and code snippets in this book are correct, some changes have been made (including the use of fictionalized, internal IP addresses) due to safety and security concerns. Thank you to my technical readers and technical consultants, including Neem Serra, Sheldon McGee, Sarah McGee, Jim deVos and the Arizona IoT DevFest community. Any mistakes are my own.

ACKNOWLEDGMENTS

Thank you so much for reading this book.

So many elements of this story were inspired by my daughter, Evelyn. She is part of a generation of teenagers who are thoughtful, engaged and determined to leave this world in better shape than they found it. *Day Zero*'s message of hope is ultimately that today's young people have the power to effect great change.

A million thanks to my fantastic editor, Natashya Wilson. I will always be so grateful for your help in building this story and this world, and for your assistance in breathing life into my fierce girls.

Thank you to the incredible team at Inkyard Press, including Evan Brown, Linette Kim, Shara Alexander, Bryn Collier, Laci Ann, Margaret Marbury, Gabrielle Vicedomini and Connolly Bottum. I am so in love with the cover of this book and I have to thank Kathleen Oudit for art direction and Elita Sidiropoulou for design. Special thanks to Laura Gianino for her tireless work spreading the word about my books.

A writer needs readers, so massive thanks to the Harper-Collins Children's sales team for all their hard work in bringing this story to store and library shelves.

Thank you to my friends and family, especially my mom, May Porter, Cassidy Pavelich, Amie Allor, Shanna Weissman and Debbie Pirone. As always, thank you to my BFF, Riki Cleveland, for friendship and always being willing to read my horrible first drafts.

To the AZ YA/MG writer community. Thank you all, especially Amy Trueblood, Dusti Bowling, Stephanie Elliot, Kristen Hunt and Lorri Phillips, for your wit and wisdom.

Thanks to my early readers, including Laura Taylor Namey, Kristina Pérez and Kaitlyn Sage Patterson. I am also grateful to Maya Rock for invaluable editorial feedback. Any mistakes are my own.

For me, the struggle of the sophomore novel was real, and no one put up with more than my wonderful husband, Jim deVos. Thank you for your unconditional love and support.

During the writing of this book, I lost an amazing friend. To Cory Weissman, it's hard to imagine life ever being the same without you. But every day I will try to honor your memory by being a little bit better of a friend, being open to new things and new adventures, and being unafraid to wear my heart on my sleeve. Thank you for all the fun and friendship.